K.J. Backer grew up on a Christmas Tree farm in Oregon, enjoying the fragrant scents of Blue Spruce and Douglas Fir, surrounded by animals, before moving to the Big Sky State in 1996. She credits her close family bonds, wild imagination, and love for books to her humble, country upbringing. She worked as a U.S. Capitol Intern in 2004, graduated from Montana State University-Billings with a History Education degree in 2009, and taught History at a local high school for five years. She has a huge love and appreciation for other cultures, adoption, travel, history, fantasy, and the written word.

K.J. Backer lives in Billings, MT with her amazing husband, wonderful daughter, and two adorable Pomeranians. *Nav'Aria: The Marked Heir* is her first novel. Follow Backer on social media and at **kjbacker.com** to learn more!

Cover design by SelfPubBookCovers.com/LadyLight

Maps by K.J. Backer (Inkarnate Pro)

Edited by Heather Peers

Proofread by Anna Genoese

K.J. Backer

Visit author website at **kjbacker.com**

Printed in the United States of America

First Edition: January 2019

ISBN-13: 978-1-7329206-1-3

NAV'ARIA:
THE MARKED HEIR

K.J. Backer

Kathy,

Happy Reading! ♡

K Backer.

For Jarica.

And for the Darions of the world.

Nav'Aria

The Camp

Mt. Alodon

The Woods of the Willow

The Stenlen

The Shazla Desert

Rav'Ar

Nav'Alodon Mountains
Land of the Trolls
The Kingdom
Lure River
Castle Dintarran
Lake Thread

PROLOGUE

Many Years Ago

"Flight, oh wondrous flight! This is fun, Zalto!"

"It is not supposed to be 'fun,' Salimna. I was instructed to teach you how to hunt today. Do not forget your instructions."

Salimna rolled his red eyes. His crimson scales flexed as he gained speed upon his older brother. Every year, the dragon hatchlings were given their 'instructions': to fly, track, and hunt. And every year they continued their learning until each area was perfected. Though Zalto tried, Salimna, it would seem, did not possess the attention span for learning.

It was all so taxing. Salimna wished that, above all, he would be allowed to roam free. Test out his wings! Explore. Waylay the rules and boundaries for a time. But alas, it could not be so. For weeks now, he had been coming up here to the steep, brush-covered cliff with his brother to be taught "the way." He looked at his brother with his sepia wings and scales shimmering in the desert sun.

His brother was droning on about something involving his heart and its inner chamber, when the pupil noticed a strange creature. His brother, oblivious to it, continued his speech. The warm wind had kicked up the unfamiliar scent. Salimna had very keen senses, it was said, while his brother boasted the intellect. He loved his brother, but he did grow bored with his "lessons." He wondered if his brother would even notice his absence?

Salimna slowed his pace. His brother, enjoying the sound of his own voice, persisted, completely unaware of his brother lagging behind. Salimna could still hear Zalto, but he began to glide lower. He slowed the rapid cadence of his wings, cautiously circling the small pool where he had the seen the kneeling creature.

"Hello," Salimna whispered shyly. When met with no response, he said it again, this time louder. His voice reverberated off the nearby boulders; his beating wings upsetting the once still water creating rippling waves.

The creature was one Salimna had never seen in his three years of life. He was unlike the typical beasts that the dragons feasted on. Salimna lacked the heart of a hunter; he found no joy in killing. Though now that he looked at the creature, he realized how terribly hungry he was. Yet he could not determine what he was looking at. The creature was pale, without scales or fur, and robed in a black material. *How curious,* he thought. He landed softly sniffing at the air, taking in the being's acrid smell of sweat.

The creature started at the dragon's arrival, taking a few steps back. After a moment, though, the creature cocked his head and said, "Hello."

Salimna instantly came closer, curiosity overwhelming him. He had always been a bit impetuous, and he was thrilled at his find. *What a magnificent day!*

The creature took a step closer. "Are you out for an early lesson, Mighty One?"

Salimna visibly trembled with pleasure at the title. "Oh, yes. I am being instructed today in how to hunt."

"Well, I hope you are not looking to hunt me," the creature replied, stepping back. Salimna missed the subtle tone of mirth in the statement.

Salimna was aghast! The sunlight glinted on his brightly colored scales as he vehemently shook his head. *Why had he said that? Now he had frightened his new friend.*

"Oh, no, Pale One. We do not hunt creatures like you," Salimna said assuredly as he crept closer. "Come to think of it... what kind of creature *are* you?"

The creature knelt, and as his pale hand rested against Salimna's crimson wing, he answered, "My name is Narco."

Youthful innocence rendered Salima blind to Narco's wicked smile which flashed momentarily upon glimpsing the dragon's scales.

"Brother, brother, where are you?"

Salimna heard Zalto's frantic call. "I must go. My brother is looking for me."

Narco's eyes searched the sky. He came closer to Salmina to peer into his deep, reptilian eyes. "We are friends now, yes?" The young dragon nodded vigorously.

"Well, then we must not tell anyone of our meeting...

not just yet, that is."

"But why?"

"Because they might not let us be friends anymore. You would not want that, would you?"

"Oh, no, friend Narco. I would not want that."

"So, it is our little secret, then?" This creature's accent was so foreign.

Salimna jumped at the thought! *A secret? How exciting!* He loved the idea, though he didn't fully understand what it meant. "Yes, yes, our secret."

"Come see me again soon, Mighty One."

"Yes, friend Narco. Soon."

The ebullient Salmina zipped into the air to catch up with his worried brother. He did not want Zalto to find his pale friend. His secret.

"I look forward to it," Narco said to himself, as he watched the red blur dissipate in the clouds.

Zalto thought he heard laughing from afar, but he forgot once he saw his younger brother swirling into view. After a stern reprimand, he puffed smoke in reproach, renewing his lecture.

***

Narco sat up as a sudden gust of wind ruffled his raven hair and cloak. He was not afraid or surprised. He had expected this after all. The beast had been so naïve it was almost comical. He blinked the sleep from his eyes; his pupils quickly adjusting to the evening shadows. A low-hanging crescent moon only partially illuminated the sky. In the dim light, he saw the looming scarlet dragon where the trees had been unnaturally parted. His lips curved into a smile.

"So, you have returned, Mighty One," Narco observed, nodding his head in Salimna's direction. The young dragon nodded eagerly. The human's heartrate pulsed rapidly. Though Narco had expected the curiosity of the youngster to get the better of him, he had not expected him to return so soon. Narco now only hoped that the next part of his plan would go so seamlessly.

Salimna moved closer, sniffing at Narco as he had earlier. His tongue flicked intermittently, exploring the foreign odors in the air. His cavernous eyes filled the blackness around the campsite. Narco hesitated at the eerie sight. *Was this creature truly as ignorant as it had first appeared? Had he told anyone of their meeting?* The human cautiously glanced around before assuring himself that there were no other creatures lurking in the darkness. The dragon did not speak, and Narco worried that he had been played the fool until...

"I do not have much time, Friend Narco," Salimna's innocent voice spoke into the darkness. "For I am not supposed to go out at night. The other hatchlings and I have strict rules we must follow." If he were not a dragon, Narco would have described his expression as sheepish, though none could describe the innate ferocity of the dragon as such.

"You have taken much risk to show your friendship," Narco replied smoothly. He raised his hand to caress the side of Salimna's face with its scaled, sharp features. He felt the creature tremble beneath his touch. "Did anyone see you leave?" Narco forced himself to maintain eye contact and a calm voice, though he itched to look at the sky for any approaching wings.

"No, no, no. No one saw me. I was very quiet. I made sure," Salimna said, though his voice wavered slightly. The young dragon seemed much more on edge this evening than he had the previous day, and Narco knew it was indeed with much risk that Salimna had come. He wondered what would have happened if he were caught. *Would he have exposed Narco?*

Narco almost balked at his proposal; again, noting the innocence of the young dragon. Yet he had been instructed that this was the only way. If his plan was going to succeed, this was the critical first step. He could not quit now. His gaze momentarily fell to his right forearm. His eyes boring through the fabric as if they would see something different this time.

"Tell me about the other dragons. What is it like growing up here?" he asked, wanting Salimna to feel more at ease with light, cheerful conversation. The dragon visibly relaxed and settled into a more comfortable sitting position so that his wings enclosed his legs. His scales glimmered in the moonlight and Narco looked at his majestic form longingly, as he only halfheartedly heard his responses. He continued to rest his palm on the side of Salimna's head, hoping to further calm him.

As dawn began to break, Salimna flexed his wings. He was clearly anxious to return to the cave where he and the other young dragons were housed.

"Before you go, I have one favor to ask of you, my

friend," Narco pulled his hand away to step back and look Salimna directly in the eye, continuing, "and in return you will gain more than my friendship. You will gain my respect." His words hung in the air. Salimna shifted uneasily, clearly unsure of how to respond. His tongue flicked the air once more. The human's words seemed kind enough, but there was something about the expression on his face that gave Salimna pause.

"What is a 'favor,' Narco?"

Narco did not miss the absence of "Friend" at the mention of his name. With a quick smile, he continued, "Before I ask it of you, tell me, are there many dragons left?" Salimna seemed startled by the question and shook his head in response.

"My brother, Zalto, tells me that our numbers have dropped over the years after the Great Drought. We have had to migrate and shift our hunting grounds. There is not as much water as there was cycles ago... at least, that is what my brother says. I do not know anything differently since it has always been this way while I was alive. There are still a lot of dragons, I think," Salimna said this last part proudly. Thinking that that was what Narco wanted to hear.

Narco nodded with a solemn expression, "It is what we have feared then. The dragons are dwindling. Then what I ask of you is of grave importance. You see, I have come here to help you. What I need then, may help preserve your kind. You could be the champion of the dragons, and forever remembered for this great deed." That seemed to work on the adolescent.

Salimna's anticipation bubbled over, and he stood with wings spread wide as if to take off. "Yes, Friend Narco. Yes, I will do it."

"Wait a moment, Mighty One. I have not told you what I need yet," Narco chided. Salimna's wings folded in again. He hung on Narco's every word. "What I need is," Narco paused, always a lover of the dramatic, "a dragon egg," he concluded in a hushed voice.

Salimna's jaw fell open, and a tendril of smoke trailed out. He spluttered, "But... But... How? Why? The females guard the nests very closely. I could never sneak in there. This is not good, Friend Narco. Not good at all. This cannot be done." The dragon's head shook adamantly back and forth.

"Ah, but you can, Mighty One. You must find a way, if you are to save your kind." Narco rested his palm upon his scaled head once more. Salimna looked at him confused. Narco explained, "We must keep an egg safe, in case the Great Drought returns. Your kind must be able to withstand any problems. The elder dragons do not speak of all the evils of this world with you, but they know. One day a storm or an evil force will come and destroy the dragons. Without this egg, your kind will be lost. You will become a fable. A legend. Dusty bones. Nothing more. No, Mighty One, you must do this. We have spoken to the elders before, but they are too proud. They do not trust we humans. But you know me as your friend. You know that I come here to help, that is all," he said this quickly, but slowed his recitation for effect. "You, Mighty One, must preserve the dragon race."

The weight of the charge fell upon Salimna, and he could see truth in the human's words. The haughty elder dragons did keep many secrets that they did not share with the young. Even his brother would not answer questions regarding the "other kind," "border," and other whispered rumors he had heard. Standing to his full height with his wings spread, he accepted. "I will do it, Friend Narco." He said it with such sincerity that Narco knew he had succeeded. The next part of his plan was in motion. He grinned at the dragon, before whispering his instructions.

As Salimna soared into the sky, Narco breathed easily rubbing his forearm, watching the idiot youth fly unknowingly toward destruction.

***

"Excellent."

The cloaked figure emerged from the shadows to come near Narco, resting his gloved hand possessively upon his shoulder. The mirthful voice whispered praise, his breath hot upon Narco's ear. With a hard squeeze, he gripped Narco's shoulder and spun him around. Narco stifled a shudder as he gazed into the depths of the hooded face. Predatorial amber eyes met his. Their gaze more threatening than that of any dragon.

The two men walked a short distance in silence to a second campsite they had set up for this purpose. Giant, round stones lined a portion of clearing near another clump of trees and vegetation.

"Is the tonic ready?" Narco knew it was, of course, but still inquired. He felt a pit forming in his stomach. The hooded man only nodded, silently waiting.

Narco's apprehension only intensified as they waited. It took two full days before they heard the rapid beat of Salimna's wings. As the dragon crested the clearing, his wingbeats slowed, landing lightly for his bulk upon the ground nearest Narco. Within his talons he clutched an immense black egg. Narco looked from the egg to Salimna.

"Well done, my friend," Narco whispered, his voice catching in his throat at the sight.

Salimna looked wretched. The task had worn his nerves raw. Two females had almost caught him. He bore a small tear on one of his wings from when he dove quickly out of view, ripping the delicate membrane on a jagged stone overhang in his fall.

Out of the twilight shadows the cloaked figure with the amber eyes came, catching Salimna off guard.

"Who are you?" he asked tersely, looking uncertainly from the stranger to Narco.

"He is my companion, Mighty One. He is a friend, too." Salimna's trepidation was evident, and Narco motioned for the stranger to stop. Narco rested his palm on the dragon as he had done previously, and he felt him begin to settle.

"May I see that?" Narco asked. Salimna released his grasp on the egg and rolled it gently to him. Narco lifted it, surprised by its size and weight already. He set it in a pile of brush that the men had gathered. It rested next to a smaller white egg. Salimna eyed the other egg but appeared too exhausted to form words.

"Here, Mighty One. Drink this," the hooded figure instructed. Salimna's eyelids were already beginning to flutter.

"This will help you rest peacefully, my Friend," Narco said comfortingly.

Salimna looked back to the stranger, then spoke softly to Narco, "Have I gained your respect now, Pale One?"

Narco's blood went cold at the blind trust in the dragon's voice. "You have, Mighty One. You have," Narco whispered, as the stranger poured the dark liquid from a leather wineskin into the dragon's great maw. Its effect was instant. The dragon's head thudded as it fell to the ground, and the creature rolled on its side in deep slumber.

Narco tried to control his breathing. His companion was characteristically silent. Watching him. *Measuring him,* Narco thought. He knew what had to be done. From the interior of his robes, Narco pulled forth a long, razor sharp blade. The setting sun's rays danced upon the clean, untarnished metal. With the blade in hand, Narco moved closer to the sleeping form.

"This is the only way," he said quietly to himself, as if it would absolve him. He knew the blood would only continue to run. This was the first of many necessary deaths if his plan was to be fully achieved.

A savage roar echoed in the distance as his blade fell to the soft underbelly of his ignorant "friend."

"Do not forget the vial! Quickly now, quickly, get it all." The hooded man stood near him collecting the lifeblood and assisting Narco in pulling the heart and lifestone from its inner chamber unique to only dragons. They hastily stored them in the large jars they had brought for this purpose.

"The ritual! Complete the ritual. Hurry, we must flee from here before the rest of them track the carcass." A gloved hand held the swirling, steaming metallic liquid up to his lips, and Narco quickly tipped his head back, drinking the vial of dragon blood in one long gulp. The hooded man than followed suit with the other vial. Narco looked at him questioningly, for that had not been part of the plan. The man simply shook his head. A chorus of bellows and roars filled the evening sky. *They know*. The two men hurriedly collected their other vials, storing them safely in their packs, along with the two eggs, then ran as fast as their human legs would carry them in the direction of the border and their awaiting mounts on the other side.

Narco could feel the blood taking effect as his legs began to pick up pace. His feet practically flew over the ground. His guilt for slaying the ill-witted dragon vanished like the desert waste behind him. Smiling broadly with pleasure at his newfound strength and power, Narco flexed his right arm. *He had all the power he needed now.*

CHAPTER 1

The Mark

Pelting rain fell in the tumultuous downpour. "Damn rain," Darion muttered, wiping the raindrops off his pizza delivery uniform. This was not an ideal night for the job that awaited. Frustrated, he kicked an abandoned frisbee out of his way in the puddle-ridden restaurant parking lot.

Tonight, would be the defining moment of his high school career! Tonight, he got the call to deliver pizza to Stephanie O'Donnell's house. The most beautiful, captivating, dream-like, popular girl in school. He had to take this chance, and the damn rain was ruining everything!

An hour earlier, Tony, the manager of The Moz, an up and coming pizza restaurant in Gresham, OR, instructed Darion to start his shift with a delivery. A late night of video games had left Darion fading fast. *This is going to be a long night,* he thought, as a huge yawn escaped his lips. Embarrassed, he grabbed the delivery slip out of Tony's large, sweaty hand and crumpled it into his fist as he walked into the restroom to rearrange his hat and uniform. Looking in the cracked mirror, he tucked in his oversized shirt. The dark and dingy restroom made it difficult to make out his features but what did it matter? He never saw anyone while on shift.

Then he remembered his first duty of the night. Delivery. He smoothed open the slip in his hand and gasped. As the paper fell to the floor, Darion frantically wetted his dark curls, splashing water on his face. His average appearance stared back at him. The boys at school were big. Active. Coordinated. Athletic. Darion, on the other hand, was tall and gangly, with tanned skin. He liked to spend his days rock climbing, horseback riding, and hiking. He had strong, lean limbs from years of adventuring the Oregon forests, amplified by his baggy pizza uniform. He had lost his other shirt, leaving him no other option but to borrow Tony's extra-large one. His green eyes were his only remarkable feature, at least in his mind. Shaking his head at his image, he took a deep breath.

What the hell. I'm going for it.

Darion had never met Stephanie—officially, that is. The girl of his dreams, yes, but as his friends put it, he didn't have the guts. He had tried though. *Once*, he admonished to himself. Last year in a Sophomore P.E. class, he'd almost had his chance. They had been playing dodgeball when she'd tripped on her shoelace. Just a few feet from her, he could make out every feature on her beautiful face. Blonde hair, blue eyes, rosy pink lips, and one adorable freckle just below her right eye. Her tight fitted tank top allowed her admirers a clear image of her perfect breasts, and small waist. Her tanned, long legs visible beneath her immodest neon gym shorts. Her cheeks were flushed from exertion and the embarrassment of falling in front of her classmates. Darion had dreamed of her in a similar position many nights, though to find her hurt tamed his lust. He was there, extending a hopeful yet trepid hand, as their eyes met. And that's when everything went black. Joey Durange had just become Darion's greatest enemy.

"Darion. You're out, man," Joey laughed, after throwing a dodgeball directly at Darion's face, knocking him out momentarily and breaking his nose.

Bastard.

Unbeknownst to him, Joey had helped Stephanie up and they sauntered off laughing about the geeky pizza boy who got in the way of the ball, while the school nurse was called in to escort Darion out. That had been a low point. His nose was now slightly crooked, thanks to that jerk.

With the rush of memories, Darion propelled himself into action. He had to erase the memories of failure.

Yes, that day sucked, but tonight... tonight is going to be a good night. Tonight is "the" night, where everything changes for this pizza delivery boy.

Darion ran out of the bathroom, yelling. "Tony, Tony, where is the O'Donnell's order? Come on! What are you guys doin' back here?" He glared accusingly at the other two kitchen staff as he slammed his fists on the counter. Joel and Andrew were fun and jovial, but at this moment, they were achingly slow.

"Hurry up you guys! I have to get this order out!"

The two men stared open-mouthed at the kid. This was the guy who never talked to anyone at work, always keeping a low profile.

"Sorry, man, we're workin' on it," Andrew muttered as he shook his head at Joel, wiping his greasy hands down the front of his apron. A few moments passed by as they pulled the pizza from the oven and packed it in a travel bag ready for delivery.

"Here ya go, kid," Joel called from the kitchen. Darion sprang out of the booth he had seated himself at and tore the travel bag out of the fat, sloth-like man's hands.

"Thanks a lot," he said, with more than a hint of sarcasm, and ran out to face the night.

***

"2457, 2458, 2459... Come on, where is 2460?" Worried he was on the wrong street, he finally saw it. *2460 Fir Dr.* He had found Stephanie's house.

He pulled into the driveway and saw "O'Donnell" inscribed on the mailbox. Darion gawked at the large, well-lit house surrounded by a white picket fence. It was much nicer than his home he realized, though he expected nothing less from his crush.

All right, this is it, he thought, gingerly lifting the steaming pizza bag off his passenger seat. *You can do this. Just be cool.*

He opened his truck door and slid out. He marched himself to the white door and knocked. Three times. No answer. He paused, deciding to try the doorbell. Still no answer. The combination of bone-chilling drizzle and lusty teenage anticipation made him impatient. *Hurry up,* he thought, growing cold and aggravated from the unrelenting rain.

Tony was strict on certain things, like attire and presentation. Imagining Tony's commanding voice: *If it is not the dead of winter, I do not want you covering up that uniform. I promise you will not die from a little rain.* Though he wished now, that he would have broken the rules just this once and worn his black rain jacket.

Knocking again, three more times... No answer. "Where is she?" he said aloud, his temper rising. Rain dripped off his hat. He knew he must look a wreck. His hair clung to his neck as rain trickled down the back of his shirt. *This was a bad idea. Tony should've delivered it himself.*

"Damnit." *This can't be happening.* He saw a large portrait window a few feet away. Stepping off the porch, he walked toward the window. This ended up being the worst thing he could have done because just at the instant he moved off the porch, he stepped on a pile of mud. Losing his footing, he skidded on the slimy material and wet grass, heaving the pizza box as he fell backwards. The front door swung open in that instant, and to Darion's horror, Joey Durange and Stephanie O'Donnell walked out to greet him. Joey roared with laughter at the sight of Darion, as Stephanie jumped off her porch to offer her hand. However, as she was inches away from his hand she stopped.

"Ewww, what's that smell?" the girl cried. "It smells like sewer!" She drew back and quickly returned to the safety of fresh air and Joey's large arms on the porch. Darion scrambled up, grabbing the pizza box. The two teens looked down on him with such disdain that he panicked. His mind went blank. He chucked the pizza onto the second stair of the porch and fled. He heard Stephanie screaming, "We don't want this nasty pizza now!" Jumping into the driver seat of his white '98 Dodge truck he sped out of the drive swerving, narrowly avoiding the O'Donnell's mailbox.

He had stepped on dog shit, fell, and fled the delivery scene like a total loser. *That didn't happen.* But judging by the smell of the truck cab, it totally had.

"No, no, no, no, no!" Darion yelled as he banged his fists against his steering wheel. Only a few blocks from 2460, the tears overtook him.

By the time he got back to The Moz, the O'Donnells had already called in to report the incident. Darion caught the sympathetic look his boss gave him. "Take the rest of the night off, kid. It is not that busy anyways, and you know just as well as I do that Andrew and Joel are useless. Maybe I will make them run a delivery for a change," he said, as he winked at the dejected teenager, slapping him on the back.

"Thanks, Tony. I think I could use it," he said, sniffling as he walked over to hang up his hat. He didn't want anyone's pity, but he was appreciative of his long-time friend and boss.

***

Tony, well-aware of Darion's longtime infatuation with the girl, knew he didn't capture her heart this evening. His heart ached as he watched the downtrodden boy's expression. He felt genuine, filial affection for the dear boy. Darion was an orphan, or so the story went. He had been adopted by the Smiths, an older couple who could not have children naturally. According to them, they had fallen in love with him the moment they saw him, though none knew exactly *where* they had found him. They had raised him since infancy and adopted him, making him fortunate. Many children are forced to bounce between foster families, and Tony was glad that Darion had not shared their fate.

Though his origins were still unknown, like all things do, the years passed by and the mysterious child's abandonment became a thing of the past. The only thing that still raised uncertainty was the inexplicable, foreign marking on the ring finger of Darion's right hand.

As a child, it appeared as nothing more than a birthmark, but as each year passed, the markings and dots became more definite. More legible. A phrase or symbol perhaps. It was the butt of jokes at school, causing Darion to find a large, black band that he wore at all times. His adoptive parents seemed unashamed of his birthmark. If anything, they didn't understand why he felt the need to hide it. They were a bit country, living on the outskirts of town, but they cared deeply for the boy, and that was all that mattered. Tony had known them for years and would vouch for them any day. They provided well for the boy, and Tony offered him a job as soon as he got his driver's license. He was well looked after, yet some injuries are unavoidable, such as tonight's events.

"High school's a bitch... do not let it get ya down." Tony waved comfortingly at the boy as he walked out the front door. "Trust me, things will work out, Darion."

"Thanks, Tony. Have a good night," Darion said, subdued. His bright green eyes were a bit dimmer than usual, bloodshot and glassy. He shrugged out of the door with an audible exhale.

***

Darion couldn't sleep. He kept picturing Joey's round, pimpled face laughing and pointing at him. He envisioned Stephanie reeling back in horror from his tainted self, covered in dog excrement. He stared at the ceiling for a time, trying to take comfort in his scenic, nature posters which plastered every square inch of his room.

That's it. Darion got up and walked across his tiny attic bedroom to his desk. He took out his notepad and pencils, flicking on his lamp. He spent a lot of nights awake. He had never been a sound sleeper. He cleared his mind through drawing. He had never shown any of his sketches to anyone. They were his and his alone. He was not sure what they meant but he knew they were not typical teenage drawings. They usually had strange markings, similar to the "birthmark" on his hand. He never willed these images; it was just what his hands and head seemed to conjure up, subconsciously. Strange creatures. Horses with horns, burly men with horse bodies, large bird like beasts, and other dark, mythical things. He didn't know why but his sketches were soothing. It was as if they were a part of him. As he filled in some shading on one of the beast's hooves, he began to think of his upbringing. Setting his pencil down, Darion slid off his black ring.

Dark lettering and symbols covered much of his first knuckle on his ring finger. *What does it mean?* There had to be a reason for it, but everyone seemed to think it was just an odd mix up in pigment. *A birthmark. How could anyone look at this and think it's normal?* Something didn't add up. More than anything he wished he knew his birth parents. *Why did they desert me?*

Like a scrap of refuse or garbage, he was left with nothing but his diaper, blanket, and strange birthmark. *Maybe they took one look at me and knew they could never love me?* On occasion, these bleak thoughts overtook his mind, but they were fleeting. Somehow, Darion knew that wasn't the case. If they hadn't wanted him, why would they have gone to the trouble to see him safely left on the Smiths' doorstep, as they told it. Maybe his birth parents were trying to protect him. Something must have happened forcing them to abandon him, and that is the one thing that kept the boy going. That, and the dream that he would one day get to be with Stephanie O'Donnell, which clearly would not come to pass after tonight's unfortunate occurrence. The image of her loose top revealing the pink lace of her bra, holding within it, her tantalizing breasts, as she had almost knelt to help him caused his pants to tighten. Feeling more frustrated than ever, he snapped his pencil in two, wishing for a different outlet for his emotions.

Sighing, he gave up drawing and climbed back into bed to catch a few hours of sleep before Monday's arrival.

CHAPTER 2

The Dream

Ring. Period one began. This may possibly be the longest hour known to man. Mrs. Roberts droned on and on about literature something or other. Darion hated to read. He hated "Literature." And he hated this class. Maybe he would have enjoyed it more had he not been assigned to sit in front of Joey Durange.

And the torment begins... He knew it was only a matter of moments once their teacher began her lesson that Joey would antagonize him for last night.

"Hey, Shit Breath. I can't believe you're showing your face today. I'd be humiliated if I were you. I thought for sure you'd stay home. Man, you'd never believe the things Stephanie and her parents were saying about you. Her dad was threatening to share the story with the news. Make sure no one ever orders from there again! You, bringing dog crap to their house and trying to sabotage their dinner. It's so nasty. What a sick prank! What were you thinking?" Joey exclaimed, clearly enjoying himself. His hateful words whispered hot on the back of Darion's neck.

Darion sat very still focusing on his breathing, optimistic about his ability to ignore assholes like Joey. He knew today would be difficult. *It's okay, I can handle this*, he thought to himself, *Ha! Is that the worst he's got?*

Continuing with a steady stream of insults, Joey concluded very quietly. "You're just a filthy orphan... no wonder your real parents didn't want you."

And that's when Darion saw red.

"No!" Darion yelled as he turned in his chair and slammed his fist into Joey's windpipe. Joey's eyes bulged, his face turning a dark purple. That silenced him for sure. It almost killed him, too. The next few minutes were a blur.

In the back of his mind he recalled being pinned down by two other classmates as Mrs. Roberts ran out in the hall screaming for help.

Darion came back to the present, in the principal's office. Seated in front of him was Mr. Pointier, a weaselly, small-framed man with bushy eyebrows. He had served in the military at one point, as evidenced by the framed photograph of him receiving a Purple Heart, with his missing arm. As much as one tried not to stare, it was always, of course, impossible.

Pointing with his stump, Mr. Pointier laid into the boy. "What was the meaning of this Smith? Any harder and you would have killed Mr. Durange." The principal, with years of experience intimidating students, stared Darion down. Seconds passed by as the two battled wills. Darion was mute. He didn't need to explain himself and even if he did, what would it matter? Joey had spoken the truth. His parents had abandoned him, and he had never felt so alone. He was suspended from school, becoming even more of an outcast, and labeled dangerous.

"Do you wanna talk about it?" Carol Smith asked her demoralized son as they drove home, having been called away from her shift at the grocery store to pick up her "violent" child.

"Not really," Darion replied sullenly.

He loved his family and was forever grateful, but Joey's words had stung deep in his heart. *Why did they leave me?* he whispered to himself, leaning his forehead against the passenger side window.

Carol slowly pulled her Honda into the well-organized garage, and before she even had her seatbelt unbuckled, Darion was already leaping out of the car and headed up the stairs for the sanctuary of his room.

***

"So, what did they say?" called Rick from the den. Carol exhaled slowly and set her keys down on the kitchen counter before crossing the room toward her husband.

"They said he is violent and almost killed Joey somebody, whoever that is. I have never even heard of this kid? Why would Darion intentionally hurt him? I know it is a misunderstanding," Carol said vehemently. She would absolutely fight to the end for this boy. Her maternal instinct had kicked into overdrive, as she had long ago vowed to protect her son from harm. She was entirely devoted to the boy who completed their family.

"Well, maybe it is good he will be home for a few days. We can talk to him and get the whole story tomorrow."

Carol smiled at the man she had known all her life, as Rick wrapped his brawny arms around her small frame, inhaling her warm, earthy scent. Her dark auburn hair was beginning to grey, but that did not matter to Rick, she knew.

"Come here, my spring flower. I know you want to comfort Darion. I want to know what happened, too, but he needs some space. He will come to us when he is ready."

Murmuring into his chest, she said, "What should we do?"

"We should do what we always do," Rick confidently replied. "Give Darion time and support no matter what." Pausing he asked, "So, what do you think about steak?" Carol chuckled and kissed her husband's cheek, fondly.

"That is why I love you, you know?"

"Why?" he asked grinning.

"Because you are steady. You always know what to say." Carol ran her palm down his clean-shaven face and kissed the knot in his chin. Laughing at their old familiarity, the Smiths began their dinner preparations, leaving Darion to the privacy of his room.

Meanwhile, upstairs, Darion was pacing, remembering. Joey's eyes bulging as his fist took him out, Mrs. Roberts screaming, Mr. Pointier's forehead beaded with sweat. The images flashed in the teen's mind, echoing his thoughts: *Why did I do that? How could I punch him? I don't belong here.*

Darion crawled into bed, snuffling his tears into the pillow, wishing away all the heartache, embarrassment, and loss.

***

Raindrops could be heard dripping one by one off the small window ledge, creating a luminescent puddle. The pungent smell of unkempt human pervaded the air in the cold, dirty cell. In the middle of the room, lay a woman, shivering. Cold and alone. The woman's hair crumpled in a mass of untamed curls. She appeared very thin in her exposed, grimy shift. Distantly, a gentle scraping on the stone could be heard. Inaudible at first. Scrape. Moments passed by. Scrape. More moments. Scrape. It slowly began to increase in volume. Louder and louder the scraping became until it turned into footsteps accompanying the sound. The footsteps stopped outside the door. A rat scurried across the room aware of the threatening eminence. The tinkling of a key fumbled in the lock, before an audible click, and the creaking door swung open.

"No," the woman softly mouthed in between gasps. She shook violently, whether from the cold, or fear, or both. "Please no."

The chorus of screams and demonic cackling awoke Darion. Tossing and turning and shouting in his sleep, Rick found his son. Grabbing him by the shoulder, he gently shook him, noting Darion's scrunched, and anguished face.

"Darion, Darion. Wake up. You're having a night terror. Wake up, son." Startled, Darion's eyes snapped open and he immediately reacted by jumping back, slamming his head on his overhanging headboard.

"Ouch," Darion complained as he held his head in his hands shaking away the last remnants of his dream. He slowly looked up to meet his father's eyes. Worry. He immediately recognized the concern, which he had only seen mar Rick's expression once before, when Darion was just a boy. He remembered he had been climbing on some rocks and had lost his footing, falling a short distance. He had been uninjured, but then, and now, were the only two times he had seen his father so concerned. It made his head pound ten times harder.

"So how are you doing, my boy?" Rick drawled in his country accent. Raised on a ranch, he apparently knew everything there was to know about horses. Though Darion could not recall if he had ever learned where his father grew up. Rick never liked talking about himself, always shifting the attention away with a question. Darion would have to ask him sometime... when his thoughts weren't so jumbled.

Rick had a calm demeanor, and Darion loved him. He always seemed to know what was really going on in his mind.

"I don't know," Darion mumbled, groggily. "My head kinda hurts," he laughed as he sat up next to his dad.

"I am sure it does," Rick chuckled. He put his arm around Darion and said more seriously, "You know we love you and do not believe one word that fool of a principal said, right?"

Darion felt a wave of relief wash over him as he

nodded. "Yeah, I know," he said quietly.

"Walk me through what happened, from the beginning."

Darion nodded his assent and spilled everything. He told his dad about Stephanie, the pizza catastrophe, and Joey's cutting remark, which seemed to dampen the very air within the attic. All the while, Darion noted his father's unswerving attention. Rick had a somber expression, and when Darion finished, the corners of his mouth seemed poised to unburden themselves of some hidden truth.

Instead, though, Rick smiled glumly. "I thought it would be something like that. Now you listen here. No parents would ever willingly give up their child unless they had no other option. You know it and we know it. Carol and I have often discussed your natural parents and what a sacrifice it was to give you up. We believe they left you for a purpose. A chance to give you life."

Darion had always thought there was more to the story and wished he knew the history. He sat mulling it over as his father studied him.

"Now, is that all? What were you dreaming about? You were sure yelling up a storm."

For a moment Darion's brow crinkled in puzzlement. He tried to recall the dream. It was obscure—like a distant memory. And then suddenly he saw her. A beautiful, frail, soaked-to-the-bone woman lying on a cold, dingy cell floor. *Why did I dream of her? I must be losing it.*

"Uh, it was nothing. Nothing. Just a nightmare, I guess," Darion mumbled while dodging his father's sideways glance. Making sense of this dream seemed like trying to piece together the shards of Carol's antique crystal bowl, which he had accidentally broken as a boy. Just as before, he wanted to avoid the situation, perhaps forget about it, and certainly not articulate it to his father.

"All right, Darion. I will let you get back to sleep then. Good night." With a pat on the shoulder, Rick stood and left his son to ponder the strange dream. Replaying it in his head, Darion shook it off, buried his head underneath his pillow and fell into a heavy sleep.

***

What's that pounding? Crankily, Darion woke up trying to identify the sound. Twisted up in his sweaty bed sheets, it took him a moment to unravel himself. Launching out of bed, he walked to the window.

"Stupid woodpecker," he muttered, glancing at the noisy bird pecking furiously at the giant oak tree outside his window.

It looked like a typical Oregon spring day, drizzling rain and grey clouds... Brushing his bangs out of his eyes, he moodily eyed his room. He could hear his parents, downstairs fixing breakfast. They must have taken the day off work.

Great. Not only am I suspended from school, but now my parents are taking off work to "watch" over me. What do they think I'm going to do? Run away? Darion wasn't mad at them, but rather, embarrassed. First the school incident with Joey, and now nightmares. He had to be comforted to sleep like a small child. Feeling lousy, Darion slowly headed down the narrow, carpeted staircase to face his expectant parents. He could tell Carol wanted to talk but a communicative glance in Rick's direction, along with his almost imperceptible shake of the head, hinted at their resolve to leave it be, at least for now.

Gratefully, Darion slumped down into a kitchen chair and immediately began shoveling down his waffles and bacon. Momentarily forgetting his problems, he groaned in pleasure at the mix of maple syrup and smoked bacon dancing across his taste buds.

After a few moments of awkward silence and now content with a full belly, he looked up, "I'm really all right. You can go to work. I don't need a babysitter."

Carol stared into her tea as she spoke, "We know that, Darion, but we have to talk to you. Joey's mom just called. They are threatening to sue. Apparently, he had some damage to his esophagus and will be in the hospital the rest of the week," Carol said solemnly.

Rick, tight-lipped and repressing approval, said, "Sounds like you punched him good, son." Carol shot him a glare.

"Rick, this is serious. They have talked to the administrators and school board in favor of expulsion."

"They want to expel me?" Darion snapped to attention. *That would be terrible. What would it mean? Homeschooling? He could transfer schools, but he knew as well as his parents, his "violent" reputation would precede him. What had he done? What was he thinking hitting Joey like that?* He had never lost control before. He knew this was bad and there were going to be severe consequences. Though try as he may, he didn't regret it. It had felt damn good to hit him.

That night Darion fell into bed, thankful for the heavy blankets and solitude of his room. He felt emotionally drained after communicating with his parents. He hated watching them fret, especially Carol. A deep, dreamless sleep overtook him. He awoke in the middle of the night, glancing at his digital clock on the night stand. *Only 1:00*, he observed happily, grateful for more hours of much needed rest. *And no nightmare like last night! Even better,* he thought, as he fell back to sleep. His gratitude must have triggered his subconscious, because out of nowhere, the dream was upon him once more.

In the middle of the room, lay a woman shivering. Cold, alone, and very thin. Her hair, a wet mass of untamed curls, trailed down her grimy shift revealing dainty extremities. Scrape. It slowly began to increase in volume again. Louder and louder the scraping became until it turned into footsteps accompanying the sound. The footsteps thudded near the door. A key fumbled in the lock. The door hinges creaked open. "No, no, no," the woman softly mouthed in between gasps.

For the second time, Darion awoke shouting trying to block out the woman's screams. Once again, he woke twisted in his sheets with his hands over his ears and his eyes glued shut. Frustrated and somewhat chilled, he sat up in bed.

What is going on? That is not a normal dream. He felt like he was there. He could still smell the dungeon cell. It felt so real. He wanted to help the lady, but that was ridiculous. *It's just a dream. She's not in real danger.* Or was she?

CHAPTER 3

The Call

The Smiths were able to placate the Duranges by implementing some severe punishments for Darion. He was perma-grounded, or as Carol put it, "grounded indefinitely." His parents also took his keys away and agreed to the condition that Darion attend two sessions of therapy per week as long as it was needed. Though Rick did mutter under his breath that it was a waste of time, and not necessary. However, with these demands being met, and Darion's acquiescence not to "seek" out Joey at school, the suggested lawsuit was dropped. Joey recovered and remained the same dumb jock he had always been.

Darion spent the next couple weeks in a daze. His days were composed of ridicule and an overwhelming authority presence to ensure he didn't act out again. His nights were restless, constantly revisited by the eerie dream of the lady in the dungeon cell. The woman's appearance and a few other subtle details seemed to change or shift. Her hair appeared less full, there were visible bruises that were not there before, and recently claw marks appeared on her pale skin. Darion wanted to believe it was just a dream yet harbored a nagging feeling it was real.

One Tuesday night, Darion jumped as thunder shook the sky. He no longer awoke yelling frightened from the dream; he simply got up and pondered the woman and her condition. It helped calm his nerves to sketch. He often pulled the images from memory and put them on paper.

Her face was the most memorable from the dream. Everything else became clouded in his mind and he could not quite capture the dark scene's essence. The woman, however, he remembered her every detail, specifically her face. Her strong jaw, ocean blue eyes, loose blonde curls, delicate nose, long lashes; she was of the utmost beauty. Strangely, something about her profile seemed familiar, like he had seen her before. He sat at his desk staring into her large, pleading eyes and took a deep breath.

I have to tell someone. This has gone on long enough.

At first, he had not thought to question it. A dream. A nightmare, what of it? Everyone gets those. But then it began to repeat itself night after night. And now the "dream" was morphing with subtle changes he could not ignore. He had done a good job of documenting these changes, and they were visible in his drawings. He had written the date on the corner of each sketch.

So far, he had sixteen drawings; all of which he began sketching after a week or so of repetitive dreams. He knew deep in his heart there was a reason these images were coming to him. It was a vision, not a dream, and he was sure of it.

Tomorrow I'll tell Mr. Boyle, Darion decided as he climbed back into bed as he did most nights after completing his documentation. His psychiatrist, one of the Duranges' conditions, kept saying he wanted Darion to open up more. Yet he speculated Boyle wanted him to open up about his parents' abandonment, the incident with Joey, and so on, but it was worth a shot.

The woman in the cell consumed his thoughts, keeping him from a regular sleep cycle. Dawn came all too soon. Dragging himself out of bed, Darion stumbled into the attic bathroom. Splashing water on his face, he looked at his reflection. *I look like a zombie*, he wearily observed. His eyes were bloodshot, and his dark circles were so intense that he looked like he was wearing black under eye make-up, like many of the "gothic" students at his high school. Grumbling to himself, he quickly turned away before he became more upset by his haggard and aged appearance.

His parents were becoming increasingly worried. Even Rick could not hide it anymore. Whenever they tried to talk to Darion, he just shut them down. He felt guilty, he truly did, but to be honest he was so tired it was easy to be bad-tempered. He didn't know how to explain the dream to his parents, as he was slightly embarrassed about it. How was he supposed to tell his mother he was dreaming about a beautiful, practically naked woman every night? There was nothing sexual about it, not like his past dreams of Stephanie had been, but Carol had always been so conservative that Darion just wanted to avoid discussing it with her at all costs. His appetite had drastically shrunk. He had had to cut an extra hole in his belt in order to keep his pants up. Each time he went to eat, though, he envisioned the hollow-eyed woman with her sunken cheeks. The very thought of her starvation and suffering sent anxiety coursing through his body, along with an inexplicable sense of guilt. He couldn't eat while she starved.

***

"I'm in a cell. I can hear footsteps. Not solid footsteps, but slow like the person has to drag a leg behind or limp down the hall. Someone," he coughed, "Someone bad is coming. I can just tell they are evil. I guess I have never seen him... until..." he said more to himself than aloud. He shook his head. "But the rat runs away every time from his voice. That's a not a good sign, I don't think?"

Darion looked questioningly at Mr. Boyle. The psychiatrist just motioned his hand for Darion to continue.

"The footsteps are right outside the door. I hear a key in the lock. The woman in the cell is shivering. She's cold." He gulped for air as he struggled to go on.

"What happens then?" asked Mr. Boyle, the psychiatrist. He was much shorter than Darion. He had very light features. Bald head, pale skin, light eyes that seemed to wobble about in their sockets. He never focused on one thing or looked the boy fully in the eye. He was familiar with prodding patients for more information by keeping them talking. As Darion described the vision, as he has begun to refer to it, he saw Mr. Boyle taking notes. *Most likely recording the "dream." Maybe he'll turn them into the police. The FBI might be better for this case.* He had come to the resolve that this was no ordinary dream. He knew the woman was suffering, and she desperately needed help. His help. Before it was too late.

"She starts saying 'no.' Quietly at first, and then the door swings open and that's when *he* enters. He has a creepy laugh, like nothing I've ever heard." Darion trailed off, shivering at the mention of *him*, lost in thought and afraid to voice the last part of the dream. Maybe saying it would make it true, and the smallest part of his soul was still hoping against hope it wasn't real. Breathing deeply, he finished, "And that's when the screaming starts."

"And then?" pressed Mr. Boyle.

"And then I wake up," Darion stated. Leaning forward in his chair he said, "Every time. I wake up at the same spot every time." He slowly brought his eyes to meet the doctor's. Mr. Boyle murmured to himself and continued scribbling on his notepad.

Darion stared at him, waiting for any acknowledgement whatsoever. When the man switched off his desk lamp and stood up without even looking at him, Darion's fists tightened. In an overtly enthusiastic voice, Boyle said, "Thank you for sharing, my boy. Hell of a nightmare. Just try and forget about it. That's my best advice," he said opening the door to usher him out.

Gawking at the man and his audacity, Darion started toward him, "What the..." but was cut off by his mother, Carol, who grabbed his arm.

"Go wait in the car," she ordered.

Pulling his arm away from hers, he followed her order and headed toward the exit. Furiously, he stomped down the stairs slamming the door on his way out.

I knew this would happen. For weeks, I've had had this vision, and when I finally told someone, the guy just opened the door and said, 'try and forget about it.' Who the hell does he think I am?

Darion couldn't believe his misfortune at having a dumbass for a psychiatrist. Holding his head in his hands, he sat on a bench on the outskirt of the parking lot waiting anxiously for his mother. Positioned across from a picturesque pond with towering trees and an abundance of chirping birds and swimming ducks, Darion ignored them all, glowering at the shadowed cement under his feet. The sun may be shining, but that jerk of a doctor had darkened Darion's mood.

Meanwhile, gesturing Carol into his office, Mr. Boyle said, "Mrs. Smith, may I be frank?" Carol hesitantly nodded.

"I believe your son has an overactive imagination. He spent today's entire visit describing a dream sequence which he claimed is real." He paused slightly, puffing out his chest, "My prognosis is that he is trying to avoid the present reality and all of its recent school displeasures by creating a new scenario in his head."

"What was the dream?" Carol asked inquisitively. Now that he mentioned it, she had heard her son tossing and turning night after night, and his bloodshot eyes were the proof of a lack of sleep. Maybe he was having nightmares like he did as a child. He was a solitary boy; he must be internalizing much of his distress. She thought back to a couple of weeks ago, when she and Rick had awoken to his yells. Rick had returned to their bed, wrapping her in his arms, as he shared about Darion's experience with Stephanie and Joey. But that had been weeks ago, it was not like Darion to hold on to something like this for so long. She felt on edge. *Why had he chosen not to share with her?*

The psychiatrist brushed her question off with a shake of his head.

"Oh, nothing original. Pish posh mostly. Typical teenage video game scenes replaying in their dreams."

Carol furrowed her brow, demanding, "Yes, but what was *my* son's dream?"

"Something about a woman in a cell—I'm going to send you home with a prescription for some sleeping pills. The boy," Boyle hesitated as he, for the first time, looked at the intensity of the Carol's gaze. "Darion," he continued. "He just needs rest. It is quite apparent by his demeanor and appearance that he's exhausted. Anything you can do to help him de-stress before bed would be beneficial. Also, tonight, have him try out a sleeping pill and I'm guessing it'll do the trick," Mr. Boyle stated confidently, as he wiped his moist, pale eyes with a tissue.

Walking out of the office, Carol wasn't so certain. She resolved to discuss the matter with Darion and Rick later that evening. Sighting Darion on the bench, she waved at him. She didn't smile, as she didn't want to encourage him that his behavior had been appropriate, though she chose not to admonish him either. Mr. Boyle was a pompous ass—she imagined herself telling him so on their final visit. Enjoying the image of herself berating the psychiatrist, she did not see the tears escaping her son's eyes in the passenger seat.

***

"There is my favorite employee! Darion, I feared you had left us for good! Where have you been, kid?" Tony called out while opening the front door to his restaurant. Darion knew his parents had called and summarized the school incident weeks ago. Carol had told Tony until the legalities and therapy were figured out, Darion would not be able to work.

"Hey, Tony, my mom sent me here to look at my work schedule. She says I need to wait another week at least before coming back."

Tony nodded. "No problem. Of course." Tony still stood opening the door, taking in, what Darion assumed, was his pale pallor and dark circles under his eyes. Darion hesitated, not wanting to enter the building to be scrutinized by the rest of the employees.

Looking around Darion asked, "Actually, Tony, can I talk to you?" as he doggedly avoided his boss's gaze.

"Uh, sure, kid. Let's take a walk. It is not often we get a sunny day around here," Tony smiled as he patted Darion on the shoulder.

As the two strolled through the parking lot in the direction of a nearby park, Darion tried to choose his words. He hadn't a clue how to broach the subject.

'Tony, I hear voices.' No, no, no that isn't how I want to come across. Instead he played out the conversation in his head. *'Tony, my birthmark is spreading, and I hear voices and I think it's all connected.' Hmmm,* he thought. *That's not bad.*

"Tony, I can't stop thinking about this woman."

Shaking his head, Darion couldn't believe that his

tongue could betray him so carelessly. That sounded all wrong. Tony had been intensely looking at him waiting for him to divulge a huge secret, and this is what the boy wanted to talk about?

"Some girl? Ha!" The huge man burst out laughing; his deep chuckles filling the empty park. "Oh, Darion. You kill me. So, you are still thinking about that Stephanie girl, I see?" he smirked as he elbowed the boy. "She must be quite a looker, if..."

"What? No," Darion cut him off. "That's not what I meant." Shaking his head, he tried to gather his thoughts. "I mean, I can't get this woman from my *dream* out of my head." Tony was still shaking his head, laughing even louder.

"I am not following you, son. What seems to be the problem? Dreaming about pretty girls never ruined my night's sleep." Tony winked, as he began picking his perfectly straight teeth with a toothpick.

"No," Darion said harsher than intended. "She's a prisoner in a cell. She has blonde curly hair and big blue eyes. She's always whispering, sometimes it sounds like she's saying my name, and then *he* comes, and she starts screaming," Darion stammered. His palms felt sweaty, and he rubbed them vigorously on his jeans as if to rid his hands of the filth the dream evoked.

He couldn't believe he had said it. He sat hunched against the stone bench avoiding Tony's gaze. This was probably going to be a repeat of Mr. Boyle's reaction. He braced himself... but he never would have expected his friend's response. Tony dropped the toothpick and leaned toward him.

"And then what happens?" Tony asked. His gaze hard. All sense of mirth vanished from his eyes, which had only moments ago sparkled from laughter, and now left Darion feeling small under the man's intense stare.

He had an unfamiliar look on his face. He had gone from a big, smiling goof to a steel-jawed, serious stranger that Darion hardly recognized. Everything about Tony had seemed to alter in an instant, leaving Darion to question whether he truly knew Tony all that well. *Maybe I shouldn't have said anything?* Darion stared at Tony, who was utterly intrigued by the dream, and began to answer all his questions regarding it. "When did the dream begin? Who knows of it? When did the mark on your hand begin to spread?" The questions poured out of Tony like a man leading an interrogation.

After a while, the two sat quietly. Tony was breathing heavily and stroking his brunet goatee. Darion just sat in puzzlement, more confused than ever. Tony had seemed interested all right, yet Darion didn't feel any better, having gained no more clarity on his life happenings. Also, Tony had asked questions about the oddest parts of Darion's ordeals. *Who cares what the surroundings of the cell in the dream looked like? What the guards looked like? Shouldn't I be figuring out why I'm dreaming of a cell in the first place?*

"Tony, do you think I'm crazy?" Darion asked after he had spilled everything, and he couldn't endure Tony's ponderous silence any longer.

"No, my boy," Tony assured Darion. "You have a good head on your shoulders. It sounds like you just need some rest. Anyways, I better be heading back soon," Tony said standing up, abruptly. "You just come back to work whenever you are ready, you understand?" Tony said as he started making his way back to the restaurant without a second glance.

Darion only nodded, feeling a bit bewildered. He had come to Tony out of desperation, and he left feeling dismissed. He began walking back to his truck.

He sounds like everyone else. 'Just an overactive imagination' or 'get some rest.' But that is exactly what no one seemed to grasp. So long as this woman was calling his name, he couldn't sleep or eat. She was consuming his thoughts.

As Darion jerked the truck door open, he heard Tony yell in a serious voice, "Darion. Make sure you do not mention this dream to anyone else, understood?" His tone and body language seemed very much in control and for the first time ever, Darion felt intimidated by the huge man. Tony added, "You know people can judge. Best keep it to yourself." Though it sounded more like the Tony, Darion had known his whole life, Tony's fluid motions still seemed strange.

"Yeah, all right, you bet, Tony. See ya," Darion said with a wave, trying to muster a fake smile.

I have to get out of here. Darion fired up the engine. He had to get away from Tony—from everyone. It seemed no one could help him. What's worse, they all seemed to be lying that nothing was going on or out of the ordinary. Darion knew better. They were all judging him, and it was only a matter of time before they started admitting it. As if on cue, the screaming in his head began. The nightmare he so often saw while asleep, was now making its presence known in the waking hours. Swerving, and driving like a madman, Darion shot out of the parking lot like a bullet.

***

Contrary to Darion's assumption, Tony was ecstatic. *It is time!*

He hurriedly entered his office and slammed the door. He was dialing the Smiths' phone number before he even realized the implications of the day's event.

"Hello," a low, bass drawled on the other line.

"Rick, hello, it is Tony. We need to talk... now."

"All right, all right, Tony, but it is not the best time. One of my horses broke through the line and I better go fetch him before the storm. It is going to get ugly out there."

"No, Rick. It is *time*."

"Time? Time for what, Tony? You are not making sense. Look, like I said, the horse..."

"Rick," Tony blared. "It is time to return home!"

Before Tony could continue, the receiver on the other line seemed to crackle and crash to the ground. He could hear Rick cursing, quickly trying to retrieve the phone as he shouted for Carol to come into the kitchen.

"Tony, come on over at once. We will be ready."

Rick slammed the phone down, and in an instant, everything became clear. Darion's behaviors and odd dreams. Maybe it *was* time to go home.

Whistling a very old tune, Rick practically skipped into the other room to find Carol shaking uncontrollably clutching a scrap of paper.

"Rick, Rick, look," she sobbed, handing Rick a half-torn sheet of paper covered in Darion's precise handwriting.

> *Mom and Dad,*
> *Please forgive me, but I need some time. I*
> *just need to figure everything out.*
> *And I hate that I'm letting everyone*
> *down.*
> *I'm going away for a while.*
> *Please don't follow me or look for me.*
> *I will come back someday.*
> *~D*

The two stared at each other in horror.

CHAPTER 4

The Signal

"How could you let this happen?" Tony roared, revealing his true self.

No longer was he the humorous restaurant owner. No, he had stripped himself of this persona, and was again Antonis Legario, the Royal Commander of the Guard, and Sworn Protector of the Prince.

"The time to return has finally come and you lose the boy? How could you be so careless?"

"Now you wait a minute, Antonis," Riccus Vershan, snapped, having also shed his false persona as Rick Smith. "You were the one who was with him last. How did you come upon the signal anyways?"

Antonis had the decency to look abashed. He took a deep breath and explained how Darion had come to visit him at the restaurant. He told them of the dream. Carol was shaking her head.

"What is it, Carolina?" Antonis asked. He looked at her peculiarly.

She cried softly, and said, "I should have told you.

Right away, after his meeting with Mr. Boyle today. Darion had told *him* of a dream. Mr. Boyle told me he was dreaming of a lady in a dungeon. I did not think it..." she trailed off. "I thought we would all talk about it tonight. I did not realize he would run away because of it. I wondered if it had to do with the Realm but wanted to have you with me before I brought it up," she said looking into Rick's steady gaze. Sniffling, she said, "This is all my fault. If I would have told you sooner instead of brushing it off, maybe, maybe..." She plopped onto the sofa. "Maybe Darion would still be here. He said he was just running by work to check his schedule. I did not think he would bolt. He must have left this in his room with the intention to run."

This last revelation resulting in more tears. Riccus gently sat down next to his beloved wife, taking her petite, soft hand in his.

"We will find him, Carolina, and then we will take him home..." Pausing, he said lowly, "To his real parents."

They stared in each other's eyes for a moment, before Carolina began to cry even harder against his shoulder. They both knew the undertaking they had committed to many years ago. Though, a bond with the young baby had formed much faster than they had anticipated. It felt like they had always been his 'Mom and Dad,' and now they had to give him back.

In a gentler voice, Antonis said, "We need to find him. The signal has come. We can talk more about this once we get him back. We have a lot of work to do and I am afraid not much time. I do not know how long the portal will remain open."

Riccus patted Carolina's knee, as she wiped the tears from her cheeks. Together they stood, and again became the Keepers of the Prince, instead of distraught, disheveled parents.

"Where would he have gone?" Riccus wondered.

The three sat brainstorming for a moment. They decided to split up and communicate via hand radios. Antonis headed in the direction of Cannon Beach, thinking Darion might be pulled to the coastline he so loved.

Carolina set out toward Mt. Hood. The boy loved a particular spot at the base of the mountain. She had taken him there as a boy, and it was always their special spot. She hoped she knew her son well enough, *or Prince Darion, that is*. She had to get used to calling him that again.

Riccus, a known tracker, retraced his son's steps back to the restaurant. Antonis said he had sped out of the driveway. Since it was an unusually sunny day, it may be difficult to track his son's truck. No muddy tracks to follow. He had no destination in mind. He opted to try his best at tracking, or at least try his best to head whichever direction he felt pulled. Darion probably had about an hour's head start on all of them. Riccus was confident however that they would find him, or that Darion's conscience would bring him back home, where Carolina had left a note explaining for Darion to call one of them immediately.

***

Darion sped up around a curvy, forested road. The

underbrush and trees were so dense that they entombed the road, making it feel like a long, dark tunnel. The bleakness of the darkened road suited his black mood. If he blasted his music loud enough, maybe he could drown out the voices in his head. He glanced at his hand on the steering wheel. The mark was no longer concealable. It had spread. The "birthmark," which used to reside on his knuckle and was easily hidden by a ring, now had taken over his entire hand. *Maybe I'm hallucinating.* The deep, black mark had transformed into hundreds of small symbols enveloping his entire ring finger and snaking their way up his wrist toward his forearm. The odd part was, he recognized some of the symbols. Many of them occupied pages in his sketch book. *That's impossible,* he assured himself, *right?*

Though he was unable to identify the cause, it was all tied together. His mysterious birthmark, nightmares, all of it; he was determined to solve the mystery. He needed space and quiet. Now that he was away from everyone, maybe he would be able to figure it out. The fresh air would help clear his head. He continued driving farther and farther from home on the windy, uninhabited road, too consumed by his thoughts to notice the deer crossing the lane.

The animal stood no chance against the large metal beast.

Darion slammed on the brakes, screeching to a halt. He scrambled out of his truck, and to his horror, there lay a dead deer. A puddle of blood spread out around the animal's carcass and its severed head. Darion stood over the animal for a long while simply staring at it. *What have I done?* His father had always told him to keep his eyes out for deer while driving.

"Damnit," he said aloud. He had never seen this much blood before. The scene before him was so raw and visceral. It was strange. As he stood staring at evident death, he had never felt more alive. He felt ashamed by the realization.

In an instant, his senses triggered. He felt everything around him. It was as if the woods were alive and connected to him. He could feel the precipitation in the air, hear the trickle of a nearby stream, and practically taste the overpowering blood that he had just inhaled through the nostrils of a coyote around the bend.

That's it. I've completely lost my mind. Darion stood paralyzed, his hands over his eyes, tears streaking through his locked fingertips.

"I'm so sorry," he whispered to the fallen doe that had lost her life because of his recklessness. He vowed then and there that he would never make the same mistake again.

He decided the decent thing to do would be to get the body out of the road, which would have been a simple act, until he saw that underneath the doe there was another leg sprouting out. He squatted down, and as he slid the deer's body to the side he grimaced as he beheld a young fawn. Its lungs had been crushed by the weight of its mother atop it, yet it still clung to life. It lay there, wheezing through its muzzle. Darion immediately saw himself through the fawn's eyes.

A murderer. Bringer of pain and death, and ultimately, a predator. Darion could not believe it. He had always been kind and cautious. Even when his friends went hunting, he would never join. He loved animals and had never killed one in his life.

As he sat next to the fawn, he tried to comfort it by caressing its head. The small creature turned its head slightly, making it clear she wanted nothing to do with the villain. He sat there with the animal, not knowing what to do but to stay by its side. He watched as the animal tried to reach out its tongue to lick her mother's bleeding side.

As the minutes passed by, the audible gurgles from the crushed windpipe began to lessen. A few moments later, there was only silence. Darion felt numb, as the sky seemed to open in judgement and the downpour began.

He stood up, no longer wanting to be there. It took him a moment to register that the lights belonged to a vehicle behind him and not the souls of the little animals exiting their earthly bodies.

Footsteps crunched behind him. Darion didn't even have to turn around. He knew it was his father.

Without words of rebuke, Rick wrapped his arms around his son, knowing the devastation that must have occurred and the heartache his son was now experiencing.

"Darion, I am taking you home. Everything is going to make sense now, I promise. You have to come with me, though."

Without even waiting for a response, Rick dragged the two carcasses off the road, and moved Darion's truck to the side.

"How did you find me?" Darion asked once Rick joined him in the car.

"It was not that hard, to be honest. I guess I know you better than I thought. I started from the restaurant and just followed my gut. It led me straight to you."

"Oh," was all Darion said.

His mind lingered on Rick's words, "Everything will make sense now." *What did he mean by that?* Darion took off his rain jacket, now soaked with rain and streaked with blood. He wadded it up and set it near his feet on the floor. Rick had mentioned that they were going home, yet this was not the right direction. Rick must be headed to a different location.

Nervously, Darion rubbed his hands together, and asked, "Where are we going?"

Rick didn't answer him. Darion looked over at his father, the twilight shadows playing across the weathered planes of his serious face. He looked different somehow. His mannerisms seemed off. Darion couldn't pinpoint what exactly was different, but it reminded him of his meeting with Tony that same afternoon. Darion felt his pulse climbing upwards. *What's his deal?*

"Dad," he repeated, "I said where are we going?" Darion questioned, his stare boring into Rick.

He wished he could determine what was different. Maybe his father was mad or disappointed in him, and that was why his movements were sharper than usual.

"I heard you," Rick stated quietly, as he took a deep breath, "Darion, we are going home. Now you just catch a few winks of sleep if you can. I have a feeling it will be a long night."

What is going on? If Darion hadn't been worried, he certainly was now. He didn't know who to believe anymore. *What if Rick was taking him to an asylum? Locking him away because he had become too much of a detriment to the family!* He stopped himself. *Stop it. He has always been true to his word. If he says we are going home, then we are. Maybe he is taking a different route, that's all.*

Feeling a little better, Darion closed his eyes. It had begun to grow dark, and the vibrations of the car lulled him toward sleep. An old melody entered his subconscience. He could hear her voice. Smooth as silk. She sang quietly, but the words were loud in his head. He was unsure if he was awake or sleeping. It made no difference now. He felt drawn to her, and she to him.

> *"Long ago, there was a man.*
> *As fortunes go, he made many few,*
> *Possessions mattered not,*
> *When the man had all he wanted,*
> *In the warm embrace of his love.*
>
> *Beauty grows and beauty fades,*
> *Men's sword arms swell but do not*
> *remain,*
> *Only love and memories can keep one's*
> *heart warm and full,*
> *This the man knew, and he knew it well.*

Long ago, there was a woman,
Who loved to sing a beautiful tune.
Her bloodline mattered not,
When the man had all he wanted,
In the warm embrace of his love..."

Darion smiled to himself. Her voice had grown
familiar over the weeks, though he wished more than
anything to never hear her screams again. She was very
talented. In the depths of darkness, he was jogged back to
consciousness by the sudden end of her song. He could
picture the tears wetting her face. He wondered why she
was crying now, just as he was getting comfortable and
enjoying the music. Slowly, she began again, softer this
time.

"Long ago, there was a King,
Whose eyes beheld a maiden, who
Had not a cent,
Though caring not,
He took her away in the warmth of his
embrace,

They lived a time quite happily,
First two, and then came three,
Darion was,
A testament of their love,
Their child's blood held that of a King
And the woman sang him to sleep,

In the warm embrace of her love..."

Her singing ceased as the cries of a mother, who has known great loss, echoed across his subconscious.

"Blood of a King!" Darion shouted, jumping upright and startling Rick.

A thousand thoughts began to swirl around in his clouded brain. He knew what he had heard, but that was crazy. *How did she say it again? 'Darion, a something or other of their love.' Their child? HIS PARENTS?*

Rick was staring at him queerly. Formulating a complete thought became a struggle, as words eluded Darion. Everything seemed to be moving, shifting, swirling, and suddenly he was out. He had finally succumbed to his exhaustion.

***

Voices woke him. Before opening his eyes, he listened.

"Well, what does he know, Riccus?" Tony demanded, or at least it sounded like Tony. *Why is Tony here? Who's Riccus? That's an odd name.* Cutting off his revelry, his father's voice replied.

"I cannot be certain, Antonis. Like I said, when I pulled up there was quite the scene. Two dead deer in the road, and a dazed Darion standing in the rain. I just took care of the situation, told him we were coming home, and brought him here. That is all so far."

"Well, what about the truck ride? You said he shouted or something in his sleep? Did he say anything in particular? Is he in a trance?"

"We have been over this at least ten times now. We will not know how much Darion knows until he tells us." At a glare from Tony, Darion's father added, "He jumped and had an odd expression. I asked him if he was all right, what was happening, and then he passed out. Not another word or sign of life since about twenty miles back."

Darion heard Carol whisper. "Do not say it like that."

Cracking an eyelid open, Darion peered out to behold a bewildering scene. His parents were sitting on a log with Tony, yet they all looked different, modified. Rick sat outlining his jaw with his thumb. Tony, whom Darion could not recall ever seeing outside of his restaurant garb, was now wearing tight-fitting pants, a shirt, and...

"Is that a cloak?" Darion laughed, startling all three of them for a change.

He sat, crossing his arms as if to ward off the chill. It was a cold night. *Why doesn't anyone have the heat on? For that matter, where were they?*

As he looked around his surroundings, he realized they were in an outdoor alcove, sitting by a crackling fire, the three of them intently looking at him. No one spoke.

"Well..." he hesitated. *What was going on?* "What are you guys staring at?" Darion followed their eyes to his hand and cried out startled, "What's happening?"

His arm had begun to take on more of the symbols. Now, not only was his finger, hand, and wrist covered, but the "mark" was spreading up his forearm. There were so many symbols, now too numerous to count, yet some of them were taking on a luminescent shimmer. His arm was actually glowing.

Feigning calmness, Darion straightened, looking from his arm to his audience. "I have lost my mind, haven't I?"

His statement and genuine confusion broke the silence. The three laughed and looked much more relieved. They all stood and took turns hugging him, glad that he was found and safe.

This is it, Antonis thought. *Time to go home and present a prince. We should have prepared him more. How did the years slip by so fast?* Gesturing for everyone to sit down, Antonis sat facing Darion.

"Darion, I am going to tell you a story. An old story. And when I am finished, things will begin to make more sense, I can assure you. I need you to promise not to interject until you have heard everything, however. Understood? It will be easier that way."

Darion looked as if he were going to argue and then thought better of it. "Understood."

CHAPTER 5

The Tale

Antonis nodded, beginning to unravel the long-awaited history of Darion's mysterious birth. Secrets that had long sat hidden in the depths of the three Keeper's minds came back to life, and instantaneously, they were back amongst their kind—the members of Nav'Aria.

"Well, I believe the proper way to start would be by introducing ourselves. Darion, my name is Antonis Legario. I am the Royal Commander of the Guard and Sworn Protector of the Prince of Nav'Aria."

Darion was looking at Tony with a doubtful stare. *What is he talking about?* Not knowing what to do or say, he just sat quietly listening, feeling rather bemused. Rick stood up next.

"I am Riccus Vershan. Keeper of the Prince," Rick stated, staring far off with a shame-filled expression. "I should have told you the truth a long time ago." He looked to Carol to continue.

"My name is Carolina Vershan. I am also a Keeper of the Prince," Carol told the boy whom she had called son since infancy. "Darion, we swore a long time ago to protect you until the time was right. Now, we are going to take you home to your *real* parents." Rick pulled her down by the elbow.

"Shhh, Carolina, it is not your place. Do not confuse the boy," he whispered loudly. He looked at Antonis, who was scowling at Carol, and shrugged his shoulders apologetically. "Antonis, will you continue?"

"What are you guys talking about?" Darion asked them incredulously. "What prince?" He had waited his entire life to learn of his birth parents, but this... this felt like some cruel joke.

"Well... you, of course," Antonis smartly replied.

That shut the boy up. His head was spinning. *What does he mean 'you, of course'? Why are they talking in circles?*

"Hey, remember I told you not to interject. This will all make sense, I promise. Let me start from the beginning."

Gruffly clearing his throat, Antonis began slowly. "Darion, we are not of this world. We come from a place called Nav'Aria. A wonderful kingdom... which you will rule one day. I know you do not believe me now, but trust me, it is incredible. Our land is comprised of many creatures. Man, unicorn, centaur, merfolk, wood nymphs, trolls, and on and on it goes. We have beautiful mountains, lakes, hills—just like here. That is why we settled on *this* place. We tried to find somewhere that remotely resembled our home, and where we would have privacy. We have found an entryway through the falls which leads to a spring, hidden amongst a copse of trees in the Woods of the Willow."

Darion shook his head. He desperately wanted to interrogate his parents rather than listen to Tony drone on about a make-believe fantasy world. What nonsense.

"Tony, do you really expect me to believe that you all brought me here through a portal? To save me? And what did you save me from exactly? Why did my supposed 'parents' give me up at all?"

He stood up and stalked off toward the edge of their campfire. He could hear the three of them whispering about him. Antonis gesticulated wildly in his direction.

He heard Carol's sweet tones, "Let him be. This is hard to take all at once," and Rick's confident reply, "He will come around. He was born for this."

Darion then, felt guilty. Afterall, these were the ones who had raised him his whole life. Even now, after all the hurt and stress he had caused them as of late, they were still here. They had come after him. They loved him. *They* were his parents. With a huge sigh, Darion turned on his heel and returned to the gathering.

"I'm sorry I interrupted, Tony... I mean Antonis," he said a bit unsteadily. He would at least hear them out, even if he didn't believe a word.

The speaker nodded his head and began his story much more formal this time. Speaking in a low voice, with his eyes focused on the fire, none could avoid how it seemed to grow and take on a tinge of green. The wilderness around seemed to be listening as well. No crickets, no rush of water, no birds chirping, no rain drops. All was still as the tale of a foreign, secret land was shared with its rightful heir to the throne.

In the days of long ago... The land, Nav'Aria, lived in harmony for hundreds of years. What you would call "mythical creatures" and man all harmoniously cohabitated in the Realm. Unicorns were the oldest and wisest of the land. They were born with an innate magical gifting. They were also known to have the longest lifespan. It was in their council that they "foresaw" the need to have a human leader. Vondulus Meridia, born with the mark, was selected to rule fairly throughout the lands, and his rule was just. The realm thrived in abundance and happiness.

Vondulus's son, and then granddaughter ruled fairly and justly. Your story begins with Aliguette, who was born with the mark and was a Meridia heir. You see, in Nav'Aria, rulers are not chosen based on gender or birth order but by the Mark. She also ruled a happy and just Realm for many cycles. She had two sons: Narco and Rustusse. Narco loved his mother dearly. He was the oldest son, always needy and insecure, and desperate to please his mother. His father, Valron, husband to the queen, looked down on the weak boy. Narco was crafty by nature and somewhat sickly in appearance, unlike his strong, strapping younger brother, Rustusse.

Rustusse Meridia was born with the Mark and became the rightful ruler of Nav'Aria after his mother's passing. Valron happily welcomed his son to the throne. It would seem the only unhappy creature in the Realm regarding the coronation, was Narco. His jealousy and malice slowly consumed him, but it was not for some time, that his bitterness festered causing him to take radical action.

For many years, the land was at peace, each species keeping to themselves, yet still in accordance with Rustusse's laws and supervision. It was not until Rustusse's third cycle, that he was forced to battle. There had been instances of unrest before, however very limited in number.

Antonis stopped and spoke directly to Darion. "You see Darion, Nav'Aria is a peaceful yet realistic realm. It is not utopia but the most tenable equivalent. Though hardly ever needed, there is an organized military presence that protects the royal family and maintains the peace. I am..." Antonis stopped and cleared his throat. "I mean, I was the Royal Commander of the Guard."

Antonis trailed off for a moment looking deeply into the flames. Riccus filled the awkward silence.

"Antonis was... I mean *is*, a great leader. It has been an honor to work so closely with him. He made a huge sacrifice by taking on this assignment." Locking eyes with the commander, Riccus said, "Please continue."

Darion looked back and forth between the men, not sure what to believe. He had to admit it was an interesting story to say the least. Maybe they were from another world. It would perhaps explain why the three always spoke so formally. They never chided him for his speaking habits, but he didn't think he had ever heard them speak a contraction in his entire life.

"Well, this is the place in our history where everything changed," explained Antonis, in an ominous tone, as he began to trace a tree branch in the dirt creating a makeshift map.

One day it was noted that there was unrest on the border of the Shazla Desert, the dark land outside of the realm, Rav'Ar. Rav'Arians are clearly named after their home. "Nav'Aria" means "of the family" so therefore "Rav" means the opposite, or literally "outside of the family." These large lizard, bird-like creatures were known to have large talons and stand larger than a full-grown man. Their scales are impenetrable, and their beaks are larger than most men's skulls. They are not allowed across the border.

In the beginning of time, when the first creatures dwelt in the lands, the unicorns made a truce with the beasts of Rav'Ar. Each group would keep to their land and never disturb the other. This treaty had lasted for many, many cycles.

However, in the years leading up to Rustusse's son's birth, the Rav'Arians had begun to run out of resources. Their food supply was low, and they began crossing the border during the night to hunt. This was a tremendous err on their part, specifically the fact that they had abducted a young centaur outside of a small village. When the parents of the missing youngling saw the large, claw footprints in the soil outside their tent, they knew the treaty had been breached. The male centaurs gathered and formed a war party to go after the young one. The war party caught up to the villains, but it was too late. What they found was terribly morbid. Before they saw the group, they smelled them. They had a potent, toxic smell as if they were the living dead. And in the middle of the dirt road were entrails and blood stains, leading the war party on to discover the corpse of the leader's beloved son. This barbarity did not go unpunished. The war party outnumbered the Rav'Arians three to one; with right on their side they laid waste to the treacherous beasts. The centaurs took the slain creatures' heads and put them on spikes along the nearby border. This night sparked the first "war" of Nav'Arian history. Back at the centaur camp, they sent out the cry of war, lighting the signals for Castle Dintarran.

Involuntarily, Darion shuddered. The hairs on the back of his neck were standing up, and as he looked at his arms, he saw gooseflesh. *If I thought I was crazy before, what does that make me now? And what does that make Tony and my parents?*

He looked at the three of them, and knew that try as he might, he could not doubt this tale. It was too specific. He had never seen the three so... real. He felt like he was being acquainted with them for the first time.

He looked at his hand, now covered in symbols. He felt his sketch book buried deep in his pocket, which he had grabbed before his hasty departure from his former home. Thinking on these things, he knew for certain this story was no *story*. This *was* his ancestry, and now he waited for the long-anticipated reveal of his natural parents. Without missing a beat, Antonis carried on, his voice growing stronger by the minute.

Forces gathered on both sides of the border. The Rav'Arians were tired of their forced exile, while the creatures of Nav'Aria were driven by the need to protect their homeland and children. It was during this battle that brother to brother, centaur to unicorn stood shoulder to shoulder, awaiting the writhing line of Rav'Arians rushing at them from across the border.

Rustusse was firm in his command. 'No one will cross the border. Let it be known in history that the vicious, blood-thirsty creatures from across the dark land invaded this kingdom, requiring my countrymen, and myself, to fight.'

It was a long, bloody battle, but the effort on the Rav'Arians' side was futile. They were outnumbered and outskilled. They had no leader. Astride his mighty companion, Trinidad the Unicorn, Rustusse welcomed the onslaught of battle. His sword arm was strong and well worked after years of training for this exact moment; besides the fact, that the mark on his sword arm propelled it into action almost of its own accord.

As the first beaked lizard ran toward him, Rustusse slashed his sword removing the monster's head before it even leveled its spear. Trinidad galloped through the swarm of creatures piercing through the dark scales with his horn. The two were a formidable pair. The remaining Rav'Arians leapt out of the way of the fearsome duo. The army's victorious cheer roared through the valley as they watched the monsters retreat, back to their land. It was not until all the monsters were beyond the line of vision, that those around the king realized there was a problem. Sometime during the tumult of the cheers, their king had been stabbed by a poison-tipped Rav'Arian spear. The culprit lay at the feet of Trinidad, who was crying for help! His panicked cries filled the ears of everyone around him.

As Rustusse slid off his mighty steed, Trinidad realized what had happened and turned in rage to face the evil adversary. He ran straight at the monster and his horn pierced through the beast's head exiting its skull through the back. Black cranial bits and feathers still clung to Trinidad's horn as he madly pawed at the ground in front of his king, standing watch. His Royal Guards rushed to Rustusse's side and stripped him of his armor. It was a clean stroke through his heart. This was a mortal wound, and the king was declared dead. The royal guards mouthed the words and to Trinidad's horror, he knew it was true. His king. His friend. His companion. Died on his watch. He was filled with immense horror and remorse. All he could do was stand watch over the fallen man.

Darion gulped. His pulse beat rapidly as the story drew out.

But just as hope was lost, Rinzaltan, the elder unicorn approached. He was too old to fight but he had stood watch at the top of the ridge. For he now knew his purpose for coming that day. It was not to celebrate the victory, but to give his life to save another.

As he approached the king, all dropped to their knees bowing their heads. Unicorns are the most preeminent and blessed of all creatures. Their powers grew with age and they were known to be very wise. Rinzaltan had seen many cycles and fathered three good colts, including Trinidad. He touched his cheek to his son's in affection. Trinidad, his youngest, and chosen to be the king's steed. What an honor!

He communicated his intention to his son in that one touch. And Trinidad fell to his knees, crying softly, "No, Father." However, he knew he could not stop his father if he wanted. His father possessed great power and had made up his mind. With his healing powers, he could have healed a dying man with the touch of his horn, yet even that exerts a lot of energy. A king lying dead was a whole other issue. It was a short enough amount of time that the king's soul fire still burned in his chest, even if his heart had stopped beating. Rinzaltan knelt before the king and with his final command he ordered his own death. None stepped up to do his bidding. None but Shale, the Royal Guard Commander.

He had led many exhibitions with Rinzaltan and known him since he was a boy. He stepped up to the majestic creature and knelt before him, bowing his head to the ground. Rinzaltan nudged him, urging him to rise. Shale stood up and after a moment met his eyes. He hugged Rinzaltan around the neck, whispering, "Goodbye, my dear, old friend," and drew his dagger at the same instance, killing him in a quick cut to the jugular.

As the blood seeped out of the wound and the slain unicorn fell beside the king, another guardsman stepped up with his wine pouch gathering the streaming blood. Hurriedly they poured the blood into the wound and into the king's mouth. For it was said that a unicorn's blood could give life. The myth was proven to be true that cold, frosty morning as the fog swept in hiding the hundreds of corpses of fallen warriors on either side.

As all the creatures celebrated the return of their king, Trinidad lay alone at the battle site, mourning the loss of his father and mentor; it was clear then, things would never be the same in Nav'Aria.

A hush had fallen over the woods and small group of Nav'Arians. Darion leaned back on the tree trunk against which he had positioned himself during the story. As Antonis concluded his story, Carolina and Riccus sat quietly. Darion had much to ponder. Though a compelling story, he still didn't know if he believed it, or more importantly what it had to do with him.

"I don't want to be rude but," Darion started, "what does it have to do with me?" He looked at Antonis, but it was his father who spoke.

"That is the next part of the story, son."

Darion interrupted again. "Well, how do I know if any of its even true? I'm supposed to believe I'm from some warring mythical land? I mean, do any of you have proof?" Darion wanted to trust them, but some things had to be put to the test before acceptance. Antonis was still looking down, but his face belied a grin as Darion was speaking. "What's so funny?" Darion snapped hotly, at his former boss. Darion didn't want to be laughed at right now and he didn't think any of this was humorous, so why did Tony?

"Now, now, Darion. Calm yourself. I only smile

because your father had warned me that if you grew to be anything like him, you would require 'proof.' He is a wise leader, which I will tell you about shortly. But before that, there is this," Tony trailed off, as he reached deep into what appeared to be a cloak's inner pocket. He pulled forth three items. A leather cord, a knife, and a scroll.

"These your father confided in me to keep safe until you had come to a certain age, and your Mark began to call you home. You clearly know that it has rapidly spread over the last few weeks. Also, the glow... that is the signal that the portal is calling. We must leave soon. Look these over, and hopefully you will begin to believe us. We would not lead you astray, my prince."

Reaching for the items, Darion paused at "my prince."

"Don't call me that, Tony," Darion said quietly. He grabbed all three items and crept back to the tree trunk, so he could examine them. The leather cord was very thick. It was an aged, black band with a large ruby hanging off a gold centered clasp.

"What's this?" Darion asked.

"That is a warrior's identification. All male warriors chosen to be in the military and Royal Guard wear one," Tony said as he tugged his tunic down to display a smaller stone against his throat. His was a green stone, maybe a peridot or jade.

"Turn the stone over, Darion." Turning it in his hand, Darion flipped the stone over. It was encased in gold, and the back was inscribed. Darion gasped.

"It says 'Darion,'" he said, awestruck. This gem was worth more than any other possession Darion had. They all nodded.

"Yes," Carolina replied. "Your father gave it to us when we left. You are meant to wear this. The ruby signifies royalty. This is your insignia. Wear this and people will recognize you before they even see your face. People of the Realm will be waiting for your return." Hands shaking, Darion nodded. He tucked the leather throng into his pocket. Picking up the knife, he tested the blade.

"Pretty dull."

Antonis laughed aloud. "Yeah, I know. I have not kept it as sharp as I should. Please do not tell your father." He smirked. "He is a stickler about such details."

Darion didn't know how to respond to that, so he examined the handle on the blade. It was a fine knife, or at least it would be once sharpened. The handle was made from an antler of some sort. On it were symbols etched with a blood-red paint, or at least what he hoped was paint. Many of the symbols he recognized.

"What do *these* mean?" he asked.

"These are old markings, Darion. Each one symbolizes one of Nav'Aria's species and their traits." Darion just stared blankly at him.

With an embarrassed cough, Rick said, "All right, let me see that blade." Pointing at one that resembled a tree, he said, "See, look at this symbol for example. This one represents the centaurs. The tree represents the centaurs because, yes, they live near trees, but also because they are like a tree. Strong and true, and their roots run deep in the land. And this one," pointing out a particular moon-shaped symbol, Rick continued. "The moon represents the unicorns. The silver brilliance gleams bright in the sky just as the majestic creatures shine in our land. They are our Elders and our guidance." Darion was nodding throughout. Now that he took the time to listen and reflect, he felt it was time to show them his sketch book.

"I have to admit that I am starting to believe you. I've been drawing these creatures you speak of and symbols for years. I thought I was just creative," he muttered lamely, more to himself. "I didn't know I was linking my heritage to my drawings."

None of them were following, and Antonis asked what exactly he was talking about. "Oh, I have secrets of my own, too, Tony," Darion smiled at the big man as he reached into his deep pocket pulling out a worn, leather sketch book.

He handed it to him, and the three huddled together to flip through the pages. In wonder, they sat pausing here or there and whispering amongst each other. The final page held a different image. A man. Carolina gasped, dropping the book.

Antonis asked fiercely, "Darion, how did this image come by you?"

Darion was puzzled by the sudden change of mood. Hesitantly, he stuttered, "He, He, He's the man in the dream. The one who hurts her..." he trailed off as he avoided the image.

It was a few nights ago. He had never before seen the man. He always woke up before he entered the cell. The last dream was different however. He had left that part out when he told Mr. Boyle and Tony. It was as if the man had sensed Darion. He could not explain it, but right at the end of the dream when he usually awoke. The man walked in and knelt beside her. He ran his hand through her now clumps of dried out, dirty hair and stared whispering one word. "Azalt."

The image revealed a man with a sharp hook nose and close-cropped dark hair peppered with grey. His eyes were dark. Even though it was a black and white sketch, his eyes gave off the color of crimson by the crackling fire. He exuded evil.

Even thinking about him made Darion shudder. After that, the dreams had ceased. He had no visual connection: Yet her voice, like the song, sounded sporadically in his head.

"Hurts who?" Antonis asked very quietly, gripping a sword handle that had just appeared from the depths of his cloak.

"The blonde woman," Darion replied.

"Oh, this is not good. This is not good at all. He is after you, boy. We must hurry." Grabbing Darion's elbow, he ushered him into the makeshift shelter and gathered the others around. "All right, we can talk later. Now it is time to move. I did not realize how serious things had gotten."

Throwing their belongings into their packs, Antonis snapped for Riccus to put out the flames. Carolina was collecting their food and putting it into another small pouch.

Antonis grumbled under his breath, "How did he find out?"

Darion, standing stupefied in the center of the group, looked to them for answers. Everyone was hustling to leave camp, but he still didn't know who "he" was. *What am I missing?*

"Who is he? What is going on?" Darion yelled, amidst the commotion.

"Narco," Riccus spat out, as he kicked earth over the flames, smothering them as their hopes of a grand, happy reunion were smothered as well.

"Narco? Wait, Narco the brother? From the story?" Riccus nodded. "Well, what does he want with her? What do you mean he is after me? Who is she?" Still clutching the book, Antonis held it up.

"According to these drawings, if this is in fact the woman in your dreams, she is your mother, Queen Lyrianna. Narco's prisoner."

Darion stared in shock. *His mother? She's being tortured!*

"Move, people! You can explain the rest later. We need to get to her." They all stared at him. "Now," he shouted.

Antonis watched Darion stuff the unread scroll into his pocket with the leather necklace; the knife he tucked into his belt. Their prince was already beginning to take his place as leader, even though he did not know the repercussions his absence may have caused the land. Antonis shook his head to clear the dark thoughts that were presenting themselves.

If Lyrianna is captured, where is Vikaris? Where is the king?

How many others knew of their absence? They had all made a pact to fake their deaths in order to safeguard the truth of their destination. Yet, if Narco was torturing Lyrianna, she may have broken. Antonis only hoped they arrived in time to help before it was too late, for he could not allow himself to imagine failure—the failure of reuniting his prince with his natural mother, the queen.

"Let's go!" Darion commanded. He no longer doubted a word. It was as if they had spoken, and all at once a haze had been lifted from his memory. It all made sense—the mark, the drawings, his heightened senses. He knew they were telling him the truth, and he knew he needed to get back to his birth family. His mother needed him. It was time to go to Nav'Aria. It was time to go home.

CHAPTER 6

The Portal

"Tony, how much farther?" Darion shouted over the fierce howl of the wind. The light drizzle had reverted back to a downpour. *Typical. I'll be ready to leave this place behind*, he thought. Darion was desperately concerned for his mother, this stranger, now the sole focus of his world. He would give anything to trade places with her. *What had triggered her capture? What did Narco hope to gain from her imprisonment?* And he realized belatedly, *Who is my father?*

Darion needed to find out more. He could feel the scroll in his pocket, and he longed to break its seal and read it here and now. Yet he knew this was not the time or place. They needed to hustle, and he would get his answers another time. Haste preempted answers, momentarily.

"Not much further, but it is hard to say for sure. The foliage has grown over the years. It looks quite different now."

They stopped on the edge of the trail, looking over the rushing water. Many years ago, they had chosen

Multnomah Falls. It was a beautiful, picturesque scene with the rushing water. As they continued on the trail, they heard the roaring waterfall. Now in the rain's deluge, their vision became obscured and the falls' beauty was lost to the night.

"What are we stopping for?" Darion asked, looking around able to only make out a vague outline of his surroundings.

Antonis nodded, "This is it. The entrance." They had crept all the way up to the top of the Falls.

"This?" Darion asked. He was hesitant, and it looked like a far drop. He had thought for sure that the portal would be in a cave or through a stone nearby. "I guess I imagined it differently," he stated.

The rumble of the water was so thunderous that it made Darion's stomach do flips. This close to the water, he could no longer tell if the droplets hitting him were coming from the gloomy sky or the crashing waters.

"Well, what do we do?" he asked.

"You do nothing but stay close," Antonis ordered, as he threw off his cloak and stood up to his full height.

The man Darion had thought of as a big oaf, was now a man of steel and stealth. He gripped his sword, and Darion stared at the chest plate that he had seemed to overlook. He made an imposing image against the sinister backdrop; his fit physique having always been masked in oversized work uniforms and aprons.

Carolina and Riccus also shrugged off their ponchos and coats, revealing simple green and brown garb. They looked austere in comparison. Darion looked down at himself: oversized jeans, tennis shoes, and a drenched long-sleeve black shirt. It was clinging to his lean frame. Shrugging, he decided nothing mattered except finding his mother.

"My prince, put on the ruby. It is time."

Remembering the gift from his father, Darion thrust his hand into his pocket and revealed a shimmering gemstone. The stone cast a red glow on their surroundings. Silently praying for it to not slip out of his fingers, he quickly latched the necklace around his damp neck, becoming startled by the warmth of the stone. It was alive.

He instantly felt stronger and energized, the warmness tingling through his veins. He could hear whispers in the dark and was not sure if they were coming from his companions or the stone itself. They all huddled around him, linking arms. Carolina was crying.

Darion huddled closer to her, and whispered, "I love you, Mom. Nothing will ever change that." Her eyes were full of tears as she looked up at him and kissed his cheek, her love for him emanating through her gaze, before turning back to the group.

Antonis bellowed in a powerful, clear voice, "I, Antonis Legario, Sworn Protector of Prince Darion command the portal to open and see Darion restored to his rightful place as the Marked Heir of Nav'Aria."

They all took a deep breath. Darion had no idea what to expect. It seemed anticlimactic. Nothing happened. They looked to each other and then back to the water. Nothing. No one spoke for a long time, each pondering their situation.

Carolina finally gasped, "He blocked it!" Revelation turning to despair across the Keepers' faces. The portal. The way home was compromised. *How would they break through?*

Riccus quietly turned to Antonis, "Do you think..."

Cutting him off, Antonis agreed. "Yes, he must be trying to prevent our return. But how did he find out?"

"What do we do now, Commander?" Riccus asked him.

"Try again, and again, until we get through." Their arms were still linked and Antonis yelled again. "I am Antonis Legario, the Sworn Protector of Prince Darion Meridia. I command the portal to open and allow Darion to be restored to his rightful place as Heir of Nav'Aria."

Again, nothing happened but the continual rush of the Falls. He tried again. And again. And again.

"Bah," Antonis angrily threw up his arms. "What is the meaning of this?" He shouted angrily to no one in particular.

Three more times they went through the ritual, and again, and again, they were denied access. Riccus and Antonis continued to stare at the water hoping their penetrating gazes would breach the blocked entryway. Carolina began exploring near the edge of the water for any herbs or berries that could be useful. Darion sat on the edge of the water on a large rock, thinking on his mother, Lyrianna. He had known there was something familiar about her. He had so many questions for his companions and his mother. His mind kept returning to the hateful man and captor of his mother. *Narco.* He felt rage. *Who does he think he is to keep me from my mother?*

Jumping to his feet, Darion stood on the water's edge, eyes closed. Suddenly, he knew what to do. Remembering his incident earlier that evening with the deer, he recalled how he had felt connected with the earth. The water. The coyote. The air. Everything. His senses had been heightened.

Riccus tapped Carolina's shoulder pointing at Darion, the boy they had raised. His dark curls were plastered to his head. His ruby necklace shone brightly, as he held his large hands out over the water. Breathing deeply, Darion became aware of his surroundings.

The sky began to darken even further. Ominous clouds crept across the sky and gathered over their position near the edge. The rush of water increased. The water began to seep out horizontally from the falls. The sky darkened further, and the water began to rise around their ankles; Darion, meanwhile, was unfazed. He was mumbling something. Antonis, Riccus, and Carolina all gathered their packs and came to stand behind the boy. They could hear him repeatedly saying one word. "Azalt. Azalt. Azalt."

The wind followed. Severe gales howled down and around the curved trail. The trees slanted under the strain of the force, many of them being uprooted. Yet in the small circumference of the group's circle no wind touched them. It was as if they were in a bubble. All the while, watching as the trees began to blow away, the sky angrily cast down lightning bolts and boomed with thunder, and the water rose to their knees. Beginning to shout, Darion's voice increased in timbre. "Azalt! Azalt! Azalt!"

A green circle began to emerge in the middle of the pool on the upper tier of the Falls. They began to hear war cries and shouts from the other end of the opening. Larger and wider the circle grew until it was only a footstep away. Darion's rolled up sleeves revealed his entire arm was alit with glowing symbols; he opened his eyes and cried "AZALT!"

The floodwater rapidly seeped through their shoes and garments, as Darion yelled, "Link arms!" They quickly responded by grabbing one another's arms, and Darion cried, "Forward!"

They jumped together into the blinding, flashing green portal in the middle of the waterfall, leaving Oregon behind.

As the portal was closing around them, Darion cried, "I'm coming, Mother!" as the gateway closed, and the lightning struck a nearby tree, splitting it into four sections.

CHAPTER 7

The Battle

"You men, hold the line. Do not back down for anything," shouted Vikaris.

Astride Trixon, the king and his steed rode down the line encouraging the warriors to stand their ground. They had been bested by the Rav'Arian demons before, but that would not be the fate of today.

For many years this war had raged on, and now Narco was going to meet his nephew's wrath. This nephew was no longer a boy, but a man fully grown. The True and Rightful King, Vikaris. A man seeking justice and vengeance; it took everything in him not to rush the castle doors himself to try and save his beloved queen. Beyond that, his son had been sent away for safekeeping, his father murdered, and his crown sat on a false king's skull.

Instead of rash haste, Vikaris had turned his anger inward. He had strategically gathered his forces and studied his foe. Found out their weaknesses. There were many, despite his uncle's dark hold on them. He had done his research and now it was time to act. He knew where to strike the Rav'Arians to have the most effective results. Their heads were the most vulnerable, having much of their body protected by an outer shell; the Rav'Arians chose to forego helmets, and this was their greatest mistake.

"The time has come, Trixon. We will defeat Narco, and I will get my family back," Vikaris said, determined.

Trixon nodded his agreement, and the king felt reassured to have his best friend here for the battle. The bond made between a warrior and a unicorn was one that an outsider would never understand. The two became one and could share thoughts, emotions, and goals. These two had a common goal; not only had Lyrianna been captured, but also Trixon's father, Trinidad. They were determined to see their loved ones released.

Many years ago, a great battle was fought between these same forces. That was the first time that the Rav'Arians had openly rebelled against the Realm. They were slaughtered. They were not well organized and had no leader back then. That was before Narco had the sadistic idea to form an alliance with them and become their "king."

He had crossed the border, in the dead of night, in search of an old, dark magic. Since he was not born with the mark, and its inherent powers, he had had to improvise. He needed assistance murdering his brother, Rustusse, Vikaris's father. Narco had teamed up with the evil Rav'Arian creatures and together, they stormed Castle Dintarran, murdering the Royal family in their beds. All but Vikaris, that is, who was whisked away by a servant and a few Royal guards. Vikaris had been eleven years old, but he still remembered every outline and crevice on his aged father's face. He had been a good man. A good king, and he did not deserve that treacherous fate.

Since that ill-fated day, the calm kingdom had been submerged into a murky time. Narco took over the kingdom, killing all of those who stood in his way, including his own father who objected to his reign. He had a supernatural strength, and the unicorns could only conjecture where his powers came from. None had crossed the Shazla Desert and lived to tell about it. It was anyone's guess as to what he had encountered there.

For a time, no one knew there had been a survivor. Many in the Realm were confused. Some had tried to revolt against Narco, but they found his twisted torture methods too terrible. He was known for killing children in front of parents, forcing parents to kill their children, and so on and so on. As the years passed by and Narco's dark powers continued to wreak havoc on the Realm, cowing those before him, spirits were uplifted as Vikaris announced his presence and claim to the throne. He was the Royal Prince, who bore the mark; therefore, he was the rightful ruler. And thus, sparked the "second" war.

He had fought a few battles, but he had never directly faced the Narco's full mass. He was hesitant to amass *all* of his allies, specifically the unicorns, not wanting to risk their lives. For if the unicorns fell into Narco's hands, Vikaris shuddered at what horrors could be concocted from their subjectivity. He had hoped to have had the war won by now and his son returned to him. When he had sent his infant away with the Keepers, he had thought at most he would be gone a few years. He did not think the boy would spend his whole life in exile. He wondered if he would even recognize his face in a crowd. He thought of him daily and prayed to the Creator for his safety—that and his wife's.

When Lyrianna and Trinidad had been abducted many months ago, Vikaris had pleaded with Trixon to meet with the Unicorn Council to see if they would use their magic to seal the portal, for the time being at least. Vikaris could not win a war, rescue his bride, and "meet" his son. It would be for the best. Even if that delayed the boy's return a year or more. At least he was safe with his Keepers, and he would not have to be subjected to Narco's cruel wicked rule.

A horn blast broke Vikaris's revelry, and he got back to action.

"Lieutenant, what is going on? Who blew that horn?"

Lieutenant Kragar shook his head. "I have no idea, Your Grace," he said, scanning the horizon.

Yelling down the line, he shouted, "Who blew the horn? Stay your ground."

There seemed to be some commotion near a section of the front line. Vikaris had commanded the centaurs and men astride horses to the front. His cavalry was strengthened by the few unicorns' presence. The ground infantry soldiers' pikes stood ready. He wanted a strong, unbreakable line. It was time they taught these monsters a lesson. Yet as he looked around, there was clearly something wrong. He and Trixon rode down the hillside to inspect the front. There was still no sign of the Rav'Arian creatures he knew were out there. His scouts had seen their prints.

One scout had had the misfortune of running into a group of the monsters. His head had been catapulted at the front line, hitting a centaur square in the chest. This is what had caused the commotion. Vikaris looked at the poor boy's head. He could not have been more than fourteen or fifteen years old. Younger than Darion... his thoughts trailed off, then he realized...

"It is a diversion!" Vikaris yelled, whipping his head around, realization dawning as he heard cries from the flank. He had positioned his men so that their back was against Mt. Alodon. No longer did the Rav'Arians live beyond the Shazla. They had infiltrated the Kingdom at Narco's command, and marched West from Castle Dintarran, where they now resided. They must have had better scouts than Vikaris gave them credit for. They had discovered the goat trails along the mountain and crept up on them from the rear. Instantly, pandemonium broke loose.

He could hear his men facing swift deaths near the face of the mountain. He needed to regain control. Looking quickly over the scene, he made a swift decision. He knew those monsters wanted him to turn his force and head for the beasts attacking his rear lines. He, however, did not see as many numbers as initially expected. He believed *this* was the decoy. They wanted the soldiers at the front to turn their backs trying to identify the source of the noise, upon whence the monsters would launch their main assault. He felt sick with nausea for the loss of the men he was sacrificing like fodder, yet he did not run to their aid.

"Hold! Hold this line!"

Nav'Arians that had begun to rush to help their comrades stopped in confusion.

"My Lord, are you sure?" Lieutenant Kragar questioned.

Vikaris nodded and stared off at the horizon, thankful for the sunrise. This was not a battle to be fought in the dark. The front line squirmed. Men and centaur grumbled and shouted out to their King, one man going as far as calling out, "Murderer!" Before he was even able to continue his curse, Lieutenant Kragar had run him through with his sword.

"We will not tolerate traitors. We follow the king's orders, and he says 'Hold.' Stand firm, all of you, or face a similar fate," Kragar said, kicking the man from his sword.

No one voiced another objection. Shortly after, the cries ceased. The king could not tell how many of his men fell before they put the perpetrators down, but it did not look like any more were coming through that mountain pass. The wind picked up and carried with it a powerful scent of toxic waste. That was the thing about Rav'Arians. Rarely could they sneak up on you, for their smell was so powerful. It announced their presence before they were even visible. They must have disguised themselves on the mountain, or else he knew his men would have picked up their odor.

Another horn blew twice. That was the signal for an

enemy army approaching. Vikaris rode out a few strides in front of his men so he could face a greater number of them. The men observed the striking figure of their king. A close-shaven, tall man with a strong jaw and emerald green eyes sat upon the majestic Trixon. The ruby at Vikaris's neck was shining bright and cast a blood-red glow over himself, and his steed. Trixon was the largest unicorn present by far. If Vikaris had been a man of average height, he would not have been able to reach his saddle. The muscles bulged on Trixon's chest and legs. His silver luminance gleamed in the dawn's early rays. He was a powerful creature, and pressed upon purpose, he was lethal. He would see this war won. Today. Standing up in his stirrups, King Vikaris cried out:

"We have waited a long time to face this group of fiends. They always dodge our movements and avoid open warfare. Why? Because they are afraid! They know we have the unicorns on our side, we have right on our side, and we are going to win. We must prevail. They are not 'of' our land, therefore they should be cast out like the toxins they are. We *will* rid this land of these vile creatures, and the treacherous Narco! He is in for a rude awakening when he feels the hammer of our might. We *will* win this war, and I *will* take my rightful seat at the throne of Nav'Aria beside my Queen. WE WILL HAVE PEACE ONCE AND FOR ALL."

At that, the warrior unicorns shrieked and pawed the earth in agreement, startling the horses near them.

"The dark days are coming to an end. That end begins today. Stand with me! Stand with your brethren, and see this battle won, so we can raise our children, and our children's children, in a world without hate. In a world that knows no evil. Narco, and the stains of his injustice, will be wiped out. Members of Nav'Aria... Arise to arms!"

With his final cry, Vikaris raised his sword in the air, his gaze sweeping over the masses. His Mark glowed brilliantly for all to see; his ruby gave his eyes a wild, animalistic look; and Trixon reared up on his strong hind legs, his muscles rippling in the sun. Many cycles later, old men and beast would still speak of the iconic moment of their king astride Trixon, charging to war.

As thousands of evil creatures spread across the terrain, rushing toward the king, he turned on his charger, and together they sped off to meet them, followed by his mighty cavalry. A cry louder than humanly possible, as many would say later, left the king's mouth as he was submerged in blackness amongst the Rav'Arians. It sounded like, "Darion." Lieutenant Kragar and those in the front line, took up the king's cry and all charged yelling, "Darion," "For Darion," "For our sons and daughters!"

The battle cries echoed, louder and louder, over the fighting.

Sword flashing through the air, Lieutenant Kragar was still able to make out his king. He wished he would not expose himself so in battle. It was hard to protect the king when he happened to be the bravest, fiercest man in the Realm.

Brandishing his sword across the back of a nearby

Rav'Arian, Kragar grimaced as the aroma of the beast's open wound hit him full in the face.

"Downright rotten, you are," Kragar muttered, as he kicked the flailing body over and rode on to the next beast. Kragar's unicorn, Seeker, was not as large, nor as deadly as Trixon, but he was still a force to be reckoned with. Together they stabbed and killed oncoming enemies, one after another.

Kragar would never forgive himself if he let the king fall. His only goal in this mission, besides overall victory, was to protect the king. He rode fast and true until he was a body's width away from His Majesty. Side by side they fought, Seeker and Trixon decimating any creature who dared come near their bloodied horns.

With a momentary lapse of opponents, Vikaris looked to his right and nodded to Kragar. He stood in his stirrups to examine his surroundings. To an unexperienced eye, it would appear to be chaos: blood, guts, and bodies littered the ground.

However, Vikaris grinned and yelled, "Victory is within our grasp. Press on!"

It seemed that many of the Rav'Arians had taken to retreat, though minimal fighting continued. His cavalry having encircled much of the Rav'Arian force in a crescent shape, joined by adrenaline-ridden pike men and young warriors, the remaining foes began to flee before they were completely surrounded. Their carcasses had begun to pile up around the King and his core group of men. The beasts could tell that the "Red" King, as they had come to call him because of his ruby, had death in his eyes and would not stop until he had run them all through with his bronzed sword arm. As the field began to clear out, Vikaris reared up on Trixon. With one last burst of energy, Trixon ran down and kicked the back of a retreating Rav'Arian and mauled it to the ground. The beast lay in tattered bloody disarray.

"Whoa, friend. Whoa," Vikaris whispered to his unicorn companion, rubbing his thick, muscular neck, which happened to be covered in a grime of dirt, blood, and sweat. "We did it, Trixon. We won this battle. They will flee and tell Narco of our might."

Trixon nodded, breathing heavily. Somberly, he looked back. *That will not scare Narco. We must find his weakness, my king. He cares not for these creatures and their losses. And for every one hundred of them we kill, he gathers a thousand more from across the border. Their numbers greatly exceed ours. His end may not come on the battlefield.*

Vikaris thought on this, as he led them back to their main force. Looking out over his men, he saw that many were being treated for minor wounds, yet they had come out on top with very few losses. The bulk of their losses came from the flank, sadly, as he had willingly allowed those men to be attacked without reinforcement.

Vikaris jumped down from Trixon, the weight of responsibility hitting him like a blow. Lives lost, victory won. It was a harsh trade, but that was the reality of war. He was pleased with his force. He was also pleased that he had learned from Trixon that no unicorns had lost their lives. *Thank the Creator*, he thought. They could not afford to lose any of their strongest allies. He noted as he strolled to his command tent, however, that many of the centaurs had gathered to the side.

"What has happened?" Vikaris demanded as he approached the group.

A female voice answered him. Centaurs were the only species who had female warriors, except for a few insistent humans and Nymphs that even Vikaris could not say no to. Vikaris never completely felt at ease about letting the women fight, yet it was either let them choose their own fate or lose the support of the male centaurs as well.

The young centaur replied, "It was one of Myrne's kin, my Lord."

The scene splayed out in front of Vikaris was one that struck home. Lying before him was a mother whose son had died in the action. The Quaigths were an old centaur bloodline. Myrne, the mother, was the Matriarch and oldest warrior of their kind. Her youngest son, Kal, had taken a spear through the neck.

No mother should have to bury her young, he thought sadly.

Vikaris knelt beside her, as every soldier, no matter the species, knelt in acquiescence to their king. Myrne gasped at his touch.

"Forgive me, Sire, for I did not see you," she whispered, bowing her head. He lifted her chin and brought her eyes to meet his.

With a steady gaze, he said, "No. Please forgive me, for it is my uncle and his rabble that have robbed you of your son. This will not go unpunished. I promise you that," the king insisted steadily, breaking eyes with hers to meet those of all the surrounding warriors. "This will not go unpunished."

Myrne nodded her head, swinging her old gray braids in acknowledgement, as her body visibly tensed with anger. "This will not go unpunished, my king," she said in low, lethal agreement.

As all eyes were turned toward Myrne and the king, none saw the brilliant flash of green over the Woods of the Willow.

CHAPTER 8

The Return

A cool, radiant sky illuminated the horizon. The burning sun was just cresting the furthest trees in view. The air smelled sweet. Pure. The rich aromas of fauna and flora were wonderfully overpowering. It was certainly a shock for the senses. All at once, Darion felt connected to his surroundings. The warm breeze tickled across his face and throughout his hair. He could hear some nearby squirrels playing merrily around the next tree trunk.

They had landed in what seemed to be a quiet copse amidst an immense forest. A small pond of fresh, clear water lay in front of him, enclosed by vast, thick trees. Some of the trunks were probably thicker than he was tall. Darion had never seen trees and forest as massive as this, and he had grown up in Oregon! Every last one dwarfed the Douglas-firs that just yesterday had eclipsed his Oregon sky.

The fall had been terrifyingly fast as they were whisked through the portal. The last few feet of their trek, however, were a gentle glide, as if they had been delicately carried by great, protective hands. They had been lightly placed on the ground, and until only moments ago, had all nestled together in a deep sleep. Darion knew there was old magic at work here. He could feel it in his bones.

Taking a few deep breaths, drinking in the taste of the sweet air, Darion sat up to examine his companions. They seemed to be resting comfortably. Rick and Carol had found one another's arms and lay in a beautiful embrace, her head and right arm resting lightly upon Rick's chest. His arms wrapped around her intimately. Antonis was sitting up against a mossy tree trunk. His eyes were closed, but Darion lingered a moment to ensure that the muscled Keeper was truly asleep.

Darion crept off quietly to explore. Walking lightly, Darion could hear everything. He heard a small beetle scurrying frantically over the leaves in front of Darion's footfall, retreating from the oncoming threat. He heard a bird from high above chirp to its partner about the stranger down below.

Suddenly, a clearing opened just beyond the other side of the pond. There he stopped mesmerized, looking upon the wonder of his new home. *So, this is Nav'Aria,* he thought. *My home.*

The image before him was nothing short of art. He had been raised to appreciate nature, having grown up with Rick as a father. He had spent his childhood camping, and hiking, and doing all things outdoors. This, however, was different. It was more magnificent than anything his imagination could create. The colors were stunning. With the forest behind him, he saw mountains to his left. A huge, looming peak that appeared to have smoke coming from the top was nearest him. An active volcano this close was unsettling, but he had to ignore it. Looking to the right of the mountains, he saw rolling, picturesque hills as far as the eye could see. He stood there in a joyous trance for some time. In his heart, he finally felt like he belonged. He was no longer an outsider. An orphan. He was in the same land now as his biological mother, he thought, wishing he could communicate with her. *Where is she?* He paused, listening for her voice.

Crunching leaves and snapping twigs caught him off guard. He spun around.

"Who's there?"

He could feel his heart pounding as he stared into the dark thicket from whence the sound had come. A tiny rabbit came darting out just as surprised to see Darion, haphazardly skittering by. Clutching his knife on his belt, he let go and exhaled loudly.

"Oh, it's only you," he said to the little terrified animal, slightly chuckling at his overreaction. *Where were his senses on that one?* It seemed that if he became distracted, he could still be snuck up on. He would have to talk to Tony about that. This was all so new. He wondered if he should head back to the group.

However, just as he was releasing his grip on his knife, a hand as strong as iron grabbed on to his shoulder and jerked him around. The sunlight was blinding as Darion tried to make out his captor; however, his eyes never traveled beyond the beast's torso. It appeared to have a man's upper body with horse legs covered in rugged, shaggy russet hair. Feeling dizzy, Darion hit the ground face first.

***

What was that? Antonis snapped awake after hearing a startled cry. It sounded like Darion. He jolted up, stomping his feet to wake his numb limbs. He must have been asleep for quite a while. He picked up his sword, which had been mysteriously removed from his sword belt, and was lying beside him. His dark eyes searched the area as he rolled his muscular back and shoulders, ready for a fight.

"Keepers, get up," he growled at Riccus and Carolina.

Darion must have risen before them. *He was just like his father, always going off on his own,* Antonis thought. He silently prayed to the Creator that the boy was all right. As the couple shook themselves awake, their sleepy smiles disappeared instantly.

"Where is he?" Rick searched the area with visible alarm in his eyes. Rising together, Rick and Carol began to scout the area for tracks in the direction that Antonis had heard the cry. A visible footprint began their trail, and they tracked through the forest and around the pond.

"Keep up. This way," Rick whispered, occasionally stopping to examine the forest floor. A broken twig here, a print there, and so it went. The group came upon an impressive sunrise in the clearing and walked right into a gathering party of centaurs. Darion lay in the center of their circle. He was not moving, but Antonis could make out the rise and fall of his chest, and knew the boy was still alive.

"What is the meaning of this?" the large man called as he barged into the circle.

The centaur who had grabbed the boy started toward the intruder, until he suddenly dropped to his front knees.

"Commander," he breathed, then looking up at Antonis he said, "Is it really you?" All the others in the patrol looked to one another in confusion but followed their leader and knelt before the stranger.

"Garis?" Antonis searched the centaur's tan and beard-covered face. "You were but a youngling last I saw you, barely able to grow chin hair. Now look at you," he said, slapping his toned shoulder. "Stand up. Stand up all of you. Now tell me, what is the meaning of this?" he demanded, pointing at Darion, and pushing his flooding memories aside for the time being.

Garis's russet coat gleamed upon his four legs as he stood hastily to address his former commander. Taking on the appropriate tone of respect as a soldier speaking to a superior officer, he explained.

"We caught this outsider wandering around. His foreign garb caught our attention, and there is the ruby around his neck. We were just about to start our interrogation of how he came across this gem. He may be working for Narco. We are not taking any chances in this war," Garis explained solemnly, then added quickly, "Sir."

Breathing deeply, Antonis nodded in understanding. He could tell Garis was nervous to be addressing his long, lost commander. He let go his anger and began to breathe evenly, remembering how intimidated and confused these soldiers were by his presence and high rank. They were all probably thinking he was back from the dead—who knew what King Vikaris had told everyone regarding the Keepers' absence all these years.

"You have done very well."

Rick started to argue, but Antonis shut him up with one look.

"This boy *is* new to the land, but he is not an 'outsider,' you can be sure of that. He did not find that ruby, rather, it was given to him... by his father. I have held onto it for many years until just recently." Antonis looked around the group as he spoke.

Darion, now awake, sat quietly in the circle, listening. Antonis smiled knowingly at him. The boy had filled pages and pages that looked just like the centaurs in his sketch book, yet he had grossly underestimated their size. And how much more lethal they looked with weapons and bulging muscles. The shaggy coats of their lower halves did nothing to diminish the ferocity of their strong legs, torsos, and arms. He chuckled inwardly as Darion scooted back involuntarily.

Garis looked the commander straight in the eye.

"If what you say is true, then that would make his father the, the..."

"The king," Antonis finished for him, smiling broadly. "Members of the Nav'Arian Guard, may I be the first to present you to the Royal Prince, Darion son of King Vikaris, and the Marked Heir to the throne of Nav'Aria."

As all eyes turned toward Darion, he straightened and pushed his sleeve up in one fluid movement, raising his arm so all could see his glimmering mark. The symbols shifted and moved along his skin in the bright sunlight. An audible gasp came from the centaurs in unison, and everyone, including Antonis and the Keepers, fell to their knees in honor of their Royal Prince.

The next few moments were consumed by groveling centaurs pledging their allegiance to Darion and his father, kissing his feet, which Antonis noted still happened to be encased in muddy tennis shoes. Antonis felt only proud, however. Darion stood tall, composed, and regal. It was evident Darion was no country bumpkin, but instead, the royal heir to a mighty kingdom. It would not be won easily, but Antonis felt a tremendous rush of hope for the land. It felt good to be home.

***

Garis and Antonis drifted to the side to watch the proceedings.

"Garis, you are the first Nav'Arians we have encountered. We have only just returned to the land, which is a different story for a different time. What I *would* like to discuss now is the war... and King Vikaris. Fill us in on the happenings of the last few years."

At the mention of his father, Darion nodded and gave a quick acknowledgement to the last of the patrol party. He motioned for them to gather with the others, and everyone cleared the way for Darion to take his seat next to Antonis. Darion, who had never liked being in the spotlight, forgot his old insecurities, his thoughts solely seeking information of his mother's well-being.

The youngest centaurs, apparently twins boasting the same ebony skin and dark, even coats, began setting out parcels of food on a log which they dragged to the middle of the circle, creating a makeshift table. As they began to prepare a plate of food for Darion, Garis began his report.

"To be honest, Your Highness... Commander," he said acknowledging them both, "this is the greatest discovery we have ever encountered. Your return signifies hope and a future. It will reignite the cause." Looking down awkwardly, he continued, "The morale has been low, especially since," he stuttered, taking a quick glance at his Prince's face, "since he, I mean Narco, took them, that is."

Darion understood. "Since he took my mother, you mean. Don't be afraid, Sir Garis, I know of her captivity. What I don't know is *how* she was taken. Will you please tell us what happened? And anything you can about my father."

Garis stared at him a bit awestruck, his Adam's apple bobbing as he swallowed, then continued. "Yes, of course, Your Grace."

CHAPTER 9

The Loss

Glass shattered noisily as a pair of pigeons fled from the exploding window panes.

"Do you think me a fool?"

Rage consumed the man though he did not yell or move. He sat still as stone at his desk. It was not an ordinary desk. To the naked eye, it looked like a table made with varying sizes and types of wood. Yet to a keen eye, one would note that the shards and pieces were in fact bone. Bones of humans and beasts alike formed a display of death and despair within the dim chamber. Prisoners were not kept alive long under Emperor Narco. He called them his trophies and their presence adorned his quarters. Vials of organs, skulls, and skeletons were his décor favorites. An avid learner of science, Narco especially loved anatomy. One day he would have Vikaris's corpse to ornament his throne room, and then his reign would have finality.

But once again, his little nephew had evaded his grasp, which this senseless guard had come to report.

A shaking captain stood in front of him. The youth was terribly skinny with a dark mop of hair. He was too young for battle, let alone to be a seasoned leader. The young man had begun to tremble and his lower lip with its pitiful attempt at a moustache was quivering. The scene momentarily took Narco back many cycles.

He sat alone under the shade of a large apple tree in the outer courtyard.

His father had once again belittled Narco in front of the entire court, praising Rustusse, the Heir. Their father had called for a duel, with wooden swords, of course. Rustusse had sprang from his seat enthusiastically before his father finished the pronouncement. Narco had been sitting, happily, or at least as close to contentment as he ever allowed himself, with his mother observing the people of the Dintarran Castle court.

"...And now for your entertainment, I would like to call my sons down for a fight to the death."

The room erupted in cheers and chuckles, for everyone surely knew they would be using wooden swords. No harm would come to either boy, at least not physically.

Narco sat still. His mother nudged him, "Narco, you must go," she quietly urged him. She stood, and all around the room, the onlookers bowed. Queen Aliguette was a handsome woman, and in control at all times. She turned toward her eldest son, as did all the eyes of the room, "Come, Narco," she said in a much more authoritative tone than she had used moments ago.

Shakily, he stood, not because he wanted to fight in this charade, but because he could never disobey his mother, whom he helplessly adored. She strode to the center of the large throne room where Rustusse was awaiting excitedly. She gave them each a nod and signaled for them to begin.

The duel lasted only a few sword strokes before Rustusse bested his older brother. Knocked to the ground, and his sword knocked away, Narco awaited his execution. Rustusse came in for the fake kill, and everyone applauded. Blurry vision from tears made it hard for Narco to be sure, but it looked as if even his mother was laughing and clapping her tiny, jeweled hands. That was too much. Rustusse bent down to help him up, smiling at him, as if he did not know he had just humiliated his older brother with his bravado. Narco fled the room as he heard his father's booming voice yell, "Once again our Rustusse has valiantly proved himself as our Marked Heir. No enemy shall ever best him."

A roaring crowd cheered ever louder, and no one noticed Narco's unceremonious exit.

Coming back to reality, Narco slammed his fist on the desk, cracking the stone casing slightly, with his supernatural strength. "Stop your putrid sniveling," he snapped at the lad, making him shake all the more. Narco stood disgusted and walked over broken shards of glass to stare out the window. A captivatingly beautiful horizon lay before him, yet all he saw was another day slipping by whilst Vikaris continued to be a threat. *I think I will pay Lyrianna a visit,* he thought to himself, smiling inwardly.

CHAPTER 10

The Letter

"No!" Darion dropped his cup and fell holding his head in his hands. The campsite erupted as man and beast jumped to surround their Prince against an unseen terror.

Moments ago, they had been calmly listening to Garis recount the last years' events, and the status of the war. The Rav'Arians had begun to move farther and farther inland as Narco sealed his reign. Their numbers continuing to rise. Garis and his group had been sent to ensure that no outsiders had entered the Woods. The King's secret camp, though always on the move, was set up beyond the Woods, therefore, they regularly searched the surrounding areas to make sure none of Narco's men found their location. Breathing heavily and fighting off nausea, Darion stood.

"It's okay," he said, motioning for the guards to calm down. He was still shaking his head though, with a troubled expression.

"What did you see?" Antonis asked, concern filling his voice.

"He's interrogating her. I don't know how much longer she can hold on. He's—" Darion frantically paced, as he spoke. "He's torturing her. All I saw were drops of blood and could hear her moans. Her vocal cords are raw... she can no longer scream. We need to tell my father and send a rescue team now." Darion stopped pacing and looked Antonis straight in the eye, as it appeared it was his turn to now seem deadly. "Narco is going to know me and my rage very soon." Darion said, cracking his knuckles as he held a fist, thinking back to how he had hit Joey, and wishing he had the same opportunity with Narco.

"She is strong, my prince. Somehow, she is still able to reach out to you with her mind. In order to do that, she must have absolute focus and clarity on one thing... you, Darion. She will fight her fight so that she lives to see you. But we must hurry," Antonis said sharply looking over the campsite.

"Garis. Take us to Vikaris and his troops. We have much to do, in a very short time."

The patrol quickly collected their items, stamped out the remaining cookfires, and gathered near Garis. He nodded his head and whistled a long, clear note.

That must be his signal to march, Darion thought. *They all seem so fluid and natural here.* He felt as far from a warrior as humanly possible; even enraged as he was, he knew he would be no match against armed soldiers. *Couldn't Antonis at least have taught me how to use a sword before we came here?* All that time he had wasted thinking about Stephanie and Joey, and other silly teenage concerns. If only he had known he was a prince... *Then I would have showed them... No, he wouldn't have shown them anything,* he thought honestly. He still felt a bit awkward. Looking down over his clothes, he knew he looked out of place. Foreign. His health had taken a hit over the last few weeks' lack of sleep, and complete paranoia over the dream. He knew his body had begun to waste away, and he looked a fragment of what his lean, yet strong build had been.

"Antonis," he called. The large man stopped in his stride and hustled over to Darion.

"Yes, my prince," he asked anxiously checking to see if something was amiss.

Caught off guard, Darion mumbled, "You don't have to call me that, Tony." Antonis waved him off as if he had not heard the wild idea.

Darion continued, "No, no, I'm fine. It's just..."

Darion felt the timing of his question would be inappropriate, yet he could not wait. Holding the pockets out from his oversized, rain-soaked jeans, he inquired, "Does anyone have something more 'Nav'Arian' that I could wear?"

Antonis looked annoyed initially, yet quickly his wise eyes took on the gleam of one who understood. "Of course," Antonis said, "You are going to meet the king. Your father! You must look the part for this monumental meeting. We can wait another moment to see you properly attired. Forgive me for not thinking of it sooner, my prince."

Apparently, Carolina had known by one look what Darion had been thinking. She surprised both men when she strolled over and threw her bag at his feet.

"What?" Darion started, then he looked at her smug smile, and knew. "You didn't?" His face broke in a huge grin, and he wrapped his arms around his adoptive mother. "Thanks, Mom," he said quietly.

With the tears hanging upon her lower lashes, she simply laughed and said, "I knew Vikaris would be very displeased with us if I did not." Antonis chuckled warmly at the exchange and ushered for Darion to hurry.

Emerging from behind a giant evergreen, Darion was pleased with his new ensemble. All stood up as he came forth, mesmerized by the firelight gleaming off his red ruby casting shadows across the clearing. His dark hair had curled in the rain, and dried that way. His bronzed skin was amplified by the rich green tunic he wore, richly embroidered with a crimson emblem of a lone unicorn on the breast. His fitted black breeches were his exact size, even considering his shrunken waist. His boots felt strong, yet comfortable. This was a much better look than his ragged clothes had been to meet his father. *The King!* He wondered when his mom had made these. His confidence swelled as he approached the group.

He gazed around the circle as the centaurs bowed their heads to their Prince. Riccus was smothering the last flames of the fire with handfuls of earth. Carolina stood removed from the group. A smile on her lips as she looked him over. She nodded her head in approval.

All eyes were on him awaiting the command.

"All right," he started then stopped, thinking back to how the military leaders he had learned about in history class had spoken; raising his voice to a tone of command, he called out, "Sir Garis, we are ready. Let's move."

***

Much of the day was spent in silent contemplation and awe. The Woods of the Willow ended up being larger than Darion had initially expected. The trees were taller than most buildings he had seen. They reminded him of the famous California Redwoods he had posters of in his tiny attic room. At some areas, they seemed to blot out the sun.

They must be very old in order for them to be this big, he thought. The colors were so vivid and rich here. He had never seen so many shades of green. The air smelled crisp, and clean. No hint of pollution.

He wished he knew more of *this* land's history. He could still feel the scroll pressing on his hip in his pocket. He had a feeling his father's words would provide him with more information. He made a mental note to try and read it before they made it to the camp.

On foot, their travels were painstakingly slow. He silently wished he still had his truck. He had a feeling this would be a reoccurring wish. He had come into a world with a raised status but fewer amenities to work with... what a peculiarity. Having spent most of his life in a different world, it was strange to be here. *Nav'Aria.*

Often throughout his life, he had prayed to know the whereabouts of his natural parents, but now that he was headed to meet his father, he was filled with apprehension. *What if he doesn't like me? What if I don't like him?* Darion was utterly lost in his own thoughts. His worries consumed him, and it was not until Garis interrupted his brooding that he realized they had stopped.

"Midday meal, my prince."

Darion nodded and followed Garis toward the Keepers. Carol had been gathering herbs and edible plants throughout the day. As the centaurs tore off grain-filled bread to share with everyone, Carol made a makeshift plate from some large leaves and placed a pile of berries, nuts, and twigs near Darion.

"I know it is not much, but you need to keep your energy up."

She and everyone else seemed to be fine with the hunk of bread, but Darion was grateful for the extra food. His growing teenage body required larger portions of food than the soldiers' rations. He had been living in a state of constant hunger since their arrival, and even before that, if he was being honest. He felt ravenous. His stomach gurgles must have been audible to those around, for they all smiled knowingly as they watched him eat his fill. Not the most exciting meal of his life, but at least his hunger pains ceased, giving him a little more clarity.

Darion reached down for the scroll; looking around, he noted that Garis and Antonis were in deep conversation. Some of the centaurs were sharpening their knives and spears, arguing on how often one should truly sharpen their blade. Darion had been initially surprised to see a female in their warband; though, after his initial shock, he noted that she seemed the fiercest of them all. She was striking, with her close-cropped hair, and tight, leather top, which accentuated her tanned breasts and toned arms. The other centaurs all seemed to do whatever she said—whether out of loyalty, fear, lust, or a little bit of all three. The younger centaurs, whilst thinking no eyes were on them, were dipping into the rations Carol had set aside for later. He could stop them, but then again, this was his first day here. No need to get high and mighty... not yet anyway. Besides, he didn't blame them. *One piece of bread will not fill anyone's stomach*, he thought, hoping their portion sizes were heartier back at the camp.

He assumed this was as good a time as any to read his father's letter. He jumped up and strode over toward a small sapling that was just outside of the circle. Unwinding the leather binding around the scroll, Darion rolled it out to reveal one perfectly scripted sheet of paper. His father kept a neat hand, similar to his own, he observed.

Taking a deep breath, he began to unravel his own history through his father's writing.

Darion,

Please forgive us. Your mother and I never intended to send you away. Know that this has been the hardest decision I have ever had to make, yet I feel it is for the best. I trust Antonis with my life, and now I trust him with yours. Since I am not sure when you will be able to return, or if I will still be alive when you make your return, I feel that I owe

*you an explanation. But believe me, I am
going to do everything in my power to crush
my tyrant uncle and bring you home.*

*Nav'Aria was a beautiful land and will
be once more. Unfortunately, it is not so
beautiful presently, with the stains of evil
atrocities marring our Kingdom. Narco has
allied with our sworn enemies, the
Rav'Arians. They are hideous monsters, and
they have always been kept beyond the Shazla
Desert. My uncle learned of the old magic in
their land and ventured there to obtain it.
This is how he was able to kill my father.*

*The thing about magic, though, it is not
intended for us mortal men. Only the unicorns
possess and wield magic, yet there is a source
of a dark power beyond the border. I will not
get into that now, but know that we can beat
Narco. So long as we have the Unicorns on
our side, he will be brought down. If we do
not kill him first, eventually his magic will be
his end.*

*I sit here now as I write, wondering of
what age you will be when Antonis passes
this on to you? Will you be yet a child? Will
you be a man? I pray to the Creator that you
are too young to read this when the time comes
to return, for that means that we will have a
swift victory, and you will be returned to mine
and your mother's loving arms soon.*

She loves you, Darion. She named you
and says she will never stop speaking to you.
Just as she spoke to you while you were
unseen in her womb, she will now speak to
you and pray that wherever you are, you hear
her voice.

The mighty Trinidad and I have been in
contact with the Nav'Arian races. Together
we will raise the call to arms for the entire
Realm. I am the true Heir to the throne of
Nav'Aria. I will take my place on my
father's throne, and once you are returned, you
will take your place by my side, as my Heir
born with the mark.

Your mother and I await you. I will have
so much to teach you, but those are things
that can wait. However, if for any reason, I
die before meeting you. Go to the unicorns.
They will tell you everything you need to
know, to wisely and truly inherit the Realm.
Honor and valor, my son.

-V

Sucking in air whilst concluding the letter, Darion let a
loud exhale escape, drawing the attention of one of the
youngest centaurs nearest him. Darion was too bewildered
to care. The lad's black eyes curiously examined the
Prince, thinking the prince didn't notice him there. Darion
feigned unawareness to continue his moments of quiet

reflection.

He wrote this letter years ago, and the war is still going on. If only Narco had been beaten sooner. He must be more powerful than anticipated. He sat quietly, thinking. His father had written this nearly fifteen years ago, thinking perhaps he was sending his child away temporarily, never fully accepting he might miss out on Darion's entire childhood. For the first time, Darion began to appreciate his parents' decision of sending him away. He knew now that they had only resolved to send their infant away due to dire circumstances. This knowledge made him ever hungrier to know this land—*my land. My heritage. Narco must be stopped... but how?*

Clearing his mind, Darion stood up. *I will get all the answers I need once I meet my father.* Reading the letter had been a strange comfort. He was still nervous to meet the king, but he was growing more and more excited as well. They were still many hours away from that reunion, however, if they kept at this pace. Looking around, he saw that everyone was beginning to gather themselves to continue their trek. He walked over to join the group, his thoughts shifting to unicorns. His father had mentioned them multiple times within the letter.

"Tony, will you tell me about the unicorns? Will there be any at the camp?"

"I was wondering when you would ask about them," Antonis chuckled. Pausing, he added, "You took learning of the centaurs in stride, all things considered," he said, winking at him. Darion smiled, glad to have the familiar exchange with his former boss and friend.

"The unicorns, though... they are a different matter." Talking in a hushed tone, he said, "Do not tell Garis, but his kind are not nearly as intimidating as they think they are. Centaurs, bah! They do not scare me at all..." His voice cut off as the lone female marched past, boldly eyeing Antonis. He glared at her, puffing out his chest, until she looked away continuing to march ahead, the pair of young centaurs closely following her.

Antonis continued, winking, "Well, maybe she does... but unicorns... You would do well to remember to never make a unicorn angry. They are the smartest and wisest creatures in our land... and they can be terrifying when provoked." Nodding his head along, Darion listened, soaking it all in.

"You see, Darion, they were the first creatures in Nav'Aria. They each have their very own gifting, or powers, you might say. Some can heal, while others have the gift of fortitude, resolve, strength, and so on. In the early unicorns' wisdom, they encouraged our Creator to make more creatures to cohabitate with them. They had seen in an early prophecy that man would rule the Realm and live in peace with the unicorns. Working together they would forge a special bond, and it would be the honor of any 'marked' ruler to choose a unicorn as his or her steed, companion, and advisor. The bond between the Marked Heir and unicorn is never to be broken. It is a lifelong bond."

Darion had been following along, blissfully thinking how wonderful it would be to meet a unicorn, when all of a sudden...

"Wait? What? I'm to 'choose a unicorn'? What does that even mean?"

That made the commander laugh out loud, causing the other Keepers to join in on the conversation, too, as they marched on the hidden trail, familiar only to the guards at the head of the line.

"Why do you think I made sure you were such a strong rider, Darion?" Rick said smiling. Darion only now realized that his somewhat old-fashioned, unconventional father in Oregon had been grooming him all along for a life in a very different land.

He had always encouraged Darion to ride and learn how to lead a horse with his legs, hardly using reins at all, even while standing and jumping, most of it done bareback. Darion had been terrified as a child, because Rick always seemed to look beyond the docile horses and choose the wildest stallion he could find for his son to ride. To this day, Darion still believed one of them, a black and white pinto, was possessed. That horse had been traded in for a sable quarter horse that Darion had loved and named Blaze. *I wonder what'll happen to him?*

Catching on to his train of thought, Rick said, "Do not worry, Darion. I took care of everything before we left. Our horses were given to a local stable, where they will have families pouring over them with love." Darion nodded, reassured. They really had been prepared for this. His respect soared for his father.

Antonis replied to his previous question. "Yes, Darion, you are to choose a unicorn. You will find out more of that at your meeting with the Unicorn Council, I am sure.

All I know is that, when the time comes to bond, you will know what to do. I know you have a lot of questions, but you have to trust us. You will learn all you need in due time. We do not want to overwhelm you... at least until after you meet Vikaris and Trixon, that is," Antonis stated, smiling mischievously.

"Oh, thanks," Darion said in an exaggerated tone. "Well, I've always wanted to see a unicorn... might as well be at a mysterious, secret Unicorn Council," he mused, causing them all to smile.

"That is the spirit," Antonis chided, as he slapped him on the back, in their familiar banter.

CHAPTER 11

The Camp

The last remnants of the sun's rays were visible beyond the distance. Evening was drawing in, and with the shadows came the renewed sense of anxiety. Darion had been distracted much of the afternoon, thinking on the letter from his father and imagining himself meeting a unicorn. *Should I bow? Do I hold out my hand? How does one meet a unicorn?* The thought was almost comical, or at least it was, until the event he had thought of all day was only moments away.

"There is the camp, Your Highness," Garis pointed out, his russet coat gleaming in the twilight.

Fear gripped Darion's stomach. This was the moment he had waited for his whole life, and he only hoped he would live up to his father's expectations.

"Here goes nothin'," Darion mumbled, and nodded to his Keepers. Antonis hesitated and pulled him aside for a moment. His strong hands grabbed Darion by the shoulders, giving him a reassuring squeeze. Darion looked in to the authoritative yet compassionate face of his lifelong friend. Antonis's dark eyes searched his and seemed to impart the magnitude of this very moment. Expecting a sentimental reflection with his old friend, Darion awaited.

"I cannot imagine what must be going through your mind, Darion. And I know you want to get this reunion started, but one word of caution. We have been gone a long time, myself included, and until we speak with your father and even after—keep your guard up. We do not know who could be working for the enemy. Keep your knife close, and trust no one beyond *us*, at least for now."

Darion's jaw dropped. He had never considered spies in the camp. "You... You are not saying that my father's troops may be working for Narco, are you?"

Antonis looked around, hushing him. "All I am saying is keep your guard up. I may not always be with you to protect you."

Darion solemnly swallowed and nodded his head. Not quite the pep talk he'd been expecting. With that, Antonis handed him a long, thin blade, and motioned for him to hide it in his boot, his dulled knife hanging from his belt.

"I understand." Darion's eyes swept the edge of camp that was just visible; the rest had already been washed away in the cover of darkness and the overhanging forest enclosing them. "Well, no use stalling. I'm ready to meet my father. Let's go," Darion said, a little louder so the rest of their group could hear him. The pit in his stomach only growing as they began to move again.

The Keepers came around, acting as Darion's "Honor Guard" as he marched behind Garis, the leader of their group. Before long, a watchman sighted them and blew one short, loud whistle. It was echoed by more whistles, and soon there were men and centaurs standing to greet the company, unsure if they were foe or friend.

***

The camp was alight with life as the party passed through. The shadows of worry melted away as the lit camp sparked Darion's curiosity.

There were so many sounds, smells, and sights overwhelming his senses that Darion had to consciously keep his mouth shut. The prince could not go gawking around at every new creature he saw... even if they were completely fascinating! The watchman who had sighted them from a rudimentary watch tower had bounded down the ladder before Antonis was able to get a greeting out. He glowered at the young man. To the youth's credit, he held his stare.

"Who are you, and why have you come here?" His voice held a slight tremor, but he stood his ground.

Antonis nodded to Garis, who stepped forward. "Excuse me, sir, I did not see you there," the youth practically whimpered.

Garis nodded to the watchman. "You did well, lad. Tell me, where are the soldiers?" He cast a disapproving glance around. "You are not the only guard on duty at this entrance, are you?" The boy blanched under the glare, even though it wasn't intended for him. He was shaking his head, but he seemed to be struggling to come up with an answer.

At that, the party scanned the area. What Darion had

first presumed as a bustling war camp, now beheld only older men, women, cooks, and a few youths hurrying around preparing cook fires, and the like. Darion frowned looking to the watch guard. The boy was stammering under the many eyes as he tried to explain the day's events. It reminded Darion of the time he had forgotten to latch the gate to the horse stall, and Blaze had gotten loose, trampling Carol's vegetable garden. His father had led a tough interrogation after that mishap. He pitied the boy being questioned by the looming Garis. His scowl could frighten the hardest of men.

"They... they... they went to f-f-fight the demons, my Lord... the day before yesterday. A scout came back a short while ago and told us to prepare for the band's return. The other guards went to assist them. They have many injured in their party and we are supposed to be ready... and be on guard. The cavalry is almost back, and the wounded will be arriving next. I was doing my du-du-duty watching out for those demons you see. That is why I asked who you were so forcefully. I do apologize, my Lord."

Antonis was nodding and told the boy to run along and tell whomever was in charge of the camp to prepare a tent for the king's son and his Honor Guard.

"His son?" the boy's mouth fell open looking between the stranger and his commander. He could only stare as Antonis nodded and Garis pushed him along to go about his bidding.

Darion watched this all with a half-interest. He was worried for his father and disappointed that he was not here when Darion had finally found the camp. *Why must I wait?* The group followed after the young guard, who was now running and calling for Seegar. Antonis thought the name sounded familiar but wondered if it could be the same man.

A tall yet stooped man stopped his lecture to a red-faced boy a few years younger than Darion on his shoddy job of cleaning a soup pot, as he heard his name being called. He turned toward the noise of the running guard, and behind him, the returning patrol.

"Seegar, sir, you must come. Garis has returned with some people. The stranger said to prepare a tent for the king's s-s-s-s-s-son."

Before Seegar could even acknowledge the comment, the young soldier was tugging his sleeve and pulling him toward the group. Seegar stopped in his tracks as his eyes found Darion's. "I would know those eyes anywhere," Seegar said softly, falling to his knees in a deep bow. Darion felt gooseflesh as the old man looked at him with such obvious reverence.

"Your Highness, we welcome you."

Onlookers paused from their chores to watch the exchange. More and more subjects began to gather around the group and the kneeling Seegar, High Councilor to King Vikaris. Darion was surprised that this man was bowing so obsequiously. He felt embarrassed by the attention it was drawing.

He stepped forward, "Thank you. Please rise," and he bent to help the old man up, taking his wrinkled, yet firm hands in his grasp. Tears were falling from the man's grey eyes as he stood and looked at Darion, smiling warmly.

"We are *so* happy to see you, my Prince."

Whispers overtook the crowd as they heard what Seegar had called the young stranger.

"Who is this man?" a deep voice called out. Many in the group were looking around, some looked hopeful, some skeptical. All eyes were on Darion. Antonis was about to speak when he caught Darion's eye. He paused, then closed his mouth.

Darion shouted, "My name is Darion Meridia, son of King Vikaris. I have just returned to Nav'Aria, along with my Keepers, to aid my father in the fight to recover Queen Lyrianna and bring down Narco once and for all."

The crowd erupted in cheers, and they all fell to their knees, bowing to their Prince. As he stood before them, he was bathed in the ruby-red light and his mark shone for all to see. He overheard their whispers of how his eyes sparkled just as their King's. Antonis reached out to Seegar, as the recollection came back to him, pulling him closer to Darion.

"Darion, this is the man who saved your father's life. He is the one who got him out of the castle before Narco got a hold of him."

Always humble, Seegar waved his hands saying, "I only did what I was obligated to do. My duty is to serve the King and his family, and that is what I did."

Darion liked the aged man already and grabbed him for a public embrace. *This man saved my father!*

"I was there at your birth, too, my prince. I have served your family for many years," the man said quietly as the two released from their hug and looked at one another. "It is good to have you home, my prince." Appearing to choke back tears and with a deep breath, Seegar stood tall and once again regained his composure. "This way, my prince, you must be wearied from your travels. We will see you cleaned and fed, as we wait for the soldiers to arrive."

As the party was led toward a large, indigo tent, the crowds stood watching and talking over themselves. Their cookfires and dinner preparations being momentarily forgotten.

"Is he really the prince?"

"Where has he been all this time?"

"He does not look like a warrior."

"How can we be sure?"

Darion heard it all, but was too overwhelmed to address the many questions and comments. He was going to need to learn to decipher between his heightened senses that seemed to come and go at whim. The overload of stimuli and information hindered his ability to focus on Seegar's words as they entered the tent.

"... a bath drawn up." Darion focused on that last statement. A bath would be very nice. He felt terribly dirty and was still getting used to the new conditions of his homeland. *Add a hot shower to things I'll miss,* he thought to himself.

***

Vikaris had heard the commotion before he saw anything. He and his cavalry had just arrived after an arduous march to camp, caring for their injured, and avoiding any additional Rav'Arian war parties. The foot soldiers, carrying the litters for the injured, would trail in for some hours still.

They had been victorious. The monsters had fled the field, as he knew they would. They served Narco, but they were not passionate for the cause. Any chance that they would be overwhelmed, and they usually fled, or at least, that is how it had always gone before. They had stayed in the fight longer than normal this time, though. It was the first time he had amassed this large of a force against the Rav'Arians' equally large numbers. Worry was his constant companion these days. The subterfuge of the mountain trail was clear evidence that the Rav'Arians—and Narco—were getting desperate. Narco was mobilizing more of them. Sending them farther north. Searching—*hunting, more like.*

They were lashing out more than ever. Vikaris's head throbbed as he pondered the uncharacteristic tactics the enemy had used at the battle. It would seem he was not the only one who wanted to this conflict over and done with. He longed for his calm, cheerful bride. She would know what to say to ease him right now. *But what was Narco doing to her? Lyrianna, are you still out there? I am coming for you,* he thought determinedly.

Trixon was silent, too, caught up in his own concerns for his father, Trinidad. It had taken Vikaris a moment to register the strong baritone voice coming from within the camp. The procession had easily entered the camp with no sign of a guard or sentry. *Not a good sign*, thought Vikaris, mulling everything over. He continued down the main lane of the camp, coming upon an amplified voice. From that distance, a normal man could not make out the words or the face, but Vikaris leapt off Trixon as he caught the words "Darion" and "returned to Nav'Aria."

The soldiers, though battle weary, mistook their king's haste for danger and spread out around the camp to encircle the indigo tent which their Lord had ran to. There were voices within. He could just make out Seegar... and...

"Antonis?"

Vikaris stepped into the tent and took the small assembly by surprise. Carolina let out a small squeal, Riccus hit his head as he tried to leap up but collided with the tray of a young serving girl, and Antonis spluttered on his wine as he launched forward to unceremoniously embrace his best friend since childhood.

In a belated and low bow, he announced, "Your Majesty, we have done as commanded. We have cared for your son and kept him out of danger until the sign to return."

Vikaris was completely overcome by emotion. It seemed like he had waited an eternity to hear those words. His gaze swept the room, but he didn't see his son. "Where is he?" he whispered, his eyes large and hopeful.

"I'm here, Father."

Darion stepped out from behind his shaded covering, where he had been stowing his belongings away moments ago.

Hesitantly, he stepped forward, his eyes on the ground. Slowly, his gaze rose. Vikaris stopped in his tracks. His son's eyes were a piercing green, just like his own. He knew without a doubt, that this was his kin. *His boy.* All of a sudden, his feet flew, as if of their own accord, and he swept Darion up in a huge, bear hug.

"My boy, my boy, you are here. You are home. You are safe now."

He basked with paternal pride. *His son! Returned!*

But the moment's joy, dampened as he thought, *If only Lyrianna were here to see him...*

***

"Why do you make me hurt you? You know this would all be much easier if you would only tell me what I wish to know."

"I would rather die than tell you anything... spawn."

Lyrianna clenched her teeth as Narco's talon-filed nails dug into her wrist. She looked away as he began his torture. This is how it always went. He would come in accompanied by his minions—their scent clouding the air, preceding Narco's appearance long before their clawed feet scraped the stone floor of her cell. She involuntarily shuddered and cursed herself for giving him that pleasure. He asked the same questions every meeting.

Where is Vikaris? Where are the unicorns hiding? How do I access their hideout?

Her bloodshot eyes looked toward the only window in the cell, a small, barred window. She imagined what Vikaris was doing at that moment. His strong, bare arm gleaming with the mark. The rugged man who had stolen her heart. She thought about their son. He would no longer be a child now, but a young man. *Would he even recognize me?* she wondered. It was during these moments that she thought of him the most. His life—and her love for Vikaris—gave her the courage to resist Narco. The hope that their boy was still out there was all that she needed to continue. Narco could never know this. Her son was her precious secret.

"Tell me where the unicorns are, and I will set you free. You know I hate seeing you treated this way," Narco said, motioning toward the guards he had brought, as if it were they who were responsible for her captivity.

She turned her gaze back toward Narco, coolly. She observed that he looked worse than usual; she had not thought that possible. His hideous, pocked face looked paler than normal, and his oily hair and coat were disheveled.

"They have beaten you again," she laughed, throatily. A full-bodied mirth erupting out of her mouth. All this time, she had been here, enduring Narco's futile interrogation. *To what gain? He has gained nothing by my being here*, she thought. *Vikaris is winning. Darion is safe.*

"Stop laughing," Narco whispered, dangerously. The creases surrounding his black eyes tightening with fury. "I said, 'stop laughing'!" he shouted, and spittle flew across her face. He slammed her wrist down on the wooden table he had been sitting at and pulled out his dagger. Pinning her hand down, he called for Dabor who had moments ago been nodding off in his chair. Lyrianna knew the troll did not enjoy working for Narco, but somehow his strange magical hold on the trolls was too strong.

"Dabor, I want you to break one of her fingers,

whichever one you would like." Narco's twisted smile spread as Lyrianna's face turned to horror.

"No, please, Dabor, fight him. You do not have to do this..." She could barely say the words, her laughter long forgotten. Her whole body shook with fear, as she tried to free her hand from his grasp. *How much more of her could he hurt?* One would think the pain would become common by now, but with the threat of each new abuse, she still writhed, trying to fight it off.

Dabor looked from master to woman. He hated his master—now more than ever. He shook his head, but to his own dismay his hands had already set about choosing the instrument to use in the process. His palm closed around a small hammer. Anything larger, and her entire hand would be broken. She was so delicate, and he hated what his master made him do more than ever. He wished as he had many times in the past few months that he could turn against the madman standing before him, but he could not.

"Do not do this," she pleaded, looking toward Dabor. He shifted his gaze, afraid that if he met her eyes he wouldn't be able to perform the task before him. Without even having to look, he raised the small hammer and brought it down in a single crushing blow. Her screams erupted, followed by Narco's spiteful laugh. Dabor closed his eyes, wishing he could plug his ears, too. Narco sat, stroking the screaming woman's hair and face.

"Good, Dabor. Until tomorrow, then, Queen," Narco murmured, his laugh echoing through the hall as he stepped from her cell. Dabor hesitated in the doorway, watching the woman cradling her broken finger. "Come, Dabor," a short command came from down the hall. Dabor slammed the cell door shut, locking it behind him.

***

Darion's eyes flew open, and he jumped out of the quilted bed. Momentarily disoriented, he looked around the lush room.

Then he remembered: the soldiers had burst into the tent, shortly after Darion and Vikaris's reunion. It had taken a few moments to calm everyone down and reveal Darion as the Prince of Nav'Aria. They had all stayed up into the very early morning hours talking and learning of each other's pasts. Darion already idolized his father. *If only Stephanie O'Donnell could see me now,* he thought, then realized that he couldn't care less about the snobby girl now.

Darion sat next to his father, the king, in the warm interior room of the tent along with Riccus, Carolina, Antonis, Garis, and the mighty Trixon. Darion had practically fainted when the magnificent unicorn burst into the tent, ready to charge any foe who might threaten the king. His concern regarding 'how to appropriately greet a unicorn' had been cast off as he and all within the tent had fled the unicorn's wake. After his parents and Tony had gone to sleep, Darion, the king—or rather his father, and Trixon stayed up late sharing about themselves—and the war. Vikaris had told Darion about his campaign against Narco. He had also told him about Lyrianna's capture.

"I am sorry I did not protect her, son," Vikaris

interjected after they had had a momentary lapse in conversation. The look in Vikaris' eyes grew pained at the mention of her, and Darion saw him squeeze his fists so tight, he wondered if Vikaris was picturing Narco's neck within his grasp.

Trixon looked over to his friend and king, nudging him gently with his snout, while avoiding piercing his skin with his razor-like horn. *It was he who was to blame,* Trixon said. Darion was surprised by the deep, rich voice filling the room. He hadn't heard Trixon speak yet and was once again in awe of him.

She had needed to send a message with the nymphs. Word had come that one of her friends had been captured near the banks of the Lure River. She had burst into the camp clearly distraught. She had news from the Northern Wood Nymphs. They are the eyes and ears of the Camp, and ever loyal to the Rightful King. Often their patrols take them as close to the Kingdom as they possibly can. Always searching for information... and runaways.

Trinidad—my brother and I were nearby when she got the news. She would not listen to my father's counsel. He had told her to wait until the men returned from hunting. This woman, you see, had raised her since she was a girl. Her parents had died early in the rebellion, and so when Sherna was taken Lyrianna was beside herself. She insisted that she needed to get closer. See if any of the nymphs closer toward the water had seen the event and knew where she had been taken.

Darion watched his father's serious face, as Trixon relayed the tale. He had begun sharpening the blade that he had entrusted to Antonis. Vikaris had commented immediately on its dullness, and Antonis had sheepishly apologized before going to bed. Vikaris's eyes looked moist, and he avoided Darion's eyes. When Darion asked him if he was all right, Vikaris spoke softly, "I failed you. I failed everyone. Most of all, Lyrianna." His grip on the blade tightened. Trixon shook his head, sorrowfully, continuing the tale.

My father would not listen to her. She demanded to be taken closer to the water. He said he would not and they would wait for the king. He went away to speak with the Council, and I, in my impudent haste to make my queen happy, cast all doubts aside, and offered to take her closer. We snuck through the back gate, lying to the guards that we were going to meet with the hunting party. Even though they should have known, unicorns never go on the hunts. We do not eat meat, nor do we enjoy the kills. But none suspected, and so we rode through the night, and made camp along the West bank of the Lure River. They must have known we would come.

Trixon halted. Shaking his head, and blew out of his nose noisily, his timbre rising.

He was there. Along the banks, he had set a trap. Sherna ran toward us screaming "No." Instantly, I knew something was not right, but by then it was too late. As soon as she set out running, two arrows pierced her heart right before our eyes. Lyrianna leapt off me the moment she saw her. I knew we were under attack and tried to get the queen's attention, but she was screaming and holding the corpse of the woman who had raised her. I was fighting off the three creatures who were standing between us. And then I saw it, she ceased her wails and stood up regal as ever. We all stopped fighting and turned to watch the queen draw a dagger from her belt.

"Imposter! You will pay for this!" she cried, as she lunged at Narco with the knife inches from his face before his troll grabbed her

and shook her until she lost consciousness. I had killed two of the three creatures who stood between us, when a silver light shot past me and straight at Narco.

At that, Narco smiled and yelled, "Now!" And then a score of twenty-odd creatures ran out and encircled my father, Trinidad. He had followed us there, quickly realizing my folly.

Trixon's voice faltered. Darion wondered if he'd go on. He had goosebumps everywhere, and he realized he had been holding his breath. Trixon concluded softly, *And, so my young prince, it is because of me that your mother was taken— and my father. I am the one to blame.*

Darion looked soberly at Trixon, watching the solitary tear roll down his shimmering, unblemished cheek. Darion had no words. He did not blame Trixon, at least not entirely. But he found it hard to articulate anything, a huge lump forming in his throat.

"No, my friend. It is I who is to blame. I should never have left the headstrong pair of you together." Vikaris faked a smile to comfort his companion, as he draped his arm around Trixon's thick, muscled neck in a comforting way. The silver mane parted slightly as his Marked arm rested, as if making way for the magical arm so it could rest purposefully on the unicorn's luminescent coat. None moved for a time, save for the flickering candle flames.

Darion could tell the obvious toll that day had taken on them both. It clearly haunted them. His father picked up the tale:

Trinidad put up a fight, slaying five Rav'Arians before he was felled. They shot him with an arrow, and then threw a net around him. Trixon charged the group. He would have killed many of them before he was caught, but Trinidad called to him telepathically. "No, my son. Get back. You must tell the king what has happened here. Do not let them take you too." Trixon hesitated in his charge as his father spoke to him. A spear shot past him, and only narrowly missed his heart as he quickly jumped to the side, receiving a shallow cut off his shoulder. "Go now, my son! That is an order!" Trinidad yelled. He could only shake his head and snort his displeasure as Narco called for the guards to capture the unicorns alive!

Narco had caught Vikaris's bride, and one of the most powerful unicorns. This majestic creature was his. Soon the rest of the unicorns would fall to his command. Trixon could see he reveled in his possession of the unicorn and was pleased with himself as he stroked Lyrianna's unconscious head. As much as Trixon wanted to spill Narco's blood, he had to heed his father's command. He took one last look at his father in the net surrounded by Rav'Arians, and another at Queen Lyrianna, who was swung over the troll's shoulder.

"I will kill you," Trixon whispered coldly as he glared down upon Narco, and from the distance he could see the man shudder. "I will come back for you, Father," he called out to him, though he could no longer see him. The beasts blocked his view, and all he could do was run back and share what had happened.

"Narco is to blame, not you, Trixon," Darion reassured him, laying his hand on his cheek. "And not you, Father," Darion said it quietly looking at Vikaris, before resting his head once more on the unicorn.

How were they able to get through? He had had the unicorns close the portal, at least for the time being, until Nav'Aria was made safe again. If there had been a sign to return, he had not sent it.

"Darion, I have to know, how did you get through the

portal?" Darion lifted his hand from Trixon and looked down sheepishly.

"I don't know exactly. I was so mad at Narco, and I kinda called on my senses, or whatever it is that I have. I just called to the waters to rise, or to open up, or well... I don't really know." Vikaris looked like he was going to say something when Darion added almost as an afterthought, "And I yelled 'Azalt'!"

At that Trixon and Vikaris both snapped their heads up and looked across at Darion. He did not miss the looks Trixon and Vikaris exchanged. He wondered if they were communicating telepathically. "Did I do something wrong?" Darion asked tersely, not pleased with their silence but also fearing that he may have angered the duo.

His father, moments ago, had been looking at him with tender love; now he looked like the weight of the world was on his shoulders—and truthfully, it was. Darion had to remember that though this man may share the same DNA, he was a very important individual to many.

"I honestly do not know, Darion. I had the unicorns close the portal after your mother was taken... until Nav'Aria was made safe again. If there was a sign to return, I am not the one who sent it, and that is what worries me."

Same with me, Trixon echoed.

The three bid each other goodnight, each consumed with their own thoughts. Darion hoped he had not overstepped or let his father down this early on. After his draining day, he should have been exhausted, but his worries for his mother and his father caused him to sleep fitfully. Fortunately, he had been functioning on very little sleep for weeks, so this was the new normal, he thought.

Now as Darion contemplated the dream he had awoken from, he had no doubt that his mother was reaching her limits.

"Father, it's her. He is with her again."

He had barely stepped forward before the king and beast were up, and weapons were drawn in the blink of an eye.

"Tell me what you saw," Vikaris said, through clenched teeth. His fury building.

CHAPTER 12

The Challenge

Antonis had slept better than he had in years. He was back in Nav'Aria. He was home.

Now as the sun's morning rays shone on his face, he smiled, taking it all in. The splendor of his homeland. He could smell breakfast cooking throughout the camp. Cookfires heating pots overflowing with meats, potatoes, and herbs he had missed, speckled the camp as far as he could see. It was a very expansive setup, and he wanted to explore this nomadic community. He had set out before his companions awoke, with the intent to speak with someone privately. When they had arrived at the camp the evening before, he had seen a face pass by in the crowd he had not been able to identify. It nagged at a place deep within him. He had been gone for many years, after all.

"Seegar... there you are!"

He shouted as he came upon the High Councilor, exiting his smaller tent nearby, clutching an armful of scrolls. Seegar, older than many in the camp, seemed to be the hardest worker of them all. He had always been that way. Ever-diligent. The old man squinted against the light, but his face broke into a smile when he called back, "Good morning, my Lord. I trust you slept well?"

"Indeed... Listen, I have a request of you."

"Anything, Antonis," Seegar replied.

"I... uh... well, Seegar, it is about a girl, or well, lady now." Antonis might look imposing most of the time, but he knew he looked nervous now!

Seegar chuckled and nodded his head, a twinkle alighting his eyes. Antonis was suddenly reminded of Darion and a similar conversation they had had recently. He knew he was being foolish and needed to get the words out. *Heavens, man! Spit it out,* he chastised himself.

"Last night, when we arrived I saw a woman's face pass through the crowd. She looked to be around my age, and I wanted to know if you know of her. She used to play the harp in the early camp before I went away. A peasant girl. Long dark hair... a pretty face."

Seegar had raised one eyebrow at Antonis mention of a 'pretty' woman. However, he was ever composed, and gave a simple nod.

"I will see what I can find out about *her.*"

Antonis gave a quick nod and forced out a "Thank you" before strutting off, forcing himself to walk slow, appearing completely at ease.

What was that about? It had been many years since he had been here, and he needed to get his hands on a sword. It probably wasn't even the girl he remembered from the night before he left. That girl had played the harp well past the sunset, and they had then shared a magical night together. But it had only been one night. He didn't even know her name, and who is to say she would remember him. Anyone from before had lived a lifetime here. Still, he recalled the passion, the feel of her soft, bare skin, the lure of her music...

He shook his head. *She is probably married off by now*, he thought. *Get it together, Antonis. You are High Keeper, and former Commander of the King's Guard. You did not return so you could pick up with an old flame.* As he sped down the hill well out of Seegar's sight toward the gathering soldiers—men, centaur, and unicorn—he missed the small form that watched him from behind a large oak tree.

It is him, she thought.

Aalil had thought she had seen a ghost the night before. She had thought he was dead. Everyone did. It had never been confirmed by King Vikaris, but he let the rumors spread regarding the Keepers and his son's disappearance. All this time she had thought him dead, and now he was back. Would he even remember her? What they had shared had been a perfect... *Stop it, it was only one night! And years ago.*

Much had happened since then. She wasn't the naïve adolescent anymore. She was a woman who had seen her fair share of fighting. Her body was hardened with muscle, not soft as it had been. She trained hard with any weapon and sparring partner she could get. *Would he desire her as a warrior instead of the musician she had been?*

She hadn't picked up the harp since *that* night. She hadn't wanted to. Looking down at her hands, she felt disgusted. Her nails were misshapen and jagged, and calluses thickened her once delicate palms. She was one of the few human women who fought. Much of her gender did not know what to think of her, while the men still viewed her as a woman, and tried to go easy on her. She found she enjoyed being with the centaurs the most. They never went easy on her.

"Why not get this over with?" she muttered. She knew they would cross paths eventually. They might as well get it out of the way on the practice field. She set off down the hill after him. Aalil spotted Antonis immediately as she crested the hill. Even though it was early, a large group of soldiers were already there. He was standing in the middle of the practice field; all sparring had stopped for the moment.

The warriors had gathered before the legendary Antonis to hear of his time away.

Not that much has changed, Aalil thought. Antonis clearly loved being in the spotlight still. He had always been one to soak up praise.

She could hear his rich, low voice bellowing, "Who here will fight me?"

He wore an overly confident smile, but when a voice, both feminine and strong, called out, "I will," she smiled watching his grin falter.

She had run the entire way and was not even winded. Years of training and battles with the Rav'Arians had strengthened her muscles. Tested her endurance. Her black hair was pulled back in a tight braid. Her worn-in leather pants and vest were immodest for most Nav'Arian women, but not for Aalil. She was a warrior. She had no time for fashion and tradition. She was lethal, and she wanted more than anything to win this fight.

Antonis looked across at his self-declared dueling partner. He was initially taken aback that a woman had volunteered.

We must be using every person we can to keep up the fight. A woman? Fighting? She could not seriously think that he was going to spar with her. And then it registered.

"You," he asked incredulously, noting the flicker of humor across her brow.

As she looked up, he knew without a doubt that it was *her.* Her clothes were different, and her body looked harder than he remembered. But her eyes had not changed. Eyes a striking shade of blue-grey stared at him confidently. Unafraid. Even as a young girl, she had not been intimidated by his position in the King's Guard. This was the face he had seen pass by. The proud set of her chin. He noted that the men were all whispering and nudging each other to get a good look at the pair... and they were backing away. She shifted on her feet, it looked like she was getting into a fighting stance.

"You do not seriously think that I will fight you, do you?"

Sooner than he could blink, she lunged forward with a bold cut toward the torso. Antonis was surprised to see that the sword she had picked out was newly sharpened. He ducked back, just inches away from her blade. He hardly looked at the weapons rack. He grabbed the first sword out of necessity... which turned out to be blunted. A practice sword.

He had thought that he would be fighting a fair partner, and that they would formally begin with the weapon choosing, introductions, and so on. This... this was completely out of line. And he reveled in it! He let out a low growl.

"I see you have still got your spunk," he said lowly, only for her ears.

She gave him a quick grin, then lunged forward again on the offensive. Her foot work was impressive, he noted, but it was no match for his brute force. He allowed her to hammer at him again and again, parrying her strikes. When she began to slow her attack to look for another opening, he launched his counter-attack. He spun around her and launched a series of sword thrusts that seemed to be wearing her down. Her lips were pressed into a thin line as she met him stroke for stroke. He was confident that he had her, though, and just as he was coming in for the final "kill," he found himself lying on the ground staring up at her self-satisfied face.

"I see you have still got more brawn than brain?" she whispered to him, her sword tip lightly tapping his throat, before standing up to face the cheering group of soldiers. They were hooting and hollering, "Aalil, Aalil, Aalil."

She tricked me, he thought. She had made him believe that he was wearing her down, and as he was going to "end it," she spun out from his sword reach and swept her leg out knocking him off his feet. *Him. Antonis. Former Commander and twice her size... bested by a girl.* She was good.

Very good. And he very much wanted to talk to her... alone.

"Here let me help you up, sir," Garis said as he reached his hand down for Antonis to grab, clearly choking down a smirk. Antonis only shook his head but took the hand willingly.

"I take it you saw that?" Antonis asked, feeling more and more foolish.

It wasn't so much that he was bested by a woman, but rather, that he was bested at all. *What has happened to me? I was the best swordsman in all Nav'Aria, and now? Now, Aalil has made a spectacle out of me.* Feeling his years as he stood up, he rebuked himself for growing lazy in his training. He was still fit from his daily exercise routine, but he had not sparred with an opponent for far too long. That was all about to change.

Antonis at full height towered over many of the men and beasts surrounding him, his muscles rippling under his tunic. His back ached a bit from his fall, but he did his best to hide it from the others. He did not want anyone taking it easy on him. The former commander refused to be pitied. He pulled the shirt off to use it as a towel. The day had only just begun, and it was already warm. He stood in a group near the weapons' rack with a group of high-ranking warriors, Garis included.

"Do not feel bad, Antonis. Aalil is one of my best fighters... And I say that honestly. She has taken us all down in the practice field and saved a few of us in the real battles. She is unpredictable. She does not follow the traditional strokes—I think she just makes it up as she goes. Call it gut instinct," Garis explained, his eyes scanning the crowd.

He nodded toward an older centaur standing at the far edge of our group.

"Just ask Tymin. He is our Training Master. She proved to be a very difficult student, did she not?" Tymin did not look amused. He only grunted and limped away from the field.

"I take it she was his favorite student?" Antonis joked. At that, all the men and beasts chuckled, and went on talking.

They are talking about me again, she thought. They always talked about her. She was an anomaly. She didn't want to think about that right now though... or Antonis's rippling muscles, glistening in the sun. His torso still bore the long, curved scar, but it had drastically faded since the night she had shared with him. She remembered tracing her fingers along the pink scar, her lips picking up where her fingers had left off... She blinked away the image.

What she wanted to know was where had he been all this time? And why did he come back? More than the memory of their romantic tryst, she also wondered what the implications of his return must mean. Her ribs still ached from the fall she had taken, nimbly missing an arrow from a Rav'Arian creature at the last battle. The battles were getting more and more desperate. Wiping the sweat from her brow, she looked again at the group of laughing men and decided to leave Antonis, and his memory, behind. She had more important things to deal with now. She nodded toward a few of the other warriors as she snuck out and headed toward the nearby woods.

Antonis had known she was watching him and did not want to give her the pleasure of gloating by returning her stare. However, he did desperately want to talk to her. The more he thought about her and their fight, the more he was reminded of a night sixteen years ago. She had been a young maiden then. Now, she was clearly someone entirely different. Someone he wanted to get to know.

Aalil, he thought, testing out her name. *You may have beaten me this time. I will not let it happen again,* he smiled to himself, satisfied at the notion.

"Do not let that first fight fool you," he yelled out, mustering as much bravado as he could. "I am still the best swordsman in this land. Who is next?"

He didn't know if he should be flattered or offended when multiple calls of acceptance rang out. One even had the audacity to call him "old man." He took out that opponent with his fist.

"First rule of fighting," he said as he stood over the young man, "Never underestimate your opponent. And secondly, never forget to use the weapons you already have."

Antonis broke into a grin when he realized that is exactly what Aalil had done. After a few more duels, he figured he had better get back to the tent and be there to greet the King when he awoke. He looked for Aalil when he left, but didn't see her. Ironically, she was the one now playing hard to get.

***

Darion knew that his father would want to depart on a rescue mission. His mother clearly couldn't hold out. But he had just met the man! The king couldn't go to a castle where Narco would surely be expecting him. It was too dangerous. Darion stood outside the main tent watching his father talk with Seegar, Garis, Kragar, and other members of the King's Guard and Council. *Look at him*, he thought. *There's no stopping this guy.*

Vikaris was a hair or two taller than Darion but looked much more regal. He was imposing yet kind. Darion knew that he must be a skilled warrior just by observing the way he moved. The man moved like a cat. Very nimble on his feet, with quick reflexes, and a dangerous expression.

"He'll be fine," Darion mumbled aloud. *He has to be fine.*

At that moment, Vikaris turned to him and called him over. "Darion, join us." All made way for their returned prince, still awe-struck at last night's reunion. "Darion, again, I need you to tell us everything you can about the visions you have been seeing. What does the room look like? I presume she is in the lower dungeons. Do you know which one? How many guards are typically with Narco?" Vikaris listed off a number of questions, and Darion was waiting for him to finish before speaking.

"This might help?" Darion said, pulling his sketchbook out from his pocket. His father knew of it but had not yet seen the images for himself. They had talked well into the night but had not found a chance to look through it. Darion hesitated. These were from the inner-workings of his mind, before he even knew of Nav'Aria. He hoped the images did them all justice.

Upon seeing the Mark on his father's hand the night before, he had remembered seeing the same design in a dream. It was one of his earliest sketches. Vikaris nodded and took hold of the book. He waved for Trixon to come closer, and the men made way almost reverently for the majestic creature. As Vikaris opened the book, he gasped, recognizing his Mark. Darion nodded sheepishly, but told him to keep looking.

"When did you draw all of these, son? Antonis mentioned you were having visions of Lyrianna recently, but he did not remark on these earlier ones."

"I've been drawing them for months now, Father," Darion explained. Trixon looked from the images to the pair and nodded.

"It is time, Vikaris." The king looked between his long-time companion and Darion, his newly returned son.

"You are right, Trixon. Where did the time go?"

Darion assumed Trixon meant that it was "time" to save the queen. He most certainly agreed with that. His father continued flipping through the book murmuring to Trixon, adding a gasp here, or a grunt there. Until he saw his wife, that is.

Darion knew which image stopped his father's progress. He had been silently studying the king and saw the corners around his clear green eyes crease. Tears filled his father's eyes, with a mixture of sorrow and rage. The most silent, calm fury Darion had ever encountered. Like a storm cloud before the tempest begins. He hardly knew this man, and he was unabashedly frightened by the look in his eyes.

The next image evoked much of the same in Trixon. It turned out that the unicorn in many of the sketches was Trinidad, Trixon's imprisoned father who had been taken away with Lyrianna. Men and beast alike began to back away from the king and his steed as it was plain that the mood had changed. The ruby around Vikaris's neck shone brightly, and his Mark around his tanned and toned forearm shimmered.

"Gather the troops," Vikaris said in a low growl.

Kragar, Garis, and the men before him scattered to do his bidding. They knew the king well. This was another battle call.

Vikaris jumped on the back of Trixon, spurring him down the hill in the direction of the blacksmith's tent. Darion turned his head as the dust cloud from Trixon's fast pace hit him, and as his eyes fell to the ground, he saw the last image his father had seen. It was a sketch of just his mother's face. He had seen it right before they came through the portal. Her lips were parted, almost hopeful, and her eyes wet with tears as she searched through the iron-railed window for the moon that was ever evasive. Her hair cascaded down her back, and though it was matted and tangled, she was the loveliest looking woman Darion had ever seen. His mother.

I have to help. He tucked the book into his pocket, checked that he had both of his blades, and then set off in a sprint to catch up with the gathering war party.

Antonis had returned to find Riccus and Carolina quickly gathering their things.

"What is going on here?" Antonis asked. Riccus sharply sucked in air as he saw him pushing through the tent flap.

Back in Nav'Arian clothes, with a bare muscled torso and sword in hand... "Now this is the Antonis I remember," Rick said, flexing his arm jokingly at Antonis. "I had forgotten how formidable you could appear."

Carolina rolled her eyes but kept packing as she said, "The king has called for everyone to gather. Rumor is, we're going to battle."

Antonis was not surprised. He knew that Lyrianna was barely hanging on, and that Vikaris would have to launch a rescue sooner than later.

"Well, I better get a shirt on then. I do not want to distract all the ladies," Antonis said, winking, trying to mask the pit in his stomach.

He had a feeling this mission wouldn't be like any other, and he knew he had to lead it. Riccus and Carolina knew their friend better than anyone, even better than himself perhaps. And they sensed his desperate ploy of humor.

"Rick, do you think he can do it?" Carolina asked as soon as he left.

"He can... I am sure of it. I would trust no one else with my life, or yours, for that matter. Look at how he took care of all of us. Darion, you, and I, we are all here because of him. He will come back to us."

Antonis hesitated before coming back into the room as

he heard their quiet conversation.

He better be right, Antonis thought. He didn't believe in himself as he once had, and before belying any other emotion, he decided to walk to the gathering alone, coaching himself along the way.

CHAPTER 13

The Shovlan Tree

As Darion approached the gathering crowd, he was momentarily stunned by the diversity of them all. He had seen only a fraction of the camp the night before. Many were filling in the clearing near the practice field. Centaurs, unicorns, men and women gathered before him.

Is that a... fairy? Though he'd seen none in his visions he could guess the luminous, winged creatures before him were the wood nymphs who hovered over the ground as they flitted around.

They peeked out of treetops, from behind tents, and their light flickered throughout the crowd. Still, being an inexperienced teenager, he goggled openly at a few females as they flew by giggling and whispering as they nodded their heads in his direction. They were gorgeous... and hardly dressed.

The trio could not be more different, each uniquely lovely. Hair and skin tones all different; they were breathtaking. He could make out the luscious curves of the fairy closest to him. Her scantily clad outfit revealed

dark, oiled skin. Her sandalwood scent was intoxicating...
it overwhelmed his senses, and his head began to spin just
slightly. Darion was growing to love this kingdom more
and more; he smiled at the nymph nearest him. She
winked at him, before scurrying ahead with her friends.
Their giggles and perfumes permeated the air.

Trying to shake off his lightheadedness, he saw his
father at a near distance, and started in his direction.
Vikaris was deep in conversation with an older gentleman.
Without hardly taking a step, a large hand clapped down
on his shoulder.

"There you are, my boy. I see you are acquainting
yourself with *all* of your royal subjects," Antonis smirked,
as he nonchalantly glanced toward the nymphs. Darion's
stomach did a somersault, as he looked toward where
Antonis was gesturing. The straps on the bold one's
lavender top had slipped off her shoulders, revealing more
than Darion would have ever hoped to have seen. She
arched her eyebrow at him, slyly. His pulse quickened, and
he knew his mouth stood agape. Antonis's booming
chuckles filled the air.

Darion quickly turned back to look for his father. He
was gone. His cheeks burned, but he wouldn't give
Antonis the pleasure of gloating.

"Where did he go?" His eyes searched the crowd, but
he had lost sight of Vikaris.

Antonis cleared his throat and spoke quietly, "That is
why I came to look for you, Darion. I know where he is
headed. Allow me to take you to him."

They began to move through the crowd. Antonis's height and presence cleared the way, but it was Darion's ruby which caught everyone's eye. Many bowed and backed away from the prince as he passed by. For most, this was the first look they had had of their newly returned Heir to the Throne. Vikaris had allowed word of Darion's arrival, but had yet to confirm via a public declaration. It had only been a matter of hours, after all, and now with news of Lyrianna's worsening state, there was not time for formalities. Antonis knew what to do and directed the prince. There would be time for pomp later.

Darion noted the hushed silence that had fallen upon the crowd. He tried to stand tall and regal as his father did. He smiled at a woman, weathered from years of working in the sun, who had called out to him with praise. A young blond boy came running out from behind his mother's billowing skirt. He sheepishly walked up to Darion, and those nearest the front gasped. The boy drew a small wooden dagger out of his pocket and tugged on Darion's pant leg. Darion looked at him and knelt to get a better look. It was a ruddy little dagger that had been worn down over the years. Darion was surprised by the inscription on the back of it though. It had been engraved by Vikaris.

"Where'd you get this?" he asked the child before him.

His mother stepped out from the crowd and bowed before Darion. She scooped up the boy and stood to meet Darion's gaze. Antonis bowed, and Darion looked between she and his longtime friend.

"Darion, may I introduce you to Lady Dalinia. Your aunt," he added, almost as an afterthought.

"My aunt?" Darion asked stunned.

The woman smiled warmly, and Darion noted the resemblance of his mother from his visions. She had long golden hair, not curly like his mother's, but the same beautiful shade. She was of average height and dressed in a rich, blue dress. The child she had lifted so easily peeked out from behind his mother's face.

"I'm pleased to meet you, Lady Dalinia," Darion said, as formally as he could muster.

His aunt! Why had no one told him he had an aunt?

He had gone his entire life feeling alone, well besides his parents—Rick and Carol—having no living relatives, which he now knew to be true, at least none in Oregon. But because of his lack of family, he had always felt like an outsider. And now here he was, meeting his mother's sister.

"As I am you, Prince Darion. We have long awaited your return," she said with a melodious voice. She spoke lower than his mother, but she was no less beautiful. "Let me introduce you to your cousin, Ansel."

At the mention of his name, she set the child down for him to give a quick bow to the prince before ducking behind his mother. Darion was still holding the wooden dagger and poised to say more when he heard Antonis grumble that they should keep moving.

"Would you like to join us? We are headed to speak with my father."

At the mention of his father, Lady Dalinia's eyes flashed, but she quickly regained her composure.

"We would not dare slow you down, my prince.

Welcome home."

At that she gave another quick curtsy and then turned to make her way through the crowd in the opposite direction, towing her child along as she left. The crowd quickly sealed up her pathway as the onlookers loomed toward Darion, staring, bowing, studying their prince.

He looked curiously to Antonis, who only shook his head slightly, which indicated they should wait to talk until they were alone. Darion remembered belatedly that he stood amidst hundreds upon hundreds of subjects, all whispering to each other after his and Dalinia's exchange.

Darion kept quiet, mulling over what had taken place. He would have to find out more about his aunt and cousin. It almost seemed like she didn't want to see the king. He was still out of his element in this new land, so he had to trust that Antonis and his father would tell him what he needed to know. Putting the meeting out of mind for now, Darion trotted to keep pace with Antonis's long strides. They made their way across the encompassing camp and through much of the crowd, Antonis bellowing for people to stand aside.

"Make way for the prince."

"Do not delay your King."

"Be gone with you!"

Darion felt ridiculous, being led and treated with such spectacle, but he kept pace with Antonis. They came to the edge of the camp where a large white tree stood. Darion had never seen a white tree before... yet he had never seen Nav'Aria before either, so he was becoming used to a constant feeling of surprise. The crowd stayed away from this area Darion saw, and he wondered why Antonis had brought him here.

"I cannot go in, Darion. Only those who bare the Mark can enter the *Shovlan Tree*."

Darion stepped up to the tree and inspected its leaves. They were not leaves at all, but small, dangling crystals. The white tree was magical, that much he knew.

Why would he bring me to this tree now? Darion had thought they were going to find his father, who was organizing a rescue mission. He knew he had to just go with it though, since nothing here made sense.

"What's in *there?*" Darion asked.

Antonis shook his head, but said nothing. Darion could tell he was not going to get any more information out of the man. *This is some sort of test*, Darion realized.

He walked slowly around the huge tree trunk, looking for an opening. Some sort of nook or cranny that would allow him in. Nothing. He absently tugged on his ruby as he walked. A thought occurred to him, and he looked down. *The ruby!*

The longer he inspected the tree, the more it made sense. He had to have the Mark to enter this tree, which he had. But anyone who had the Mark also had a royal ruby. He stopped directly in front of the tree and lightly pressed his palm against it. Stilling his mind, he attuned to his heightened senses.

He could smell the now dried sweat on Antonis. He could hear the blacksmith's hammer pounding vehemently in the distance. He could hear quiet whispers from some nearby nymphs he had not earlier detected. And he could hear—

"My father is in there," he blurted. *I hear him.*

Antonis only lifted an eyebrow but didn't otherwise move. His chiseled jaw set in determination, as if he were having to keep himself from speaking. Darion closed his eyes again and focused on his father's voice. The tree began to vibrate, and Darion noted that it was not a steady rhythm but syncopated, as if the tree were trying to communicate with him through the pulses. *Beat. Beat. Beat beat. Beat. Beat. Beat beat beat. Beat. Beat. Beat. Beat beat beat. Beat beat beat beat. Beat.* Slow pause. *Beat.* Darion traced his hands along the tree as he listened to the pulses. He noticed that the further left he went the more sporadic the beats became. The further right he moved his hand, the stronger they grew, pulsing, directing him toward something. He listened carefully and continued moving along the tree toward his right. *Beat. Beat. BEAT. BEAT. BEAT.* As he was coming around the trunk, his foot slipped into a small hole at the base of the tree. He opened his eyes to look at the hole.

That couldn't be it, could it? It was an awfully small hole, but he slowly traced his hand down the tree and knew it was the entry point. *BEAT BEAT BEAT!* The beats rose in crescendo the nearer Darion approached. He got down on all fours to inspect the trunk and shook his head. Now that he had at least found the opening, he hadn't the slightest clue how to enter the magical tree.

"You really can't help me?"

He looked to Antonis who stood a few steps away. The Keeper shook his head, keeping his back to Darion.

As much as Antonis would like to help, this was the first of many tests which were to come Darion's way. Vikaris had instructed him to bring him to the Tree. A messenger had intercepted Antonis as he headed to the gathering, and so he knew he had to fulfill the role of Keeper. Darion had to learn to use his newly discovered senses. After all, baring the Mark didn't necessarily mean one would become leader. The original Unicorn Council had seen to that many cycles ago. There were a series of tests one must pass, in order to solidify the title as the True Heir. Antonis had decided to leave that part out, at least until they returned to Nav'Aria. No one, to his knowledge, had ever failed the tests, so he had seen it as more of an oversight, than an issue. He began questioning this notion. He realized he may have made the wrong decision. Had he prepared the boy enough? He didn't know how to wield a sword, true, yet he did have many other skills that Antonis and the other Keepers had seen to. Determination. Perseverance. Humility. Kindness. He was skilled with animals and loved nature. The Keepers had trusted the unicorns' foresight in choosing a safe haven for them. Their time in Oregon had been well spent. Darion may not have grown up in Nav'Aria, but the more Antonis thought about it, he was confident in the prince's upbringing.

He watched as the boy he had known since infancy scowled at the base of the tree. His long, lean body hardened by a life spent outdoors. His dark hair falling into his intelligent green eyes. Focused on solving the problem before him. Antonis knew Darion was working through it all. *You can do it, Darion.*

***

Darion lay on his stomach inspecting the area, when he had a thought. *How deep is the hole?* He tentatively moved his hand into the base of the tree. He really didn't want to have his fingers bitten by some vermin nestled inside, so he hoped his instinct was right. As his hand moved through the shallow opening, he heard a distinct clink, like a lock. The beats stopped. He froze. Waiting for something to happen. Moments passed but revealed no change. No crevasse opening a door. He exhaled loudly.

This is stupid. Why wouldn't my father have just told me about this tree? Or better yet, have brought me with him? He had to go storming off on Trixon and leave me behind.

Darion knew he was being childish. His father was worried about his mother and preparing for battle. There was much Darion still did not know about his father or this land... and it was time he started figuring things out for himself.

He mentally reviewed everything he had learned about this tree. His father was in there, somewhere. The tree had pulsated, as if communicating with him, leading him to the hole. And then there was the opening, which sounded like a lock, when he placed his hand through it. *My marked hand*, he realized. *So, what am I missing?* he wondered.

While he lay there with his hand in the moss and dirt, the white tree became bathed in a red light. *The ruby!* As the tree was turned to crimson before his eyes, he put his unmarked palm against the tree once more, and stated,

"My name is Darion Meridia, Prince of Nav'Aria." The tree began to rumble against his hand. He quickly pulled his hand out from the base of the tree and jumped up. The tree was trembling and changing between all shades of red. Darion stood mesmerized as the once crystal tree vanished, and there stood a red maple tree, the largest he had ever seen, with a wide opening at the base. It appeared to be a stairwell. He looked back to Antonis, who only nodded. He was tightlipped and glassy eyed.

Darion knew he had done it. Darion drew a deep breath and looked back once more to see Antonis smiling at him, before he stepped into the Tree's opening, and cautiously walked down the large earthen staircase. The opening sealed as soon as he was through it, cutting him off from the world above. His senses were flooded. It smelled so fresh down below the earth. It surprised him. He could hear a worm wriggling away to the right of his head and what he assumed was Antonis' steps walking away from the clearing above. His ruby radiated enough light that he could find his footing along the stairs, which turned out to be tree roots, carpeted by moss, in a cascading fashion. As he continued farther and farther down into the earth, he could hear more voices. A light was coming from down below, and so he quietly stepped out onto level ground, and emerged into a large cavern below the white tree at the surface. Whatever he had expected to find, didn't include this!

The king had been laying out his battle plans, when he heard the opening from above. *He has done it*, he thought.

Vikaris had not doubted his son necessarily. He had

hoped he would find his way through the Tree's barrier and come to the meeting. However, he did not know him. This boy was his son, yet a stranger. He didn't know what his physical or mental capacity were. He only hoped that he would pass the tests and emerge undoubtedly as the True Heir. Vikaris was relieved to see Darion walk through the opening into the great cavern. His footsteps reverberated off the crystal floor, as he walked toward Vikaris. He recognized the look of wonder in his son's eyes.

"Welcome to Shovlan, Darion. The great cavern of creation."

Darion could only nod to his father. He wanted to look at every detail of the vast cavern, his eyes widening as he took in the marvels surrounding him. Every nook and cranny more ornate than the next. The rich carpentry and stone work were breathtaking. There were rooms beyond rooms, just waiting to be explored. Chandeliers of scented burning tapers filled the room with a warm glow and a dizzying bouquet of sage and cypress, causing his head to become fuzzy from the overpowering scent. The crystal floor, he noted belatedly, was a mosaic piece which would have been at least as large as his old gymnasium. He wanted to study it, that is, until his eyes fell upon the five majestic creatures before him.

"Welcome to Shovlan, Prince Darion," came a voice almost as old as the cavern they stood in. Darion bowed low. Before him stood five unicorns and the king of Nav'Aria. Nothing could have prepared Darion for the immense awe he felt now. He recognized Trixon, who stood closest to his father. He focused on the one who had spoken, however, for it was a female. He, in his naiveté, had not thought about the existence of female unicorns.

Of course, there are female unicorns, you idiot, Darion scolded himself. As the eldest unicorn bowed her head to him, the other four did as well. Vikaris then gestured for him to come to the great table and take a seat.

He approached the largest table he'd ever seen. It was made entirely out of a rich blue stone, a rare one he assumed, for he'd never seen anything quite like it. The vast oval shaped table only had three chairs at it. Very plush and formal looking, but only three. Darion wondered at first why such a large table would have so few chairs, and then it hit him. Only those with the Mark (as well as the unicorns) were allowed down here. They could only seat three marked heirs, one per generation. The unicorns clearly did not need the chairs. So, he sat. His father sat beside him. And the unicorns, towering before them, gathered all around the table, to look at their prince—and the impressive map which was laid out across the exotic stone table.

Darion's eyes swept over the map. Nav'Aria! His country, so surreal yet here before his eyes. He was able to now visualize exactly *what* he was the "prince" of.

"This map was drawn by a master artisan from the castle long ago," the eldest unicorn stated. She was not as large as Trixon. Her lavender eyes appeared to be lined with coal and boasted long, dark lashes. Her white hair was blinding. She was so white... and powerful. Now that Darion stood before her, he recognized an enormous power emanating from her. He was still learning how to handle his new senses, but there was no mistaking this being's aura of strength. Of wisdom.

Darion could feel their eyes boring into him. He made a point not to gawk at the unicorns, as much as he wanted to, like the other youths at the camp. He made quick glances instead as if he were a painter, and they were the canvas. His eyes beheld everything, leaving no detail unnoticed. His hands itched to sketch the scene.

After enduring an awkward moment of silence... "How rude of us," the eldest unicorn said, turning at once to face Darion. "We must have introductions." Thinking more to herself than to the assembly, she stated, "I do not think I have ever had to introduce myself." She chuckled quietly looking them over.

"My name is Elsra. I am the Regent leader of the Unicorns, and the eldest. I have lived many, many cycles—unicorns' lifespans being much longer than any other being. Back to the days of old, I have seen the kingdom grow in prosperity and happiness, before the Fall, that is. Those were dark days. Days that I hope will be remedied now—with you."

Darion bowed to her, overwhelmed, and almost intoxicated by the amount of power and knowledge her very essence exuded. Next to her at the table stood a slightly larger unicorn, but also female he realized noting the lavender eyes and multitude of thin braids in her mane. "I am Xenia, daughter of the slain Trinity, granddaughter of Elsra... and Rinzaltan," she concluded softly. Her voice sounded like a songbird—sweet and clear. She gave off an aura of peace, calmness, and serenity. Darion felt himself smiling warmly as he gazed into her eyes.

Startling him out of his reverie, the largest of the gathered unicorns spoke next in a low, booming voice. "I am Drigidor, the second mate of Regent Elsra." Darion was surprised by this, because he seemed younger than Elsra.

What does he mean by second mate? And why say it? Darion observed that though Drigidor was bulky and looked strong, his aura was not nearly as powerful. *Deceiving to the eye. Antonis was right about their "gifts."*

"I am Triumph. Named in honor of my father Rinzaltan, *First* Mate of Regent Elsra, and sacrificial *hero* for King Rustusse," a tall, proud unicorn stated. Darion did not miss the smoldering look he and Drigidor shared. This unicorn seethed with righteous indignation, though Darion had no idea why. He gave him the shivers.

Those two definitely don't get along, he thought, slightly stepping back from the unicorn. Triumph's eyes were a piercing blue as were Trixon's, while Drigidor's were a deep brown.

Yet the lowest, strongest voice of all spoke next, not aloud but instead into Darion's mind, telepathically.

And I am Trixon, son of Trinidad, grandson of Rinzaltan and Elsra, and escort to his Majesty King Vikaris, the TRUE KING of Nav'Aria.

Vikaris watched the introductions with curiosity. He had never seen them introduce themselves, for there had been no need. Everyone had heard of the Unicorn Council members—that was, except for Darion. He had had to contain a proud smile when Trixon introduced himself, for he had heard it in his mind as well.

Trixon was his best friend and confidante. He had bonded him at a very early age, and they had shared nearly every experience together.

"And I am King Vikaris Meridia, the Marked Heir and Lord of Nav'Aria, and of all the beings within it. May I formally introduce to you my son, Prince Darion Meridia, the Returned and Marked Heir to the throne of Nav'Aria."

The unicorns all shuffled at the last part of Vikaris' statement, but none spoke in protest. *He will be the True Heir of Nav'Aria*, Vikaris thought. *His instincts were solid. Darion had already surmised his way into the Tree. He will pass the other tests... He has to.*

Trixon looked him in the eye, giving him one strong nod. He hadn't even communicated with him; his friend just knew him that well.

Sitting, Vikaris motioned to move forward with the meeting. "Now that we have that out of the way, how are we going to save my wife?"

"And my father?" Trixon echoed. Their eyes falling upon the castle image upon the map, just south of the Lure River. Just south of where they stood now.

CHAPTER 14

The Hour

A single, solitary star was beginning to shine as twilight turned to evening. Trinidad stood alone in his cell; one of the rudimentary cells at the very base of the castle. His holding was below Lyrianna's. That much he knew. There was no window, but he could see the glimmer of the stars off the pool of water in the great space beyond the dungeons. Castle Dintarran had been built around a small natural spring. In this section, the outer wall windows ushered in the moonlight to brighten the vaulted ceiling overlooking the spring. Trinidad could never see more than a gleam from where he stood behind his bars, but that had to suffice.

Keeping a unicorn locked away from nature was the deepest, and most destructive torment imaginable. Trinidad had to keep his wits. He reminded himself every day that he had to stay strong, though it was becoming more and more difficult to remember why. His coat no longer had the unique sheen that his majestic race boasted. Instead, he was covered in dirt and grime, and his mane had been shorn. The stubble that now grew back was ragged and lined with fleas. Though he could not see the vermin, he knew they feasted on his wretched body. He had lost the will to try and shake them from him. It expulsed too much energy. So, he tolerated it.

He had once been the mighty Trinidad, Eldest Son of Elsra and Rinzaltan, second in command in the Unicorn Council, bonded to King Rustusse, and father to Trixon, bonded companion of King Vikaris.

And now, here he stood. Imprisoned. Tormented. Broken. Narco had seen to that.

Upon capture, Narco had had Trinidad drugged. He lived in a constant state of apathy; there was no way to avoid the mysterious drug. His captors had cut off his horn, and each day under the watchful eye of the Rav'Arian sentry, a troll came down and pressed a yellow, syrupy liquid to the base where his horn had been. It was before this time though that his lethargy began to wear off before the next drugging. Between twilight and the dead of night, he had moments of lucidity, and they were vital to his escape plan.

He could communicate to Lyrianna in these moments and hear how she fared above. Trinidad didn't let his mental activity register on his face, however. He tried to remain as impassive as possible while he communicated with her, lest they find out that he had a few hours a day of mental clarity. He thought back to that first night that he had been captured. They had kept him in the net for hours. He had been clubbed and kicked until he lost consciousness. Powerful as he was, he had not been able to fight off the Rav'Arians' repeated blows.

He had come to while they were removing his horn. The memory was not one completely riddled with pain. He had left Narco with a scar that day, too. One that he knew the wretched man hated.

He had awoken to men and beast standing above him, his head held in a troll's arms. They had not expected him to arise that early, much to their dismay. As the blade hit his horn, his eyes snapped open and he jumped out of the troll's arms, slashing across his abdomen, spilling his foul guts. A nearby Rav'Arian was slashed across his upper body, but able to escape without a mortal wound due to its strong exterior shell. Narco, who had been overlooking the removal process intently, froze like a coward when Trinidad gained consciousness. Narco was run through the head.

His healers had been able to save him, yet the left portion of his jaw and cheek had been greatly damaged, and he still bore a hideous scar along the side of his face. Whatever power Narco possessed had not been able to save him his vanity, again giving Trinidad some small pleasure. Trinidad had known him as a boy, after all, having been bonded to his brother. Narco had always been a weakling, and practically overcome by his insecurities as a youth. This scar only added to those. No matter the dark strength Narco had come upon, no amount of outward physical strength could wholly compensate for his inadequacy within his inner core. Next to Rustusse, there was no comparison. Except perhaps Vikaris, who was the strongest willed man Trinidad had ever met, and the True King of Nav'Aria. Narco knew that deep down his "powerful" control of the Realm was all a tenuous ruse. None of it was really his, and having a shameful scarred face only added to his feelings of weakness. How

*could he be the strongest, and greatest leader of Nav'Aria baring
such proof of defeat?*

Every time he came to inspect or question Trinidad,
Narco intentionally presented his right side so that the
unicorn couldn't see the damage on the left. Trinidad
relished those moments, for they were few. And they
reminded him of his victories, before he was robbed of his
most prized possession. *His horn.*

A unicorn's power was mainly emitted through his
horn. Without it, he was still strong, or would have been if
afforded adequate nutrition. But his gifts were gone. He
could not command the earth and elements as he had
once done; he could not communicate with anyone,
except Lyrianna, for she was close enough in proximity.
What Narco didn't know however, was that Trinidad's
powers were housed in an earthly shelter as well. The
Shovlan cavern could restore him his powers and assist
him with regrowing his horn. He didn't know of any living
unicorn that had ever a need of the Shovlan power stores,
but he knew they were no myth. They beckoned to him.
He could feel the Tree's pulses; though far away, he knew
his powers could be returned. Narco could not know that,
though, for if he did, there would be no stopping the man.
After all, the cavern housed the greatest of all Nav'Aria's
power, for it was the cavern of creation, where the spirits
of deceased unicorns went to rest. The crystals along the
Tree's branches were the souls of the many unicorns that
had passed on, waiting to join their powers together to
bequeath to one of their kind. They together, could

restore his power, if he was found deserving. They together could make one strong enough to take down Narco once and for all, though the crystals would not act of their own accord. One must show such sacrifice and valor that the spirits are awoken to help share their powers. Trinidad wondered if he could be found deserving.

I have to get there first... Do not get ahead of yourself, Trinidad, he told himself.

He had spent too many days being despondent and genuinely depressed over the loss of his horn; that was, until Gruegor had died trying to save him. Gruegor had been sent with two others, presumably by the King, to rescue Lyrianna and Trinidad. He had been coming off his sedative and was disoriented when he heard Gruegor's calls. He had not reacted quickly enough, to warn Gruegor of the Rav'Arian sentries. There were always at least two guarding his cell, if not more. Trinidad still didn't know how Gruegor had come upon his cell, but it didn't matter, for before they could even communicate, Gruegor was decapitated by the Rav'Arian monster who stood guard. The towering, black, bird-like creature made not a sound as it mercilessly killed the man, watching Trinidad intently as Gruegor's life blood flowed under Trinidad's cell. Trinidad scolded himself every day since the incident, when he had broken eye contact with the beast and shuddered as the blood pooled under his hooves. He had stepped back then, and the cackle from the guard was a sound that Trinidad had not forgotten. Humor. The beast had found the incident humorous. It had only strengthened Trinidad's resolve that every last Rav'Arian had to die. However, that instance had also provided him hope, for even though Gruegor had fallen, Vikaris *was* trying to save them. Trinidad had to do his part and try to help the king as well.

Trinidad had not known Gruegor, but Lyrianna had been deeply affected. Narco had immediately brought the head to her cell for identification. She feigned ignorance. And later suffered a terrible beating, but she never told him who he was. She would take that to the grave, she swore to Trinidad, and made him promise to do the same. He had been married to her sister. She would not give Narco the pleasure of knowing he had killed one of her relatives. She only used Gruegor's death as fuel, as Trinidad did, to get out. Narco had claimed Gruegor's head now adorned the palace ramparts, though neither Lyrianna nor Trinidad could confirm it, they didn't put it past their insane captor.

My Queen, Trinidad called out to Lyrianna telepathically. *Give your report.* Each night he called to her, and she gave her run down of the day's events before he was drugged again. She always spoke first, in case he was drugged or they were caught communicating.

Trinidad, a sad, weak voice replied.

Trinidad had to keep himself from shock each time he heard her speak. Lyrianna had been the most beautiful maiden in Nav'Aria. She had had many suitors, and though she had come from humble means, she had become the wife of the True King. The Nav'Arians loyal to Vikaris, loved her. She had the most beautiful singing voice, sweet and melodious. It pained Trinidad to hear her now.

I have been waiting for you, Trinidad. He came again today... I did not give him anything.

Trinidad noted the pause. *What did he do to you?*

She sighed. *It does not matter,* she replied softly. *He cannot break me. Though he may break my body, and though I may never see my husband again, I have reason to be hopeful.*

Trinidad didn't know how to react to this. *Was she becoming delusional?* They had been in captivity for months, and he knew she couldn't hold out much longer.

Before Trinidad could voice his concerns, Lyrianna simply stated, *He has returned.*

Who, my queen? But Trinidad knew as soon as he asked.

She confirmed it with one word, *Darion,* before growing quiet.

Had she fallen asleep or worse? Trinidad didn't know, for she didn't respond to his series of frantic calls.

He hadn't heard the name Darion in a very long time. He worried over this news until he saw Dabor, the troll, approaching with the serum. *Darion.* He was not supposed to return until the unicorns deemed it safe enough for his return. *Surely, they had not called him back?* As the large troll approached, he shook off his worries. *She must be delusional.* He knew his focus had to be solely on getting her out safely, not questioning whether or not the prince had returned. He rolled an apathetic eye toward the troll, masking any emotion or concern. He had not learned as much as he had hoped from this day; he only hoped Lyrianna could hold on.

Let it be so, he offered up in prayer to the Creator before he was sent into a void of numbness, the potent drug taking hold of his senses, and the queen and her son slipping away from his memory.

***

Antonis hated being kept out of the meeting. He respected the king and the Unicorn Council, yet he was so curious as to what they would decide. He felt obligated to go and help in some way. All these years he had spent in comfort, safely tucked away, unlike his comrades here. Pleasure, harmony, normalcy linger only in their memories. The war still waged on! Narco must be stopped. That everyone could agree on.

"We have to find his weakness," Antonis mumbled as he paced nearby the place of the crystal tree. No one beyond the Marked Heirs and Unicorns could actually *see* the Tree. Antonis had only paused once Darion had. Vikaris had described what would happen, and true to his word, Darion had stopped dead in his tracks at the sight of the tree. He found the entry point, leaving Antonis behind.

Not for the first time in his life, Antonis kicked at a large stone, his frustration getting the better of him. He felt restless and insecure with his returned place in Nav'Aria. *What was he now? Commander? Keeper? Tony?*

He heard a rumbling and knew that the meeting was concluded. He quickly turned back toward the opening and fell to his knees in awe. Resplendent in light and power, his king, prince, and entire Unicorn Council approached him. Antonis gawked as he saw the Tree's crystals materialize and shine brightly, seeing how they paled in comparison to the white coats of the unicorns. Vikaris and Darion were bathed in red as their rubies glowed for all to see, and their Marks were illuminated. While not one to give way to headiness, Antonis knew that he would never forget this moment.

He had only seen Regent Elsra once when he was a boy. The unicorns had taken great measures of concealment, especially after Narco's coup. No one could know where they were. The magic that they possessed protected them from Narco, and it is all that he sought. The Shovlan Tree only appeared to someone approved by the Council, which had historically only included the Marked Heirs. Its location constantly moved. The fact that they were all gathered here before Antonis spoke volumes. He shuddered at the significance of this moment. Trixon nodded to him, and he shakily stood up.

"Antonis." Elsra nodded to him. "Come closer." He swallowed hard, but moved forward. "And you can come out, too," she called to someone behind him. He turned and saw Aalil guiltily nod as she came over from the tree line. She must have followed him there, keeping a distance, but watching the proceedings. Antonis knew that she would be aware of the unicorns' secret lair, but unable to see it, having most likely only ever seen the unicorn warriors—no females. Antonis knew how she must be feeling as she hesitated near him, clearly considering how to approach. *Bow? Stand tall? Say something?* Antonis had experienced the same uncertainty the first time he had seen the Council as a boy. Never in her life had she seen a female unicorn or felt such supreme power, Antonis knew.

Lavender-eyed creatures searched the humans' faces.

"Who are you?" Elsra asked.

Aalil appeared terrified. Antonis smirked at her. *Not so confident now, are you?* He was glad for it, for though he'd never admit it, his tailbone did hurt from their earlier fight. Clearing her throat, she said quietly, "Aalil."

"What was that, girl?"

"My name is Aalil, Great One."

"Oh, I know your name. What I asked is 'who are you'?" Elsra's eyes searched Aalil's face, coaxing her. Aalil looked up confused, at first, but then nodded as she looked at her King.

"I am a faithful servant of Nav'Aria, and loyal subject to the True King, Vikaris. I have been one of his warriors for many years. I await your command, Oh Great One," then looking and bowing to Vikaris, "Your Majesty."

"Now that's better." Elsra murmured. The large creature on her right looked at her. It was obvious that they were conversing telepathically.

After a moment, Trixon became agitated and snapped "NO," aloud. "Let me go. This is all because of me. I will not allow someone else to go in my stead. We have already covered this."

The air grew crisp, and in an instant, Trixon was on his knees before the roiling vehemence of his grandmother.

"You 'will not allow' you say. Do you dare try to defy me on this?" Elsra's voice filled their minds, and all trembled before her power. Trixon knelt before her but did not capitulate.

"I only meant, that I do not want to risk anyone else's life because of *my* folly."

Trixon held Elsra's glare. He did not back down. "Grandmother, you know I do not want to overstep, but this is my father we are talking about! Antonis has been gone a long time."

Surprising them all, Elsra relaxed and smiled at Trixon. Her eyes sparkling. "I see Rinzaltan in you," she stated proudly. Antonis thought he detected an eye roll from Drigidor, at that. Trixon stood back up, and Elsra looked at him, and then all of them gathered there. "Trixon, is right. In part, he is responsible."

Vikaris started at this, "Now wait..."

"I did not say it is 'because' of him, however..." She turned a knowing eye on the king. "We are all responsible for their capture. We could have done more, yet this is not *our* fault. This is the fault of Narco. Of evil. Trinidad knew what he was doing when he came upon you and Lyrianna. He knew the risk, and he took it." As she turned her gaze to Antonis and Aalil, she continued with, "And now I will ask you to take a risk. Vikaris trusts you Antonis more than anyone else. If anyone can bring them back, it is you... and Aalil."

Antonis's eyes bulged, as did Aalil's.

"Why me?" Aalil blurted out. A look of horror on her face, as she realized she had just spoken out of turn to the Great Regent.

Elsra chucked warmly, saying, "Exactly. Why you?"

Confused more than ever, she turned to look at

Antonis, whose glare warned her to not press the issue further. *Why her? She will only slow me down,* he thought bitterly.

"Forgive me, Great One, but..."

Antonis whispered for her to stop, knowing that it would only lead to trouble trying to argue with the Eldest Unicorn, but she looked at Elsra for more meaning.

"We have chosen you, young one, because, though you are a bit rash, you are clearly devoted to Nav'Aria... and to him." She nodded toward Antonis. Aalil's cheeks burned, registering the implication. "Who better then to keep an eye on him?" Antonis felt like he had been hit in the stomach at her words. *Devoted to me?* Antonis and Vikaris burst out laughing.

"Let us go discuss this further in my tent. We must find Seegar," Vikaris said, after catching his breath from the laughter. Antonis felt flushed, and Aalil looked as if she wanted to crawl into a hole and die. Things were looking up, Antonis thought to himself, standing a little taller after the pronouncement.

Darion took it all in in stride. He felt proud of Antonis. His long-time friend and mentor, now being chosen for this mission. He was also worried though and wondered about his position as leader of a rescue party. As they strode toward the camp, Darion caught his father's eye.

"What am I supposed to do, Father?" Vikaris' eyes sparkled with paternal emotion.

"Soon, son. You and I have a lot of catching up to do.

There are things you still must learn about our land. Your responsibility now is your training, as Elsra and I discussed before you entered the Shovlan."

Darion only nodded, knowing that was all he going to get for an answer at the moment. He looked back at their procession, and as he neared the camp he thought he saw his aunt's face pass through the crowd. She didn't smile as he caught her eye. He'd have to ask his father about her. Later, though. For as they entered the camp, a horn blew.

CHAPTER 15

The Kingdom

Edmond stared out the window of his little hut. *Keep your head down. Work the land. Do not ask questions.* This is what he had been told ever since he had been born thirteen years ago.

Growing up in a divided kingdom was difficult. Confusing. Dangerous. He had so many questions. His parents always shushed him when he inquired. They always said, "We just have to get through it, Edmond. Just get through it."

Their dull eyes were void of hope. Though he didn't know any other life, his heart broke for his parents who worked so tirelessly. He knew they had been born before *the Fall.*

What must their lives have been like? No one could talk about the forbidden topic. The trolls saw to that. They had their ways of keeping tabs on the workers. Edmond shuddered at the thought. *If the other king was so evil, why then did the trolls and Rav'Arians abuse the workers?* Edmond had always been taught that Narco was the rightful king. The *only* king. The Emperor.

Deep down, Edmond knew this was a lie. He could never say it out loud, but he knew in his core that what Narco did was wrong. He tortured people. He killed for fun. His beasts slew and devoured on a whim any creature they wanted. Edmond tried to shut off his mind as he pictured his younger brother, Anton, running back from the fields one day, screaming.

The Conderra family had pilfered grain and gotten caught. The product of each harvest was taken up by the villainous overlords and given to Narco. The people meanwhile were starving. The Conderra family was only doing what was needed to survive. Every worker stole grain when they could. How else would they make it through winter?

That dreadful day, the workers were called to the fields to watch as the Rav'Arians killed each family member and proceeded to eat them. "Justice," they said. Stealing from the Emperor, as Narco liked to be called, was treason. The trolls beat the drum with each death. The final family member, Stevan Conderra the father, stood proudly, and as the beasts approached, he called out, "Run, my friends. Do not settle for this life any longer. Go to Vikaris!"

At the mention of the name, the nearest beast shrieked and slashed out, killing Stevan instantly. That moment was one Edmond would never forget. It was forever burned into his memory. Vikaris. He mentally noted the name of the "other" king. He had never heard the name before, but knew from what he could gather that there was a "rebel" king to the north.

More and more food stores were raided by the Rav'Arian hordes before marching to battle the "foe."

Thinking back, Edmond considered. If only he could get to him. He looked over at his parents, who sat staring aimlessly into the small hut fire. There was little talking in his home. Little of anything really. They worked most of the day, ate what they could find, and slept. At night, Edmond would stare at the ceiling and dream, serenaded by his family's soft snores. One day he would be a warrior for the other king. He would save all of those who had been left behind. Those who had fallen under Narco's oppressive rule... And he would kill *every* last Rav'Arian.

"I swear it to be true," Edmond whispered aloud, his dark eyes shining with emotion as he blew out the last candle flame and tucked in for the night.

***

"Whose horn?" a soldier called as the king's party passed him. Darion, Vikaris, and Antonis rushed into the heart of the camp.

At the horn blast, Vikaris had signaled for Elsra and the Council to return to the Tree until he said it was clear. He wouldn't dare expose them if he could help it. Trixon had cantered into the camp ahead of the three to ensure the king's safety.

As the party approached Trixon, they saw Garis holding the arm of a shaggy-haired adolescent. "My king, a patrol found this boy wandering south of the camp." Kragar stood by with Seeker, the warrior unicorn, menacing as ever. The young boy avoided the hard gaze the lieutenant and commander directed at him.

"There seems to be a lot of that at late," Vikaris said, winking at Darion. "And who might you be, lad?"

"Where is my brother? Let go of me!" The boy's gaze smoldered at the group, flinching as Garis's iron grip tightened on the boy's arm.

"Answer the king," Garis growled, shaking him slightly. The centaur's muscles tensed.

"And show some respect," Kragar said lowly. Hard as steel. His sword arm flexed as he spoke. His chiseled jaw, though speckled with grey stubble, revealing his age, was no less deadly when tested. His slate eyes bore into the boy, who had the sense to look down at the last moment in acquiescence.

Raising his hand, Vikaris nodded to the commander to release the boy. Standing to his full height, he peered over much of the gathered crowd. Brushing off his pant legs, the boy managed to appear sheepish when Trixon strode over to stand in front of him. *Who are you?*

The boy trembled at the deep voice which entered his mind. "I am Edmond," he said, looking up, still managing a brave face, even though his rapid breathing gave away his fear of the lethal men, unicorns, and centaurs.

"Why were you outside my camp, Edmond? You are an outsider, it would appear." Vikaris's face hardened as he spied his uncle's black and red royal crescent on the boy's robe. "... from the kingdom, are you not?"

"Yes, Your Majesty. My brother and I fled the Stenlen to find you." Vikaris nodded for him to continue. Remembering the Stenlen, one of the small villages outside of the Kingdom grounds, near the Lure River. He knew the area was now occupied by Narco's agents, and the people there were his captives. Many had turned against Vikaris, to ensure their own survival, and so Vikaris could not trust anyone. He had made the mistake, early on, to take anyone who escaped at their word. After the second assassination attempt, he did not blindly accept his former subjects on their word alone. The unicorns scrutinized those who entered. They scoured their minds and analyzed the purity of their hearts.

"I came to pledge my allegiance. I mean, we both did. May I please have my brother back? He is young and scared." Edmond's dark eyes pleaded with the group before him, as he visibly tried to keep himself calm.

"Where is his brother?" No sooner than Vikaris could inquire, Seegar walked forward holding the hand of a small emaciated boy, donning bandages around his leg and forehead.

"Forgive me, Sire, but I have just patched this boy up. It would appear his brother has been inquiring after him..." The ever faithful Seegar had taken the younger child, fed him, bandaged him, and gleaned information from him in his tender care.

"Their village was overrun by Rav'Arians, Sire. They are orphans and appear to have been traveling for quite some time."

"Is this true?" Vikaris asked. Fervor overtook fatigue and worry, and at once, Edmond appeared much older.

"It is," he said tightly, his chest rising ever faster. "Narco told the creatures to make an example of us, because of the martyrs." A frown appeared between his eyes as he continued, "It started with Stevan Conderra. He was killed for stealing food for his children. He yelled for us to run and find you. After his death, more workers began to revolt. One man, Keller, called for us all to flee in the night. My parents refused. They said it was too great a risk. 'We must just get through it,' was their anthem. We were one of the only families to remain in our huts that night." He stopped his tale, looking away. His eyes shutting for the briefest of moments, as if trying to block out the sights of the recalled memory.

"Go on, boy." Trixon nudged him. Vikaris felt himself nodding in encouragement, fearing for his subjects.

"One of the Stenlen guards, a large troll, came across the party and before they could kill him, he sounded the alarm. Most of the group was rounded up by morning, and we were gathered to face the Rav'Arians. My parents pleaded that since they had stayed behind, they should be given mercy.

"'Mercy,' the creature spat. 'Give mercy. Narco's mercy,' as he stabbed my father's throat with his long talon. My father's blood..." He paused, looking at his brother. Seegar noted his meaning and led the boy to one of the cookfires nearby. "His blood spurt out onto my mother's face, and she screamed. The creature said he had more mercy for all of us, and he pushed her to the ground. The troll swung his club and crushed her skull. They began killing everyone."

"How did you escape, then?" Garis asked, looking the boy up and down, noting for the first time it would seem his large muscles and height. Vikaris was doing the same. *If this tale is true, this boy should be given a hero's welcome.* Trixon cautioned him to wait until the boy was finished sharing, before welcoming him arms wide open.

Edmond smiled a half smile, and said, "Well, it was not hard. I had found a knife years ago, in the field, and had it in my pocket. When I saw my parents murdered, I just grabbed my brother and ran. One guard was sent after us, but I was faster than him. I drew him out from the area, and as he began to tire, I threw the blade at his head." Aalil and Antonis gasped in unison. "He died, I mean, I killed him. And I kept running, carrying Anton, until *this patrol* found us," Edmond finished, pointing at Garis.

The bronzed military leader again looked over the boy, surmising his abilities as a potential recruit. Admiration clear on his face.

This boy is not as immature as he first appeared, Trixon murmured. Vikaris nodded; Darion could have sworn he winked.

Vikaris said then, quietly, his pulse rapidly climbing, "Then they have not forgotten me in the kingdom?"

"No, Sire. Well, they are not allowed to talk about you. I only just learned your name this year. But everyone knows that Narco is an evil king, and what he says about the 'other' king cannot be the whole truth."

"And how old are you, Edmond?"

"Thirteen, Sire," adding quickly, "almost fourteen."

Antonis whistled at that. "You are huge! With proper training, we could make a warrior out of you." Aalil elbowed him, loudly whispering that it was not size alone that made a warrior.

Vikaris had heard enough. He stepped closer to Edmond after seeing Trixon's peripheral nod. "And you said, you wished to pledge your allegiance? Then do so, boy. I think we could find a place for you in our training camp if you are interested in fighting?" The boy's eyes lit up, and he nodded eagerly.

Vikaris smiled at Antonis. "It looks like you just found your new pupil," he said, clapping his former commander on the back. Antonis was grinning wide, gesturing at the boy and whispering none too quietly to Aalil. "Look at those arms! Such potential!"

***

"You've got to be kidding me," Darion brushed past Antonis, agitated. "My new sparring partner? He's just a kid. I'm the prince. Can't I have someone a little older? More experienced? I actually want to learn, you know."

Antonis whistled through his teeth sarcastically. "Oh, I see, now that you are the Marked Heir, you think you are better than that orphaned outsider out there? You know more than him after being here... what... a few days?"

Darion hesitated, and his cheeks flushed a light pink. Antonis stepped closer to Darion and puffed out his chest saying, "You listen here. That *boy* knows more than you will ever be able to learn from me. He has been living under Narco's rule his entire life. He has grown strong from working as one of Narco's slaves. He is willing, and he killed a bloody Rav'Arian." Spittle flew with emphasis. "You two have a lot in common, and it would do you good to make a friend." Exhaling angrily, Antonis added, "Though, I suppose I can find someone more *worthy* of your time... Prince. I will take the boy on, and you can find your own instructor."

Antonis stormed out of the tent and left Darion feeling small. *What am I doing? Antonis is right. I have only been here a matter of hours, and already I'm acting like a jerk,* Darion thought.

Darion didn't notice the tent flap open again, until King Vikaris tapped his shoulder. "I see we will have to work on your senses. First lesson on staying alive: pay attention. Do not ever let anyone sneak up on you." The skin near his father's eyes creased in a good-humored smile, though. His smile reminded Darion of Rick. Being here with Rick and Carol—the only parents he'd ever known, to now spending time with his biological father, the king, only added to his confusion and taught nerves. He felt like he was letting Carol and Rick down. He had seen how the smiles hardly reached their eyes as they watched him with Vikaris. He knew they were hurting, and he wanted desperately to talk to them—to assure them that he loved them no matter what, but everything was so complicated now. He was the prince. This was his father.

And I don't measure up at all, Darion thought morosely.

Darion sat down on a giant cushion, feeling even more deflated than before. "I don't know if I can do this. It's all so foreign to me. I am such an outsider." Darion hated showing weakness... especially to this man—this stranger. He felt overwhelmed.

Vikaris squatted beside him. "I cannot imagine how difficult this must be for you, Darion. I wish you could have returned during a time of peace, and acclimated at your own pace, but that is just not how it worked out.

You are here now, and if you are going to survive this conflict, you will have to begin your education. Today."

Darion looked at his father more steadily, "What about my mother?"

"You let me worry about her," Vikaris stood straightening his belt. "Trixon and I have been talking, and we agree that you cannot stay in camp. It is too dangerous. Our survival depends on keeping our camp hidden, which we do not seem to be excelling at presently. We have to move, as well as mobilize for our next attack. When the rescue mission begins, I cannot worry about you *and* focus on saving your mother. That is partly why I sent you away in the first place."

Darion flinched at the callous mention of it. *He already wants to get rid of me?* The shameful self-doubt that Darion had thought was behind him hit him full on. After hours spent wondering what it would be like to find his birth parents, his father was just planning on sending him away again.

"Darion, know that I want you here with me... I truly do, son." Darion met his eyes, and Vikaris held his gaze. "I promise, I am sending you somewhere safe, not to be hidden away this time, but to begin your training." Darion remembered the unicorns alluding to his tests to become the true heir. He sighed. He would have to trust his father's word.

"Where?"

"The Isle of Kaulter," Vikaris replied. "The unicorn homeland." Darion felt his mood lighten. He was being sent to live with the unicorns! "Before the Fall," Vikaris continued, "unicorns lived in harmony with humans. They lived in the Kingdom, as well as in Kaulter. After Narco's rebellion began, however, Elsra and the others found it prudent to stow their young away. Eventually, we sent both our young and old there for safekeeping—those who would go, at least." Darion thought back to the few elderly persons or children he had seen in the crowd that day.

"Only a small retinue of unicorn warriors remain with us. Narco, you see, always expressed a sadistic fascination for the unicorns, even as a boy. His jealousy that his brother had been bonded with one, and that he could not, drove him mad. That is why we fear so much for Trinidad." Vikaris' eyes grew hard and stormy. Then, turning back to Darion, they cleared as he continued.

"No one knows where the Isle is. The unicorns use the Tree or Portal, as transport. It is beyond our world. The unicorns' horns and gifts access the portals, as do our rubies," Vikaris noted, looking at Darion's brightly shining stone.

"It is believed that Narco seeks Kaulter. This is why the unicorns are so secretive, and rarely show themselves beyond such protection. I think that was the first time anyone in my camp has seen the Council, and you saw how quickly they were forced to leave today. We will not take any chances with them. You must go to them though, Darion. This has always been foretold, that when you returned, I was to send you to them for training. There you will learn what it means to be the Nav'Arian Heir... just as I had to learn. There, you will become the greatest warrior our world has ever seen. You will bring peace to our world once more." His green eyes shimmered as he spoke.

Darion didn't want to break it to his father, but he knew that what he said was impossible. *There is no way, I'll become the 'greatest warrior' and 'savior of the world.'* He was a gawky teen who had grown up in a different land—easy compared to Edmond's upbringing. Darion felt spoiled. Soft. Not a hardened, capable warrior. He had a lot of catching up to do to even come close to navigating this new world. He looked at his father who nodded at him, assuredly. Darion cleared his head and stood. Whatever happens, he would try his hardest to become what his father said. A man his mother could be proud of.

"Will I still get updated on Mother's rescue?"

Vikaris nodded, then reached out his arm, and Darion grasped his forearm, Marks touching. As their marks linked, a clear white light shot up through the tent, the interior tinted red by their alit rubies.

Trixon cocked his head in mid-conversation with the blacksmith. Turning toward the king's tent, he nodded his head. *The pact has been made. The prophecy has begun.*

CHAPTER 16

The Isle

"This way, this way. We must not keep them waiting," Seegar chided, as his charglings gawked at the giant waterfall they had just burst from. Darion stood wide eyed, as he took in the spectacular view of his new home, the wondrous Isle of Kaulter.

Grudgingly he admitted that this *was* a pleasant change from the war camp. The verdant forest was surrounded by rolling hills as far as the eye could see from the high vantage point on the bridge. Sheep dotted the plains, while the cattle roamed. He had not seen many animals since coming to Nav'Aria and now realized that the livestock were kept here. They would otherwise give the camp location away.

He stood over a hundred-foot drop, the waterfall emptied into a pure, cerulean pool. The clearest water he had ever seen. Edmond and his brother stood quietly behind him, making sure to keep their eyes down in the presence of their prince.

"Come on, come on, Sire. We really must not keep

them waiting. I assure you, you do not want to see Regent Elsra in a temper," Seegar added, winking at the boys. Darion nodded but couldn't seem to tear his eyes away from the water. It was the same color as his mother's eyes. *So honest and transparent.* The younger boys bumped into him, interrupting such musing.

"Sorry, Sire," the small boy squeaked. Darion hadn't spoken to either of them, and as he was about to, he noted Edmond sliding his arm in front of the boy. As if for protection. Darion met his eyes for a moment, registering a strength in them that again evoked insecurity in Darion. He quickly turned toward Seegar.

"Let's go," he told the white-haired servant, with more force than he had intended. *I don't care what Antonis says about this kid. He's too... too... too Nav'Arian—that's what.* Darion didn't trust him.

Seegar had generously offered to accompany them to Kaulter. Apparently, he was always responsible for the transport of children. It seemed he had a soft spot for them. Darion was glad for him. Saying goodbye to his father had been difficult, but his heart hurt more for his parents, Rick and Carol. He had a terrible sense of foreboding that he wouldn't see them again. He had just learned that Rick and Antonis would be going on the rescue attempt. He sent a silent prayer, hoping that someone up there would hear him. He had pleaded with Carol to come with him, but she declined. She said this was something he had to do on his own. He hated leaving. His father, the king, had been absolute in his decision, however. Darion could never have swayed his mind, and after further consideration, he realized he didn't want to. He needed to learn from the unicorns, in order to be valuable to his loved ones... and Nav'Aria.

Trixon had also reminded Darion that he was the True Heir, and should his father fall, Darion would be the Rightful King. He needed to learn, and fast!

The four of them traveled a worn dirt path away from the cliff's edge and waterfall, and toward a large wooden structure near the horizon. The unicorns had come here directly after being dismissed from the War Council. Darion could have gone with them through the Tree, but that would leave the other three behind. Seegar had known of another portal point similar to how he had arrived in Nav'Aria. Trixon had accompanied them to the portal entrance.

As the portal had closed in the rock embedded stream, Trixon had entered Darion's mind, saying, *Learn fast, my prince. Trust your senses. Guard your mind.*

Just over the crest of the last hill, Darion and the others came upon their destination. As the sun's rays danced along the shimmering coastline, he swore he saw mermaids swimming out in the water from his viewpoint, jumping and splashing about. *No, that's crazy,* he thought. *It's just dolphins or fish.* The harder he squinted, he could make out arms. *They're waving!* His mind was instantly distracted from self-loathing and practically imploded with curiosity. *I get to live here?* He smiled slightly at Edmond, who looked equally impressed... even more so. Edmond's widened eyes met his for a moment. Catching himself,

Darion halted his smile, and returned Edmond's look with a haughty one. He tried to look nonplussed and acted as if this were not the most spectacular view he had ever seen. He was the prince, after all.

The wooden structure on the horizon turned out to be a giant wooden fortress partially encased in an immense, hollowed tree trunk. It would have engulfed his old school! Nearby the massive building stood a lone, white crystalized tree. *The Shovlan Tree!*

Darion had not known what to anticipate, but he had not accounted for how many other creatures—humans, nymphs, centaurs, merfolk—would be there, too. Now, as they approached the wooden fortress, he realized that there was an entire village. Seegar had mentioned that he accompanied children here. He hadn't really considered just how many, but it did make sense. A war camp was no place for the young or the old. Those who weren't able to fight or work in the camp, but were loyal to Vikaris, were sent here. All had to be approved by the unicorns, of course. If the children were not sent here, they could possibly fall prey to Narco's monsters and become his slaves, as Edmond's family had been.

He looked at the siblings from the corner of his eye. He didn't know what it was about him, but he didn't like Edmond. He was too... *too muscular for one thing*. He reminded Darion of Joey Durange, the bully from school. Though Edmond did not appear malicious as Joey had been. In fact, he was a bit dull for Darion's taste. And just as Darion thought it, he realized how ridiculous he was being.

What do I have against him? He's an orphan. His parents just died, and here I am, judging him. And then it hit Darion. *I'm jealous!* This kid looked Nav'Arian. He looked like *he* was the prince, not Darion, who looked alien in this world.

A giant band of younglings charging ahead pulled him out of his brooding thoughts. Darion was struck by the levity of the group. Beast or man, they all ran and played together, hooting and hollering as they went. Darion loved the diversity of the place already. It was truly magical, like something from a story. He couldn't believe he was really standing here.

"This is where your father grew up, Darion. Your parents were married just over there." He pointed toward a shallow cove near the cliff, where a simple wooden arch stood.

Before he could ask more about his parents, the four were met by the rushing kids. "Seegar, Seegar," the kids shouted.

"Hello, children," Seegar said, as he waved his hands, in a kind yet silencing motion. "I have brought a *very* special group today, and we must go straight to see the Regent. Will you walk with us?"

The children all nodded their heads, as their curious little faces turned toward Darion, Edmond, and Anton. Darion met their eyes and smiled. His heightened senses once again allowed him to hear the whispers. *Who do you think they are? Why are they so special? Do you think he brought us gifts? Of course, he did—Master Seegar always brings gifts!*

The party continued toward the wooden enclosure through the square. People had come out of their homes to see them. Young children of all kinds ran up to them. Elderly humans, and centaurs hobbled over to their neighbors to gossip about the latest group. And throughout the encampment unicorns came forth. Hundreds of them! Darion could not completely tell with those before him, but he knew that many looked to be female. Young colts peered from behind their mothers' legs. Darion's heartrate rapidly increased as they began to approach the structure. Awaiting the group were Elsra and Drigidor on a raised platform. A few feet away from them stood Triumph whom he had met at the Council. Darion shivered under the unicorn's fierce scowl.

"Members of Nav'Aria," Elsra spoke, and the crowd hushed. "Today, I have the privilege of introducing you to our newly returned Prince Darion!"

Many in the crowd gasped, much like the war camp onlookers had. Elsra nodded her head at him, and he stepped forward. He turned toward the crowd and gave a little wave. He had never been trained in diplomacy. He had no idea what Elsra expected but he hoped his wave would be enough.

Continuing she said, "King Vikaris has sent him to us to begin training. Please welcome your prince... and his friends," she said, as she looked toward the other boys. The crowd cheered, and many of the young kids who had accompanied Darion's party, now knelt before him. Some of the older women had tears in their eyes. Darion wondered how many of these women were widows because of his uncle. He tried to look as stoic as possible but hiding nerves of this magnitude would require training. He was standing on a dais with three of the most powerful unicorns and before a cheering crowd of "his" subjects. He was suddenly glad he had opted to go to the bathroom before entering the portal.

"Seegar, lead them in. Show them their quarters. We'll be with you momentarily."

Darion noted the tone in her voice as she stared sternly at Triumph. Darion had a feeling they were talking about him. If only his heightened senses would allow him to intercept their telepathic communication. It seemed they could control who their audience was. Drigidor pawed his front hooves and exhaled noisily. Seegar didn't miss any of this, and quickly ushered the boys in. Young Anton looked as if he might faint.

***

"Have you ever seen anything like this?" Darion couldn't mask the wonder in his voice as he stood within the interior of the fortress. Edmond shook his head no. If he was surprised that Darion had spoken to him, even if indirectly, he didn't show it. Darion looked at him from his peripheral gaze and noted that maybe Antonis was right. Edmond seemed to take everything in stride and had a calm countenance. Darion envied him. He was just barely able to hold it together. He had come through a portal to land in a fossilized tree trunk full of unicorns and centaurs! He continually had to pinch himself to make sure this was actually happening... and to not embarrass himself by passing out. *Maybe some of Edmond's calmness could rub off on me,* he thought begrudgingly.

The vast space boasted an ornate wooden frieze along

the entire rotunda. Feeling mesmerized, Darion stared, his eyes feasting upon the fascinating art. It began with very sparse detailing, and eventually added more and more creatures and detail to the image. It told of the beginning of time, in accordance with the unicorns' plea to the Creator to make humans, as they had seen it foretold in the signs. Darion wondered if they regretted their decision now. Humans had become broken. Narco had seen to that. Darion shuddered thinking of his dreams—of his mother—forced to endure captivity under that maniac. Even his name sounded slimy. Darion didn't want to think about him right now. His eyes fell upon another large map, like the one he had seen in the Shovlan Tree. He wanted to look at it as well, but just then a young maid arrived.

"Ah, Alice," Seegar said. "Good to see you. I trust your parents are well?" Seegar, it would appear, knew everyone everywhere. The red-haired girl nodded, giving him a hug.

She turned to face the boys, and Darion almost laughed aloud, when Edmond sucked in his breath at the sight of her. *She's pretty, I'll give him that.* Bright red hair, with amber colored eyes, and the palest, translucent skin Darion had ever seen. She looked to be around fourteen or fifteen. Not quite Darion's type, but pretty. Her eyes seemed to linger on Edmond for a moment too, before blushing and looking back to Seegar.

"I have the guest rooms prepared. Right this way, please," she said in a honied voice. All of a sudden, Edmond didn't look nearly as sure of himself. Darion enjoyed the moment tremendously.

Darion had the largest room by far. It was more like an apartment, really. Seegar was to stay a while as Darion adjusted, and he had his own separate room adjoining Darion's. Edmond and Anton were taken elsewhere. Edmond didn't even acknowledge Darion's farewell as he was quite fixated on Alice, who was telling them what to expect for the evening. Seegar chuckled as he watched them go.

"I like that one. Strong spirit," he said quietly. Darion smiled at that as he watched them. Maybe the kid wouldn't be too bad after all.

CHAPTER 17

The Altercation

"My Lady," Trinidad hesitantly called out, after another despondent day. Again, Trinidad's mind was clearing up from the sedative, and he had a short amount of time before the guards came back. Along with calling out to Lyrianna, he always tried to communicate with any nearby unicorns. Unicorns were able to detect each other's presence from a great distance. Unfortunately, after losing his horn, and with it, most of his powers, his calling distance had been severely shortened. He tried, nonetheless, for he knew that Vikaris and Trixon would be doing everything in their power to conduct a rescue mission. And he also knew that was exactly what Narco was anticipating.

Since becoming Narco's prisoner, he had learned a lot more about the way he led his "Empire." It was much more methodical and sadistic than they all had once thought. Narco had captured any living creature that he could before they made it to Vikaris's troops. He had created a hierarchy in which he was the law. But more than that, he considered himself akin to a god. He expected his people to worship him. He had put the Rav'Arian creatures directly below him. They, then the trolls, served him, though Trinidad could not identify what power he held over them. *What kept them from turning on him?* There were no remaining unicorns or centaurs in Narco's holdings, besides Trinidad himself, at least that he knew of.

It had been rumored that the remaining merpeople of the lake were under constant watch. Fishing quotas were set, and if these were not met, Narco would order one of the merfolk to be captured and hung out to dry above the dock. Many had fled, but Narco had trapped them in the Lure River after commanding a crew to build a dam.

At one time, he had had more beasts under his control, Trinidad was sure. He had seen many varieties of bones as he had been led down to his dungeon. He knew that the centaur clans were fierce and would never bow to Narco in submission. Trinidad respected their integrity but still mourned their suffering. Their end would not have come quickly. Therefore, the humans were his labor. All three groups—Ravarian, troll, human—filled Narco's ranks. The women, children, and elderly worked the land to ensure he had enough food to feed his troops. He had no advisors that Trinidad could find. He knew there was something hidden, though, but he had never seen another human with Narco. There was something that he could still not see. *What power had Narco found? How was he able to rule?* Fear, mostly, is what kept the humans at bay, Trinidad knew well. Fear was a powerful motivator, but so was hope.

He contemplated the differences in Narco and Vikaris. One was like night, where the other was the day. So different. And yet Trinidad feared for Vikaris. They were losing. They had *been* losing for years now. Somehow Narco had the upper hand. Trinidad had to figure out how. As he continued to contemplate all of this, he listened for Lyrianna. *Where was she?*

And that's when he heard it. A faint call at first, but it grew. Suddenly his ears rang with the noise. He glanced around nonchalantly, as his heart about leapt out of his throat. He didn't know how they were able to tune him in, but all at once, he heard voices. He heard his family! *Elsra, Triumph, Drigidor,* and wait, *Darion!* Trinidad desperately called out to them, but it seemed they were unaware of him. *How could that be?* He tried to think less of how this was happening and pay attention to what they were saying.

Silence. Silence, Elsra growled. *You overstep, Triumph. You will remember that this is still my Council, and before it, your prince. Please forgive him. Fear of Narco and his spies, has caused him to become hardened. He did not mean that, Darion. You are our prince, and your training shall begin, as is expected.* Trinidad could hardly breathe. If he was hearing this correctly, however it was possible, that meant that Darion had returned! He felt the prickling of goosebumps traveling down his spine. He had to let Lyrianna know. They had to get out of here. *Her son was in Nav'Aria!* He was safe with the Unicorn Council... presumably in Kaulter.

Thank you, Regent Elsra. My father instructed me to come to you for training, and for my education of Nav'Aria. I know I don't know as much as you would like, Sir, Trinidad guessed that was directed toward his forceful brother Triumph, *but I swear that I'll work hard. I won't let you down. I may be an outsider, but for the first time in my life, I feel like I finally belong. Nothing will keep me from fulfilling my duty now. I will become a warrior, as my father wants, and I will see my mother again when she is saved.* Trinidad's heart soared! That was Vikaris's son all right. He could hear it in his voice, but more than that, in his resolve. He couldn't quite make out Elsra's response, for the communication began to fade away. No, he could have yelled, but he didn't want to draw attention to himself. Soon it was quiet again. Trinidad momentarily panicked, wondering if he was hallucinating from the drugs. But no, he knew he had somehow heard from them, and he knew it was just what Lyrianna needed.

Again, he called out to her, "Lyrianna?"

"Yes, Trinidad, I am here." She sounded groggy, as if he had awoken her.

"Lyrianna, listen to me. Before they come, I have to tell you something."

"I have to tell you something, too, Trinidad," she said sadly. He started at her tone. Just as he was going to inquire, he heard the keys coming toward his cell. He had to hurry.

"Lyrianna, listen to me," but she cut him off.

"I am dying, Trinidad. I feel it. The end is near." *Was she whispering, or was her breath failing her?*

"No, no, Lyrianna, you have to listen to me I have news!" He could barely contain his frustration at his inability to go to her. "I have news of your son," he yelled at her through their telepathic connection.

"Yes, my son," she said, her voice catching. "Take care of my son." Her voice was broken and barely audible. He could hear in her voice that this was not a simple case of hopelessness. Something had happened. Something terrible. And *he* did it.

She was silent. Trinidad feared the worst, and in that moment, Narco stood before him. "Enjoying your little chat?" Narco said full of malice.

Trinidad, who had always feigned delirium in his presence, knew the gag was up. He reared his head puffing out his chest, towering before Narco. Trinidad smirked as Narco was forced to take an involuntary step back.

"What do you want, Scarred One?" Trinidad retorted. He could see that Narco struggled to keep his countenance while hiding his scar. Narco's eyes burned with fury.

"I want to take you on a walk," he said suddenly, surprising Trinidad. "It has been quite a while since you had proper exercise. Why not today? A little fresh air might do you some good, wouldn't you agree?"

Trinidad was instantly on guard but did indeed long for air that was not filled with the fetid smells of dungeon and Rav'Arians. He didn't know what Narco was playing at, but he knew he would most likely not like the outcome.

***

Lyrianna lay on the ground, disheveled. Trinidad could not fit through the doorway to her cell but resolutely tried, nonetheless. Narco stood beside her and kicked her in the stomach. She let out a low moan but didn't wake. Trinidad was glad that she was still breathing, but he knew she would not last in her present state.

"What did you do to her?" he demanded of Narco. His eyes staring stormily at Narco. The man blanched at the unicorn's fury, but swiftly recovered and motioned to the guard. The troll grabbed the halter they had tied on him and jerked him back from the doorway. Narco walked toward him.

"You coward," Trinidad whispered. "You would not dare face me, unless drugged and chained, with your toadies here," motioning toward Dabor, the troll, "to protect you. You are weak, Narco. You have always been weak. And you know it." The last phrase he enunciated slowly. Deliberately.

A corner of Narco's mouth lifted to form what Trinidad assumed was a smile, though it looked more like a snarl on the ugly man's pocked and scarred face.

"You are wrong, Trinidad. You are the weak one," Narco said snidely, looking at Trinidad's wasted form. "Say what you like, but do not think for one minute that I am weak. In fact, very soon you and I will be spending a lot of time together. You will come to obey me, just like everyone else." He held Trinidad's halter, whispering close, "I choose you, Trinidad. A Nav'Arian leader must have his unicorn, right? You were fit for my brother; who better than to bond to me?"

Trinidad had to forcibly keep his temper down. Narco couldn't know just how much that thought terrified him. Looking away from Narco's vile face, Trinidad spotted a red stone hanging from a cord around Narco's neck. At first glance, it appeared to be a ruby, as the Marked Heirs had always worn, and which Narco had always coveted. On closer inspection though, Trinidad noted that it was not a gemstone, but rather a vial of liquid.

"Ah, and this brings me back to what you were saying," as he followed Trinidad's eyes, "you mistake me, Trinidad. I am not weak. Not in the least," he chuckled, as he fixed his shirt to cover the necklace once again. "There is still much you do not know, Oh Mighty One," he whispered, with a chilling voice. Trinidad shuddered at the title.

He gestured to his guards. "Take them."

Just then, Trinidad felt enormous hands on him, pulling his halter toward a door farther down the hallway. He wasn't familiar with this part of the castle, but he believed that door led to the south wall. He frantically tried to turn his head to see what they were doing to Lyrianna. He breathed relief when he saw another troll emerge with the frail Queen in his arms. *He knows,* he thought. *He knows about Darion and the rescue that is most likely underway.* Trinidad wished more than anything he could communicate with the Council again.

Narco stood watching his guards lead his prisoners away. *And now I have you, nephew,* he thought, as he clutched his vial and watched the door close behind the once majestic unicorn and broken queen. *Now, I will have all of you.*

CHAPTER 18

The Secret

"Hurry up, old man," Aalil snapped.

After meeting with the Unicorn Council, the two had been instructed to leave immediately. Riccus had joined them, and they were to meet up with members of one of Garis's patrols. From there, they would head toward Castle Dintarran.

"We are the same age!" Antonis shouted back, as he caught up to the lithe warrior he had once shared an evening with many years before. "Why they grouped us together, I will never know," he grumbled. He had been surprised to see her face in the crowd, when they first returned. Now, he wished he hadn't.

She was smug, bossy, and downright unappealing. Time had not been kind to her. She still had a certain appeal: leaner and harder, but attractive nonetheless, he grudgingly admitted to himself as he eyed her tanned bare arms, fortified from years of battle. Her braid loosened from their quick pace; he caught himself staring at a loose strand of hair, almost tucking it behind her ear. *Stop it,* he reprimanded himself, making a fist and glaring at her, as if her loose strand of hair was a ploy to entice him. No, it wasn't so much her beauty but her attitude that had changed. No longer the sweet harpist he had known. *He wanted a soft, beautiful woman, not... not this formidable warrior woman before him.*

"I think she was talking to me." Riccus winked. Antonis stopped and nodded embarrassedly. Rick arrived at the clearing where Aalil was waiting, not so patiently.

"Hurry up, *both* of you. We have a long night before we reach the edge of the Woods, and I for one would like to..." her voice cut off as she motioned for them to be quiet. Instantly all three drew their blades and waited. Antonis had been away a long time, and he berated himself for letting his senses dampen so much. *Get it together, man, she's not worth the distraction! You are on a mission... from the king!*

Now that she had pointed it out, he did hear a sort of rumbling sound nearby, though it was hard to hear over Rick's heavy breathing. He glared at him, mouthing "old man" as he eyed his rising chest. Rick just scowled and gave a level look around them, waiting.

Aalil had two blades drawn: her sword in her right hand, and a curved dagger in her left. That seemed a bit over the top, he thought. It was probably just an elk or deer. Garis himself said they had not seen any Rav'Arians this far out, and that they purposely swept their tracks after a battle keeping their lair hidden.

In a flash, Aalil spun around and threw her blade past Antonis's head, piercing the eye of the approaching troll.

Antonis whistled as she nearly clipped his left ear.

Oh, I love this woman, he swooned. *She might be a bit bossy and rough around the edges, but I like a girl who can handle herself,* he thought, all at once forgetting his earlier doubts.

As soon as she had thrown the blade, Antonis heard the corpse fall behind him. He grinned at her, then turned to study the creature. As he knelt to inspect it, a loud crash sounded behind him. Rick had just been tackled by a crazed swarm of cloth.

"Let go of me," it yelled. Riccus struggled to pin the hidden limbs that were covered in the rags and cloth. A foot kicked out and struck him in the groin.

"Oww," Rick muttered as he rolled over. The hooded stranger began to stand, and Aalil was suddenly there—faster than Antonis could even blink.

With a blade under the chin, Aalil ordered it to remove the hood. "Not too fast now. I do not give warnings," she coldly stated. Antonis's heart melted. He came to stand right beside her, as Rick stood up, straightening his tunic.

"Who are you?" Antonis said, searching the hooded being.

"Ahahahaha," the creature cackled. Still unable to see it, Aalil flicked her blade to the hood revealing the stranger's head. "So, the rumors *are* true?"

"Morta," Antonis spat, instantly recognizing the pale, freckled man before him. "Morta Evess. The Traitor." He raised his blade toward the man's thin throat.

"Now, now, it is all perception, Antonis. You know this. I am no traitor. I serve the Meridia family, same as you."

"No! *Not* the same as me," Antonis flicked his cheek with his sword for emphasis, enjoying the sight of blood appearing on Morta's freckled face. To his credit, the small man didn't even flinch. "You serve the imposter. The murderer! I serve the Marked King."

Wiping the droplet of blood with his robed sleeve, Morta croaked, "You always were a man of integrity... But, wait, I thought you were dead?" Morta inquired, feigning surprise. His sneer made the hairs on the back of Antonis's neck rise. He had the sinking suspicion that his return had not been kept secret after all.

"What do you want?" Antonis asked harshly.

Morta glanced at the blade below his chin and raised an eyebrow. Antonis stepped back and lowered the knife edge; Aalil and Riccus kept guard. Antonis motioned for him to sit.

"What do you want, Morta? Why are you here?" Antonis glowered at him. The man sat mute, watching him. *This man! This treasonous bastard who brought down the house Meridia. Do I kill him, or bring him to Vikaris?* Antonis mulled it over as he stared at the monster perched on a boulder. *His head will suffice,* he concluded, tightening his grip on his sword.

Morta had served as Rustusse and Narco's instructor at the palace. As the boys grew older and Rustusse was sent away for training with the Unicorns, Narco was left alone with Morta. Whatever those two shared, it was not normal. Their deep, dark secrets of power and take over began in that little school room. Morta was the one years later who snuck the Rav'Arians into the palace, leading to

Narco's coup. He was responsible for the death of Rustusse, for Vikaris's conquest, and Darion's secret life away. *I should kill him. Now.* Antonis flexed his fist, staring at the villain's thin throat.

"You do not want to do that," Morta chided, "Though killing me will give you instant pleasure, I am sure, you will miss out on my message from the Lord Emperor."

"What message is that?" Antonis said through clenched teeth.

"Ah, ah, ah. You did not think it would be *that* easy, did you? If I give you the message, what guarantee do I have that you will not kill me?"

"None."

"Alas, that shall not work for me. You see, Narco thought you would say as much. It turns out, he remembers you quite well, Antonis. Or is it Lord Commander? You always were a bit of a hothead. Did you enjoy your time in Oregon?"

The hair on Antonis's entire body began to tingle. "What did you say," he asked quietly, unable to mask the tremor in his voice.

"Oh, Oregon. That is how you pronounce it, correct? It took us quite some time to track you down... but we did." He smiled darkly. "We have been watching you for years... Tony."

Antonis leapt forward, punching the man in one quick jab. Aalil and Rick were on him in a second and pulled Antonis back. Morta, looking surprised that he was struck, sat up, and Antonis was glad to detect a glimmer of fear in his eyes. "You are bluffing," Antonis stated.

"That is the gamble. Am I bluffing, Lord Commander, or am I telling the truth?" Morta paused theatrically, eyeing the surroundings, and asked, "And where *is* Darion?"

"Do not say his name, you son of a bitch!" Rick roared, grabbing for his throat, his eyes blazing.

It would appear it was Rick's turn to be held back, as he exploded with the most colorful language Antonis had ever heard... and he had been a soldier much of his life! Aalil dragged Rick away, but not before his boot connected with the Morta's kneecap, dropping the man, who moaned with agony in response.

Antonis, feeling much more satisfied and in control, pressed on.

"What are your conditions then, for this message?"

"And here we are," Morta coughed. "We have finally come to it," Morta stated, slowly rising to his feet. "Narco will release Lyrianna and Trinidad on the condition that I am returned—alive and well, and that *you*, Lord Commander, take their place."

Throwing his head back, Antonis let out a full, throaty laugh. *As if he could believe that.* He looked up to catch his companions' eyes. Aalil's mouth was agape. Rick simply would not meet his gaze. "Wait, you two do not seriously believe that Narco would make good on his word, do you?" Neither answered. Morta smiled even wider, revealing blackened, decaying teeth.

Fuming now and utterly disgusted, Antonis asked, "And what if we do not meet his *conditions?*"

"They die." At that, Antonis hit him on the back of his

head with his sword hilt.

"What was that?" Aalil started. "You have to keep him talking."

"I have heard enough," Antonis said darkly. His eyes searching the woods for any other lurkers.

"We should go back. Take the traitorous bastard with us. Vikaris will want to interrogate him. How did he know about Oregon?" Riccus's words coming out in a rush. He was always so calm; this meeting had clearly left him shaken.

"No," Antonis looked from Aalil, the woman who evoked strange feelings in him, to Riccus, one of his best friends and fellow Keepers. "Every moment we wait puts Lyrianna and Trinidad in more danger. We have to follow the plan. If Narco thinks Morta is in Vikaris's care, so be it. We will free the other two before the 'conditions' ever have to be met." The pair exchanged a look before nodding their agreement.

Aalil hesitated, then said quietly, "But, would you do it? Would you surrender yourself if what he says *is* true?"

Antonis met her eyes. "For my queen? Without hesitation," he said fixedly. He thought he saw Riccus nod subtly.

"Now we move. We have to meet up with that other patrol before it gets too dark." Antonis searched the unconscious prisoner for any weapons before binding his wrists and throwing the small man over his shoulder. Aalil crouched down before the troll, retrieving her knife from its eye. Antonis watched as she wiped the blood on its front tunic and spit on its face as she kicked the corpse away. "Filthy traitors," she muttered.

***

"You see, Darion, when our world came to be many cycles ago, the Great Creator saw it in his vision to create the sky, water, plants, and living beasts. He saw it fit to charge the unicorns, his first living creation, with the task of overseeing our world. This we know from the First Horn, as Tribute came to be called. He was the land's beacon. What was right and wrong, was set forth by him, in accordance with the Creator's wishes. This early period was known as the 'Formation.' A quiet, peaceful time. The unicorns ruled over the other species, and the land was free of pain and sorrow.

"According to the story, one night, Tribute went to a small spring, and as he gazed at his reflection, he was startled. For there he saw *man*. He saw a human in the reflection who appeared to be on his back. Riding him. Tribute was disturbed and took this as a vision. He went into the Shovlan Tree and did not come out for nearly three cycles. No one outside of the Unicorn Council knew if he lived anymore, as the other unicorns took up the leadership of their peaceful realm.

"When he finally came out of his self-enclosed isolation, revealing himself to all of those in the Realm, he was not alone. Riding Tribute was a young man with a gleaming ruby around his neck and a shimmering arm full of symbols. This man was Vondulus, first of his name, the first King of Nav'Aria." Seegar pointed at one of the images farther down the frieze in the rotunda. Darion had asked if he could learn more about the history of the land,

and Seegar, an avid historian himself, had been more than happy to oblige.

The next image showed unicorns kneeling before a man.

"Tribute came out of isolation, declaring that the Creator had seen it fit to create humans. Tribute credited his vision as a sign and remained in a state of meditation for a year or two. He explained to that during that time, unbeknownst to the rest of the Realm, a child had been sent to him. For three cycles he had raised the child—the King. Finally, he invited some of the elder unicorns from Kaulter and revealed to them his gift from the Creator. Many balked at the strange, two-legged, furless creature. Though eventually they all believed the tale, once they saw Vondulus's arm, that is. Its markings held symbols that spoke the Creator's direct commands. Only the Creator could bestow these marks as a gift that shone as brightly as the Creator himself. With Vondulus and Tribute also came years of writings and prophecies that had been deciphered from his symbols." Breaking from his tale, Seegar looked back at Darion. "You will soon learn more about Vondulus. He has many written works that you will need to familiarize yourself with before becoming the True Heir."

Darion was about to ask about that last part, but Seegar hurriedly picked up his story again, looking almost embarrassed. Darion could only wonder why, but quickly became swept up in the story once again, fascinated by the tale.

"Before their King, the first unicorns knelt, swearing

fealty to him. To protect him, to oversee peace in the Realm, of course at the discretion of His Majesty. The unicorns realized that this would allow them to live amongst the Nav'Arians without having to rule them any longer. Their task now would be to serve the King and honor the Great Creator by protecting him. Tribute and Vondulus maintained a closer relationship and began the tradition of 'bonding' between House Meridia and the First Horn's family line."

Darion was spellbound by the information. He wanted Seegar to explain every image and motioned him to keep going.

"One more, my prince, and then we have to go to your first lesson." Darion felt a flutter in his stomach at the mention of it, but before he could get too worked up, Seegar continued. The next image was of a tall, spired building. It appeared to show a gathering of creatures outside the large gate. *A castle*, Darion thought. *It is stunning.*

"This is your rightful home, Darion," Seegar said, pointing to the castle.

"My what?" Darion said in disbelief.

"This is Castle Dintarran. The home of the Meridia royal family." Darion's eyes searched the image, memorizing every fine detail. *It was breathtaking. It had looked impressive on the map he had seen, but this? This was incredible.*

Clearing his throat, Seegar explained, "Once the king was named, the unicorns took him to the spring where Tribute had had the vision. There the Great Creator had told them to have Vondulus enter the water and immerse himself in it. When his head broke the surface, the party all stood stunned at the red light that now bathed the pool. Around Vondulus's neck was a large gemstone. A ruby. Nothing of its kind, had ever been seen in Nav'Aria. From that day forth, it was proclaimed that every Marked Heir would wear a ruby, just as the First King did. At the birth of each Marked child, they are taken to that special spring."

"But where?" Darion questioned, clutching the stone at his neck, feeling its warmth radiate into his fingers.

"Why, Shovlan, of course," Seegar answered matter-of-factly, as if there could be any other possibility.

"Shortly after Vondulus's arrival, the Creator sent forth a multitude of humans that now populated the Realm. The unicorns, with the assistance of trolls, centaurs, nymphs, and humans built the castle you see here. Thus, beginning the 'Blessed Period.' Peace still spread across the land, but now the creatures had a leader. They had a purpose. Vondulus created structure and a government. His people loved him. He was blessed by the Creator himself. He encouraged creatures to find a livelihood and pursue interests that would best provide for the good of the Kingdom. Creatures came forth and became farmers, builders, healers, teachers, and so on. Civilization flourished under the First King. He even created an army. Although no one at the time understood its purpose, it was as if Vondulus knew there would come a day when Nav'Aria had to be ready to fight against a threat from outside, or rather, from within."

Darion thought again of Narco.

What man could do such horrible things? He ran his eyes along the frieze. He would ask Seegar to explain the rest later. Though his nagging contemplation pressed. How could one man tear all of this down? *What propelled Narco?*

Coming back to present, Seegar sighed. "We should go, my prince. It would not reflect well on me, if I were to make you late for your first lesson." Seegar brushed off his green robes, turning to leave, but Darion stopped him.

With the insecurity that still comes with adolescence, Darion had one more question that he had been considering. He quietly asked, "Is the Creator of Nav'Aria the same as God in my old home?" Darion would be the first to admit that he had not attended church as a boy, but many of his peers had. *Had they been right in their beliefs? And could the Creator, as Seegar said, have created all of this? All this world, and his last?*

Darion had never professed his belief in a higher power, at least out loud, but he had always felt one. Without realizing it, Darion knew that he believed. It was in the crisp inhale of an autumn day, or the tingling of a warm summer breeze. The rich swirls of color in a sunset, the thunderous sound of rushing water, the quiet afternoons with his old horse. The draw of nature for Darion had always been strong, and, well, spiritual. He had always known there was something guiding him. Seegar simply smiled and put his arm around Darion's shoulders.

Looking into his shining emerald eyes, Seegar said, "I think you already know, Darion. Whatever name you used there does not matter. It is what you know and believe in your heart that truly matters."

Seegar's serene, matter-of-fact attitude quieted any insecurities Darion had. Feeling at peace about his origin and purpose, Darion allowed Seegar to lead him to his first lesson.

Bring it on, he thought.

CHAPTER 19

The Upset

"Vikaris," Trixon murmured, "is there a reason we have been staring at her tent since sundown?"

Vikaris wearily wiped his brow and shot a sidelong glare at his companion. He had had a very long couple of days. They both had. He noted his friend's drooping eyelids. Vikaris couldn't believe how many people he had sent away. After the Council meeting was disrupted by the arrival of the boys from the Kingdom, Vikaris had known he could not put off sending Darion away. He had immediately sought out Seegar and Trixon, and through him, Elsra. Darion must have his training. He had to be ready for what was to come. As much as Vikaris hated sending him away again. This boy. This, well, man... He could not let his emotions overrule what was right. Darion had to be kept safe and receive his training, so he could pass the other tests. After a curt goodbye, so as not to cry in front of his only child, he hurried them off to the portal and to safety in Kaulter.

He had then sought out the Keepers and Garis to

discuss the rescue mission the Council had agreed upon. Vikaris had been in many meetings like this before, and much to his chagrin, they had all fallen flat. His bride was still held by that treasonous snake. He tightened his fist just thinking of it, his green eyes glimmering in the twilight. Yet this time was different. *This time*, Antonis was the one leading the rescue, and there was no one Vikaris would trust more. After all, he had entrusted him—and the other Keepers—with his infant son. They had not failed him, and he knew in his heart that they could not fail at this. He felt wetness on his cheeks and realized he had begun to cry thinking back on the last image in Darion's sketch book.

His wife. His beautiful wife. A shell of what once was. Could she hold on? He longed desperately to hold her and kiss her. Take her in his arms, nurture her back to her glory, and never let her go again. He quickly wiped the back of his hand across his eyes. *This is not the time for tears.* All that image did was strengthen his zeal to crush his uncle. He wished he could go to her and lead the mission himself, but Elsra forbade it, or at least attempted to order the King about. When Lyrianna was taken, he had practically ridden to the castle and given himself up in exchange for his wife that very day. Garis and the Unicorns had had to hold him back, until Elsra could talk sense into him. *Be rational, Vikaris,* he remembered her saying. Narco wanted him dead so he could be the unrivaled king. Vikaris absolutely could not give himself up under any circumstances. Without Vikaris, the rebellion would die, and Nav'Aria would be lost forever.

Or at least that was until Darion returned... Vikaris wondered if his death would really be such a crushing blow.

Would the war wage on if Darion were at the head of the "rebels"? Could Darion do it?

He thought back to his son, his foreign accent and mannerisms, still *his* son nonetheless. He had gripped Darion's shoulders as he stared into his eyes for one brief, final moment. In his son's emerald eyes, he saw his strength and Lyrianna's goodness. Though a stranger in all but name, he saw such potential in the lad... as did Trixon. He saw what he would become. *A leader.* Vikaris had been unable to speak in that last moment, overcome by emotion, but he still hoped he had imparted his love for Darion.

The magnitude of the day's events weighing heavily on Trixon and Vikaris, as they both recalled saying goodbye to yet a second group. Vikaris knew that Trixon felt just as guilt-ridden seeing another group sent off to remedy his folly. While Darion was portaled away to safety, Antonis, Aalil, and Riccus were being sent right into the heart of danger itself. After they could no longer see their friends, Vikaris ordered his senior officers to spread the word, "the camp moves at dawn." Too many wanderers were encountering their perimeters. They had to keep moving to avoid Narco's clutches. Now at their new camp destination, as the day faded into evening, all he wanted was to fall into his bed. Yet, here he waited. *Here.* Outside the burgundy tent, with the gold trim that he knew so well. He had given *this* tent as a wedding gift. He had pleaded with them to move to Kaulter but was denied each time. He continued to stare at the entry way to the tent, willing the occupants to walk out. He was hesitant to ring the bell outside the plushily curtained entrance. So, he instead, sat, and waited, and watched. As he always did.

Gruegor volunteered for that first mission, Vikaris. That was not your fault.

Trixon gazed upon his king, their eyes meeting. He knew this man better than he knew anyone else. He could read his thoughts at a glance: a tilt of his head, the crease of his brow. He knew he had always carried the guilt of Gruegor's death with him, feeling responsible, and he knew that part of the reason was because Lyrianna's sister, Dalinia, blamed him. Trixon knew this was *her* tent, and he knew that every time Vikaris sent out another mission he would come and sit outside her tent, as if it were a vigil for his lost brother-in-law.

What Vikaris didn't know was that every time *he* sent out a mission and waited here, morose in his memories, Dalinia snuck out the back and watched from a neighbor's tent. Trixon shook his head thinking on how strange humans were. Either unicorns were just better at communicating, or they rarely had conflict with each other... though he knew it wasn't the latter, recalling Triumph and Drigidor's tension. *No,* he thought, *maybe unicorns are not much better after all.*

"All right, that is enough," Trixon bellowed, loud enough for the general vicinity to hear. The moonlight beginning to gleam off his pure coat and twinkle from his majestic horn. He whinnied loudly and bucked to his back feet, demanding the acknowledgement that every unicorn from the line of the First Horn deserved. He rarely lectured his king, but he was terribly tired and did not much care at the moment... As for Dalinia, he wanted to make her squirm a little. He did not appreciate the dark thoughts she directed at him *and* his King.

These two will resolve this, and resolve it now, Trixon thought. Vikaris looked wide-eyed at Trixon, as if he were a stranger instead of his longtime friend.

"What are you doing?" he whispered tersely at him. "You are going to wake everyone up!" A few of the nearby tent flaps had already begun to open as neighbors gazed out at their king and his fearsome steed. His eyes met children's faces ducking out from behind their tents and the men at the nearest cookfires gazing curiously.

"Dalinia," Trixon boomed. Trixon smirked as the woman jumped, startled at her name. It would appear she'd thought the unicorn didn't know of her presence. He blew out his breath noisily. *Humans,* he grumbled. *Always assuming they are so much greater than the rest. What a silly woman to really think she could hide from the King's Unicorn.* He was about to tell her so, when he looked at Vikaris, and noted the hot glare he was directing at Trixon, as the firelight danced upon the ruby, casting a red glow to the king's already fierce eyes. Trixon hesitated. His father always had told him that he was too rash. Maybe he had been a little dramatic rearing up like that.

'She has been watching us, the entire time you have been watching her tent, my king," he told him, guiltily, as the tall woman approached. Trixon was pleased to see her cheeks were flushed with embarrassment or anger, he could not quite tell, though she held her back stick straight and maintained a proud stare as she approached.

"I was only just coming home from dinner with the Lasters when I noticed you watching my tent," she replied smoothly, looking with outward disdain for Trixon. He knew she blamed him for the death of her husband as well. He had, after all, been the one that got Lyrianna and Trinidad captured, as she liked to point out regularly.

"Quiet, woman," Trixon snapped, more harshly then he had intended, his temper rising, "You dare lie to your king?"

Suddenly every tent flap opened as onlookers sought the source of the commotion. Vikaris placed his hand on Trixon's now heated neck. "Enough," he whispered tersely at Trixon. *Maybe I did overstep... But I will not apologize to her,* Trixon thought proudly.

He nodded his head and took a step back, allowing Vikaris to stand in full view of Dalinia, his sister by marriage. Dalinia had lost some of the smugness and now avoided eye contact with the man before her. All around, people bowed their heads in respect to the king and Trixon, all accept for Dalinia. Her contempt for him was palpable. Though just when she was formulating a curt response, Ansel ran out from the tent and flew for his uncle. His childish mind still not understanding the proper etiquette for one's king, not that Dalinia was a prime example of proper decorum.

"Uncle," Ansel blurted as he hugged the man's legs. He had always idolized his uncle. He and every other child in the "rebel" army, that is. Vikaris was a remarkably good looking, powerful leader who loved his people—and his people adored him, Trixon knew his cutting figure stole the breath of many women. Though Dalinia was blinded by her husband's failed mission, choosing to hate the man—and Trixon—whom she held responsible.

"Come in, come in, Uncle," Ansel said, pulling him by the hand. Vikaris took the opportunity to smile at the boy, with his infectious positivity. Trixon nudged closer.

"I would love to... that is," Vikaris paused, looking at Dalinia, "if that is all right with your mother?" The smile on his face not meeting his eyes any longer. There was a tension here. Where there had once been friendship and familial affection, now stood distance, formality, and dislike.

"Of course, Your Majesty. We are lucky to have you grace us with your presence," she lied smoothly, while eyeing the onlookers nearby. Trixon stamped his foot at that. Losing the grip on her facade, she muttered, "And bring the Unicorn as well." With that, she spun on her heel, and vanished behind the curtain.

Ansel, clueless to any tension, smiled dreamily at Trixon. This was one of the happiest days of his life. *A unicorn,* he thought, *in my tent! Wait until my friends hear about this!*

***

Darion knew that he should be studying. The Council had provided him with ample materials to study the history of Nav'Aria, though try as he might, he couldn't concentrate on the books. His mind kept wandering back to the frieze in the Main Hall. He longed for Seegar to continue with the oral history. He had always been an auditory learner. Even as a boy, he could zone in on any sound near him. Learning about his heightened senses explained a lot about why his experience with education had been difficult. Hands on activities, no problem. Reading was another thing entirely. It wasn't that he couldn't do it, he just didn't *want* to do it. He wanted to be with a Nav'Arian rather than locked away in the musty earthen den they called a library.

It was unlike any library he had ever seen. The room was at the foundation level of the building and the only light came from two inadequate wall sconces. Reading in the dim candlelight strained his eyes. Electricity had been another thing he completely took for granted while growing up. No computer, or light switch would aid him in his studying now; he was all alone in this chamber smelling distinctly of dirt, dust, and fungi.

"This blows," he said angrily, pushing the large, ancient tome written in Vondulus's hand away. He closed his eyes and rubbed his temples, thinking back to the images he had seen in the frieze. Maybe no one would notice if he took a break from studying for a while... But then he remembered Elsra. *She was intimidating!*

Seegar had presented him to the Council as he had been instructed to. Darion's training was to formally begin today. He had imagined physical training, being mentored by a warrior with a giant broadsword or battle ax like he had seen in the movies. He had barely been able to hide his disappointment when Elsra said he would have to read the ancient tomes before moving onto the next phase of training. He had a sick feeling that she would know if he lied and said he finished them. He had spent much of the day here, according to the much shorter candle sticks. Darion had yet to finish one book.

"I'm going to be down here forever," he complained to himself. He glowered as he remembered Edmond being led away by a giant centaur to begin his training as a soldier. "Bah!" He stood up quickly and walked to the door, his hand hesitating as he felt an overwhelming presence in his mind.

Not so fast, my prince. It was Triumph. Darion shivered. He knew the unicorn, for whatever reason, didn't trust him. *How does he know what I'm doing?* Darion wondered. *And, where is he?*

I have been instructed to oversee your studies, Prince. His last word sounding forced. Darion gaped, stepping away from the door. *He can read minds?* He was instantly amazed—and terrified—by the great power of the unicorns. Darion stood immobile, suspended in time, unsure what to do next. Should he reply? Should he sit? Should he open the door and discover where the angry unicorn lurked? His hesitation was short, for quickly the door burst open, and in the doorway stood Triumph looming angrily over Darion. He filled most of the doorway. *I'm trapped*, Darion thought, despairingly. Darion swallowed his fear and stood up straighter, returning what he hoped looked like a glare. Triumph and Darion stood like that for a moment, glaring at one another, and then suddenly... laughter. The unicorn was laughing. At Darion.

"What's so funny?" Darion shouted at the creature, feeling his cheeks color. Triumph's posture completely relaxed, and he didn't seem as threatening as he had a moment before. His sheen coat rippled as his throaty laughs coursed through his body. He shook his head, freeing the silver strands of hair that had covered his eyes momentarily as he burst through the door. His cool aquamarine eyes peered at Darion.

"You *are* your father's son," Triumph said aloud, with a note of respect. "No one else would dare stand up to a unicorn, as you did, except for a Meridia." Darion relaxed, too, running his hand through his dark locks. He had not had a haircut since well before the first dream, which was months ago. His hair had grown longer, almost to his shoulders. With his red tunic tucked into tight black breeches and tall, knee-high black boots, he felt so foreign when he saw his reflection in the mirror. Tanned skin and piercing eyes, dark tendrils curling around his forehead and neck. He barely recognized himself. He still felt awkward, though not as much as before. He felt out of place, yes, but not unwanted. He also felt annoyed. His glare returning.

"Have you been spying on me all day?"

"I would not exactly call it *spying*. Like I said, I was 'instructed to oversee your studies.'"

Darion eyed him. Throwing his hands in the air with a note of exasperation, he fell back into his seat. "Triumph, these books will take me forever to read. Some of the writing has smudged with age. It's hard to piece it all together."

He knew he sounded like he was whining. But he didn't care. He *was* whining. To a unicorn. Feeling like an idiot, he covered his face in his hands, berating himself. Slapping himself a few times to wake up, he looked up to meet the unicorn's steady gaze. Triumph's head was cocked to the side as if he were analyzing the specimen before him, trying to make sense of it.

"Well I suppose I could help you with some of that. I was, after all, instructed to..."

"Yeah, yeah... Oversee my studies."

"Right. Well, where did you leave off?"

"Vondulus was explaining his economic system. I think." Darion paused. "I kinda nodded off during that part."

"Right, well, where were we... You see, 'Vondulus believed that everyone should participate actively in his Kingdom. All worked, and all were rewarded.'"

"Wait, you have it memorized?" Darion asked, surprised. His tired eyes widening and sparkling with hope.

"Well, of course; I am on the Council, am I not? We all know them from memory... We would not want the information lost if the books were destroyed."

Darion didn't know whether he should be impressed or furious that he had been cast to the belly of the building for much of the day when he could have had Triumph instructing him all along. Either way, he was relieved that he didn't have to try and read the small, chaotic script in the poor light any longer. Vondulus had not been one to waste paper, as Darion had noted after trying to decipher one of his journals. The margins having all been written in, making his writing difficult to comprehend.

Darion settled back in his chair, and eagerly listened to more of the history of his land.

***

Trixon instantly regretted initiating this interaction. As soon as they were behind the tent, Dalinia's ghastly behavior only worsened. The child, oblivious to his mother's vehemence, talked on, showing Vikaris and Trixon his new rocks, wooden sword, everything! Meanwhile, Dalinia busied herself at a tray, slamming glasses while supposedly pouring cups of tea for her guests. Trixon knew he would receive no form of hospitality here. It was his folly that had gotten Lyrianna captured in the first place. Dalinia seethed with hatred when she looked upon him. Trixon noisily blew from his nose as he settled himself in a comfortable recumbent position. He smiled inwardly as Dalinia turned her nose up at him and tried unsuccessfully to step around him. He took up much of the tent. Without drawing more attention to the "beast," she was forced to take the seat nearest him. Trixon had done this on purpose, but he'd never admit it. An air of mischief had always surrounded him. His father, Trixon remembered fondly, had been genuinely shocked when the king took him as his steed. *Son, you must not act out, as you are so fond of doing. Restrain yourself.* He smiled to himself thinking of his father's lectures; that is, until he remembered that because he had not heeded his father's advice, Trinidad was now in

Narco's clutches, and had been so for quite some time.

Growing irritable and ashamed, Trixon muttered, *Creator help us!* Vikaris glared at him as he often did when Trixon got in one of his black moods. Trixon was renowned for his boldness on the battlefield but struggled mightily with tempering it during moments of diplomacy.

Calm yourself, or you will have to wait outside, Vikaris said to him. Trixon nodded curtly, then rested his head on his front legs, pretending to sleep.

Vikaris sighed, before looking back to his unhappy sister-in-law. She had just told Ansel to go to bed, and the boy, though obviously crushed, kept his emotions in check and wandered off to his bed in the back of the tent, after bidding them goodnight.

The child is more behaved than you, Vikaris chided him. Trixon grumbled at the King that he was treating him unfairly.

Dalinia observed, knowing they were communicating—most likely about her. She glared. It was evident she only felt hate for Trixon, but she truly did not hate the king, Trixon knew that deep down. When she looked at him, her eyes bespoke great pain. Regret. Betrayal. Her emotions were muddled when it came to *her* king.

Clearing her throat, Dalinia asked, "And to what do we owe the pleasure, Your Majesty?" Trixon could feel Vikaris flinch, from the daggers in her forced tone. Her face pinched with obvious strain barely maintaining civility.

"I wanted to see how you two were getting on," the

King said. "Are you well? Ansel appears happy as always."

The words erupted out of her. Standing up, she yelled, "Happy? Without his father? No! How could we be? Continually on the run... We are not doing *well*, Vikaris." Her scolding shriek hung in the air, and Trixon's eyes opened, all pretense of him sleeping forgotten. He let out a low rumble that made the tea cup splash in its saucer near her. Suddenly, fear etched her face.

She dropped her gaze and fell back into her seat, less than gracefully. "Forgive me, Your Majesty. I... I should not have said that."

She paused, clearly hating her betraying emotions and the tears she was no longer able to contain. Vikaris went to her. Trixon watched as Vikaris knelt beside the trembling woman and took her hands. She wept openly, unable to stop the torrent of anguish spilling forth. If Vikaris was surprised by her vulnerability, he didn't show it. Pain appeared on his face as he held her hands and told her it was all right. His eyes moistened, and he apologized, too.

Gasping and momentarily stunned, she whispered, "What did you say?"

"Dalinia, I am *so* gravely sorry. Gruegor was my friend. I carry the weight of his loss and the capture of your sister every waking moment. I..." He faltered, emotion catching in his throat, and the light amplifying the moisture in his eyes. "I love you and Ansel as I loved Gruegor. I promised him I would care for you both if something should happen, and I have failed you. I am sorry."

He looked down, sadly. He was telling the truth,

Trixon knew. His helplessness wearing through his haughty royal persona. This was not some far off, unfeeling monarch. This was her friend. Her brother in marriage. And Trixon watched the realization take hold in her eyes—*he was grieving, too*. Still sniffling, but the tears subsiding, she placed her hands on the sides of his face and kissed the top of his head.

Almost so quiet that one might wonder if it was only a dream, she whispered, "I forgive you."

Trixon smiled inwardly, feeling rather proud of his interference once again. Now, he *could* sleep.

CHAPTER 20

The Ploy

The path before them stood empty. Pine needles and rocks littered their way, as a warm breeze blew through and rustled the overhead trees. The sky was clear as the nightfall colors emerged on the horizon. Rich reds and yellows as far as the eye could see. Aalil longed to stand for a moment to soak it all in. The quiet. The sunset. The masculine smell of Antonis on her right. She shook her head slightly, feeling her long loose tresses against her back, her mind wandering once again to that night long ago. Picturing his brawny arms clutching her body to his as they reached simultaneous climax—his breath hot on her neck as he kissed and held fast to her. Her pulse quickened at the memory.

They had kept a hard pace throughout the day. Antonis and Riccus took turns carrying the traitor. Their respite was short since they still had not found the patrol. As the men stood stretching their arms and drinking from their water skins, her eyes fell on the pale man writhing in his bindings. They had bound his ankles and gagged him once he regained consciousness. His unending diatribe of horrors that the Emperor would inflict if they didn't meet his conditions were tiresome. Aalil had raised her knife at him, but Antonis caught her before issuing the killing strike. Their nerves were all wrought, and the man was lucky that he had only been gagged. Antonis's boot now pressed into the man's back, holding him face down. They didn't want so much as to look at the vile traitor. Rick offered to check for tracks, leaving them alone for the first time since Antonis had returned. Well, nearly alone, besides the bound man under Antonis's heel.

Aalil, still staring at the sunset emerging from the break of trees, could tell Antonis was looking at her. She felt a flutter go through her and wanted to curse herself for acting like a silly maiden. *HE HAD LEFT WITHOUT A WORD!* Too much had happened over the years.

We cannot just pick up where we left off, she scolded herself. Or could they? She avoided his eye, though all she wanted was to have him lift her with those bulky arms and wrap her arms and legs around him for a heated kiss. She bit the inside of her cheek, trying to distract herself with the minor pain it brought. *Stop it!*

Antonis watched her, unsure of what to say. He noted the small crescent shaped scar on her right cheek. Why had he not noticed it before? What had happened to her over the years? What was it about this woman that made him so flustered? He was never at a loss for words, but when he was around her, he felt like... like... like a damn teenager. *Like Darion.*

He turned to her, twisting his heel into Morta's back. The man moaned, but Antonis ignored it. He lifted his hand to brush that stubborn strand of hair off her forehead. She lifted her hand to cup it around his, and they leaned toward one another, searching each other's eyes wordlessly. Longing to see what could still be between them. Her lips parted slightly in anticipation... his heartrate leapt...

"Well, this got awkward," Riccus announced, in his straightforward way. Aalil blushed furiously and took a step way back. Antonis spluttered as he choked in surprise. He kicked Morta again for good measure, glaring at Rick, who in turn gave him one of those 'what did I do' shrugs.

"Did you find anything?" Antonis asked gruffly, trying to regain his composure and hoping his voice sounded like someone in command. He was having a hard time catching his breath, and he silently berated himself. *Get it together, man!*

"As a matter of fact, I did. Follow me." Riccus spun, ducking behind the thick grove of trees from which he had only just emerged. Aalil zoomed past Antonis before he could see her face. Grunting and griping to himself, he grabbed Morta by his collar and lifted him easily, slinging him roughly over his shoulder once again.

"See that," Riccus pointed at a dying ember of what looked like a recent campfire. "And that," he pointed at some droplets in the dirt that upon inspection appeared to be blood. Antonis nodded along, his nostrils flaring at an unidentified aroma.

"What do you make of it?" he asked.

"Well..." Riccus hesitated, as if unsure, his forehead dotted with perspiration.

Antonis didn't understand what was so difficult. "It looks simple enough. Whoever made this fire probably was cooking a rabbit or bird, hence the little blood," he said pointing at the droplets.

"If that was the case, I would smell the hide. The burnt flesh." Digging with his callused fingers, he pointed out, "See. No bones. No nothing. Just a little fire. Which makes me think, someone's meal was cut short, ending before it even began."

"Soldiers are injured all the time. The patrol has to be nearby. A little blood does not seem worth worrying over." He paused, noting the glint in Rick's eye that he had been withholding from his voice. "Does it?"

Rick nodded his head slightly, a sorrowful look in his eye, pointing past the blood. Antonis, motioned Aalil over, forgetting at once their near kiss. She took over guarding Morta as he walked into the thicket that Rick had been nodding toward. And then he saw it.

He hadn't realized what that smell was until he got closer, again cursing his laxed senses. The visceral smell of blood and a fresh corpse hit him. The toxic, and cloying scent of the enemy hung in the air near the body. There was a lot more blood here, puddling out from the fallen soldier. Whatever happened to him did not look pleasant. It looked like his stomach had been cut out, or rather eaten while likely still alive. Antonis saw no other mark on the man. Antonis looked away, willing himself to not be sick. The man, what was left of him, appeared to be young. Maybe a couple years older than Darion. He reached down to close his eyes, unable to avoid the fact that his face still held the appearance of one being tortured. His death had not been the clean, honorable death that a soldier dreamt of. It had been savage. Barbaric.

"Rav'Arian," he growled, knowing that this was not of 'this world.' The perpetrator would not be far. The blood droplets, he now realized, had most likely dripped from the beak of a Rav'Arian that had left after having its fill. He took off his cloak and draped it over the fallen soldier, wishing they had the tools and time to bury him properly.

"To the Creator you go, and to the Creator you will stay. Your pain is gone, and no evil can ever be dealt upon you again, my friend. You can rest now, soldier." He said the burial words numbly, wondering where the creature went. He stepped out of the thicket and approached his companions.

"Sit him up," he said darkly, spitting at Morta's crumpled form. "Where are they?" Antonis demanded. "Where is the rest of the patrol? Where are the Rav'Arians?"

The bald, pale man, who Antonis had thought was writhing from pain and fear, was instead laughing mirthlessly. When they pulled the blindfold and gag from him, Morta chuckled lowly, his red-rimmed eyes staring up at them.

"This was all part of the plan, was it? Is this an ambush then?" Antonis flexed dangerously, as his companions pulled their weapons free, taking a defensive position and scanning their twilight surroundings.

Morta shook his head. "Not for you," he murmured, enigmatically.

"What do you mean? For who then?" Antonis felt a pit in his stomach. The man screwed his face into what Antonis interpreted as a sadistic smile.

Rick and Aalil looked fearful as Morta answered quietly, "For the *traitor*, of course."

***

Lyrianna and Trinidad had been bound and left upon the ramparts of the Castle. Narco had had them taken up there hours ago. The wind howled from this distance, and he could visibly see Lyrianna shaking. He noted her damp rags that had been a dress months ago. She had not had a change of clothes, or any hygienic care that Trinidad could tell. Her eyes were closed as she lay on her side, pressed up against Trinidad for warmth. His gaze was fixed on the wooden door they had been led from. The troll on guard dozed, sitting on a stool that looked like it might collapse under its bulk.

Trinidad looked upon the apathetic guard, feeling indignant that the troll did not guard his formidable query with a watchful eye, whilst on the other hand, praised the Creator that he was presently lucid and without supervision. He was about to nudge Lyrianna quietly when a blood-curdling scream shot through his mind. He groaned inwardly at the shrieking voice filling his ear drums.

"*Get back. Stand behind me,*" he heard... *Wait, was that*

Vikaris?

"We have to go now, my liege." My son! Trinidad's heart soared, but fear gripped him, too. *What is happening?*

"Ansel, we cannot leave Ansel." He knew then who had been screaming. It was Lady Dalinia. He looked down at Lyrianna as he listened, unsure of their connection since his horn had been mercilessly shorn, limiting his communication and powers. Just then, he heard, *"Mama?"* *No*, he thought. Whatever it was, he knew the boy was walking into an ominous scene.

"No," Dalinia screeched, *"Not my boy. Let go of my son,"* and he heard crying, and Trixon, *calling for help, telepathically to anyone nearby. "Help! Help! The Rav'Arians are here. The king is surrounded. Dalinia's tent—to arms!"*

Trinidad shook involuntarily at the news, and then it all made sense. Narco's smirk. Their presence atop the towers. He had ambushed the king. He had finally found his hideaway, and when Vikaris was brought forth, he would be greeted by Lyrianna's corpse, *and mine*, Trinidad thought. *Where is Darion?* Trinidad felt his throat close with fear. *Narco cannot win. He must not the boy.*

Just then he heard steel on steel as Vikaris, he assumed, engaged the assailants. He heard mad crying from the woman and the guffaw of his son, *his colt!* He would know that sound anywhere. *His son. His king. In danger. He had to help. He could not succumb entirely to helplessness while they were under attack. He could not lie here as Narco plotted their deaths.* Nudging Lyrianna, wordlessly, he breathed a sigh of relief when her eyelids fluttered.

"My queen," he murmured to her. *You have to wake up,*

but do not move. She pressed into him slightly, to acknowledge him. He relayed what he was hearing. She had been unconscious most of the day and had only come to a while ago. She was very weak and had barely enough energy to move. Trinidad still didn't know what Narco had done to her today. He writhed in anger as his eyes saw the multitude of bruises and scars she now bore.

She made no other sign that she had heard him. "The king and your sister are surrounded, my queen." Whispering on, he said, "We have to get out of here."

One eyelid cracked open at that. *"How?"* she mouthed. Contemplating his next move, he froze.

"No, let go of him. Let go!" A woman's cry was suddenly cut off and followed by a loud thud. His unexplained connection to his son went quiet. He feared he had lost them. The quiet lasted a matter of heartbeats, before he exhaled in relief. Trixon was in command of the room. Reinforcements had arrived, and Trixon was yelling for them to take the King to safety.

"We need to interrogate them. Leave one alive."

"What about the one with the boy?" a voice asked.

"Leave him to me," Trixon said with a lethal edge.

Trinidad's breath caught. He had never heard his son use that tone. So... commanding. So... menacing. The connection then faded, and Trinidad was left with his worries. Lyrianna's eyes were on him. They searched for some meaning from his silence. He feared she knew the fate of Dalinia. His eyes moistened as he tried to focus on his present imprisonment and avoid her gaze. They had to get off these ramparts... and now. The sooner Narco learned of his failed attack, the sooner he would appear to take it out on his captives. That much Trinidad knew. Narco was never late when doling out punishments. Lyrianna's frail condition couldn't take another thrashing. Trinidad trembled as he wondered whose body would swing from the ramparts this night.

Searching the rooftop without appearing to was difficult. From his vantage point, he could only see one guard, the sleeping troll, near the door in front of him farther down the walkway. He dared not twist his neck around to bring attention on them, but he had to know if any other guards were atop the tower walls. He nudged Lyrianna, who appeared to be dozing off again. Her eyes opened, and in them he noted her understanding. She knew. She knew someone she loved had just died. He didn't know for sure, and so avoided broaching the subject. There would be time for mourning later, but at present they needed to move.

"Can you see anything behind me?" he asked quietly, hoping she could peek over his broad shoulders.

She attempted a sly look. Trinidad held his breath. He cursed Narco for cutting his horn. The majesty and power of the unicorn was its horn. And that was lost to him now. He could have had them out of here in no time, had he possessed all of his strength. Among the unicorns, Trinidad was one of the strongest... or had been, he thought morosely. *He could command minds!* He could have controlled the Castle guards with one look, but instead he reflected on what Narco had said earlier: *I choose you, Trinidad.* He tasted bile as he recalled the evil man's words.

No matter what happens, he thought, *I will never serve Narco.* Serving Narco would be a fate worse than death. He would get Lyrianna out of here and sacrifice himself if needed. But ever Narco try to bond him, he would realize the might of Trinidad's resistance, he thought darkly.

Lyrianna took a slow, drawn-out look as she contrived a yawn. Appearing to be confused by her surroundings, then lying back down, falling asleep. She immediately told Trinidad that there were two men standing guard, behind them from the opposite tower. They stood in their direction yet appeared to be having a heated exchange and were not actually watching their captives. Again, Trinidad felt minor irritation at having been underestimated so easily. *He would show them,* he thought. These guards had forgotten the strongest element of the unicorn's powers... his mind. And Trinidad's was completely alert.

***

"You see, Darion, Vondulus had been sent by the Creator to lead Nav'Aria, and lead it, he did. With an established line of power, the Marked Heir, with the assistance of the unicorns, made it impossible for anyone else to lead, that is..." Triumph faltered, breaking his eye contact with Darion. "Well, until Narco that is." Darion could feel tension fill the air.

"That's what I don't understand," Darion interrupted. "If the Creator created Vondulus, did he know that someday Narco would seize power and ruin everything? Why couldn't he or the unicorns stop him?"

"That is a tough question, Darion. The truth is, we will never know until we ask the Creator in our next life.

There was no prophecy about Narco per se, but... there was one about..." Triumph cut off his explanation, checking himself. He shook his head, "I am not the one to share the truths of prophecies, at least not yet..." Triumph hesitated, as if contemplating it. Thinking better of it, he continued as if nothing had happened, "However, I will say, that whatever Narco possesses is not natural; it is not of the Creator's doing. It is a dark power. It pulls from the Shazla Desert, or beyond."

Darion cocked his head. He must have looked confused.

"The Shazla Desert... the home of the Rav'Arians. *Outside* of our Realm. It is believed that Narco went there before murdering his brother. He was away for a while." Darion vaguely remembered this from Antonis's story before the Portal. It made sense, the more he thought of it.

Dark magic. But what kind? And how?

"He had told his brother that he wanted to study with the trolls. He was ever the student, and Rustusse allowed him to go. He never went to the trolls, however. We, the Council, believe that he crossed the border and encountered something... something powerful enough to upset everything we have here. He still uses that knowledge against us. He has somehow cowed the trolls and made an alliance with the Rav'Arians."

"But why couldn't you stop him? I thought unicorns were supposed to be all-powerful?" Darion noted the growing ferocity in Triumph's eyes. He added lamely, "I mean, I'm just wondering what he did to you all... just trying to understand." Darion slowly scooted his chair back just for good measure.

Triumph took a moment to collect himself, before starting off on the lad. With a deep sigh, he admitted, "It is a question that has rankled me for years. How does he do these things? Can we really stop him?" Darion's eyes widened at the unicorn's admonition, Triumph hastily continued, "Our minds and ability to communicate with one another from far distances are our greatest powers. The unicorns, then, have various levels of strength, intelligence, influence, and power—just as you humans, Darion. Rinzaltan, besides the First Horn himself, was the most powerful unicorn. A mighty warrior, and he sacrificed himself for your grandfather, Rustusse. Our horn, and our blood, is said to have healing powers, and our heart's blood can bring someone back from the dead. He willingly sacrificed himself for *your* family." Darion thought he detected a note of bitterness in his tone. Darion only belatedly realized that Rinzaltan was Triumph's father.

"I'm sorry," Darion said quietly.

Triumph's clear aquamarine eyes seemed to consume Darion as he looked him over, then nodded. "Thank you, Darion," he said, seeming to believe him. "You see another power some of us have is the ability to measure the purity of a person. We can detect emotions, and that is why we only 'bond' to the purest humans, thus far, the Marked Meridias," adding slowly more to himself, he said, "Though, sometimes I can be a harsh critic of character." Darion remembered how Triumph had snarled at him upon meeting him in Kaulter, calling him a 'spy.'

An awkward silence hung in the air. Darion mulled this over and wondered how Narco's sinister nature had been overlooked. He wanted to ask more about the desert, or if they had ever considered crossing the border to find out what Narco had found there. Before he could, Elsra's voice surrounded them, booming in their ears and echoing off the chamber walls. "To the Council Room. Immediately!" All thought of study was quickly pushed aside as the pair hurried from the earthen library to the Hall. The severity in the regent's voice made it clear that tardiness would not be tolerated.

CHAPTER 21

The Captive

Darion searched the faces. He knew something had happened. Seegar had gone back to the Camp in Nav'Aria, so he only recognized Elsra and Triumph. Edmond wasn't present. He felt himself slumping down, trying to become invisible before the gathered Council that consisted of ten or more unicorns on the platform. The feelings of insecurity crept up, threatening to take hold. Triumph turned to look at him, surprisingly calming his nerves. Darion straightened his shoulders; his hand rested on his dagger at his belt as was becoming his reflex. Whatever had happened, he could handle it. He had to.

The large chamber was lit with hundreds of candles as the sun had set for the evening. A cool breeze caused the flames to dance and cast strange shadows as they moved. Elsra stood to address the crowd which had gathered. She waited for everyone to quiet down, her intelligent lavender eyes sweeping across the diverse crowd that quieted almost immediately as she did so.

"The Camp has been ambushed!"

A stunned gasp echoed through the hall. Every head snapped to attention. Elsra paused. Her anger and emotion spilling forth. Darion felt a tremble of fear run through his body. He could sense the panic in the room. His head felt light with the intoxicating smell of candle wax, the earthen floor, and the bodily sweat from such a large gathering.

"Reports are still coming in; however, Trixon was able to contact us. It would appear, that a small force of Rav'Arians attacked the camp." Looking at Darion, she hesitated, and fear reigned for a moment. He thought of Carol, Rick, Antonis, and Vikaris. He thought of dear old Seegar, who had just returned to camp. He could tell by her tone some had died, and he held his breath as she continued, "They found the King and Trixon with Lady Dalinia, without a guard." She hesitated. He tasted lead. He knew.

Here it comes, he thought. *It was too good to be true here. My father is...*

She turned to Darion, causing all of those gathered to turn their gaze toward him. He held his breath. "I am sorry to say that Lady Dalinia was slain, along with many sentry guards outside of camp. Also, there is a missing patrol that is feared to be among the dead. Families will be notified once we can identify those lost."

Darion felt like he had been punched in the gut. "Dalinia," he whispered. And just like that, his only extended family was taken from him. Then he remembered the boy. *His cousin. What was his name?*

He racked his brain, and he heard Triumph whisper,

Ansel.

Not even phased that the unicorn had been reading his thoughts, Darion called out, "What about Ansel? What about my cousin?"

He caught an almost imperceptible flicker cross Elsra's eyes. "They took him," she said throatily, emotion catching in her voice. He heard whispers, and gasps of horror near him. "And," she went on louder, steadier, quieting the crowd, "Trixon has gone after them—alone. We have not had a report since."

At once the room was in uproar. Centaurs, humans, even the usually composed unicorns—all calling out their intent to help. Crying, angry whispers, and a call to arms reverberated across the room. Women clamoring toward the front to see if their husbands were among the dead. Trying to quiet the room was a challenge; Darion then heard a horn. One of the guards had blown it as a warning to hush them all.

"We are sending a force of warriors to aid the camp. I will get more information and relay it as it comes, but otherwise, no one..." She paused for emphasis, her magnified voice echoing, as she commanded, "I mean *no one* leaves Kaulter. The mainland is not safe."

Darion felt completely helpless. *What could he do?* His father had told him to come here and train. He had said he couldn't risk being in the same area as his father. *Had he known?* Darion wished again that he was older and stronger so that he could help. He met Triumph's eyes and knew that his training had just been expedited. He would need to learn... faster. Become a warrior. Become the True Tested Heir bearing the Mark should his father fall.

***

The sound of ragged breathing was all that sounded in Trixon's ears. His breathing.

He had been tracking the Rav'Arians for hours. It was well after dark. They had grabbed the boy and gotten away amidst the chaos as soon as a team of warriors had come to surround the King. Unfortunately, they had also split up, and their toxic odor clung to everything in the entire vicinity. Identifying the path of the one carrying Ansel was becoming an infuriating challenge.

Not all had escaped his ire, though, Trixon thought darky. He had run one completely through as he had begun tracking them out of the camp, zigzagging around campfires and tents, passing the frightened onlookers. The one Rav'Arian he had slain had screamed terribly as Trixon's unforgiving horn pierced its abdomen. He relished the sound. Hate was his only comfort in this moment. Narco had sent those creatures into *his* camp and nearly succeeded in surrounding the King. He had captured Trinidad and Lyrianna, and Trixon would make him pay.

Oh, sweet Creator, he would make that man pay for what pain he had caused.

Trixon was completely out of his mind with rage. Had he been thinking more clearly, he may have thought that it was unwise to leave his king after being so recently exposed to danger; however, Trixon felt compelled to save the boy. Narco would not have him, or worse, those savage creatures would not make a meal of him. Worrying that this was exactly what they intended made him hasten his pace. A sheer gleam of sweat coated him as the moonlight fell upon his shimmering white coat and mane. His horn illuminated the way before him. He knew he was extremely exposed in the dusky forest. His white coat amongst the dark trees and shrubs. Yet, the Rav'Arians left such a taint. The smell was putrid, and he tracked them easily.

One by one. He would make them pay.

"What was that?"

"I do not know," Riccus paused, "but it sounds big." He held up his hand to silence any further comments as Aalil and Antonis knelt beside him. Antonis had dropped Morta during their journey, accidentally, or at least that's the story he held to, knocking the man's head on a rock. He had not awoken.

The small party made their way back as quickly as they could in order to warn the camp of the nearby Rav'Arians. They only hoped they weren't too late. Antonis kicked himself for not interrogating Morta better when they had first come across the man. He hadn't come back to Nav'Aria only to lose his friends... or the war.

"There it is again," Aalil whispered. The sound was drawing nearer, though quiet. To a trained ear it was clear that something—something large—was moving at a rapid pace through the brush and headed straight for them. Rick motioned for them to follow, quietly.

Trixon heard something to his left and veered slightly in his determined gait. He aimed toward the sound and ran full speed.

"Get back, get back," Riccus cried, as Trixon broke through the brush with a loud bellow. The party was stunned. Having the aggression of a unicorn turned against them was something they were completely unfamiliar with. It was petrifying.

"Wait, it is us…"

Trixon reared before them, barely stopping his hooves from colliding with the man's face. "Antonis," he breathed out.

He had been tracking the Rav'Arians, or so he had thought. *Why had he come here?* He was glad to see friends, but he was confused by the smell. *Had he lost the trail? The smell was everywhere, yes, but his sense of smell was one of his strongest gifts.* He had always had keen senses and rarely lost a trail like this. Bewilderment and anger took hold. "What are you doing here?" he snapped, his anger now directed at them since his prey had eluded his grasp for the time being.

Antonis, unfazed by his tone, said, "We came across *this*, on the onset of our mission," as he said it he kicked the unconscious man, so his face came into full view.

"I should have known," Trixon denounced, stamping his hoof. Morta's pale face exposed under the unicorn's bright, shimmering coat.

"The Rav'Arians know of the Camp. They are

coming," Antonis was explaining when Trixon cut him off again, to speak to the party telepathically.

I know! They found us. I was in Lady Dalinia's tent with the king when they rushed in. They killed her and took Ansel. I am after them, or, he paused, *at least I thought I was. The trail led to you...* He paused again, berating himself for his poor tracking skills.

Antonis and Aalil looked shocked, but as trained warriors, they took it well. Riccus interrupted.

"Morta had been with them and a troll. He smells of them," he said, pointing at the man. "I have been sick with the smell of him all day."

I have to keep after them before they... Trixon stopped. They all knew what he was going to say, thinking back to the fallen sentry who had been feasted upon and left with his life's blood and guts spilling about him. Antonis felt sick again at the refreshed image.

"We'll help you," Antonis said firmly, standing to his full height. Trixon hesitated. He would need to keep a fast pace. He looked them over. They were three of the best warriors and Keepers of the Realm. He found himself nodding. *Bind him on my back,* he said motioning toward Morta. Antonis made a face but did as directed, muttering all the while, "It feels wrong. This... this hideous traitor strapped to the king's steed."

The feel of the man *did* make Trixon's skin tingle, as if his pure white coat had been sullied by the dark aura wafting from him. He was evil. *Unmitigated evil.* Trixon hated him. He hated the feel of him on his back, but he knew that his friends couldn't carry the weight and keep the pace he would set. He also knew that he could not leave Morta behind. *Oh, no,* he thought. *I look forward to having a conversation with this one soon.*

"They could not have gone far," Riccus said in his calm drawl as he staked out the trail with Trixon. He was the best tracker in the Kingdom, and though he did not have the same innate powers and heightened senses as many unicorns did, Trixon still greatly admired the man. He had missed him. After some backtracking, cursing, and fumbling for Trixon's "light," Riccus found what he believed to be the trail; the party ran into the night to rescue the newly made orphan from his living nightmare.

Creator, guide us, Trixon whispered, as he and his companions set off.

***

Narco sat in a chair near his bed in his dimly lit chamber relishing in his near victory. Moments from now, the war would be finished! He could feel it. Morta had assured him that he would not return without Vikaris, now that they had located the camp. It had been a constant thorn in his side for nearly three cycles. The damned unicorns aiding in his hiding. Constantly shifting their location from the Tree, to Kaulter, to Camp. They were always one step in front of Narco's clutches, and he had sacrificed countless Rav'Arians to capture them. Even with his strengthened physical power, the ability to command the Rav'Arians and search the signs—with Morta's assistance, for the Mark, Vikaris always evaded him.

"But that's all over now," he murmured to himself,

pleased with the notion of Vikaris splayed out before *his* throne. Narco's dark, oily hair fell into his eyes, and he brushed it away with his long, talon-like nails. He had them filed just so. As he brushed his hair, his fingertips fell across his cheek. His mood darkened, as he remembered his scar. His slack face. The unicorn would regret that attack. He wouldn't kill Trinidad.

Oh, no, he thought. *Trinidad is mine. I will bond the beast and have the mightiest steed since Vondulus's time.*

Though, that was assuming his horn would grow back. Morta had assured him it was possible.

Narco had intended to take Lyrianna as his bride after killing Vikaris, yet now he considered his long-held fantasy. It might be more enjoyable to kill her instead... slowly, right before Vikaris's eyes.

During her imprisonment, she had been... difficult. He remembered the countless times she had had to be beaten for not giving in to his advances or answering his questions. She had been firm in her resolve. *Yes*, he thought. *I will take another bride. Lyrianna will die.*

He eyed the woman he had taken to bed to celebrate his near victory. A child, really. The scared girl with the blackened eye, and straw-like hair trembled where he had left her moments ago. The sheer sheet barely hiding her nakedness. Bruises already visible from the strength of his grip upon her arms. As he looked at her, he noted her pert adolescent breasts and thought back to Lyrianna's full bosom he had seen so often falling out of her shift. Even underfed and held captive, her body maintained some of its magnificent shape. She was a woman unlike any other.

Though she was filthy and injured from her *visit* to Castle Dintarran, she could still make a lovely bride. *Maybe killing her would be too easy.*

No, I will not kill her, he thought. *The thought of us together will kill Vikaris a thousand times over.* He smiled, satisfied with his plan, and crawled back into the bed, his cackling laughter masking the girl's muffled whimpers as he pulled her to him.

Taking the girl yet again, he pictured Lyrianna's face as he strangled her newly returned son before her eyes. *Yes, he would kill Vikaris and then capture and kill Darion.* Lyrianna would capitulate after that surely. She would have nothing else to live for after that, and then she would be his. His broken, beautiful queen. *He would have all of her then.* Climactic spasms wracked his body as he pictured the woman, nearly forgetting the girl thrashing beneath him.

***

Trinidad and Lyrianna had been concocting a plan while pretending to still be in a drugged state. The charade was harder to keep up, than one might imagine. Trinidad itched to get up and use his sharp hooves to pummel the guards. Lyrianna disagreed and said there had to another way. Force would not work in this case, and he had to admit that he agreed with her, begrudgingly so. The troll would awaken as soon as he tried to make a move. No, they would have to use stealth.

As they contemplated, Trinidad worried that their time was slipping away. He knew the ambush had failed, and he knew that it wouldn't be long until Narco found out. When he did, he would most assuredly burst through the door near the snoring troll, and the game would be up.

"I will do it," she whispered to him. They had agreed that the two humans were the target. The door they guarded was farther away, but it would lead to the exit. The troll would need to be dealt with as well.

"You will do what?" he replied, sternly. He was not about to put the queen in more danger than she was already in. He was glad to see that she had recovered some of her lost energy. The prospect of escape had seemingly reignited a fire in her. Yet, she was still so frail.

"I will distract the guards," she said, quietly.

How? he asked, only then noticing the rags barely encasing her still-full breasts and hips. She discreetly pulled the strap down from her shoulder and shook out her dirty hair.

No, he communicated at her. He would not allow her to traipse herself before them like a common street woman. *No, he would* not. *There had to be another way.*

He was shaking his head resolutely before realizing it, and now checked to ensure the guards had not noticed. One was using his hands most emphatically to tell a story. The other waited on his every word, laughing loudly, at what must have been the punch line of his joke. Their faces etched in the moonlight, Trinidad wondered if they could not just sneak up on them? They really were the worst guards ever. *Imagine, revelry before duty!* Interrupting Trinidad's inner rant, Lyrianna continued...

"Trinidad, I will distract them. Tell them I need to make water," she said discreetly. He eyed her wondering if it could work. He played it in his mind. As she got up, their eyes would search her immodestly clothed shape and one would happily oblige to take her, maybe hoping to run his hands over her a bit while the other assumed the unicorn was still drugged. *After all, what is a unicorn without its horn? I will show them*, he thought darkly.

"What happens when he takes you to 'make water'?"

"He dies," she said simply, in such a confident tone that he was taken aback.

How?

She made a low sound in her throat, and he noted the ferocity in her gaze. Only earlier, he had feared she was dead, and now, he feared for whomever met her wrath. *Trinidad,* she communicated, *My son is here. No one will keep me from him. Not these guards, and especially not Narco. We are leaving, Trinidad. Tonight.*

For the first time in a long time, she sounded like her old self. Not the victim that she had become in the last year of imprisonment. She was the queen. *His Queen.* And she was no longer discussing the plan. She was ordering him, and he would obey. The stump from his horn tingled, as he felt the power of his resolve calm him.

With his phantom horn, he felt empowered, too. *Darion has returned. We are leaving... now!* They spent a few more moments finalizing their plans, then she stood up.

Due to the late hour, the dark aided her surreptitious approach. She was almost upon the men before they noticed her.

The guard with the obnoxious voice, exaggerating yet another story, now stuttered and stopped. His comrade looked at him expectantly, then noted his gaze and followed it, until his eyes fell upon her. Trinidad struggled to feign his stupor, upon seeing their eyes hungrily taking in her near-perfect form. The moonlight spilled upon her blonde hair, and shadows danced across her light dress, only making her appear lovelier, despite the dirt and grime.

"And what do we have here?" the stout guard elbowed his comrade. "Our sleeping princess has awoken." He stepped closer to her, "What can we do for you?" he asked, his spittle hitting her cheek.

Trinidad watched from his peripheral as she lifted her head and managed to give the two such a look of disdain that the main guard backed away. She demanded, "I have been up here for hours. I need to make water," as the men looked to one another, confused.

"We were told not to let you leave here," the stout guard replied, strongly.

"... or to talk to you," piped the younger one, the main guard shooting him a shushing glare.

Trinidad had waited until he knew their eyes had passed over him and were back to examining the disheveled queen. Once she held their focus, he began to make his move. Because he had lost weight while in captivity, he didn't make much of a sound as Lyrianna scolded the men for keeping her from relieving herself. She spoke loudly to hide his footfalls. He had crept about half way when he saw the side of one's head turn toward him. He knelt quickly and hoped that the shadows would obscure the distance between the men and unicorn. He felt the man's eyes pass over him, and from the corner of his eye, saw Lyrianna step toward the man, placing her palm on his face. The young man started at her touch.

She lightened her tone. "Please," she said helplessly. "It has been hours..." She cocked her head at them, and said, "You do not wish for me to suffer, do you?" she pouted, changing her tone completely as she looked at the ignorant youth. Trinidad had begun to move again, and almost laughed before he caught himself. *Humans!*

"Well, I suppose we could take just her, right, Mandel?" Lyrianna smiled inwardly while keeping up her pouty disposition. She tried to make her eyes large, innocent.

Mandel, the guard, sighed. "All right, princess." He looked around, "But we will have to hurry. The Emperor would not like to find you missing if he comes to check on you."

At the mention of Narco, she felt her smile falter. "I will be fast," she said sweetly, her smile not meeting her eyes.

Trinidad had been listening to the exchange while creeping ever closer.

"What happening?" a voice boomed. Trinidad's pulse quickened as he jumped up. The troll had awoken to find his captives ready to pounce on the unsuspecting guards. The guards groped for their swords. Before the troll could close the distance, Trinidad stood up to face him. The guards goggled. Mandel looked wounded as he glared at Lyrianna, the younger guard looking as if he might run himself. Lyrianna looked from both men, dangerously, backing away like a caged animal. Her eyes landed on a metal rod that was used to snuff out the highest lanterns. She grabbed it and swung it at Mandel's head, surprising him with her quick reflexes. He fell back, howling. The younger guard stood transfixed at the formidable beauty. He swung his fist at her, attempting to cuff her and bring her down without much fuss. As his fist swung, however, she brought the rod up quickly, striking him under the chin. The sound of his teeth slamming together was audible. Bright red liquid sprayed out from his mouth as he stumbled from the blow.

Trinidad hoped she was able to hold them off, as he stood eyeing his foe. The troll was much larger than he had initially thought. The creature stood to its full-height, bare-chested and menacing as it loomed over him with its large metal-ridden club. Its ashen skin stretched tight, revealing bulbous, blue veins riddling its torso. Its yellow eyes gleamed in the darkness.

Trolls. Instant loathing filled him. The traitorous population of trolls had sided with Narco's forces during the Coup. Before the Rav'Arians had ravaged their home in the mountains, their leader N'olf had sworn fealty to Narco, and thus, turned against their former allies, the unicorns, centaurs, and the Marked King, Rustusse.

I wish I had my horn! His powers were significantly lessened without it. He was still strong, but his ability to communicate to and thereby influence another's body had been incapacitated. Trinidad studied the slow walk of the troll as it strode toward him. He noted that he favored his left leg. *Maybe recovering from an injury on the right?* Trinidad wondered. He would use that to his advantage.

"What happening here," the voice boomed.

Trinidad charged the lumbering troll before it could set up a stance. Trinidad rushed full force into the troll's right leg, hoping to knock him off balance. He saw the club rise in the air before it soared past him, narrowly missing his head as he had ducked at the last moment. The troll let out a pained cry. His jaw grasping at the air above Trinidad, revealing a foul cavern of blackened, jagged teeth. The unicorn reared on his hind legs as the stunned troll swayed unsteadily, trying to put weight on his injured leg. Trinidad took advantage of the opening and landed heavy blows upon the troll's head and shoulders before the troll swung at Trinidad's face, knocking him down the parapet.

Lyrianna rushed to him, holding the rod. The two guards had been hit hard, still reeling, Mandel was trying to roll to his knees. She swung at his head again as she passed him. He fell heavily to the ground with a loud thump. The youth's mouth and tunic were soaked in red blood from his mouth wound. He didn't attempt to rise.

"Trinidad," she yelled, going to his side. The troll had hit him hard, causing him to let out a moan. As he slowly managed to stand on shaky legs, Lyrianna turned to greet the enemy. The troll towered above her petite frame, and she looked unsure of her weapon as she eyed his club. The beast snickered at her as he puffed his large chest; his pectorals rippling as he laughed. She puffed up, too, in response. Standing before him, she held up her rod, brandishing it at the creature in a valiant effort to protect her struggling friend.

Trinidad's head felt foggy, as if he had been drugged again. He had hit the stone wall hard. Pride swelled in his chest, as he looked toward the small woman guarding him against the foreboding troll. Lyrianna lunged, seeing the troll's massive arm rise for the hook, but was cut off as Trinidad's hooves assaulted the guard. As the troll's swing was thrown off balance, Lyrianna seized the opportunity to jam the rod into its gaping mouth, stunning the creature, as it choked on the cupped end. It swung its head, sending her flying to the side. Trinidad feared she was dead after she hit the stone wall, harder than he had done moments ago. She didn't move. He watched the troll warily as it struggled to pull the rod from its mouth. It appeared to be stuck, the cup lodged around his decaying molars. Trinidad didn't hesitate, coming around and charging the creature's right side once again, knocking it onto its back, the rod still lodged in the troll's mouth. Trinidad jumped atop the creature, and as he watched the beast struggle, he almost felt pity, that is until his eyes returned to Lyrianna. She still had not moved. He raised his right hoof, and with all his force, stomped it through the troll's eye, breaking through his cranium and piercing its brain.

The massive creature's struggle ended almost instantaneously, and the roof was quiet, save for the laborious breathing of the incapacitated youth. Trinidad carefully stepped down from the troll's corpse, wiping his hoof on its cloak. His white shoe stained with the troll's oozing blood. Staggering with the exhaustion that comes after a struggle, Trinidad nearly fell beside Lyrianna.

My Queen, he murmured in her ear, *are you all right?* His breath caught, as he waited for her reply.

"Trinidad," she moaned, cautiously sitting up, her hand gingerly feeling for any broken ribs. "Is he..." She stopped, as she looked at the mountainous corpse. She slowly tried to stand, wincing as she did. "We have to get out of here," she said, urgently. They had made a lot of noise; surely a guard would come to inspect the commotion.

Trinidad motioned for her to hold on to his mane while they made for the back staircase, carefully avoiding the fallen soldiers. As they passed by, the youth's hand shot out and grabbed Lyrianna's ankle, pulling her toward him. She gasped, and before she could react, the boy released, falling back gurgling, asphyxiating on his own blood and swollen tongue. They both took a moment to collect themselves, breathing rapidly.

Quietly open the door, then stand back, Trinidad ordered. He knew that they were near the rear of the castle. Below these ramparts, were the kitchens, and traders' entrances. The farmers and merchants had been a very active part of Castle Dintarran back in Rustusse's day. They had had their own entrance which fit the large grain wagons and spare quarters for the instances they wished to stay at Court. All were welcome at the castle. But that was a long time ago, and Trinidad wearily searched the opening as she pulled the lever. Not knowing what would greet them in the desecrated castle, they stepped into the dim, stone stairway, one step closer toward freedom.

***

Darion had slept fitfully that night, unsure of his future. His family members were all in danger while he was here amongst strangers in Kaulter. His plush, feathered bed with its canopy had at first felt like a safe refuge, but now left him feeling claustrophobic. He got up and went to the desk. He considered sketching with the parchment there but decided against it. It didn't feel right. He didn't want to draw; he wanted to act. *To do something*. He began to pace nervously. *What can I do?* He thought back on Elsra's speech. Dalinia was dead; Ansel missing. He sent up a prayer for Ansel, hoping that Trixon would find him safe. If he was going to be useful to anyone, he had to become Nav'Arian, and fast. His mind wandered back to the frieze that had fascinated him. What was it about the images that drew him?

It was the earliest hours of morning, before the birds' songs came and the sun's first rays danced above the horizon. He lit the lantern on the desk and slipped on his boots and overcoat. Carefully, trying not to make a sound, he reached the door and peeked out into the hall. A female centaur had been on guard when he went to bed. He didn't know the rules here and thought it best to avoid the guard, just in case he wasn't supposed to leave his quarters. Without Seegar to ask, he didn't have a good guide for Kaulter. Then he remembered Triumph. He supposed he could ask him but soon pushed the thought away. *That unicorn is... unapproachable!* Darion decided to keep his questions to himself, for the time being anyway.

Looking down the rich, dark mahogany hall, he saw the guard's tanned back was to him. He looked to his left and saw the great stairway. If he could quietly slip around the corner to the stairs before she turned, he would be free to wander the castle. He held his breath for another moment, then launched himself into the hall as quietly as possible, walking on his tip-toes to keep his heeled boots from ringing across the floor. He had almost made it to the stairs when he heard something clatter to the ground. Cursing to himself, he hurried around the corner, barely avoiding the guard as she looked to identify the source of the sound. Darion assumed she had dropped something. He made his way to the Great Hall with the historical frieze that had captured his interest without giving the noise a second thought.

Darion's time in Nav'Aria had been a whirlwind. He had only been here a couple of weeks, yet he could not remember the last time he was alone, except for the last couple of evenings while he slept. So much had happened; it was just too much to digest. After their quick portal trip to find Vikaris, he had spent a brief amount of time getting to know his biological father before being sent off again to safety here in Kaulter. He missed his mom... Carol, that is. He thought of Rick and Carol and wondered how they would now fit into his life. He wished he hadn't been such an ass these last few months. He knew he had been an ungrateful nightmare to be around. If Carol were here, he could apologize and tell her how much he loved her. She and Rick were great parents. They always knew how to calm him down when he was in one of his moods. He felt remorseful after spending so many years wondering about his birth parents, instead of being thankful for his adoptive ones. *Why couldn't I appreciate them more?*

He hoped again that they were safe at the Camp. Lost in thought, he didn't notice the shadow that passed behind him as he stepped into the sweeping room.

A great fireplace stood at the end of the Hall. Its embers had long ago burned out. The room had a cold dull glow to it without daylight. The moon's beams broke up the shadows erratically. He looked around, almost afraid to move. He thought he felt a presence. The hair on the back of his neck tingled, and he searched the darkness with his eyes, willing the flame from his lantern to grow.

At once, the flame rose to the brim of the lantern, almost scorching his hand. He focused on it, and the flame leveled out to a reasonable height. Holding it up, he held it out to search the gloom; a sound made him turn, and he came face to face with Triumph, the imposing unicorn he had already spent a grueling day of studies with.

Relief flooded over him, until he noticed the unicorn's face, intense and bathed in red by Darion's ruby. His blue eyes taking on a fiery glow.

"How did you do that?" Triumph demanded, eyeing the lantern.

Darion didn't like his tone. He wanted to ask why the Unicorn was spying on him again, but instead replied, "I have no idea, honestly," studying the flame. "I wanted it to get bigger because I thought I heard something," he looked at him, accusatorily. "Then it did. It almost burned my hand, so I wanted it to level out, so the flame wouldn't leave the rim, and so it did."

Truthfully, Darion was just as surprised by it as Triumph. *How did I do it?* he wondered.

"Have you ever done anything else like this?"

Darion thought about the waterfall back in Oregon. Before he answered the question, he asked instead, "What are you doing here? Spying on me again?" His tone clipped, his nerves raw after being startled. He didn't like Triumph's constant interrogations.

Triumph eased off and took a step back. He touched his horn to the lantern closest, which set off a series of light. At once, the Great Hall's sconces were lit, and Darion could easily see the frieze above. Darion thought the unicorn's questioning had been a bit impudent, since he could obviously do a lot more than make one little flame grow. Maybe Darion hadn't even controlled it. Maybe it was just a breeze that made it swirl up. Darion turned toward the portion of the frieze where Seegar had ended the history lesson.

"As I said earlier," Triumph lectured, "I have been instructed to oversee your studies."

"At night? Don't you sleep?"

"I think I could ask you the same question," Triumph snorted. "My quarters are just below yours. I was not able to sleep, and then I heard the floorboards squeaking. I knew you were awake, too." Breaking eye contact, he admitted belatedly, "I did 'spy' on you, I suppose. Not in the way you might think, but I just checked into your thoughts, once I thought you were up," Darion cut him off.

"'Checked in'? You can do that?"

Triumph nodded. "It is odd," he replied. "Typically, we can communicate with others, but we cannot read all minds. Your mind, though, seems so readily accessible." He added, "We will have to address that right away. You would not want the wrong person to enter your mind."

Darion shivered at the thought. What was it his father had said to him when he left? 'Guard your mind, Darion.' *Easier said than done*, he thought.

"So, what else have you done?" Triumph nodded toward the candle, coming back to his initial question.

Darion relaxed once again, surprisingly comforted by the daunting unicorn's presence. He was one of the largest unicorns, and Darion, oddly, felt safe with him near. Though he wasn't sure if he *liked* him and his pestering, it *was* nice to talk to someone. He felt lonely here at Kaulter, and admitted to himself, that he would rather be badgered by Triumph than pacing his room alone.

While still staring at the magnificent castle on the frieze, Darion thought back to Oregon, before he had known of Nav'Aria. He told him of the dreams, Joey Durange, whom he had punched after his venomous remarks, of the dying deer in the road, and of the moment he realized he could sense the animals around him. Then he hesitated. He still didn't know what he had done at the waterfall. He thought about keeping it to himself, but then realized by the look Triumph was giving him that he would be able to search his mind if Darion held anything back. He could, as he had said, 'access' his mind quite easily.

"And then there was the portal," he explained. "It was stuck. Tony couldn't get it to open, and I got really mad because I found out my mother was in danger, and so I just," he stopped, thinking of how to explain it, "I don't know, I just commanded the water to rise and yelled something... and it worked."

Triumph cocked his head. *What did you yell? We had purposely closed the portal to keep you safe. How did you access it?* The last question more to himself, than to Darion.

Remembering Trixon and Vikaris's reactions, he hesitated. He had a strong feeling that it was something significant. Something bad.

"I yelled 'Azalt'!"

"You what?" Triumph thundered, the fireplace suddenly alit with shooting flames, as Triumph towered over the boy. "Where did you hear *that* word? Does Elsra know of this? Come with me. NOW!"

Darion had no choice but to follow Triumph, paling under the wrath of the unicorn. Trixon and his father had appeared worried, but not mad. *What had he done?*

CHAPTER 22

The Bond

"Mother, I need to speak with you, right away!"

They were standing outside the largest door, Darion had ever seen. This was in a separate wing of the wooden fortress. Regent Elsra, it appeared had her own luxurious apartments. *Why did I have to leave my room?* Darion had been berating himself the entire way. Triumph smoldered, and Darion feared for his own safety.

You idiot, he thought. *You couldn't just stay in bed? Your big, soft wonderful bed? No, you had to go wake the whole place because you wanted to see the frieze. Really? The frieze? Now you're going to be killed by angry unicorns all because you wanted to secretly study some art? Damnit, Darion!* He knew he was in trouble, and when he realized Triumph was going to wake Elsra, beads of sweat broke out above his brow. *They can't kill me, right?*

The door burst open, and in the large doorway stood an angry Drigidor. "What is this about, son? It is the dead of night." Drigidor's voice resounded in the wooden corridor.

Darion continued his internal berating as he stepped behind Triumph to avoid the glare consuming Drigidor. Antonis had warned him never to make a unicorn angry.

Triumph barked a forced laugh, "I am not your 'son,'" he replied coldly. Standing even taller than before.

Darion knew these two didn't get along, and he hunkered down to be as unnoticeable as possible. He didn't want to get involved in this family squabble. *Maybe he could just sneak...*

"What is *he* doing up?" Drigidor looked above Triumph's shoulder to Darion failing to conceal himself.

"Shit," Darion whispered, as the reality set in. Now he had two angry unicorns focused on him. Swallowing hard, he felt a trail of sweat run down his back. He tried to look calm. Well, somewhat calm.

Triumph smarted off that Darion was not of his concern, and to wake Elsra. Immediately. Drigidor refused, saying she needed her rest. Triumph stomped his foot so hard that Darion's teeth chattered from the reverberations.

He opened the portal. HE knows.

"Who?" Drigidor asked, now showing genuine interest. "What are you talking about?"

Through clenched teeth Triumph replied. "Narco. Opened. The Portal. Wake Elsra NOW!"

The color in Drigidor's white face drained, which Darion had not thought possible; for once, Drigidor didn't argue with his wife's quarrelsome son. He hurried out of sight to wake his partner, the Council Regent. After a few moments, light flickered in the room as the lanterns were lit, and Darion heard a throaty voice call out, "Enter."

"We're going in there?" Darion whispered terrified to Triumph. He had for a moment thought that they could be friends, and then Triumph had turned on him over "Azalt." *What had he done?* He asked himself again.

Darion hadn't considered what a Unicorn's room would be like. Upon entering he was struck by the fact that it was the nicest room he had ever seen—human or not. Rich silks and plush carpets and draperies were strewn throughout the ornate room. Incense burned, flooding them with earthen smells of sage and cypress. It reminded Darion of a Persian setting, like something he seen in a history class... not that he had paid much attention to history in his other life either.

Elsra's mane cascaded down her neck and back. Long grey and silver tendrils curling as they met the surface of the satin divan she lay upon. Her lavender eyes sparkled in the candle-lit room. A servant entered from an inner chamber and offered Darion tea. He recognized the red-headed servant as the one who had first shown him his chambers. He could not remember her name though. *Edmond would know*, he thought, but this was no time for jest. Darion felt terribly uncomfortable. He had disturbed their sleep and had now entered their rooms. It was such an intimate setting that he felt the color rising in his face. He could not quite meet her eyes, though she bore hers into him.

"What is the meaning of this?" She directed her question toward Triumph, who was staring out the window nearest Darion. The horizon aglow with the returning sun.

Triumph cleared his throat. *Was he hesitating? He is intimidated by her!* Darion was, too, for that matter. He leaned against the wall, hoping he could escape notice.

"Darion was just telling me that when he came through the portal, he shouted 'Azalt'!"

Drigidor gasped. Elsra, however, didn't seem phased. Darion had kept his eyes down but looked up to see her staring not at Triumph, but at him.

She smiled at him. Triumph looked at her questioningly. "Well?" he pressed.

"Trixon already told me," she said. "It would appear, that Narco somehow linked to your mind, Darion... that was what he and his men chanted the night they overtook the Castle."

Darion gawked at her. No one had told him yet that Narco had entered his mind. He shivered before he could catch himself. He was going to ask what it means, but his breath caught when he saw Triumph's severe gaze. The unicorn had been positive that his mother was going to give the boy a sound verbal lashing for being so reckless...

"It would seem like a good time to instruct your new pupil on guarding his mind, Triumph. Save economics for another day." With that, she nodded at Drigidor who escorted them back to the door.

Triumph and Darion both gaping at her reaction, or lack thereof, as the solid, wood door slammed closed.

***

Vikaris stood peering over a map with Myrne, the centaur

Matriarch, in an enclosed grove. Armed centaurs encircled the two. Security was at an all-time high after the most recent attack. Vikaris felt edgy and vulnerable without Trixon. He had never been separated from him for more than a matter of hours. The bond he and Trixon shared was one of supernatural orchestration. He couldn't shake the feeling that Trixon was in grave danger. His companion had always been headstrong; that is what had drawn him to Trixon in the first place. He appreciated that quality, for he too could also come across as headstrong at times. Yet he needed him here. *Where are you?*

"It is the only way, Sire," Myrne stated. "Sire?" She looked up from her intake of the map to see her King lost in thought. Again, she questioned, "Sire?" growing alarmed when he still didn't reply. His forehead was contorted, and he looked to be in pain.

She moved closer, placing her weathered hand on his arm, concern in her eyes. "Are you all right, Your Majesty?" Her braids made a soft, tinkling sound as the beads clicked together, swaying in the light breeze.

"Yes, yes," Vikaris tried to laugh off his startlement. "Sorry, what were you saying?" She looked at him, worry creasing her brow. When she did not respond, he admitted quietly, "I was replaying the attack in my mind." Dalinia's panicked face haunted him. "I am all right, Myrne," he said, none too convincingly, "I really am. Now, what were you saying?"

She smiled at him warmly, her chestnut eyes aglow with intelligence. Knowing that he was indeed all right, if only a little shaken up by the previous day's encounter, she restated her plan.

"We must amass a full force—including the unicorns—and march on Castle Dintarran once and for all. It is the only way, in my estimation, to defeat that bastard." She coughed out the insult at the end, remembering to whom she was speaking to. "Forgive me, Sire," and Vikaris could only smile. He liked Myrne for her ferocity on the battlefield and her savvy mind. She was one of his highest advisors, and he valued her opinion. Though he wondered, *is it really time for a full attack?* The war had been going on for years, yet he still didn't feel ready to risk his people's lives—both those in Camp and the Kingdom. There would be no going back once they marched on the Kingdom. All other battles had been fought in the open; urban fighting was something he had been trying to avoid. Including the unicorns was also something he'd tried to avoid.

"This is exactly what Narco wants us to do," he cautioned, eyes boring into the map. "We are still missing something... but what?" He said it more to himself than to Myrne.

Stepping away, he examined the map from a different angle, glancing at the border along the Shazla Desert. The key to Narco's power had not yet been identified. The unknown ate at him. *How had Narco risen to power all those years ago, and kept it? What control did he have over the Rav'Arians, trolls, and those forced into servitude within 'his' kingdom?* None who had tried to cross the Shazla for answers had ever returned alive. Vikaris *knew* the answer waited beyond the border, but he wouldn't risk another man's life to die in vain being attacked, or worse yet, eaten by the Rav'Arian demons all on a hunch. Yet here he was. *What should I do?* This is the moment to act, and yet, he hesitated. *Blast you, Trixon,* he thought anxiously. *I need your counsel.*

He had kept his troops movements and battles restricted to open areas. Attacking the Kingdom, full-scale, that would be a different story altogether. Civilian subjects, like Edmond's family, would surely be caught in between both armies. Vikaris wasn't willing to risk their lives, or his wife's, for that matter. The unicorns had been mostly kept safe at Kaulter. If he was to march, they would need to bolster his forces. *Is it really time for that?* Pondering the map and Myrne's counsel, he shook his head slightly.

Myrne waited for his reply. She watched him silently mulling over the dilemma. His green, predator-like eyes ate up the map and space surrounding the castle. She knew what he was thinking: Were they ready? Could they really defeat Narco after all this time?

"As always, Myrne, I appreciate your candor. I will hold off from making my final decision until Trixon returns. However, in the meantime, prepare for battle. We are..." he paused. "*I am* going to defeat that 'bastard'."

Myrne felt a shiver of trepidation as she looked upon her king. The man she so loved and respected, so lethal in every way.

She nodded to him, and he spun on his heel, heading

back to camp toward his tent. A contingent of his best soldiers followed him wherever he went after the ill-fated attack at the last camp.

"Prepare for battle," she whispered, sending up a prayer to her Creator and ancestors.

***

"You have to be faster, Darion," Triumph commanded.

Darion stood in the practice grounds outside the Kaulter Fortress. He and Edmond, the village boy whom he had accompanied here, sparred with practice swords. Darion reasoned Edmond had the advantage because he had grown up in Nav'Aria and had been swinging a hoe and scythe for years. His toned arms, with a sheen of sweat, made him appear much older.

Darion shot him a glare. "Are you sure you're only thirteen?"

Edmond only smiled, edging him on with another offensive strike. *The smug prick,* Darion thought, as he backed away again from his "enemy's attack."

Darion had grown up in Oregon, horseback riding and playing video games; he was no match for Edmond. At least not yet.

Barson, the bronzed swordsmaster called for the two boys to "halt." He stepped up to Darion and adjusted his grip on the sword. Barson looked every bit the medieval swordsman—tall, lean, tanned, and with just a touch of grey at the wings. His hazel eyes bore into Darion intently, as a wolf would observe its peers—its young. He looked over Darion, calculating the boy's capabilities. He intimidated the shit out of Darion.

"My prince, you have to tighten your grip. Believe that the blade is an extension of your arm. Do not think about it. Let it lead you." He modeled what he instructed with his own sword, moving swiftly through a series of parries.

Darion had begun working with Barson briefly. Studying the sword. Holding the sword. Learning the forms. Since the attack at Camp, however, his training had been expedited. He had gone in two weeks from holding a sword for the first time to having a sparring match. Blisters marred his palms where he gripped the blade. Bruises lined his limbs from various strikes and falls. His study of Nav'Arian history would have to wait, as his arms training took precedent. He had heard Elsra and Triumph whispering about the "test," and something or other about the "True Heir."

Darion felt the wall go up between himself and Triumph. He had confided to the unicorn—started to trust him even. That was before Triumph's outburst, dragging Darion before Elsra in the middle of the night. Darion felt betrayed. He didn't know how Narco had entered his mind or if his family was safe. He had a score of questions and felt anxious with worry. All he knew for sure was that he needed to learn, and quickly. The problem was, there was so much to learn such as how to shield his mind while literally shielding himself from an enemy with a sword! He thought back to when Carol used to make him rub his tummy and pat his head, or was it pat his tummy and rub his head? Either way, survival in Nav'Aria was much harder than his nursery games with his mom. *Couldn't my parents have prepped me better?* he thought darkly. *Couldn't have made time for a little fencing lesson back home, huh Dad? Who am I kidding?* Darion thought. He would have never gone for "fencing" back in Oregon. He knew his parents, had tried their best with him. And now it was his turn to return the favor. He *had* to learn. *Focus! What is Barson even saying...*

Darion blinked, casting aside his worries and focusing on the blademaster. Barson had ordered Edmond to take a break and polish the swords. Edmond had a natural gift for fighting—*of course, he does*, Darion thought. He was a strong, challenging opponent for Darion, a novice to swordplay. Darion liked him, but he was too stubborn to admit it—at least, at the moment. He didn't trust anyone in Kaulter—especially after Triumph let him down. Feeling lonely, he wondered what Edmond was doing after practice.

Stop it. Focus, you idiot. I don't need friends. I need to learn— that's it.

Barson picked up a practice sword. "Again," he clipped, nodding for Darion to attack. The crisp morning air tickled the back of Darion's neck, which had become moistened with sweat. Barson grinned wolfishly as Darion countered one of his wide arcing slashes. The fight was on!

Though Triumph continued to tell him to go faster, Barson murmured instruction, praise, and critique as they went along. "Good, Darion. Use your feet. Remember, your opponent will be using a real sword. They will not have blunted edges. Use whatever it takes to get away from their sword tip." He lunged forward, his sword nearing Darion's throat. Darion stepped and leaned back as the sword narrowly missed him. That would have been a death blow in a real fight.

Again, Triumph yelled out to him to be better. "Work harder." Darion heard a loud thud, as Triumph kicked the wall encircling the practice ground with frustration.

Heat rising in Darion's chest, he spat, "That's easy for you to say. All you're working is your mouth over there. I don't see *you* doing much else."

Barson dropped his guard. His mouth falling open, before catching himself. Darion noted that the instructor immediately backed away from him, as if contaminated.

Oh, fuck, Darion thought to himself, as realization dawned on him. Frantically thinking up his apology, his senses suddenly noticed the force coming his way. It was too late. Once again, Darion had spoken too quickly. He needed to learn to keep his tongue in check. He felt him, before he saw him. Triumph was there, atop Darion, knocking him off balance with his back haunches. Darion tumbled gracelessly to the ground. Arms up, trying to shield his face from imminent death, he waited. *He didn't kill me!* Darion lowered his arms and looked in horror as the enraged gaze of Triumph met his. The unicorn's horn mere inches from Darion's face. He could make out every detail this close. Silver tendrils of mane blew slightly in the wind, beads of sweat dotted the hairline from Triumph's mad rush to the sparring ground. The whiskers near Triumph's muzzle quivered as he spoke.

"Then fight me, my prince." Darion didn't miss the note of condescension as Triumph sneered at him, backing away. Darion shuffled to his feet. *What do I do?* He looked to Barson for guidance. *And I thought he was intimidating,* Darion thought, near panic. He had the practice sword still in his grip, but Triumph wasn't wearing armor. He had only fought men so far. *Can I hit him? Will he hit me? How do you fight a... a unicorn?*

Before he could think of what to do next, Triumph rushed him, hitting him full on with his broad chest. Darion fell hard landing on his tailbone; he breathed out noisily. Momentarily stunned and unable to breathe, he could only stare. He lost his sword upon impact. *A lot of good that blunted piece of wood did.* He now sat a few feet away from the gleaming terror before him. Darion heard the hush whispers of onlookers. He glanced around to see Edmond wide-eyed near Barson as a crowd gathered near the front of the field. He noted that Elsra and the Unicorn Council were striding up. *Surely Triumph wouldn't continue this berating in front of Elsra? Would he? Should I yell for help?*

Get up, Prince, Triumph barked, as he pawed the ground. He began pacing before Darion. He reminded him of a lion he had seen at the Oregon Zoo a few years back, pacing before the cage. Its gaze was deadly. Darion stood up, brushing off the dirt from his pants, stalling for time. *What now?* He rubbed his palms together. They were clammy with sweat, and he welcomed the dirt. He jumped forward grabbing his sword, then quickly backed up, giving the creature a wide berth. Darion recalled what Barson had told him: *Let the sword lead you.* He took a deep inhale, smelling the fresh sweat on himself and his opponent. The soft breeze carrying the cloying perfume of Elsra, and the... the dirt.

That's it, he thought. The soil had become loosened after the shuffle of many feet moving back and forth. Triumph loomed before him, ready to pounce. Darion had to be faster. He kicked quickly, causing a dust cloud to envelop Triumph's head, temporarily diminishing his view. Darion jumped to the side, knowing that Triumph would rush headlong where Darion had just stood. He whirled around to face Triumph's right flank, and slashed, his blunted sword making contact. Triumph snarled and whipped around to face him. Of course, the blade didn't pierce his skin, but Darion hoped it would leave a welt. A big one. Triumph again charged Darion; yet again, Darion anticipated his move, hearing his opponent's movement before he could even see it. His heightened senses were on full alert, and he feigned again to the side, then turned back and rushed Triumph's left, smacking his underbelly. Triumph reared at that swinging his back around, bashing Darion for the third time this round. The air abandoned Darion's lungs as he landed heavily—again. Coming in for the final blow, Triumph stood atop Darion, poised to run him through. Darion feared he may actually do it. His ruby warmed at his throat. He gasped. Darion brought his hand up smoothly and grabbed the horn, yelling *"Denont!"* in one fluid motion. His ruby glowed brightly as Triumph became encased in a red glow, frozen, as if time had been suspended.

It was Triumph's turn to gasp. Faltering, he moved back. *How did you... I thought...* His eyes widened in shock, and then supreme awe. *I,* Triumph stuttered, *my prince. I apologize. I do not know what got into me.* Triumph continued backing away and slowly lowered his head and gaze submissively. Not a breath could be heard outside the arena. All stood still.

Darion stood up hastily, embarrassed by the onlookers. He met Elsra's eyes, and she, out of the entire crowd, seemed to be the only one who wasn't surprised by the exchange. She nodded to him, encouraging him to go on. That gave him the confidence he needed. He had done the right thing. Darion examined Triumph, one of the largest, and deadliest unicorns alive. A formidable foe to say the least. Yet now, instead of feeling fear and anger toward Triumph, Darion felt an appreciation *for* him. A warrior of his capacity was one to uphold, not antagonize. Triumph deserved respect. It was as if all at once he knew him completely. He knew Triumph's heart. His utter devotion to his mother. The memory of his father. To Vikaris, and thereby Darion. He knew all there had been, and all there could be of Triumph. The great hidden pain that Triumph tried so hard to hide, causing him to continually lash out with mistrust. Darion strode to Triumph, gently lifting his chin so that their eyes became level. He nodded to him in respect. In that one collision of their strong wills on the practice field, Darion had countered his enemy's kill strike with one of his own.

He had bonded Triumph.

CHAPTER 23

The Cage

"I hate this," Trinidad murmured to Lyrianna. They had escaped only hours ago, hiding in an abandoned coal shed not far from the castle. They had made their getaway in the night, and had been prepared to flee—that was, until they saw what Narco kept hidden on this side of the castle. They couldn't leave now. Not without a little more investigation, that was.

"We have to free them, Trinidad. This is our only option."

He knew he could never sway her determined mind. He didn't have to like it though. Especially not when she was rubbing him down with remnants from an old coal trove. His pure white coat—granted, it had not been clean for months now—was sullied with blackened coal dust. She intended for them to be well hidden when they made their move, completely covered herself. Her long golden locks were now blackened and tucked beneath her dark shirt collar. The two made an odd and filthy pair. He knew they were not safe here. He had heard Narco's feral yell that morning as he discovered his captives had escaped. *We need to get out of here,* he thought worriedly.

He looked out of the crevice of the wooden shed toward the cages in the old Traders' loading area. Where once bustling merchants and farmers had brought their wares and crops to share with the Meridia family, now stood two unbelievably large cages full of young prisoners. All females. Trinidad shuddered when he thought of their purpose.

Lyrianna knew their purpose all too well, and she meant to free them—or die trying. A year of captivity told her what Narco intended to do with young females, and she didn't hesitate for a moment. "We are not leaving without those girls. I am their queen, Trinidad. I cannot abandon them. Not to *him.*" Her fiery gaze signaled that there was no alternate plan. No more discussion.

The cages sat apart from each other. One cage held all human cargo; the other a mixture of centaurs and nymphs. The nymphs' backs were bloodied; their wings looked to have been torn off. The prisoners huddled, unaware that they were being watched by more than lustful guards.

All through the morning, Trinidad and Lyrianna studied them. Watching the changing of guards. They were mainly Rav'Arian, troll, or the occasional human. She snarled when she thought of the humans. The other rabble she could understand, but humans? *How could they turn on Vikaris? On me!?* she had demanded forcefully to Trinidad. He grew just as angry as her watching the traitorous guards, their hideous intent for the girls only too clear. They watched the one human's eyes as he greedily looked the girls over. Trinidad's focus shifted to study the troll on guard. *What was in it for him?* They watched as he circled the cages, and then stopped before them. Lyrianna stifled a gasp; prickling hairs stood up along Trinidad's spine. The troll pointed out a young centaur with luxurious auburn curls spilling down her bare back, her large breasts exposed having had her shirt torn from her upper body. Her pale skin flowing almost seamlessly into her ivory fur upon her four legs. *That one,* the troll said gruffly.

"Look away, my queen. You do not need to see this. Please, turn away," Trinidad cautioned, without success. Lyrianna stood, looking horrified yet transfixed at the crevice, as she watched the female pulled from the cage. Her back legs lunged out at her captors. She gnawed, scratched, snarled, and kicked, but to no avail. Trinidad and Lyrianna watched hopelessly as the troll dragged the centaur by her hair—her lovely thick hair—into a corner of the enclave to use her. His intent becoming known as he lowered the front of his britches. His grey, veined skin was a stark contrast to the pure ivory hindlegs he straddled. The centaur's legs frantically kicked, but the creature's strong hands held her still as he took her. Lyrianna retched in the coal pile and covered her ears in a desperate attempt to drown out the sounds coming from beyond the cages. More than anything, Trinidad wished he could do something for the girl, while also getting the queen out of harm's way. *This is no place for Lyrianna.* Trinidad's rage turned molten as he heard the guards on duty cheering on their comrade as he concluded his business. The centaur's screams dropped in octave to throaty moans.

"Bring her," the beaked Rav'Arian called out. Lyrianna shot back up to look out the crevice, watching in horror as the troll dragged the victim by her hair again, toward a newly lit cook fire. Her screams intensified with each step.

"No. They cannot," Lyrianna managed before retching again. Trinidad could only stare in stupefied horror. *It was already too horrific to think of that beast raping the poor child, but now, to watch them eat her, too?* He couldn't sit by and watch this. It was too much. It was all too much. This evil must be punished. He was beaten. He was bruised. He was tired, and he was without his horn, yes. But he was not without his wits. He looked around and saw that now that the cook fire was being tended, the guards—human included, had gathered around. He watched as they tied the girl to a stake. Her four legs were bound tightly. The guards were consumed in their task, paying little attention to the cages, and though Trinidad was sickened by the display, a plan began to formulate in his mind.

Yes, he thought, *let them tend their fire. For that will allow me time to tend mine.*

***

"Here," Riccus called out. "We need your light again, Trixon."

Trixon stepped soundlessly through the dense vegetation and met Riccus on what looked like a game trail. It was freshly trodden.

"Injured," Rick said lowly to Trixon. The unicorn

nodded again, respecting his companion's superb tracking skills. The Rav'Arian's gait looked uneven, as if one limb was dragging from an injury, or from carrying a prisoner perhaps. Trixon took a deep inhale and noted the faint smell of rotting filth.

"It is close," Trixon murmured, and Rick nodded, motioning for Antonis and Aalil to get down. Antonis had dealt Morta a severe blow with his sword hilt after he commented on Aalil's attractive frame. The traitor was unconscious once more, just the way they all liked it.

As the party knelt, they listened for the enemy. As if on cue, a small sound filled the silence. Trixon saw Riccus and Antonis look to Aalil questioningly, her eyes widening.

The boy, she mouthed to them. *Ansel.* The sound started again—the boy was crying. The wind carried the sound to them. Antonis looked at Trixon, who looked grim—all signs to hasten their action. *We need to intercept them.*

Trixon spoke into their minds. *Antonis and Riccus, you come with me. We will surround them. Riccus will start first, because he is the quietest of us all. Once we are in a sound position, I will tell you to strike. No matter what, we get the boy to safety. He is our top priority. Understood?*

The two men nodded. "What about me?" Aalil asked, her tone biting.

You watch the prisoner. If we are unsuccessful, you take him back to the king. Aalil looked as if she was going to argue, but thought better of it after catching Antonis's eye. It would not do anyone any good to have her arguing like a petulant child. Of course, she longed to be in the fight.

But she respected Trixon, and she was a trained warrior—she knew not to go against her commanding officer... Trixon knew she had a history of defying orders to save civilians and the like, but he put it out of his mind. Aalil had her orders, and he had to trust that she would follow them. He had his own trajectory to contend with.

Aalil sat down near the prisoner, whose face they had covered with a spare linen. She nodded to the men—Trixon included—as the party spread out, beginning their descent upon the adversary.

Riccus had been boyhood friends with Gruegor. He was completely consumed with determination to rescue his friend's son. He couldn't imagine the trauma Ansel was experiencing, seeing his mother killed, and being abducted by this monster. He remembered when Darion had been that age... his thoughts strayed. Shy yet mischievous, Darion had always been so observant, not hot-headed like other little boys. No matter what would come, Rick knew in his heart that Darion would always be his adopted son—*his* son. He worried so much for him and prayed that he was all right in Kaulter. Thinking, too, of his springflower whom he had left back at Camp. *Creator, protect her. She is my everything.*

He crept quietly along the greenery, catching his breath when he heard a sound to his right. A moment later, a slight yellow bird with black markings hopped down from the low branch on which it had been preening. It looked around to its left. Startled, it flew off. He looked back at his pathway. Clear. He could not hear or see anything, but the tracker in him knew his prey was close.

Lowering down to all fours, Riccus crawled, ducking behind a large, mossy tree. Just down below, he could make out the top of the Rav'Arian's head bobbing up and down, clearly at work on something. He continued to creep closer, avoiding the small brush and twigs that might give away his presence. He moved silently. Deadly. He got into a close, defensive position, then waited. He knew Trixon would give the signal once he and Antonis were in position. From his vantage point, he could see the creature. Meticulously, it reached for items from a small pack that it carried and laid them out in a line. Riccus couldn't exactly make out the objects. He could hear the boy's snuffles from here. It took every fiber of practiced control not to rush the creature with or without his friends' help. He could see Ansel, though he was propped against a shaded tree and the shadows hid his face. Riccus squinted his eyes, trying to get a better look at him. He appeared banged up. The child's knees looked bloody, and his clothes were torn. Riccus concluded that the boy had been dragged for some of his journey. Ansel looked weak. His head drooping, and though his face was hidden by the lack of light under the tree where he had been tethered, Riccus knew they didn't have much time. The Rav'Arian had begun fire preparations, and Rick had the sick fear that the beast was prepping for a meal.

He hesitated. Trixon had said he was to wait for his command, but he didn't want to wait one more second. *Where are they?* He bounced the blade in his hand then thought better of it. He would wait. He had a bow slung around his back, and he stealthily withdrew an arrow from his case. He notched it, aiming directly at the beast's head. When the command came, he would be ready.

Antonis stumbled along, silently cursing himself for being a big, bumbling oaf. Trixon was right in choosing Rick to be the silent leader. Antonis tried to be stealthy, but it seemed that every twig, small stone, and dried leaf was positioned directly in his pathway. He hoped he didn't give away their attack. He drew his blade, prepared for what lay ahead.

Trixon verged closer than any of the others. From his vantage point, he could see the Rav'Arian clearly. He circled the tree where Ansel was nestled. He spied Rick's form from across the way; his heightened senses detected Antonis crashing closer, and Trixon knew that he needed to make his move before the Rav'Arian noticed the loud noises coming from his side. Trixon led the three-prong attack. Riccus would be the archer, and Antonis would rely on his brute strength. *But what about the boy?* He needed to get out of the wooded area, and fast. Though Trixon could not see Ansel, hidden from view by the towering tree, he could sense the boy's waning strength.

Antonis, you're too loud, he called out through his mind. He looked toward Riccus, and though he knew the man could not see him from that distance, he felt that Riccus knew he was there. *Listen carefully,* Trixon said quietly. *Rick is going to shoot rapid fire at the creature, to draw him out, and shift his focus. Creator, help us! You better be ready, Antonis, to then rush him—as loud as you want. While he is distracted, I will gather the child and take him back toward the direction of Aalil. I will return quickly, but that leaves you on your own. Can you handle this task?* He felt, more than heard, their agreements to the plan. Taking a deep breath, he said, *Now!*

Riccus, a seasoned fighter and archer, had not seen battle for years, but he clearly had been an avid hunter during his time away. Trixon watched as he mechanically squinted his left eye, drawing the bow string back. He, as was his habit, bit his lower lip, and let out a low whistle while releasing the arrow aimed at the Rav'Arian's head. And with that, they moved closer.

The creature spun around in the last instant, having heard the whistling arrow and narrowly avoided getting hit through the eye. Instead it grazed the side of its head. A scream filled the quiet, and all at once the beaked lizard rushed headlong toward Rick. Another arrow struck the creature in the chest, followed by another in the gut. Still the creature didn't slow, and Rick appeared to be preparing to run. Notching a final arrow, he shot this one cleanly through the creature's right eye. Still it continued toward him. He jumped up, drawing his blade, backing away from the edge. He wanted to draw the beast farther away from Ansel and Trixon. As the beak emerged over the edge where he had just been kneeling, Trixon made it to the boy. In a blur of white, the pair dashed to the safety of the woods—and Aalil.

Riccus focused on the fight, exultant that it had actually worked! Ansel was safe.

The bird-like monster stood taller than he had initially

expected. Its clawed fist wrapped around the arrow in its eye, pulling it out with a sickening sound. The moist pluck that came out with the arrow revealed an eye ball that had been impaled, and thus withdrawn. The creature didn't even look at it but threw the arrow to the side. Then, in quick succession he pulled the other two arrows from his body and moved toward Rick with surprising agility. *Creator, help me! The arrows did not even slow him down!* Rick knew the creature was too close now for the bow, and he braced himself in a defensive stance. He was not as skilled with the blade as others, but he was no novice either. He calmed his breathing and waited. *No matter what, Ansel is safe. And Darion is safe. Narco had been denied both.*

"Do your worst, little birdie," Riccus said tauntingly at the Rav'Arian, its beak clicking open and closed angrily.

Antonis, having heard the command to fight, knew that his "quiet" approach was no longer necessary, and he sprinted toward the encampment. As he made it into the opening he saw all at once the fight in front of him. Trixon had found the boy and galloped steadily toward Aalil, Ansel clinging to his mane. He looked terrified, but stable on the unicorn's back.

Antonis looked toward the clearing edge and watched nervously as the beast rapidly gained on Rick's position. Spitting and rolling on his toes a few times, he prepped for the fight. He ran toward the beast, whose attention was now solely on the kill before its beady eyes. He knew Riccus had been a solid fighter in his day, but feared for his friend all the same. Riccus jumped backward, narrowly missing a clawed swipe to his face. The Rav'Arian, or so it appeared, had no blade. As Antonis approached, he struck the creature's back with a heavy cut. He felt his blade cut through the creature's cloak, and thickly encased form. He knew that Rav'Arians had a very strong exterior, much like the exoskeleton of a beetle, upon their back. He had only meant to antagonize the beast from attacking Rick. The creature spun around to face him, and without hesitating, Antonis thrust his blade again, this time toward the creature's exposed front. From the corner of his eye, he saw Riccus make a cut toward the beast's arm. Both men struck their opponent, and Antonis lunged away, but as he did, he noted that Rick's blade did not come free. The creature had pinned the blade, and therefore Rick's hand as he had struck.

Grasping Rick's arm, the creature swung his heavy claw upon Rick's side, gaining a guttural cry of pain from the man. Antonis growled at the beast, and in a whirl of practiced swordsmanship, began to make several quick slashes. His moves were too fast for the beast to follow. The creature had been forced to drop Rick in order to stave off the other man's attacks. Antonis, completely consumed with the task at hand, didn't see Rick crawling unsteadily away from the danger. He cut the creature's mid-thigh, sliced open its belly, and spun back, giving himself enough distance to throw his blade directly through the beast's neck.

Take that, you sack of shit, Antonis thought smugly, pulling from his store of Oregonian swear words.

The creature fell, spasms wracking its body as its

clawed hands shakily tried to grasp the blade that had now opened its neck. Black tar-like blood gushed out. The creature's beak opened and closed, gasping, and then fell silent. The threat was over. They had won.

Filling his lungs with deep breaths, Antonis looked back to see his friend clutching his side, red blood in stark contrast to the Rav'Arian's gore seeping through his torn shirt.

"Rick. How bad is it?"

Riccus, with his customary look of nonchalance, shrugged his shoulder as if to say, "Not too bad." Though as he moved, he winced, breaking through his bravado. Antonis knelt by his side and moved Rick's hand to look at the wound. All in all, it wasn't too deep. There was a lot of blood, but it appeared to be only a surface wound. As Antonis ran back to grab his pack, which he had dropped as soon as he made the clearing, he was startled to find Trixon already beside Riccus.

"And you said he was the silent one," Antonis mocked, looking from the unicorn to his injured friend, hoping to lighten the mood. *Rick has to be okay.* Trixon inspected the wound while Riccus explained the fight. The unicorn looked to him and nodded, "You did well, Commander." A ripple of pleasure overtook Antonis at the praise, though he chided himself for acting like a young soldier. *Of course, I did well*, he thought. *I am the former Commander. A trained killer and Keeper of the Realm. I have to do well, or else.*

He looked at his friend and thought with gloom, *Maybe it did not go so well.* Rick's face was beginning to take on a sheen of sweat, and pale pallor.

"All right, Keeper," he directed toward Rick. "Let's get you sewn up." Field kit and water pouch handy, Antonis cleaned the wound where the Rav'Arian's claw had raked his skin, leaving four parallel gashes. Threading the needle, he began the messy business of stitching his friend back together. Rick gritted his teeth, as Antonis slowly began to close the jagged talon marks. Riccus eventually passed out from the blood loss and pain, but Trixon assured Antonis that he would be all right. After having cleaned and sewn the wound, he wrapped cloth around Riccus's torso, and as gently as he could, draped him over Trixon for the march back to Aalil and Ansel.

Before they left, Antonis had searched the Rav'Arian's belongings and gathered a few peculiar items. He could only guess at their savage purpose.

***

"Carolina," a voice called out. Carol turned to see none other than the always bright and poised Seegar. A smile lit her face but didn't reach her eyes as she took in his expression. She feared he brought bad news of Riccus or Darion. Had she known as soon as they'd returned, that her family would be split up and put in perilous danger, she may not have been as thrilled to return home. She shook her head, banishing the dark thought. Darion was where he should be: reunited with his father, which was a joy for all to see.

Yes, it is a joy, she reprimanded herself. Though she remembered the last weeks differently than most. She remembered that first night, holding her husband—her rock—as they tried to make sense of their new life. As he cried, tears of joy, and fear after seeing Vikaris embracing Darion. *Darion—their son.* He had been so brave that day, and every day since then. He had met Vikaris, *and... and... he had forgotten about them,* she thought, her heart aflame with so many competing emotions. *He had forgotten about Rick—the only father he had ever known.* Darion was blinded by Vikaris's larger than life presence. And for the first time in Carol's life, she knew envy.

"What can I do for you, High Councilor?"

Seegar seemed to stand a bit taller at the mention of his title. He proudly bore that title and had for a long time. Yet with the skin creasing near his eyes, and his lips pressed firmly in a line, Seegar looked tired... and worried.

"The king has received news of your husband. Please, come with me."

Her heart leapt into her throat as she followed him quickly toward the king's chambers. Her stomach tightened with fear. *Please, Creator. Do not take my husband, too.*

"Ah, Carol," Vikaris called as she entered his tent. "There you are."

"What have you heard, Your Majesty?" She could not deal with the petty formalities in this moment. Vikaris nodded toward the seat next to him, and she felt her legs go numb as she moved to her chair, none too gracefully.

"I have heard from Trixon. They are headed back as we speak. They were successful in rescuing Ansel, and..."

"And Riccus is with him? I thought they were headed to rescue Lyrianna? What has happened to my husband?"

She inquired, her pulse climbing. She heard Seegar cough subtly behind her but didn't care. She knew Vikaris was holding something back.

He broke eye contact for a moment, and then quietly spoke, "He is alive, Carol, but injured." She felt the gooseflesh form across her whole body as the king spoke. "Apparently, he and Antonis defeated the Rav'Arian that took Ansel, though before it was killed the creature clawed Rick's side during the fight. Antonis cleaned and sewed the wound, but it is not healing correctly. Trixon has tried touching his horn to the infected tissue but still it festers. Rick has fallen into a..." He stopped, searching for the word. He rubbed his hand over face, clearly hating to find himself speaking with yet another wife whose husband may die.

"A what? Fallen into what?" The panic evident in her voice, her eyes pleading as they searched his.

"A coma. He has not awoken since yesterday's attack."

She shuddered. Knowing the severity of something like this. She gripped her auburn braid as if it were some link to Riccus. He loved her hair, and always chuckled when she nervously ran her hands through her hair.

"There is more," he quietly continued. She looked up, her eyes brimming with tears, unwilling to cry in front of Vikaris. She took a deep calming breath and nodded for him to continue.

"The wound is... strange. Trixon said the skin around it has become blackened. Instead of healing it seems to be decaying." That did it. She covered her face with her hands, feeling the tears run down them. *My Rick! I cannot lose him. I cannot lose him. I cannot lose him,* she repeated, unsure of whether she was praying or simply stating a fact.

Before the blackness took her, too, she had a thought. As one of the most well-known horticulturists in the land, the symptoms sparked a memory as she tried to search her mind. Something she had read about that could counter-attack even the most virulent wounds. *What was it?* She tried to search her clouded brain.

Vikaris grabbed her hands. "It will be all right, Carolina. We will get to the bottom of this. I have already sent a message to Elsra. She will know what to do."

She nodded, eyes still closed. There is a cure, she just had to find it.

***

"Stay here," Trinidad said through gritted teeth. "Lyrianna, please," he said quietly. "It is too much of a risk." He couldn't risk her life for theirs, after everything they had gone through to escape, he was going to see the queen safely home.

She turned to face him. Even covered in soot, he could still see her face flushed with anger. "I most certainly will not, Trinidad. Now let's go!" He glowered at her a moment longer, trying to think of something to say that would convince her, but knew he had to act quickly if he was to save the centaur. He whispered frantic instructions to her as she was already opening the door.

It was a storm-ridden day, with clouds gathering in the west. The overcast light cast shadows upon the ground. *This will play to our advantage,* Trinidad thought, since Lyrianna had so meticulously blackened his coat.

Though he feared for her, he knew he could not look back lest he give her location away. Leaving the shed first, he had ordered for her to wait until he got to his position, able to then distract the guards, before she headed toward the cells.

As he drew closer toward the gathering of the guards, he could make out the faint tear stains on the female's cheeks. She had fainted as soon as the flames began to grow. They now licked at her hooves and pale fur, as the guards began to lower her before the fire. It was still a small enough fire, but Trinidad had only mere moments before her agonizing screams would fill the morning air. Her long tail was mere inches from the dancing flames, her ivory coat taking on an eerie orange glow.

Trinidad stuck to the shadows, snaking his way toward the men. He spotted a chicken coop a few yards from his location which became his target. If he could get to it unseen, he could kneel below it out of sight and set the trap. As he got closer, he could hear a strange sound coming from the Rav'Arian. It sounded like some kind of incantation. Dread soon filled Trinidad's chest. He had read about something like this many cycles ago. He could not place it, but he knew that this was a dark magic, brought from beyond Nav'Aria. He shuddered, and practically fell before the coop. He knelt there, trying to steady his breathing.

Whatever it was that they were doing, it could not happen. He would not let this happen. He gathered his thoughts. Focusing on the image of the fire that lay just beyond his hideout. He pictured the faces of the men and beasts. He remembered the screams he had heard from the centaur. And then he projected into their minds.

Where is she? he howled in as menacing a voice as he could muster. Spears and weapons fell as their master's voice filled their minds. He heard more than one mug shatter to the ground as the group waited, listening.

Trinidad waited a moment longer for effect. In a slightly softer voice, *I said, where is she?* He could hear the scuffling of boots as guards began to elbow one another.

He heard one gruff voice whisper, "What was that?"

You dare question the voice of your Lord. Bow before me, scum. You who would rather pleasure yourselves and fill your bellies with MY bounty. You miserable lot, who would let HER get away and think I would not come searching for the reason. And then to find you all... Here... His voice trailed off, leaving the impression that he was watching them, that he was very displeased with them.

They all knew who "he" was, or at least who they thought he was. Narco. He dared a glance around the corner of his hideout, and he was pleased to see that some of the guards were visibly shaken. More men were coming out from the inside of the guard room nearest the fire. The centaur had been dropped to the side, discarded as those on duty gathered. Listening. Their eyes roving the area. Tiny, crackling sparks shot toward her. Any closer and one of them would set her aflame. He willed her to wake up. The guards seemed to be searching for Narco, trembling with fear. All but the Rav'Arian. The creature's head was cocked as if it were trying to solve a puzzle. Trinidad didn't want to give it enough time to figure it out, so he bellowed.

You will report to my throne room at once. The false queen's absence must not go unnoticed. All other soldiers have already been called before me. YOU, he said with emphasis, *are the only ones NOT in attendance. Leave the centaur alone and get to my chambers now if you wish to live through this day.*

At once, there was a smattering of petrified trolls and men, running into each other, barking orders, and haphazardly making their way toward the back staircase that led to the inner cookhouse, kitchen, and the interior of Castle Dintarran. All left but the Rav'Arian. Again, it was looking this way and that, with an undetectable expression on its hideous face.

Trinidad knew what he had to do. If that Rav'Arian caught whiff of Lyrianna near the cages, it would be on her in a matter of moments. She could not overpower it, though her strong will made even Trinidad wonder sometimes. Only last evening he feared she wouldn't survive their ordeal; now he feared for anyone who stood in her path.

As he stood preparing to run out into the courtyard to face his foe, he heard a small yelp. *The centaur!* The Rav'Arian drug her back toward the cages, now that the crowd had dispersed. Trinidad peered around the chicken coop, startling a pair of hens, who clucked in alarm, thinking meant to steal their precious eggs. The beast neared the cage. The red-headed centaur's spirit was returning; she immediately began kicking and growling as she was dragged. And then just as the beast rounded the corner, Trinidad heard the commotion stop. *Lyrianna.*

"Hush now, listen to me," Lyrianna told the human chattel in the barred enclosure. "We will get you out, but you must stay very quiet, and do exactly as I say."

"Who are you?" one woman asked, appearing to be the oldest and the leader amongst the captives. She appeared just slightly older than Lyrianna herself, though the grime and grit on her face may have made her seem to be older. Lyrianna felt as dirty and disheveled as they after months of captivity and an added layer of soot.

"I am your queen," Lyrianna said softly, with her strong, yet kind voice. At once the women, some who had been in a state of semi-sedation with lolling heads, looked toward her. Hope filled their troubled faces. Others: skepticism.

The older woman stood moving closer. "Can it be?" she whispered. Lyrianna lifted her chin, and though covered in filth, none could mistake the queen's exquisite profile. The women bowed their heads in unison.

"We are saved," a small voice called out. "Bless you, my queen. It is you!" A middle-aged woman reached through the bars, and kissed Lyrianna's hand.

"Yes, now as I was saying, I am here to get you out..."

She heard the beast before it filled the space. She told the women to stand and to try to block her view. The Rav'Arian was dragging the poor abused victim back to the cell of centaurs and nymphs, making Lyrianna's blood run cold. The female made quite a fuss, and Lyrianna hoped she would not be further harmed.

She watched as its clawed hands grappled at its waist

for the keys. *The keys! If I could only get the keys somehow.* She knew Trinidad had called to the men's minds. She had heard it, too. His plan had been to scare them all away. Apparently, it had not worked for this creature. She surveyed her surroundings. She needed a weapon, and now.

As she crept along the bars, she discovered a lone blade near the corner where the poor Centaur had been taken earlier. It would require her to jump up in plain sight of the Rav'Arian. She had been a good fighter, that is, before she was taken. Her husband had instructed her with the sword early on in their marriage, so that she would be prepared for a moment such as this.

Relying on someone else to protect you is the fastest way to get yourself killed. We are at war, Lyrianna. You must be strong. Watch, and wait for the enemy to tire. Look for their weakness. Vikaris's instructions run through her memory, adrenaline coursing through her veins. She looked down at herself, remembering her malnourished state. *Can I even hold the blade steady, let alone attack a creature such as this? Where is Trinidad?* she wondered, fearfully. Looking back and forth between the sword, and the now occupied Rav'Arian, she decided to act. She was tired of being incapable. Held back. It was time to move.

Just as she was beginning to rise, she saw the gate swing open and the beast roughly push the Centaur back into her cell. The creatures within all climbed back, away from the opening, fear in their eyes. Although, as the creature began to close the door, he toppled over. A black force hitting him!

Trinidad! Without hesitation, she ran to the corner retrieving the blade, and rushed toward the fight. All the women—human and other—were on their feet. Knowing that moments like this did not come often, they needed to be ready to run.

Trinidad might not have a horn, but he was certainly not defenseless. His force knocked the unsuspecting Rav'Arian off his feet, and before it could gather its wits, Trinidad used his hooves to trample the beast's chest and head. Blow after blow, Trinidad was relentless. As the beast swiped a clawed fist at Trinidad, the unicorn was forced to jump back to avoid the poisonous talons.

"Look out," a nymph's shrill cry rang out from the cage, Lyrianna spun on her feet, just in time to see two more Rav'Arians approaching behind her. She planted her feet, tightening her core, and raised her sword in a defensive posture, just as Vikaris had taught her. The injured Rav'Arian clicked its beak, mocking the frail queen. Trinidad rushed it again, yet the Rav'Arian jumped back not taking the full hit as before. The two of them stood blocking the cage door, so the females trapped within could not escape without rushing right into the menacing Rav'Arian.

Trinidad knew they were losing precious time. His ploy with the soldiers would be very short lived, and most likely raise the alarm for the whole Castle if Narco heard of it. He had to finish this, quickly. Lyrianna couldn't take on an opponent in her condition, let alone two!

He glanced at the cell and noted that many of the

centaurs looked strong, and healthy, some bearing the Quaigth mark. *Warriors. They have not been imprisoned long*, he realized. The door was open, he only needed to get this Rav'Arian out of the way, so they could assist he and Lyrianna.

He quickly turned, looking as if he was going to run. The Rav'Arian stood, dropping his guard, long enough for Trinidad to kick his hind legs full force into the creature's body. The cracking of bones was audible, and the form fell back, in a daze, its head slamming to the ground as it fell. This was all the opening the dozens of captives needed as they poured out from the cell, encircling the Rav'Arians that now threatened their Queen.

Lyrianna had been successful in evading her enemies thus far but had not been able to strike another opponent. She was barely avoiding their simultaneous attacks. A front kick from the creature on her left, sent her flying toward the wall.

Her opponent stepped toward her, and she was forced to scoot backwards, unable to stand just yet. She looked toward the humans in the cell closest to her, helpless to save them. They all stood solemn watching her through the bars, and then their eyes began to widen and look beyond she and her attacker. Flashes of brown, black, red, and gold swam before her. A swarm of life came to her aid, and in an instant, the Rav'Arians went from thinking they had bested her, to facing dozens of enraged centaurs and nymphs. They were surrounded! One small nymph stayed nearby, and Lyrianna heard jingling. *The keys!* This small wretch, not more than a child, had done it! She had the keys and was beginning to work at the humans' lock.

Trinidad came to her then and nudged her with his muzzle. *Get back, my queen. We will finish this.*

Lyrianna stood, slowly sucking in a deep breath. The force of the kick had most certainly broken at least one of her ribs. She could only hunch over as she held a hand to her side, nodding as she moved to assist the nymphs.

The Rav'Arians were soon overwhelmed. Though one had a sword, it hadn't struck any of its opponents. So fierce were the attackers that in a different time and place, the scene would have been comical.

Trinidad joined the battling females. The largest centaur landing a rear kick to the nearest Rav'Arian's groin, just as a nymph jumped on its back. The broken nymph stabbed its fingers into the creature's eye sockets, clinging for all it was worth. The Rav'Arian's head shook, frantically trying to free the creature from atop his back, but his claws could never reach up because of the multitude of centaur kicks it faced. It soon toppled over succumbing to the captives' unrelenting attack. The largest centaur nodded toward the last of the warriors. The red-headed centaur limped over and with a nod from the elder drew a thin cord from her belt. She wrapped it around the creature's neck, while black blood poured from its torn face, strangling the creature until its life had left its body.

Go back to whatever hell-hole you came from, Trinidad thought, darkly.

The other Rav'Arian didn't seem to go down as easily,

and Trinidad rushed to help. This beast had its blade drawn in a defensive posture, making small threatening arcs. Trinidad paced before the beast, hoping to distract it and look for an opening from the blade. As he did, the circle of centaurs pressed in, encroaching upon the beast's space. And then at once, Lyrianna stood at the center, blade in hand.

No, Trinidad called to her, but it was to no avail. He could tell she favored one side, due to her injuries, and that she was drawing the beast out so they could overtake it. She couldn't stand fully erect, and he knew she was injured. *Get back, Lyrianna. You do not have to do this.* At this close range, he could see her jaw tighten at his words, but otherwise she stayed immobile. Eyeing the beast. She was the only one with a weapon, and Trinidad knew this would give them an opening. His gaze never leaving hers, he began to make his way through the crowd, trying to reach the creature's blind spot.

Lyrianna's sword arced. The centaurs nearby hesitated, looking unsure whether they should continue their attack. *If they attacked, would that help or hinder her movements? Would it knock her or the creature off balance?* Silence permeated the air. Lyrianna spun, ducking as the whoosh of the sword went above her head. As she knelt low, she swiped cutting across the beast's legs. It emitted an unintelligible sound yet continued its foray of slashes. Rolling out of the way, the creature's sword clashed on the stone. She staggered, gripping her side, *her injured ribs,* Trinidad thought, worriedly. *This has gone on long enough,* he thought, rushing the oncoming Rav'Arian, slamming into its side. As he did so, the centaurs surrounding the fight moved in and pummeled the toxic creature. One quickly pinned its sword arm. Trinidad watched his queen rise sword in arm, limping and bruised, and filthy from the coal dust, as she made her way for the kill. Her allies restrained the creature's arms and legs. Lyrianna jumped onto its flailing body. Slamming her sword into its chest, cutting off its frenzied movements in one strike. She fell back, and Trinidad was there. He felt her lean on him heavily.

It is over, my queen. Well done. You can rest now. Lyrianna did not—perhaps could not—respond. The fight had undoubtedly consumed her last bit of energy, and she collapsed.

"Hurry! Place her on my back. We must flee," Trinidad commanded to the motley gathering of women.

CHAPTER 24

The Intercourse

"Careful with her," came a terse whisper, somewhere outside of Lyrianna's sub-conscious. She tried to crack her eyelids, but the instant she saw the blinding light, she scrunched them tightly closed again. She tried to listen. *Who is that speaking? Where am I?*

"This is a very old path. We do not have time to move slowly. If the guards catch us here, that could be the end of our hideout. Of our people!"

"Drama does not suit you," came the terse whisperer. "*She* is the most important person to ever step foot on this path. So be careful!"

Lyrianna tried to open her eyes again. This time the dense tree branches overhead momentarily blocked the sun's direct light. She cracked her left eye open, then her right. She was completely surrounded, that was for sure. Wrapped in a strange quilted fabric, it felt as if she were inside a large leaf or cocoon. Everywhere around her smelled of earth—smelled fresh. Even herself! She tried to take inventory of her body. After months of captivity, molestation, beatings, and a complete lack of hygiene, it felt almost foreign to be clean. She knew she would never fully forget her time as a captive. She shuddered at the thought.

Suddenly the whispering voice revealed itself, belonging to none other than the beautiful red-headed centaur. All around her stood the women from the cages. Her litter was gently set down. The women around her looked as beaten and battered as she felt, and she knew if she saw her reflection, her bruises would tell the story of her own abuses. The other voice must have belonged to the nymph nearest the centaur. They both were failing to disguise their frustration with one another.

As if all at once, the sequence of events leading to Lyrianna's freedom returned. She remembered the guards on the tower, the cages, Trinidad, "Where is Trin..." her voice gave out. Struggling to clear her throat and maintain consciousness, her eyes jumped around looking for... She needed him. Feeling close to panic, then she heard the rich voice she had come to love.

"I am right here, Your Majesty," Trinidad said quietly coming from her right side. She looked over to see him standing behind the centaur, relief filling her. The last time she had seen him, he was covered in soot. His freshly cleaned coat gleamed in the light.

"You look good, my friend," she whispered. The warmth in his eyes bespoke the mutual affection they now shared after months of imprisonment. Though his horn was gone, and his mane was short, his presence was still impressive. The nymphs, humans, and centaurs parted as he made his way closer.

"Did we..." She was again unable to formulate her words. Her eyes fluttered with fatigue. Their battle with the Rav'Arians had depleted her last ounce of strength.

"We did, Your Majesty," he concluded. "We saved them all. We are away from the castle, and with the assistance of these former prisoners," he said, nodding to the centaur and nymph, "we will take you to the king," and even softer, he added, *and to your son.* Her eyes opened briefly at that, tears filling her eyes, before falling back into a deep slumber.

As she lay there, one lone tear traced a path down her cheek. He nuzzled her face, wiping it away, before her litter was picked up again for the continued march. He cared more for this woman then most other living souls. During their captivity, he had been time and time again impressed by her resilience and courageous spirit. No wonder Vikaris had been drawn to this captivating woman. She *was* Trinidad's queen. The True Queen. And Trinidad loved her. He watched her sleep peacefully, a serene smile on her lips. Taking his place next to her as her litter barers began to pick their way quietly through the forest, he felt a lightness ease the tension in his shoulders and neck. He was filled with hope as they neared the safe refuge of the Camp.

We are coming, Vikaris and Trixon, he thought. *We are coming, Darion.*

***

"What do you mean 'they are gone'?"

Narco stood in his throne room, after being surreptitiously pulled away from his bed and the conquest of the young maiden's body. He had a splitting headache and was in a very foul mood. *Playing with her was supposed to calm me down after today's news—what is happening?* Even sex had lost its allure it would seem. The adolescent had bothered him with her tight, childlike body and hushed whimpers. The whole time he had been with her, he became more and more angry that it was not Lyrianna's body beneath him. He wanted a *woman*. He wanted the full breasts of the rebel queen. He wanted real resistance. A fighter with passion! The peasant had caved in her struggles giving in to rape far too soon, and no longer held any appeal to him. He felt so disgusted with her that he almost couldn't finish the deed. He was striding toward the chamber door, ready to have a guard remove the wretch, when he heard the forceful knock.

"Sir. The outer guards are asking for you. They say it is urgent." Narco pulled his robes back on, nodding to the servant. "Shall I have her wait, Emperor?"

Without a look back, Narco strode out flicking a hand as if at a pest. "Kill her."

The girl screamed as soon as he was gone. Narco's pace slowed, and he thought about returning to bed, musing to himself about the sexual pique a mere scream could bring. Nothing aroused Narco more, than seeing fear, true fear in the eyes or voices of those before him. That's when he felt at his best—the strongest! Not weak, like his father Valron had treated him. *He had shown him— and I'll show Vikaris, too.*

As he walked his mind returned to Lyrianna. She never fully gave in to the fear—yes, she had the momentary anxiety of the pain awaiting her during the torturous interrogations, but fear of *him*, that never came. No matter what, she never gave in to his advances. She had never broken. He respected that, in a sadistic way. She reminded him so much of his mother, Queen Aliguette. He had always loved his mother. He had always wanted her to... he knew it was unnatural in many eyes, yet in his mind it was beautiful. Narco had long fantasized about them being together, if only his father had been out of the picture. He blamed the imbecile for not slaying the Queen's Unicorn, Trinity, to save Aliguette when she had died from a hunting mishap. He had made sure *that* unicorn suffered when he seized power. He made her regret her careless and selfish act of not saving the queen with her own heart's blood.

Narco craved a woman like his mother—like Lyrianna. *I have to her. All of her.* He had waited to take her fully. He had seen much of her body, yes, and tried to have his way with her on more than one occasion, but she was different. He wanted her to come to him willingly after she was rid of her taxing husband. *Vikaris's death would break her, and then I will have her forever.* His mind filled with scenes of Vikaris's death as he made his way to his throne room.

Narco eyed the cage guards, listening to their tale of hearing him commanding them to appear in the hall. While the guards had left their captives, the females had escaped, and the guards had only now found out what that news would mean for their futures.

"Let me get this straight," Narco said with a forced smile, for this was the second time today his prisoners had gotten away. "You heard *me* in your minds, and so you came running to the throne room, is that it?" His filed nails clicking together as he punctuated each word.

The battle-worn men, all looked down as if they were once again youths receiving an admonishment from a superior officer... albeit, a sadistic one.

"And not one of you thought to leave a guard behind? Just in case?" His condescension and fury oozing forth in his quiet words.

The most seasoned of all the guards looked up at that. "Forgive me, Sire, but we did. The Rav'Arians stayed behind. We came to you, as we were instructed." At the smoldering glance he received from Narco, he added, "Or we thought we were instructed. Once we found that you were not here, we went back and found their corpses. That is why we're here now, Sire. The guards were attacked! The prisoners are gone." He and the men all took a step back, bracing themselves for the rage that was sure to follow.

Narco grimaced at the realization that Lyrianna had not only evaded his clutches but she had now "saved" the female chattel. It had to have been her. He knew she would have been the only person noble—brazen— enough to try it.

Now that is the woman I want, he thought, pondering.

If she and Trinidad had stuck around to save the prisoners, then there was still a chance of catching them.

A smile parted his ugly face. The men dared not breathe, fearing their punishment would be next.

Hours before a different guard had come running with urgent news. He had whispered to the nearby advisor, who stood at the foot of the throne in Morta's absence. The advisor, Porris, paled with the update. As the squat man spoke, Narco knew what had happened!

"NO!" Narco let out the most savage, animalistic cry of his life. *Not her! They'll pay. I'll rip their throat out for losing her.*

Narco fell to his knees. His guards witnessing his collapse as he fell to the floor, covering his face to hide the tears. Mumbling to himself and flailing on the floor, Porris had tried to assist him. That was a mistake, for Narco swiped his fiendish nails, slicing Porris's neck. Just a surface wound really, but the aged advisor reeled from the pain, tripping on his robes. Like clockwork, Narco stopped. Shakily standing up, he pointed a finger at his men, including Porris.

"Bring her to me. Bring me the unicorn. If you fail in this, *your* heads will be my newest castle adornments come nightfall." His voice quivered with rage and loss. "They cannot have made it far. GO! What are you waiting for? FIND THEM NOOOOOOOOOW," Narco bellowed, before collapsing into his throne, unabashedly crying.

None before would have dared laugh. Certainly not his closest soldiers who saw his most abhorrent practices on a regular basis. They had all seen what Narco and the Rav'Arians had done to their Kingdom. The horrors were not stories at all. They were living breathing realities, the worst of which sat madly muttering upon the throne. He didn't care what they thought of him right now, so long as they obeyed. *Find her, must find her,...* he had sat muttering to himself until he spotted the servant girl, and dragged her to his chambers.

The irony was not lost upon him. Here he sat, again, learning that his captives had escaped. Coming back to the present, he looked disgustedly at his incompetent guards, eyeing the oldest one. "WHY ARE YOU STILL HERE? GO! As before, you worthless piles of scum, find Lyrianna and Trinidad. Bring me those captives—or you will all die! They are miiiiiiiiiiiiinnnnnne!"

The men ran out before his tirade concluded, not wanting him to find any other fault in them.

Narco watched the men run to do his bidding. As he sat upon his throne, he contemplated his position... Victory had been within his grasp, and now... *And now what?* he thought. For a man who was strengthened by dark magic and nearing immortality, he did not feel strong. In his deepest inner core, he still felt second best. Like he was out to prove something. If only he had Lyrianna as his queen and Vikaris and Darion's heads on spikes. Then, he could celebrate. Then, he would know true happiness.

This room amongst all others evoked the strangest feelings in him. For this was the room where he had watched his mother, Queen Aliguette, all those years ago. His beautiful, powerful, intimidating mother. There she had ruled Nav'Aria. And there she had announced that Rustusse would take over the Kingdom after her, instead of Narco—her eldest son. Narco's skin grew cold at the memory, and he had to keep his hand from rubbing his bare right forearm.

Narco looked at the sniveling Porris, who was shakily dabbing a handkerchief to the earlier cuts on his neck. "Where is Morta?" His voice was deadly. "He should have been here by now."

Their plan was slipping through his fingers. Narco imagined how it would feel to wrap his hands around Morta's frail neck, squeezing the life out of him—slowly—hearing the vertebrae popping underneath his grip. This had all been *his* idea. Narco fumed. Morta had never been away, and the clarity that comes from one's absence is a wondrous thing, Narco realized.

For years Morta had instructed Narco to wait before launching a full attack on the Camp and leading to the conquest of Kaulter. Never quite ready. "Soon, soon, my Special King," Narco remembered Morta's special name for him since boyhood. As the man had allowed, as he put it, Narco to explore his sexuality. Their relationship had always been close. Intimate. No one else had given him any attention as a boy; no one but Morta. He had always been there for Narco, but it wasn't love they shared. Now, as Narco thought about it, he grimaced at the sudden clarity.

What is in all of this for Morta? Why does he want me to wait?

He remembered Morta telling him before he left: "Soon we will have everything in place for you to become the most powerful ruler this Realm has ever seen." Narco didn't like thinking on this. He already was the strongest ruler the land had ever seen. Had Narco gone against his aged tutor, he might already have been celebrating his victory. *His wedding!* Morta had instructed Narco to wait until his return before initiating a full-out attack, to lead Trinidad and Lyrianna to the ramparts to await Vikaris's capture, and to enter Darion's mind and bring him back— though all that had led to was the Realm having another Marked claim to the throne.

This war has gone on long enough. Narco was done listening to Morta. He was finished with the tutor who had concocted the decimation of the Meridia Kingdom, leading to Narco's coup cycles ago. *I am no one's puppet.*

"Bring me the chalice."

"But Sir..." Porris stopped, horrified. He had just disobeyed the emperor. His hand flew back to the cuts on his neck.

"What did you say?" A savage snarl overtook Narco's face.

"I," Porris stopped, clearly unsure of what to say next. Narco motioned for him to continue. "Morta instructed me to keep the chalice hidden until he returned, Sire."

"He did, did he?" Narco said softly. "Take me to it. At once," he commanded the nervous advisor.

He would view, through the magical liquid of the chalice, where, in fact, Morta was. He would locate Lyrianna, Vikaris, and Darion and bring destruction upon them all. He would be the strongest leader this Realm had ever seen.

"No, on second thought—" He thought back to the

proud, and evasive Trinidad. "—let us first go and visit *the* chamber. We mustn't forget my pets." Narco smiled evilly at Porris, who looked near collapse. Narco assumed Morta had also told him to keep the Emperor away from them as well. Morta typically tended to them. Well, no matter now; Morta was gone, and Narco had a feeling that his special occupants were ready to be battle-tested very soon. *Very soon indeed.*

***

As soon as they were outside, the men stopped near the cages. "Now what?" one guard wheezed, as they stood to catch their breaths. Running in this much armor was difficult for the youngest and fittest of men. They were neither. The youngest soldiers were busy terrorizing the villagers into working and defending the Realm, or at least that is what the latest propaganda had alluded.

The oldest of the group, Carn, spoke first. "Now we track," he said, looking at them all in turn. "Find them *now!*" The men rushed to the cages and began inspecting immediately. Carn took in the open area. Across the way he saw an old coal shed. His mind was already putting the series of events together as he started for it.

Our prey is not far, he thought darkly.

CHAPTER 25

The Assassin

Sweat, saliva, and blood mixed together, coating Darion's mouth, as he rolled and jumped in one fluid movement, spitting as he regained his footing. Edmond, his sparring partner and begrudgingly Darion's only friend, let out a little laugh before passing it off as a cough. He had clipped Darion hard with his shield after failing to cast off his attacks. Darion glared at him before falling back into the "dance of death," as the Swordsmaster liked to call it.

Barson had been working with the two lads tirelessly day in and day out. The boys had gone from using blunted blades, to now working through the various strokes with sharpened swords. After hearing of the attack at Camp, training had been expedited. Triumph oversaw all of it, but in a new way. Gone were Darion's feelings of resentment, or intimidation when he felt Triumph's presence nearby. Now, it was as if Triumph had always been there. As if Darion had always known him. It was comforting, really, having Triumph so undeniably devoted to Nav'Aria—to Darion and his family. The bond that had taken place days before was completely a surprise, and somewhat of a mystery to Darion... and to Triumph.

Darion had no idea what *Denont* meant, only that he had read it scrawled in a sidebar in Vondulus's journal next to an image of a horn. Suddenly the word had popped into his head mere seconds before bonding the unicorn. He secretly feared that it was Narco again entering his mind, but Triumph reassured him that that was impossible. Narco could not enter his mind once in Kaulter; the barrier of the secret island allowed them safe distance from the villain. *Why do you think he has never invaded us, Darion? He cannot find the Isle.* Darion wished, not for the first time, that the island was larger so that the entire rebellion population could just live there... just leave Nav'Aria to Narco and make a new home with his parents here. Deep down though, he knew it could never be so. One look into Vikaris's eyes told him that. His father would never stop until Narco was defeated.

Elsra had been the only soul *not* surprised by the bonding. When pressed by Triumph, she simply said, "Make sure he is ready."

Furthering that conversation was out of the question. Triumph knew when to press his mother, and with everything associated with Darion, she was very tight-lipped. Triumph had even wondered aloud to Darion if it hadn't been her who had planted the ancient word, *Denont,* into Darion's mind. Though bonded to one now, Darion would still never be able to understand the underlying tensions associated with Triumph and his family, or rather, unicorns in general.

Another round of sparring began, pulling Darion from his contemplations. *Good Darion. Lean back. Your right shoulder gives you away. Focus.*

Edmond came at him with a solid cut toward his middle. Darion, hearing Triumph's coaching, leaned back before ushering in a quick block, spin, and thrust that cut into Edmond's new leather grieve.

"Hey," Edmond glowered, "not my new grieves please! This is the nicest thing I have ever owned." Darion laughed at Edmond's sudden vanity—it turned out, the guy had a great sense of humor. Darion ignored his warning though and launched a series of quick cuts and jabs. Edmond dropped the fake pout and fell into step once again. This was going to be their final duel, Barson announced. The afternoon light had given way to evening, and Darion knew Barson had a family to get home to. Darion had other training to get to as well. He nodded in agreement without taking his eyes off his younger, yet stronger opponent.

In the past week, Edmond and Darion sparred daily. Their comradery grew, and they shared quick glances and laughs about Barson, the other practice combatants, and anything else that popped into their minds about life at Kaulter. Darion was grateful for a friend, yet he knew he couldn't become distracted or weaken as an opponent just because he fought a friend. Triumph had reminded him that allegiances sometimes change, and you never know who will be at the other end of your sword one day. *It is best to protect yourself by becoming the best at* everything you set out to achieve.

With one final swing, Edmond came out victorious, again, slashing across Darion's chest plate with a "kill stroke."

"Bah!" Darion threw his sword down at the same time Edmond did. Both boys laughed at their follies of the day and quieted as Barson came for his last words of wisdom. *More like rebuke,* Darion thought. *Here it comes.*

"That makes 3-2. Edmond won the day. Darion, your footwork is quickly improving, but *that* shoulder. You have to lean back. Let the sword lead you. You give yourself away too often."

Darion's cheeks reddened at the critique. Edmond was smirking, self-satisfied at his win. He stood tall, confident...

"And you," Barson directed a glower toward Edmond, in a gruff voice. "What are you smiling about?" Edmond's cheeks now matched Darion's.

"For every mistake Darion makes with his upper body, you make one with your legs. You two are quite the pair. Never have I seen an odder duo of fighters. It is the *dance of death,* not a pig wrestle, boy. Step lightly."

Darion and Edmond looked sheepishly at one another, knowing that Barson viewed them as outsiders who lacked the natural finesse most Nav'Arian soldiers had. Triumph pawed the ground on the outer fence, and Barson made a deep sound in his throat.

"Oh, Triumph. Do not try to tell me you thought that was a fine match?"

Triumph ceased pawing and slightly tilted his head,

avoiding eye contact. Darion shot him an angry scowl for concurring with Barson.

"Sellout," he muttered.

Barson softened his tone, "I am not saying I have not seen improvement, I am just saying that every mistake Darion makes with his arms, Edmond makes with his legs. Together, you make *one* fighter. It is as if you are both compensating for the other's lack of skill. I think fighting alongside each other, you could be unstoppable, but I do not think this is an appropriate match as far as training. Tomorrow, you will have new sparring partners. It is good to have new opponents. A fresh perspective." With that, Barson nodded to them and turned on his heel. Case closed.

Both boys looked glum as they walked silently back to the arms shed to return their practice swords. They had had a great day of training, in their opinion. Darion felt that Barson was being too hard on them.

Doesn't he know who I am? Darion thought, hotly, the adrenaline from the match still coursing through him.

That's exactly why he is doing this, said Triumph. Darion wasn't surprised by the response. He had not been talking to him directly, but Darion knew that Triumph's presence was now always there, welcome or unwelcome.

You are the Marked Heir to the Throne. You have to be ready. Barson is trying to make that happen. You would be wise to listen to his instruction.

But, he doesn't have to be so pushy, Darion thought grumpily.

Yes, he does, Triumph whispered. *You never know when you*

will need to fight for your life. You are the Marked Heir, Darion,
which means you are also the most 'marked' target in all the land!

Darion hadn't thought of it that way. A shiver
overtook his body as he thought about just how many in
the Kingdom probably wanted him dead. He knew all eyes
were on his father, but had he really thought of the
implications to the realm if *he* were imprisoned or killed.
He looked at Edmond, who seemed to be lost in his own
thoughts, too.

Darion lightly pushed him, forcing away Edmond's
grim expression. "Come on 'winner,' let's go see about
some food. Maybe that cute maid you're always looking at
will be there!"

Edmond's worries over sparring completely faded. His
face warmed with a different type of nerves. "Do you
really think so?"

Darion snickered at that, and the two boys, followed
by one large unicorn, traipsed into the dining hall for their
evening meal.

None noted the pair of eyes that had been watching from
behind the cluster of trees near the arms shed. The amber
eyes flickered with mirth. *The target is almost too easy*, the
shadowy figure thought, creeping out of concealment.

***

Seegar stood waiting. He had been tipped off by one of
the sentry guards that Trixon and Antonis's party were
close. Their return trip had been slowed dramatically by
the comatose Riccus and the greater distance of Camp's
new location. Trixon had reported to the king that he was

having to step gingerly to not upset his invalid's wound, while Aalil and Antonis were then forced to carry Ansel and the other prisoner. Seegar had no idea who the other prisoner could be, but he had faithfully obeyed Vikaris.

He knew Carolina would be beside herself with worry. She had been out all day in the forest, picking anything she could. That woman baffled Seegar. She heard her husband had faced an enemy and was now in a coma, and then ran off to the forest to pick greenery. Seegar knew she was one of the most renowned herbalists in the realm, but could she really find something to counter the coma Riccus was in?

If Trixon could not find a cure for the infection, how could Carol, a mere human, hope to do so? Maybe instead she should prepare herself for the inevitable. Seegar wanted to believe that she would find the remedy, yet he was also a realist. He had not been High Councilor for this long by being a dreamer. He had seen too much violence and bloodshed over the years to rely solely on hope. He was more of a pragmatist. He believed in her abilities, but he also knew the depths of the Rav'Arian horrors. He had been there the night of the Fall. He had seen the bloody coup d'état that overtook Rustusse's house.

Shaking his head to clear the unwanted memories, he walked toward the entry gate. The guards there searched the night for any looming threat or undetected presence. Vigilant as ever after the raid. Vikaris had called them to arms and to move the camp, but after hearing that Trixon and the other party were near, he had stalled the move. He had sent the main Camp onward toward the East and commanded his Lieutenant Kragar to run the camp while he was away. Once joined by Trixon, he and the small party would join the main Camp once again. Seegar hoped it was the right decision. He had advised for the king, at least, to return to Kaulter. Though, he didn't ever question his king, for Vikaris was a true leader—always honorable. Still, Seegar hoped that other Rav'Arians weren't lurking in the dark. His thoughts were, not for the first time, troubled...

***

Darion and Triumph talked late into the night. Ever the teacher, Triumph spoke of the common people, and the social dynamics within the Kingdom. Having grown up in a democracy, Darion had never considered the implications of a monarchy—let alone a tyrant such as Narco. With his station came great responsibility, but he also wondered *why* the people were content to move into the future as a monarchy. He didn't voice his thoughts, for he feared Triumph would think his thought pattern treasonous. Though Darion did wonder. *Would he really become king one day? The people wouldn't actually want that— would they? Do I want that?* They were before the frieze again, the great fire crackling as the nights began to cool even further. Darion sank into the plush chair and his thick overcoat.

Staring at the frieze, a lone figure caught his eye. *He's remarkable*, Darion communicated. A centaur of old. A formidable, epic presence, unlike those he had met. Though still formidable, thinking back to his first encounter with Garis, he hadn't seen the likes of this.

Triumph followed his gaze, having grown accustomed to his young prince's scampering thoughts. One might be quick to think Darion was easily distracted, but after the bonding, Darion had proved that his thoughts typically had a purpose—a target. Triumph had praised him, telling Darion that his mind processed rapidly, making connections from the most random of details, and that Triumph was impressed. *The unicorn was impressed!* Darion wasn't ashamed to admit that that acknowledgement had lifted his spirits. Darion felt Triumph's overwhelming pride and loyalty filling him—healing much of the anxiety and pain he had stuffed down for years. Triumph felt like a father, uncle, mentor, and friend all rolled into one. Having Triumph with him made Darion want to try all the harder. Triumph made Darion want to be Nav'Arian.

"Who is that?" Darion asked, thinking that such an impressive figure could have easily taken over the Kingdom.

"That is Elmont. The eldest of the centaurs. It is said that he stood over nine feet tall, almost as tall as the trolls." Darion had yet to see either, so the comparison was lost on him, but he could tell that it was a mighty figure.

"Now, don't get me wrong, I'm glad my dad is king and all, but why..." Darion trailed off, eyeing his companion's large stature. He didn't want to set Triumph off again. That unicorn had a temper like none other.

"Why did the Creator choose Vikaris over Elmont to rule? Is that what you are thinking?" Triumph could have read his mind, Darion figured, but appreciated him asking instead.

"Well, yeah, talking about our society and stuff. It just makes me wonder why *us?*"

"Many have asked the same question over the cycles of our existence. How could the unicorns willingly give up their position of power? And if they planned to, why not give the trolls, centaurs, or even the nymphs a chance at ruling? Why did the Creator choose the humans? None of us will truly know until we meet Him."

Darion knew that Vondulus had been created, and began the Realm, for he had read much of his diary—and learned from Seegar's recitation. He still felt uneasy about the history though.

"Do you think, after having Narco, the people and creatures would even want a king anymore? Are any of the other creatures," he hesitated, "resentful of us?" He had to know. It was his Kingdom after all! He wanted to know what he was up against.

"Resentful? Of you? No, my prince." Triumph said immediately. "Who could resent the Meridias?" Then he was the one hesitating.

Darion studied him. "Triumph?"

After a long pause, Triumph responded, "Well, no one in Kaulter or the Camp resents your family. Those left in the Kingdom, however..." Triumph paused. Darion thought of Edmond and how he had described his upbringing there.

"They would have to resent us there," Darion stated, quietly. "How could they not? Because of us, particularly my father's 'rebellion,' they are penalized. They starve under Narco, because he desires to kill my father more than anything in this world. He needs to feed the Rav'Arians so that they continue searching for him. Isn't that right?"

Triumph's gaze dropped low. He stared at the embers of the dying flames, thinking back to long ago. "Before the Kingdom was split, in my early years, the Meridias were revered," Triumph broke off. He had explained that the lifespans were longer in Nav'Aria, than what they were in Darion's other universe, "it feels like a lifetime ago," Triumph mumbled to himself. Darion studied him. He knew their conversation had taken a turn. He had hit upon a sensitive topic. He dared not breathe.

Triumph's aquamarine eyes became glassy, losing focus, as if he were looking inwardly, remembering a time long forgotten. Darion didn't want to embarrass his friend. Whatever Triumph was thinking about must have been painful. He had never seen him break his haughty façade. Not like this. Darion waited silently. Triumph would continue when he was ready. After a long pause, punctuated by the crackle of burning twigs, smoke began to cloud the room, causing Darion's head to feel light.

Triumph then began his tale. "You know about the night of the Fall?" It was a rhetorical question that needed no response. Darion nodded, his throat seeming to close with trepidation. Triumph cleared his throat, shaking his mane as if to cast off old memories.

Well, what you do not know is of my role in it. I was on watch that night. I was a rising guard at the castle and had recently been promoted. That was my first night back, however, because of my,

Triumph's voice cracked. Breaking. Darion looked at him, and this time he saw tears freely falling. He moved closer to Triumph, realizing that what he was about to say was something that must have weighed heavily upon him for years—for a lifetime.

Triumph shook his head and blew his nose noisily. The sound making Darion's ears ring.

I had just returned from my 'leave.' The hairs on Darion's neck prickled. *My wife, Selestiana, had given birth to twin colts. Our first.* Triumph met Darion's eyes. Pools of pain. Darion's breath caught. Pain that had been masked. Pain that Darion now recognized as so deep that it had become an extension of Triumph. Darion knew that this tale was not one Triumph had told often.

My colts were born early. Twins often do not go the full term, so I have been told. I had had to leave my post suddenly. After spending time with my family until Selestiana was comfortable, I returned to my fellow guards. She was staying in the village outside of the castle. Explaining, *At that time, the village was filled with the guards' families.*

Darion's expression must have changed, prompting Triumph to add, *Though, many of the species kept to themselves even during Rustusse's reign, it was not uncustomary to see all gathered together, as we are now. The 'Empire' as Narco likes to call it, is now more divided than ever. The Rav'Arians guard him and the Realm, while the trolls take advantage of the other creatures, man and beast alike. It was not always so,* Triumph finished quietly.

Darion hadn't once considered that Triumph might have had a family. That *all* of the guards might have families. *You selfish prick*, he chastised himself. *Never once did I wonder what it's been like for Triumph. For any of them. I've only worried about myself.* Suddenly his cozy life in Oregon, didn't seem that unjust. Now that he thought about it, he recalled seeing a couple little centaur younglings running around, baring a striking resemblance to Garis, with their russet coats, proud postures, and already strong sword arms. The soldiers' wives and children must all be here.

Darion nodded slightly at his friend, staying mute. Hoping that Triumph would continue.

His companion began speaking aloud, very softly, "That night, the night of the Fall, is one that I will never forget... for many reasons." Triumph shed his tears unabashed.

"My comrades had bought a few tankards to celebrate the birth of my children." He smiled sardonically at Darion. "Yes, Unicorns can drink alcohol. We have a better tolerance than you humans, that is for sure. That is, we usually do. That night, I had ingested a large amount from my trough as the guards continued to congratulate me. When the alarm came," Triumph sniffed loudly, staring directly at Darion. "I was asleep. I was completely inebriated and sleeping off my comrades' good cheer..." His voice broke. "All while my king and his family were slain." His expression grew so dark, Darion was fearful to move.

"After the commotion spilled out of the castle, I saw my family—Trixon and Trinidad, with Seegar and young Vikaris being ushered out through an interior door near my post. I honestly was so drunk that I thought I was dreaming. I lay there in and out of consciousness, undisturbed." Triumph sucked in his cheeks, taking a shaky breath.

"In the early morning hours, I awoke to the tumult. The fighting had continued through the night, and to my greatest regret of my life, I had slept through it. Drunk on cheap ale." His timbre began to rise as he punctuated each sentence.

"As I slept, the Rav'Arians crept into the Village and killed and captured anyone they could find. I awoke before dawn and knew something was wrong immediately. Though my head pounded, I fled from the castle. I saw many of my comrades' corpses littering the ground as I ran by. Narco and his minions had led the coup and celebrated in the Feast Hall after securing the Castle and Village below. They chanted, 'Azalt! Azalt! Azalt!'" Darion's eyebrows shot up at the word, his skin tingling all over. "That is why I was so angry when you said it the other night," Triumph admitted, darkly. "It is an old word. Something Narco dug up in his studies. It means "Arise, and fight. Arise, and see who will be the victor." Darion sat stunned, the meaning causing a wave of nausea to sweep over him. Triumph picked up his story, his eyes growing glassy once more. "When I got home, I found," he stopped.

Darion felt a cold sweat run down his spine. His ruby sparkled, bathing them in a scarlet glow, as Triumph told of the bloody scene awaiting him.

"Selestiana had fought until the end. I know that," Triumph said it so fiercely that Darion swallowed hard, believing him without a doubt.

"In our home, were two Rav'Arians. They were near the doorway. She had killed them before they could abduct both of our colts. Zhoe, my boy," Darion heard the faint whisper of a father's pride in the name. "Zhoe had bled out by the time I found him, just like his mother. The beasts had clawed them across their necks and..." Triumph let out a small sound as his voice continued to crack, emotionally. "Selestiana had slain one though, for her horn was covered in blackish tar, and the beast's stomach had been cut through. She was ferocious, my wife..." he trailed off again. Darion felt his own tears streaming down.

"My girl," Triumph's voice completely broke now, and Darion put a palm against his friend's neck, with a gentle pat, Triumph rubbed his cheek against Darion's shoulder.

"My girl, Zola. She looked just like her mother," he said this part almost to himself. With more force, he continued, "She was taken. I tracked down the Rav'Arian that had taken her. The white strands of hair still hanging from his talons... and the blood," his voice rising to an edge as sharp as a knife, "dripping from his beak." The unicorn swallowed, loudly. "I killed him. Slowly. He took everything from me, and I tore him apart... I buried my wife and son outside the village, with the help of a neighbor. I intended to head straight to the castle to kill Narco then and there. I was crazed with grief, as you can imagine," he looked at Darion, briefly. "But then I heard my mother's voice, beckoning me to come to her. In my fury, I hadn't even remembered that she had been present at the castle. I marked a place near their graves for Zola, though without her body, I could not give her a proper burial... and I fled. Here. I found Trinidad, Trixon, Elsra, and the others..." His blue eyes filled with such loss, tears falling freely. His voice broke and entered Darion's mind.

Can you imagine, Darion? Knowing that because of you, your family was killed. Because of my weakness as a father and husband, they were KILLED! Can you imagine what that does to someone? He exhaled loudly, breathing so fast that Darion feared his heart might burst. *This,* Triumph spat, *this I have to live with. This is what makes me get up every day. This pain. This rage. So, Darion, to answer your question, yes, the people and those left behind do resent your family. But it is not you that they resent. There is just one that we resent. Just one that we hate. Narco. My story is not the worst of it, though. There are hundreds of stories just like mine... and worse. That is the Fall, Darion. That is when our peaceful Realm was massacred by that sadist. That stain upon the Meridia name. Those left behind, or who have been unable to get away, are now Narco's slaves. He uses the Rav'Arians to keep them in check, and he overworks them to the point of starvation and exhaustion. We have smuggled out all that we can, but there are still so many out of our reach. This, Darion, is why I fight. Though I will never—ever—forgive myself.* Triumph paused refocusing on the fire. *I know, through the help of your father and the Unicorn Council, that the villain here is not me, but Narco.*

Darion didn't know what to say, yet he wanted to reassure his friend. He lifted his hand to brush the tear from his companion's cheek, as he did, his heavy sleeve slid up revealing his mark, luminescent as ever. As he touched Triumph he closed his eyes, rested his forehead against Triumph's, and replied quietly in his mind, *We will defeat him, and he will answer for his crimes. HIS crimes against your family. I promise you.*

Just then a blinding white light filled the room, and Darion felt an odd sensation on his arm. He looked to see his Mark growing rapidly as if someone were compelling the design. With it came a series of strokes so unique that Darion wouldn't have been able to recreate them without intensive study.

"What the," he started, as Triumph blinked rapidly trying to clear his teary eyes. "That looks like..." he began, his words drowned by a blood curdling scream filling the air.

"Mother!" Triumph yelled, quickly ordering Darion to stay behind him, as they ran toward Elsra's chambers.

***

"There you are!" Vikaris exclaimed as he spotted Trixon carrying Riccus's comatose body, Antonis and Aalil close behind. He ran to his friends, wrapping his arms around Trixon's neck in a tight hug. The only other time he had been parted from Trixon, since their bond, was when Trixon had run off with Lyrianna, resulting in her capture. *I am glad you are safe,* Vikaris said quietly. Trixon's ferocity and passion is what had drawn Vikaris to him at an early age. They understood each other. Respected one another. *You did the right thing rescuing, Ansel. I forgive you for leaving... but do not do it again,* Vikaris instructed.

Trixon rumbled in his mind, not necessarily agreeing. He belatedly noted that Trixon was carrying Riccus and Ansel. He quickly reached for the boy and gave him a fierce paternal hug. The boy let out a cry, gladly going to his uncle's arms. Emotions were raw. Seegar ushered them into the king's tent for refreshment and medical attention, knowing Carolina was waiting.

"This way, this way," Seegar said, drawing them into the interior of the large tent. It was already late, and candles and lanterns lit the tent.

Inside the opening, Carolina stood vigil. Her face pale, eyes rimmed in red, as if she knew what would be before her eyes any moment. Vikaris gripped her shoulder as he passed her, to set the boy down. He had been shocked to see Riccus.

Antonis entered followed by Trixon. Vikaris rushed to help him lift Riccus from the unicorn. "Carol," Antonis breathed out, as he saw her. Vikaris knew he was thinking she looked to have aged a cycle in the short span since he had been gone.

"Let me see him," Carolina sounded on the verge of panic or tears—or both.

"He is here, he is here," Seegar soothed, as he directed Antonis to set him on the cushions before them. Servants stood ready to assist them, and quickly set to the task of stripping Riccus's clothes and cleaning his body. From Rick's festering wound wafted a foul odor. Blackened skin and red streaks ran across Rick's abdomen. Carolina let out an anguished wail and fell to his side, clutching at his limp hand.

Vikaris felt helpless, but knew he would only get in the way. Medicine was not his forte. His giftings were found in leadership and on the battlefield. All he could do was pray to the Creator and learn more of the incident from his friends. The party stood there solemnly, as if in silent prayer, all praying for the fearless, good-natured Keeper. Vikaris's eyes brimmed with unfallen tears as he watched Carolina gingerly lift Riccus's face and press her lips to his forehead.

Vikaris knew that this was, *again*, his fault. He hated himself in that moment. First Lyrianna, then Gruegor, then Dalinia, and now Riccus! *How many must fall for me? And for what?*

Trixon nudged him then, pushing him toward the other room, not allowing Vikaris his self-indulgence of guilt. *Thoughts like that will not help Riccus... or defeat Narco.* Seegar had seen to Ansel. The boy was also in need of medical assistance and rest. He nodded to his High Councilor as he moved to the next room, knowing that Riccus and Ansel were in as good of care as any under Carolina and Seegar's watchful eyes.

As they entered the next room, Vikaris was startled to see Aalil behind Antonis. He had briefly noted her presence, but not the bundle she carried. That is, until she threw it as his feet.

"You need to look at this," Antonis said forebodingly, as he, Aalil, and Trixon all glowered at the hooded figure at the foot of their King. Trixon let out a low snarl. Vikaris heard him before he saw him. As Antonis pulled off the brown makeshift hood, Vikaris reeled in hatred.

"You!" He reached for his sword without a moment's hesitation. Morta's reddened eyes practically glowed in the candlelight. He lay there, wriggling like a worm in his bonds. Laughing. *The bastard was laughing as Riccus lay there in the throes of a poisonous death.* It was too much! Vikaris struck out at the man with his sword cleanly removing his left hand without so much a twinge of remorse. The severed hand twitched briefly, before falling still in a puddle of blood. Morta's chuckles turned to spasming cries of pain.

Antonis kicked him squarely in the stomach while Aalil drew her blade.

"Enough!" Trixon yelled so vehemently, that Vikaris shot back, startled. He had never heard Trixon yell like that.

"If we wanted to kill him, we would have already done it, Vikaris." Trixon glared harshly at him. "If you kill him, Riccus dies. Darion may die. We need this…" Trixon pawed the ground, "this *vermin* for interrogation. For information."

Trixon was right, of course. Vikaris knew it but would show no contrition. *This man is responsible for the death of my father! Of my family! This is the monster who filled Narco's head with tales of power and treason. This is the man who had stolen everything from me.*

Vikaris held Trixon's fiery gaze, until finally acquiescing. "Fine," he said, then looked at Antonis. "Cauterize the wound. We will keep him alive. I will know *every* detail of the castle, my wife, and of my uncle before his heart stops beating."

Trixon nodded, as Antonis reached for a blade and the nearest candlestick.

***

"It will not heal," Carol said, with hooded eyes, as the

moonlight filled the tent. Her dark circles aging her greatly. "There has to be something we can do—some way to help him," she implored. Seegar stood helpless. *There must be something....*

Carol continued her frenzied speech, "Maybe there is a root or plant that we need... it could... could counter the effects. I need time to gather. Yes—a plant substance. I can kind find it. I will find it. There has to be something." Her eyes pleaded with Seegar, as if pleading with the Creator himself.

Seegar knew that 'time' was the one thing they didn't have. The pallor of Riccus's skin, and the croaking sound of his shallow breathing demanded urgency. Seegar, seeing her desperation and noting the fervor of his king from the previous night, knew the only thing that could possibly help Rick was not here.

"We must take him to Kaulter. At once." Seegar said in an absolute voice. He knew she had neither slept nor eaten since she had heard of the attack days ago. She had stood vigilant near her husband. She would not be able to keep it up much longer—let alone, traverse the woods alone to find an elusive cure. *No, we need to leave... immediately.*

As if in echo to Seegar's response, the king agreed, stepping into the room. "Then, we will head to Kaulter," Vikaris responded, having heard his High Councilor's pronouncement. "Send a messenger now. Our soldiers will remain under Garis's charge. Narco must not find them." He looked over at the bunk where Ansel was sleeping. The poor boy's world had been completely shattered, and Vikaris watched as even his sleep was terrorized by the memory of the recent events. Vikaris again prayed for peace to come to the boy—at least during sleep. As if on cue, the boy's worried face softened, and he fell into a deep slumber. Thanking the Creator, Vikaris began his preparations.

This was it. We're finally retreating to Kaulter. He prayed for his wife and for Trinidad, hoping that she could hold on. If only there was room for all his followers, but he knew that Elsra kept her limits on her population for a reason. It would do him no good to have everyone starve. No, he would retreat, but his force would stay here ready to attack as needed.

Now that Antonis and his party had returned, Vikaris was helpless to what to do for Lyrianna and Trinidad. No rescue was coming.

You have to hold on, darling.

***

Lyrianna stirred. She could smell the cool, dewy air around her, and see the stars above. A rare shooting star streaked across the night's sky. Looking over, she saw Trinidad hovering near her right shoulder.

"Where are we?" she asked him quietly. She knew they were away from the castle and vaguely remembered the overheard conversation hours ago.

Trinidad whispered in her mind. *We are on a very ancient trail, my queen. The nymphs and centaurs are taking us to Vikaris.*

How, she mouthed. *How would they be able to find his Camp?* Vikaris was constantly on the move and using the secrets of the unicorns to conceal their hideaways.

One of the centaurs, the red-headed one, apparently is from Elmont's house. Lyrianna's eyes widened remembering stories told of Elmont, the eldest and most powerful centaur. Narco had wiped that line out cycles ago. Myrne's kin was now the oldest centaur clan.

She glanced at the red-headed centaur. The one who had been horrifically abused. A bloody patch on her scalp showed where the hair had been torn as she had been dragged. Her pale skin revealing her battering and bruising as the hours passed by. *As does mine,* Lyrianna thought. Her body felt oddly clean, though; someone had managed to bathe her. Unfortunately, she knew she would have permanent damage from the abuses she had taken. Her little finger, for example, stood stick straight and had not healed properly. Another finger was completely numb on her other hand, having sustained nerve damage. Her arms bore the spidery marks of the host of cuts and slashes she had endured over the last months. She wondered how this proud figure before her, seeming to lead the party, had been so ravaged by the monsters earlier, and still held her head high. *Will I ever be able to do that again?*

She must be of Elmont's house, she admitted to Trinidad. Then added, *How is it that they are all still here? They could have come to Camp earlier,* she stated, wishing to understand.

They said they have been watching Narco and smuggling supplies into the Kingdom to aid those there for years. They have built up their own resistance, it would seem, at least until a supply drop went awry and they were captured.

But why not let us know? We could have helped them!

Lyrianna thought, utterly baffled.

Trinidad shook his head subtly before the leader of the group came before her vision. A nymph shuffled nearby as well.

"We did not believe the rumors, Your Majesty," said the centaur.

Lyrianna made to sit up. She had been carried in a litter for much of the night. "What rumors?"

The red-headed centaur nodded to those in the front and called to make camp. Their enclosure was a netted area surrounding the fruit, fir, and pine trees. Fireflies swarmed overhead alighting their path. The "trail" was remarkable... and populated. As Lyrianna looked around, heads popped out from all over.

"Allow me first to introduce myself, Your Majesty. My name is Cela, and I am the leader of this party. We were captured recently, and thanks to you, we are now free. Please forgive us for not coming to your aid." And then, in quiet lament added, "If only we had known you were imprisoned."

Lyrianna grabbed the woman's wrist and smiled warmly at her. "No one here should apologize for what Narco did. But tell me, why are you all still here? You could have joined us. Many of the centaurs and nymphs are with us, yet I have never heard of you all surviving. You may have relatives still living at our Camp," she said, her eyes rising to look over the dozens of faces emerging from the trees.

Cela studied her for a moment before speaking, plainly struggling to keep her emotions at bay. "After the Fall, we were cut off from our species. Many of us fought *that* night, and our families were the ones imprisoned by the Rav'Arians. We," she nodded to those around her, "had escaped, and have since been aiding the villagers." Then she looked solemn. "We were told that you were killed. We were told that Vikaris had also been killed, and that another has been fighting to keep the rebellion alive. None of us truly believed it, though we did not have any substantive evidence that you were alive either. We did not know how to find you, and we could not leave our clansmen to Narco. All we know is what the Callers tell the community, and what news is circulated throughout it. From what we have gathered from the Mighty Trinidad, it is all untrue," she said, almost questioningly.

Lyrianna's temper rose thinking of Narco's lies and propaganda. "You mean, the people in the village, do not know that Vikaris—their Rightful King—still lives? That my husband is fighting for them?"

Cela shook her head. "No, the young are indoctrinated now, especially since Narco's commandments were sent out with the Callers."

"What Callers? What Commandments are you speaking of?"

"The Callers come out once each week with a patrol, and all are forced to gather to hear the latest 'news.' They speak of Narco's noble efforts at protecting our Realm against the treasonous rebel trying to destroy the Meridia family. They have completely manipulated the history, and the people are told that Narco is the last of the bloodline. That a rebel from a faraway land had killed Rustusse and

Vikaris before escaping to the North. Not all believe it though, Your Majesty," she said reassuringly as she took in Lyrianna's lethal expression. "But any who speak the truth, or against Narco, are mercilessly tortured, and their families are put to death. The people are overworked, and starving. They have no other option but to cow down and 'believe' the Callers."

Cela, whom Lyrianna had seen mercilessly raped and beaten earlier, seemed strong and her voice grew harder as she relayed Narco's hold on the Kingdom. Lyrianna felt the heat rising in her body, growing angrier with every revelation.

"Narco's 'Commandments' came out a few years ago... No one is allowed to speak the names of the former Meridia family members. None can go to school, unless they join the military. There they can be given an education approved by Morta, Narco's lead advisor. None can question Narco or speak to the Rav'Arians. The people—and beast alike—are heavily worked... and taxed."

"Those poor people," Lyrianna whispered. She had heard dark stories from survivors of the Kingdom over the years, but nothing this extensive. Taking in the battered women before her, she wanted to ask why there were no males with them, but Cela beat her to it.

"Early on," Cela added, "they took our menfolk. Killing most of them."

"But why..." Lyrianna cut off, the bile rising in her throat as she realized why Narco would want so many females left behind.

Cela saw understanding in her Queen's eyes and nodded. "He wishes for a new generation. A new empire, where the young grow up only knowing him as the leader. By killing off most of the males who had raised arms against him, he now has had cycles of young males brought up only learning about himself, and his 'love' for them, as he calls it."

Lyrianna felt sick. She wanted to ask more—to know more! All this time, they had feared those who remained did so willingly. Then they had begun to learn—through a few escapees—that some were enslaved to work the land. But nothing, nothing, like this had ever been shared with her or Vikaris. Hot tears flooded her eyes, and hate filled her heart.

Damn you, Narco, she thought bitterly. *I should have ripped out your coal black heart.*

"We need to keep moving, Your Majesty," Cela pressed. "As you know, we were captured recently. Narco's monsters do not know of this Trailhead yet, but we were captured not far from here. We must keep moving. Some of the nymphs have heard 'calls,' that they had once written off as echoes of old and now believe to be their sisters and brothers calling from the trees in the North. They are calling from a place of freedom. We must hurry to them. We still have a very long journey before us, and we are low on provisions. We must not delay."

***

Darion and Triumph rushed to Elsra's room. The door stood open, and loud wails and sobs came from inside. Guards filled the hall, rushing to the chamber.

Darion felt goosebumps run the length of his entire body, afraid of what awaited them; however, nothing could have prepared him for such a grisly array.

Darion smelled it before he saw it. Blood. Everywhere. It reminded him of hitting the deer, back in Oregon. It seemed like a lifetime ago, but his heightened senses brought it all to the forefront of his mind.

He could smell the cypress and sage incense burning; He could smell Elsra's lavender oil she washed into her mane; he could smell a puddle of blood that spilled out from the corpse of Xenia, Elsra's granddaughter.

"What happened?" Triumph whispered, full of raw emotion at the sight of his niece's body, rushing to his mother's side, only moments after telling of his slain family.

Elsra wept, kneeling on all fours, her muzzle reddened with blood as she rubbed the spot where Xenia's horn had been cut. Darion noted the deep slit across the neck, revealing the source of the blood. Xenia had been murdered, as well as, her horn shorn at the very base. Drigidor, he noted belatedly, lay beside Elsra, a guard beginning to attend to his wounds. He had various slashes across his chest and neck, though he was still alive. Darion could see the rapid rise and fall of his chest. A trickle of blood came from near his horn's orbital, as if a knife had begun to saw at it.

I'm gonna be sick. The room and its cloud of blood and incense made Darion nauseated. Since all were naturally focused on the Regent and unsure of what to do next, no one noticed Darion vomiting in the basin nearest the door.

Elsra looked up, as if seeing everyone gathered in her room for the first time. "Guards," she shouted, regaining some of her wits, "*find* the assassin!" Many of the guards—human, centaur, and unicorn—had already begun to search the halls and had ordered for the emergency chimes to be rung. "*No one* leaves this building!" Elsra's voice shouted in the minds of all of those gathered before her.

Darion tried to comprehend the scene. Splayed soup bowls and grains on the floor near the bodies. The blood... so much blood... and the unicorns.

Triumph murmured soothingly into his mother's ear as she nuzzled Drigidor, her shoulders shaking—whether with sorrow or fury—or both. The guard attending Drigidor's wounds gave her a hopeful smile, explaining that the cuts were shallow, and though he had lost a lot of blood, he would live. It appeared he had fought off the assailant.

"Elsra," Darion said softly, not wanting to disturb her in her grief yet needing to know what had happened. His pulse quickened. His Mark tingled in his shirtsleeve, and as he rolled it up, he saw that new symbols traced up his arm. His ruby glowed bright. Something was amiss. Obviously there had been a murder, but he felt something foreign, besides himself. *A foreign element.* Something out of place. He began searching the area near the spilled meal and came upon the bowls. The smell was fetid. *Why hadn't he noticed it before?* It smelled... unnatural. As he reached for one, he gritty black sediment collected at the bottom of the bowl.

He gasped. "Poison," he said, holding the bowl out for Triumph to inspect.

"Show me," Elsra commanded, rising and coming to stand near Darion, looking every part the Regent and no longer the grandmother in mourning. Her luminous eyes, taking on a darker purple hue in the light, bore into the bowl.

"Who brought you this meal?" Darion asked without pause, his mind already clicking the events into place.

Elsra stood stunned. "My maid, Alice," she said softly. Darion pictured the beautiful auburn-haired teen with the golden eyes that had apparently waited on Elsra for the past few years. "You think she is responsible?" Elsra's eyes widened, searching his and Triumph's. She murmured to herself, but with Darion's heightened hearing he made out her words. "I am the most powerful unicorn; surely I would have detected an evil presence within her my own home!"

Seegar had told Darion that Alice had been an orphan. On a secret Kingdom patrol one day, a Camp soldier had found her wrapped in a tiny bundle near a fig tree. With her was a tiny stuffed doll, and that was it. The guard had brought her back to Camp, and Seegar had sent her to Kaulter to be raised by a kind family there. She had worked for Elsra, for the last few years.

Darion, though surprised, prodded. "Where is she?" Elsra, it was clear, was having trouble believing that Alice could do something like this. Looking around, she suddenly frowned, "She is not here."

Darion looked to the nearest guard. "Find Alice the maid. Find anyone from the kitchens, too. No one leaves here. Do you understand? Tell your commander." The guard paused staring at him, and then back to the mighty Unicorn Regent, obviously wondering from whom he should take orders. "What are you waiting for, *GO!*" Darion said with more force than intended, yet the effect was worth it. The man ran down the hall to find his fellow guards.

Darion knew he was the Rightful Heir, and this act of treason had been committed against his bonded companion's family. He also knew that if an assassin attacked the unicorns, an attack upon him was imminent. He loosened the blade at his belt. His goosebumps returned, but this time he didn't feel fear. He felt ready. He rolled his hardened shoulders, tested from his time training with the sword, ready for the fight ahead. Triumph nodded at him, his eyes blazing with rage. Triumph also stood ready.

***

"What is that sound?" Antonis asked, his soldier's instincts reacting as the chiming of a bell reverberated off the Village square and echoed into the hills. Sword in hand, he guided Trixon who carried Riccus, with Vikaris, Seegar, Carol, and Aalil down the worn path to the Fortress. Seegar and Vikaris had made quick preparations and led the large party, having only enough time to send a sentry guard from the Portal entrance to the Isle of Kaulter, where he was expected to announce their arrival and the need for immediate help. Leaving in the night after Carol had made known that Riccus couldn't wait another moment. They emerged in Kaulter, expecting aid, yet what they found was far from reassuring.

Beacon lights twinkled throughout the square and near the Fortress. Armed soldiers—unicorns and men alike—ran past the party without a second glance as they rushed toward the source of the noise.

"Darion," Vikaris breathe. He took off at a dead sprint. Antonis cursed and charged after him, followed closely by Aalil.

Trixon yelled for them to wait. He couldn't run for fear that he would further hurt his charge. "That damned man! What is he thinking running off like that?" Trixon demanded loudly. Seegar, looked as if he was going to remind Trixon of his impulsive flight a matter of days ago, but after one look at his smoldering gaze, Seegar chose to remain silent, instead shifting the sleeping Ansel in his arms.

"He will be all right," Seegar said instead, and Trixon didn't know if he meant Vikaris, Riccus, or Ansel. He hoped for all three and he picked up his cadence, ignoring Carolina's whimpering caution to be careful.

Antonis arrived close on Vikaris' heels, shocked to see the king denied entry by the Fortress guards.

"What is the meaning of this? Make way for your king!" Antonis bellowed, staring them down angrily. Before they could answer, Vikaris pulled off his cloak revealing his large glowing ruby. The guards stepped back, gasping before falling into a salute.

"Your Majesty," they said in unison.

"We did not know it was you, Sire," one guard squeaked.

"What has happened?" Antonis interjected, eyeing the nervous guards and the scene before them. Guards marched up and down the halls, and many of the Fortress staff, kitchen workers by the looks of them, were seated in rows under close guard in the Great Hall.

"There has been an attack. In the Regent's chambers. No one is to come or go in the building," the youth gulped, eyeing the king—and then Antonis. "That is, besides you, Majesty."

Vikaris nodded at him, "I have a party coming up the main pathway. Riccus, the Keeper, is very ill. He needs medical attention right away. You *will* allow Trixon, Riccus, Carolina, Seegar, and my nephew to pass." With that, the king began running toward Elsra's chambers. Antonis gave the guards one lingering stare, for good measure. The youth gulped, nodding.

Vikaris searched for Darion with his eyes sweeping the room and exhaling after seeing him. He hadn't realized he was holding his breath. The boy looked older in only the few days they had been apart. *He was not a boy, but a man.*

Darion stood in his fitted black shirt, the sleeve rolled up on his Marked arm, his dark features with piercing green eyes making a striking figure as he ordered the guards about. His sword hand flexing near the handle. Vikaris felt relief and pride flood his body.

"Darion," he called out, striding toward him.

"Father!" He ran to the man's embrace, and all quieted in the room as they saw the intimate reunion between father and son. As Vikaris withdrew from the hug, he caught the eye of Edmond standing nearest Darion. Vikaris nodded to him, remembering the boy.

And then his eyes fell upon Elsra, lying near Drigidor and a body covered in a large dark sheet. The pungent aroma of blood filled the room.

"What happened?" he asked, coming to stand near Elsra. She stood, tilting her head in the direction of her interior chamber, where they could speak freely. Vikaris, Darion and Triumph followed. Vikaris saw Darion and Antonis nod at one another.

Elsra walked to the window. The sun's rays beginning to cast out the shadows from the night before.

"Xenia is dead," she replied, not taking her eyes from the shining horizon. "Drigidor was hurt, but those tending his wounds believe he will be all right."

She explained how another unicorn, not of the family line, but a strong healer all the same, had come forward to help tend Drigidor's wounds. His most severe cuts were already binding themselves, with the assistance of Greca, the young female unicorn, though such work had greatly sapped her strength and she had had to be escorted out to rest from her using her "gift."

"How? Who?" Vikaris's questions tumbled out all at once. Xenia had been one of his mentors during his studies in Kaulter. Her kind laugh, and humble intelligence had helped him through many difficult days of lessons.

Elsra raised her chin sharply, indicating for him to stop so she could explain.

"Last night, I had invited Xenia to sup with us. It was late, and I wanted to discuss Darion's progress as well as any news from the Camp." She met Darion's eyes briefly before continuing.

"Alice, my servant, brought us our evening meal as usual. I had told her there would be another unicorn joining us, and she had said she would have the kitchen make my favorite soup," she scoffed.

"The vile wretch!" Triumph grumbled. Vikaris was surprised by the anger emanating from Triumph.

Elsra nodded as if in agreement, before continuing, "After she had left the meal, I received a note from a guard saying there was a message from Camp. From you, I presumed." She looked at Vikaris. Her violet eyes were large and shining with unshed tears. "I told him I would come with him, for I wanted to invite Triumph to join us. I knew he had been instructing the prince, and I wanted to see how they were doing."

"After receiving the note, I saw Triumph and Darion immersed in a deep conversation, and decided to return to my supper, leaving the pair undisturbed." Pausing, she shook her mane, before continuing, "When I returned, my room was quiet. It was strange to not see a guard or hear any conversation spilling from within. As soon as I walked in, I saw the reason for that. The guard's throat had been slit, just as my sweet Xenia's had been... before... before..." She paused, unable to speak the words.

Darion took over. "Before her horn was cut."

Vikaris's blood boiled. He felt Trixon joining the party, awash with his own fury.

Elsra nodded to her grandson before continuing, "It appears Drigidor put up quite a struggle. Though the assailant tried to remove his as well, he fought off the assassin. He is very groggy, however, and has not spoken since the attack to identify his attacker."

Darion had brought in the bowl and held it up now. "That is because of *this*." He pointed to the poisonous resin at the base of the bowl.

"Lei," Elsra explained, "one of our main healers here has identified it as a sulfurous substance, found near the Shazla Desert. He says it can be deadly if consumed in large quantity, but its main symptom is fatigue and lethargy. One or two drops can knock out a large beast, such as a unicorn or troll, and can kill a smaller victim, such as a man." Her eyes held Darion's before looking at Vikaris.

"But why the horn?" Antonis interrupted from the doorway, Aalil elbowing him to remain silent. Vikaris nodded for the pair to join them.

Triumph's voice thundered, "It appears Narco's agents have a farther reach than we thought." Vikaris felt the hairs on the back of his neck rise, as the meaning of the unicorn's words took hold. *He has breached Kaulter?* Fear gripped Vikaris, as he looked toward his son. *Narco cannot have him,* he thought fiercely, stepping closer.

"The horn is for Narco?" Antonis' expression was one of incredulity. "What could he possibly want with a unicorn horn?"

That is not all, Trixon added telepathically. He had inspected his cousin's wounds. *Her lifeblood has been collected,* he shared, given the interspersed droplets that made their way out the servant's chamber and then out the window. The guards were examining the trailed blood as he entered.

Suddenly all understood. The assassin, whom they now presumed to be Alice the servant, had taken Xenia's horn and lifeblood to give to Narco. The dinner bowls had been inspected. It was clear that she had intended to take all three diners' lives, and thereby, horns. Elsra shuddered.

"She must not leave the Isle," Elsra said coldly, all those before her nodding in agreement. "What is her motive?" Elsra wondered. "How had Narco gotten to her?" Looking around, she noted that they all seemed to be searching for meaning in the tragic event.

"The portal," Elsra said suddenly. "With the horn, she may be able to use it. I must speak with the guards immediately." She looked them all over sternly. "No one leaves here," Vikaris, though the King, nodded along with the rest at the elderly Unicorn's command.

"No one leaves here," Vikaris agreed.

CHAPTER 26

The Reunion

"Where is he? I need to see him," Rick said softly. His
country drawl even more recognizable now that he was
weakened with injury.

Carolina smiled, staring with wonder at her husband.
He is alive. That was all that mattered to her, well, that and
Darion. Sickened with fear, she had spent the night
worrying for her husband and filled equally with dread for
Darion. Having been abandoned by Vikaris and Antonis,
and then forgotten by Trixon once arriving at the fortress,
Carol, Seegar, and Riccus made their way to Lei's
medicine chamber on one of the outer wings of the
unicorn home. The chiming warning bells had had
everyone on high alert, and rightly so, for she now knew,
there had been a murder.

"Antonis went to fetch him, Rick. Just hold your
horses," she chided, lovingly. After learning of Xenia's
death and the terrible attack, Elsra questioned why the
king had returned. Remembering Riccus, he had explained
how Rick had been injured by a poisonous blade in

Ansel's rescue.

Without hesitation, Elsra called for the cover on her granddaughter's corpse to be quickly removed. She called for Lei to come. He collected some of Xenia's pooling lifeblood—still warm—and laid cloths soaked in the unicorn's blood onto Riccus's wound. Almost immediately, the blackened skin began to take on a healthy pink hue, and by morning he had come out of his coma. Once again, the healing power of a unicorn's blood amazed the onlookers.

Before Elsra left to return to her wounded husband, Carolina called for her. Crying softly, she said, "Thank you, Elsra. I am so sorry for your loss."

Elsra held her gaze and said even softer, "At least her death will now hold some meaning. Xenia would have given her lifeblood willingly if she knew she could heal someone with a mortal wound. That is just how she was... That is how her mother, Trinity, was. This," Elsra nodded toward Rick, "this, has made something beautiful out of something terrible. She would have liked that." And then she had glided away, as Carolina had rushed sit at Rick's side.

Interrupting her thoughts, Darion ran in, followed closely by Triumph, and then his Edmond.

"Dad," he said without hesitation, running to Rick's side.

"There you are, son," Rick drawled, his hazel eyes shining. *His son.* Nothing would ever change that feeling, Carolina knew, even though he was Vikaris's heir. "You look strong," he said, sizing Darion up. In just a short while, they could tell that Darion had grown—in his training. His confidence. "You look... Nav'Arian." Riccus said, and Carolina knew his heart was swelling with pride—much like her own.

"I figured it was time," Darion said laughing, running his hand through his long hair, and falling back into his and Rick's easy exchange. Darion smiled over at Carolina. "Hi, Mom," he said, hugging her tightly. Just then Vikaris walked in, smiling at the familial warmth they shared.

Riccus struggled to sit up, and before Carolina could admonish him, the king did. "Stop that," Vikaris said, pressing the Keeper down with a firm but loving hand.

Rick's stubborn voice squawked, "There you go again, ordering me about. If I want to bow to my king, then no one can stop me." Carol, Darion, and Vikaris all shared a knowing smile, as Riccus glowered teasingly at them.

"Oh, I see," Riccus said, jokingly. "I am out for a couple of days, and now everyone thinks I am an invalid. Bah!"

They all smiled at the levity, knowing that Rick's coma was anything but comical. The thought of what might have been remained unspeakable. Rick, Carol, and Darion spent much of the day catching up, as Vikaris was in and out with his royal responsibilities. Alice had yet to be found, and it chilled them to think that the murderer was still out there. For whatever reason, the unicorns could not locate her. Even with their telepathic and mind-scanning powers, none could find her. It was as if she had vanished.

Guards followed Vikaris and Darion closely wherever

they went. None were as resolute as Trixon and Triumph though, who did not leave the royals alone. Vikaris had informed the Keepers of his interrogation with Morta. Carolina had been too overwhelmed with Riccus's care to give the prisoner a second glance. The king informed them that he had left Morta with Garis and the soldiers at camp. They were commanded to keep him alive, but to keep him bound so as not to escape. They would send word if they discovered anything else through his interrogation.

Elsra, Trixon and Triumph had had their own catching up to do, sadly, while planning the burial of their beloved Xenia. It had been a long while since a unicorn had been slain. Their lifespans expanded that of humans, and they rarely died from wounds such as this—at least, not since the Fall. Though many still fought in Vikaris's army, as Trixon himself did, none had died in battle for many years. The Rav'Arians seemed to avoid them, something that Vikaris and the Council had long speculated about. Was it only coincidence, or had Narco ordered his beasts to spare the unicorns?

It was a quiet few days in Kaulter while everyone tried to make sense of the attack—to learn from it, and to locate the perpetrator. The guards stood ready. The villagers were instructed to limit their activity, and a nightly curfew was implemented until Alice was found. Security to and from the Isle was on high alert.

Three days after the attack, Vikaris had come to visit his

son, whom he found with the Keepers. A less confident man may have been jealous of the affection the three shared, but Vikaris certainly was not. These were his dearest friends, and he knew that they had taken supreme care of *his* son. *Their son,* he thought, watching them. *No,* he countered, looking at Darion, who shared such a striking resemblance to himself. *Our son.*

As the group discussed Darion's training and the future of Nav'Aria, as well as the bleak condition Lyrianna and Trinidad must be facing, they were interrupted by a loud knock on the door.

Antonis pushed in unceremoniously, followed closely by Trixon, and then...

Filling the doorway stood an emaciated horse without a mane. Though with closer inspection, none could mistake him as a common horse. His aura remained powerful and spoke for itself with his weary presence, even he was lacking his horn. Riccus and Carolina gasped in unison. Trixon lent his weight to help support Trinidad.

Vikaris was out of his seat and at the door in a moment's leap. "Where is she?" Goosebumps ran the length of his body, and his spirit soared as he sprinted down the hall.

A small group had gathered outside a nearby chamber, many of them women—nymphs, centaurs, and human. All parted, mouths dropping open as the king, evident by his glowing ruby and Marked bare arm made his way toward the entrance. Cela stood guard at the door and backed away as soon as she saw Vikaris.

"My King," she breathed, as he pushed past with nothing but a quick glance. A rush of whispered voices filled the space as soon as he departed.

The room within was quiet and filled with a honeyed fragrance he would recognize anywhere. Walking in to see his wife—was a moment he would never forget—his eyes filled with tears. *His love!*

Lyrianna, propped up with fluffy white pillows in a plumed canopy bed, alit with joy as their eyes met, but she didn't get up to greet him. Her golden hair hung in wet tendrils from her recent bath, splayed across the pillows. She smelled of verbena soap and lavender as he rushed to embrace her. Without a word, he kissed her—*his wife!*—embracing the woman he loved. The stubble from his chin tickled her lips and cheeks in a familiar sensation, causing her to laugh as she always did.

"Is it really you?" She placed her hand on his cheek as if to make sure he wasn't an illusion before her eyes. "I have dreamed of this moment for so long," she whispered, tears streaming down her lovely face.

"It is me, darling. You are home. You are free... but how?" His bright green eyes were full to the brim with joyful tears; his love for her was soaring. She smiled at him dreamily, and stroked his tear-stained, unshaven face.

"I am free," she whispered, and lightly pulled him down to her, where he kissed her again freely before traveling down the nape of her neck and exposed portion of her chest. He wanted to kiss all of her. He wanted her. His desire for her so strong, that is, until... he looked at her. Really looked.

He gasped. "No," he sobbed. His face contorting in pain, and Lyrianna appeared confused at his sudden change.

He pushed her newly washed hair aside to see her more clearly. He could make out Lyrianna's clavicle and chest bone, so apparent was her lack of nourishment. Her pale beautiful skin told a story of agony and abuse as he perused the spidery scars which lined her arms and portions of her chest. He looked at her hands. Her once beautiful hands, now scabbed; her fingernails were ragged. Her crooked and bruised fingers told a torturous tale. The realization drawing him from his revelry.

"What did he do to you?" His voice was so low, Lyrianna strained to hear him. His tears spilled across her hands and the sheets. His wife looked down at her hands. She looked shy, almost, not meeting his eyes. He gently tipped her chin up, and kissing her tears away, and holding her in a tender embrace.

After a moment like this, she pushed him back and looked at him levelly. "He did not break me," she said in a strong voice, full of determination and triumph. *She is still there,* he thought, nodding vigorously.

"No, he did not," he said, filled to the brim with love and pride in his queen. They clung tightly to one another, crying the tears that had not been shed for some time. Relief and exhaustion overtaking them, they fell asleep in one another's arms.

A hesitant knock sounded at the door. Vikaris, annoyed at the interruption, belatedly remembered his son. *Darion,* he thought!

He looked over at his majestic wife whom had also awoken at the sound. They had hardly spoken in their moments together. They had just held each other and drank in each other's kisses. There was still so much he wanted to know, and likewise, so much he needed to tell her.

"How selfish I have been," he said, rising. "Darion will want to meet you."

Lyrianna's eyes widened. "He is here? He is really here?"

"Forgive me for not telling you sooner, my love. We have much to discuss, but first," he cut off, as he went to the door. He knew it would be him. He knew Darion had waited his whole life for this moment, and he could not deny the boy this reunion any longer.

He held the door open, smiling encouragingly at the man on the other side. "Come, Darion," he whispered to his son, closing the door once again on the gathering of growing onlookers. "There is someone very special I would like you to meet," Vikaris said, as he pulled Darion into the room, guiding him with a firm hand on his shoulder.

Darion had a huge lump in his throat. One look at his father confirmed it. *It's true! She really is here!* Lyrianna was free. She was safe.

"Come in, Darion," he heard the soft yet melodious voice, he would recognize anywhere. "Come in, my son," and then he saw her. *It's her!* She *was* the woman from the dream. The most radiant, beautiful person he had ever set eyes on. *My mother!*

He stopped at the foot of her bed, unsure of what to do and afraid to disturb her, fully aware of her frail condition. He was probably more aware than anyone here, having suffered through the dreams—or visions, as Triumph called them.

"I have waited so long to see you," she said with the most beatific smile Darion had ever seen. He made his way over to her, his heart pounding, and wrapped his arms around his mother; she held his head and hummed softly, as if he were a babe. He felt for the first time whole. *Now*, he thought, *I am home.*

Vikaris, overcome with love at the pair of them, sat on the other side of his wife, wrapping his brawny arms around the two who held his whole heart. *Narco did not get them. No matter what,* Vikaris thought, *Narco will never take my family from me again.*

***

Trixon and Triumph stood outside the door, sharing a smile of relief. They had taken over watch of the door, having told the females to go get care for themselves. The unicorns were astonished by their poor, grimy, and emaciated conditions. Their stories would have to wait, though, for their health took precedent. All had gone, except Cela, who had stubbornly and faithfully remained. Her bloodied scalp, reddened welts, and tear-streaked face bespoke severe pain, and yet her eyes told a story of victory. She stood before the unicorns boldly and declared that she would not leave her queen's side. They had acquiesced, of course, though Triumph had sent a servant to find Lei, so she could still have her wounds attended to.

The two unicorns could now know some peace themselves. Trixon's father, Triumph's brother, was alive! Trinidad was resting, and though his horn was shorn and the Unicorn Council was desperate to hear of their imprisonment and escape, everyone was happy in the knowledge that they were all safe for now. *They were free.*

***

As the guards continued their militant search, and the three devoted companions guarded the King and Queen's chamber, none noted the pair of shimmering golden eyes outside of the bedroom. Spying from atop a high perch in the lofted ceiling, hidden within the shadows, Alice watched. A smile of malice touched her lips, twisting her pale and dotted face.

CHAPTER 27

The Sacrifice

Guards rushed the halls, and again, the Fortress was filled with chiming warning bells, awaking all within.

Elsra rushed with her contingent of guards toward the source of the noise. Fear filled her veins as she galloped through the Fortress—*her Fortress!* Her guards sprinted to keep pace with her. Someone else had died under her roof. Under her watch. *Please, Creator. Protect Vikaris and Darion, for without them we are doomed!*

Centaurs, nymphs, and humans frantically called for help, running in and out of Lyrianna's room. Elsra's breath caught before walking in. Death hung in the air. She smelled it immediately, and dread seeped through her as she remembered the similar scene just days before.

The blood leaked through, though hands held the cloth firmly in place. It seemed there was nothing to be done. This mortal wound was already taking its toll, and the fatigue that comes with death was setting in. Only a few breaths of life remained.

Moments before, Carol intervened between Alice's blade and Vikaris's heart, taking a wound directly to her own chest. The obsidian blade was long. Any seasoned veteran could have told her that it was a mortal wound, though none did. All those gathered before her stood in a hushed, eerie silence. Fear occupied their breath.

Riccus, still recovering from his own terrible wound, had collapsed at Carol's side, weeping. Carolina gently stroked his hair. She knew it was fatal. She had only moments left, and she knew she needed to say what was in her heart before the Creator took her.

This was only Rick's first day back on his feet, and she hoped that he would find the strength to go on. *He had to go on.* Vikaris had called for Riccus and Carol to join Darion and Lyrianna for the evening meal. Lyrianna herself was still weakened by her months of malnutrition and torment and had not yet left her chambers.

Attempting to clear her throat, Carol croaked, "Watch over him." Lyrianna knelt on her other side, tears falling freely, holding her hand. Carol knew he wouldn't make it in time... Darion had been running late from his lessons with Triumph. She knew he would never forgive himself for not being with her.

"Please," she pleaded before Lyrianna. "Watch over *our* son." She stared straight, and clear into Lyrianna's teary eyes. Lyrianna, dignified as ever, nodded once, with promise in her eyes, giving a light but firm squeeze of her hand.

Carolina looked back to Rick now, lightly tapping his head for his attention. He looked up, their eyes meeting.

"I love you, Riccus. I will always love you. Tell Darion..."
She trailed off, wheezing...

Riccus grunted, groping for the words to say. *My sweetheart!*
I am losing her, he thought terror gripping him. *Creator, help*
us!

"You cannot leave me. Wait for Darion," he pleaded
with her. His bloodshot hazel eyes held hers, until they
began to fade. *Damnit, I am losing her!* He looked
beseechingly at the unicorns gathered there. Elsra and the
others wanted nothing more than to help, their powers
were restricted to binding wounds and using other sources
of power with the senses. Knowing this though, Elsra had
still called for a guard to fetch Greca. A mortal wound,
especially one to the vital organs, could only be spared
with the lifeblood of a Unicorn. Carol would have never
allowed one of them to die in her place; they knew it, and
so did Riccus. Xenia's blood had long since grown cold
and would not help them here.

"Wait! Carol, you have to know how much I love you.
I have always loved you. Not a day will go by without me
loving you." His weathered face, clean shaven as always,
was saturated with his tears. His eyes were filled with pure
and intense love as he gazed upon his dying wife.

Carol's lips flickered into a faint smile as her hand
lifted to rub the knot in his chin affectionately. "You think
I do not know that," she smiled, speaking in a whisper,
and then as quickly as it had come, the smile disappeared,
and her hand fell away.

With that, Carolina was gone.

***

The solemn crowd watched as a husband mourned his beloved wife. A King and Queen mourned a friend. And a son arrived too late to say his goodbye.

Vikaris spoke a soft prayer over the woman who had raised his son and given her life for his, thanking the Creator for his wisdom and grace.

***

"Wait! Wait up for me!"

Darion turned, astonished at what he was looking at!

"Edmond?" he spluttered. Before him, Edmond was cantering down the trail astride Soren the Unicorn. Darion remembered meeting Soren at the sparring ground previously. He and Edmond had taken a liking to one another. Both being young and strong, they seemed adept in their shared skills for fighting.

"What are you doing here?" Darion demanded, trying to sound angry but in truth thankful for the company. He had been on the road for many days, so many in fact, he had lost count. Besides Triumph, Darion was completely alone.

"Soren and I came looking for you after..." Edmond trailed off, his eyes dropping to the ground.

"After my mother's funeral, you mean." Darion choked, though not unkindly.

He had sat for her burial, and then he and Triumph had snuck away in the night. They had contemplated the voyage before news of Carol's death, after a discovery during one of their lessons, along with news of the powers

Narco had used upon Trinidad. The latter alone solidified in their minds what had to be done.

Darion couldn't stay anyways. The forlorn look in Rick's eyes had nearly knocked him flat on his face with grief. Darion pictured Lyrianna standing with Vikaris, Antonis near Aalil—her tears breaking through her warrior visage, and the most anguishing view, of course, was that of Rick holding Carol's lifeless hand as she lay in her silken wrappings within her coffin.

The experience—the memory—it was all too overpowering. Darion knew that he had to end this before anyone else he loved died too.

Alice had been caught and gladly confessed her heinous crimes. She had been near the portal with a bag containing a bloodied horn and a vial of Xenia's blood, though the vial had shattered to the ground during Alice's struggle with the guards.

She had admitted, only after heavy interrogation led by Vikaris and Antonis, that she was the illegitimate daughter of Morta. He had visited her in her dreams for the past few months and had begun grooming her for her crimes. He had taught her to shield her mind from even the strongest of the unicorns, Elsra herself. Her treason was one of the biggest tragedies of Elsra's life, according to the unicorn. After exacting as much information from her as they could, Alice was executed. Her throat was slit, as she had done to countless others. Barson carried out the punishment witnessed by Vikaris, Darion, and a small party, including the Unicorn Council. Her body was thrown off the steep cliff of the Isle rather than buried.

No grave marker would ever stand for her. No one would ever mourn her.

Dread and dismay had filled the leaders' minds at Kaulter. The Isle was supposed to have been protected from Narco. He shouldn't have been able to read or enter anyone's minds there, his dark powers limited to Nav'Aria, or so everyone had thought. If Narco's agent Morta had been able to enter Alice's mind, what was stopping him from doing the same to every living being in Kaulter. *Or had he already?* The Council had discussed this possibility endlessly after Carol's death. New parameters were set, and the portal protected around the clock. Everyone feared, however, that it was too late.

The Isle was no longer safe from the horrors of Narco. Triumph and Darion had decided then and there that the time to act was now. They had to do whatever they could to stop Narco and save the ones they loved.

Edmond only nodded at his friend. Though he was large for his age, he was still just a young boy speaking with the Marked Heir.

Darion shrugged, conveying many emotions in his face. Edmond, a perceptive youth, said quietly, "I am sorry for your loss, Sire."

"Don't call me that," spat Darion, giving Edmond a half smile. Edmond looked sheepish at first, but then he realized the admonishment was only in jest.

"Where are you going?" Edmond asked, curiously. It seemed Soren was asking Triumph the same question, as his companion filled him in. It had taken Soren some time to track the pair down, though he had gladly agreed to Edmond's proposal. Triumph had been one of his mentors; yet he too felt compelled to help. Soren knew that his mentor had not fled, and so he and Edmond had packed up shortly after Darion and Triumph and taken off. Following the Marked Heir and his companion's trail was easy for Soren, as tracking was one of his biggest gifts.

We are going to the Shazla Desert, Triumph's voice boomed in their minds. Edmond's eyes grew large with momentary disbelief. Darion thought he was afraid. And then he noticed the skin tightening around the corners of the boy's eyes. An expression he recognized. *No, he's not frightened. He is exultant!* Darion remembered Edmond's story, the first day he had met him. His family had been killed by Narco's creatures.

"We're going to find out what dark magic Narco has been using so we can defeat him once and for all. We must find a way to use his powers against him." Darion stared hard into Edmond's eyes, and then, Soren's. The unicorn was a hair shorter than Triumph and not quite as menacing, though Darion knew he was just as powerful. And intelligent. A worthy ally to have accompanying them on their trek.

"Care to join us?" Darion asked, feigning a casual expression.

"I thought you would never ask... Sire." His friend smiled, as Soren pawed the ground.

"You'll have to stop doing that," Darion chided.

As the sun began to set, the two pairs—riders and

unicorns—continued up the sloping trail and around the bend toward the hazy border of the Shazla Desert. What would come, none knew for certain, though Darion felt, for the first time in days, at peace. He was at peace with what was to come. He knew he had been loved all his life by four amazing parents. Meeting Lyrianna had been dampened by the loss of Carol, though he was eternally grateful to meet her at last. He knew in his heart, he wasn't the unwanted orphan his insecurities and dumbasses like Joey Durange had helped conjure up. He was Darion Meridia: Son of Vikaris, the True King of Nav'Aria; natural son of Lyrianna, Queen of Nav'Aria; and the adopted and loved son of Riccus and Carolina Vershan. He would always carry Carol's memory in his heart.

"This is for you, Mom," Darion said quietly, looking at the breathtaking amber sunset displayed before him, as the creviced and dried border drew nearer. "This one's for you."

Triumph reared up, echoing Darion's words, as did Edmond and Soren. *For Carol! For Rinzaltan! For my family! For Nav'Aria!* With that, they crossed the border, entering the Shazla Desert.

EPILOGUE

The Winged Ones

And though none have sighted the winged creature, tales of old remain.

> *Once the world was whole, and winged*
> *and horned creatures roamed together. Though*
> *unicorns were made firstly by the Creator, He*
> *saw fit to create companions. The Winged*
> *Ones lived for some time in harmony with the*
> *Horned Ones. As time wore on, the Winged*
> *Ones took to the skies and found new lands*
> *farther from the Horned Ones. The two*
> *councils amicably agreed that the space was*
> *necessary for hunting, and better for both*
> *species. The two parties had never fully*
> *accepted the other, and the distance helped. It*
> *is rumored that there was an incident between*
> *the Winged and Horned creatures long ago.*
> *A young winged creature attacked the*
> *spawn of the horns and thus began the*

unofficial break. The two kept to their areas,
vowing to never speak of each other again,
honoring their boundaries and common
Creation... This then, is the only mention of
them. I, hereby, seal this content with my
stamp, so that none other than I, the Unicorn
Elders, and the Creator, will know of their
existence.

—Final excerpt found in the sidebar of Vondulus's
study journal, entitled "Fables"

Acknowledgements:

Thank YOU for reading *Nav'Aria: The Marked Heir.* There is much more to come in the sequel, *Nav'Aria: The Pyre of Tarsin!* Visit **kjbacker.com** for more information and updates!

If you enjoyed this book, please share an honest review on Amazon, Goodreads, and anywhere else you can! THANK YOU SO MUCH, READERS!

To the FANTASTIC individuals who helped with this book in its creation and fruition:

To my late Grandpa: My obsession with unicorns began with the painting you left me.

To my Dad: You read the worst of the worst—fragmented sentences, unfinished chapters, all the first draft ugliness—yet in it you saw the potential of a great story and pushed me to finish it. Thank you for believing in me… and for setting me on the path of fantasy as a child.

To my Husband: Thank you for encouraging me, supporting me, and helping me with formatting. Because of you, this book is a reality.

To my Daughter: You are as much responsible for this book's completion as anyone mentioned here—

maybe even more so! It is because of your strength, resilience, and joyous spirit that I found the final inspiration needed to write the rest of this story. I look forward to sharing it with you one day (when you're much older)!

To my Mom, brothers, extended family and friends: Your love and encouragement over the years means so much. Thank you for being my greatest supporters.

To my former English teacher, friend, and editor, Heather Peers: YOU were the first non-family member to read the book. I remember meeting you for coffee, and thinking, "she's going to hate it. That red pen is going to RUN out of ink, by the time she's finished with it." But that was not the case! YOU believed in me. YOU read my story—and loved it and prodded me to get going on the sequel. It is because of YOU that I began to think of this story as an actual book, and not just a hobby. And the funny part is, I started writing THIS book while substitute teaching in YOUR CLASSROOM. You are as much a part of Nav'Aria, as I am. Thank you from the bottom of my heart.

To Anna Genoese, my proofreader: Without your polishing skills, I don't know if I would have ever felt confident in releasing this book to the world. You made it look and sound just right. THANK YOU!

To LadyLight and Rob at SelfPubBookCovers: The cover art is amazing! I know it is said, "not to judge a book by its cover", but I'm pretty sure people will—in a good way! Thank you for your help, and for making sure EVERY TINY concern I had, was addressed. You have my highest recommendation—and sincerest thanks!

To Kelsea Schreiner and Josh Wirth, Marketing/Website Design: Thank you for believing in this book, and the importance of having the *right* website, social media presence, and overall vibe! I have learned so much from you both and look forward to sharing this book with the world.

Nav'Aria⁂
The Pyre of Tarsin

K.J. Backer

"You will never find me!"

Dew glistened upon the green blades of grass spilling forth across the lush meadow. The sun's rays warmed Tarsin's face as he smiled, listening to L'Asha's lilting voice intermittently calling to him as the breeze carried the sound to and fro, teasingly.

They were playing their favorite childhood game: the honkey in the meadow. One had to hide and make all oddities of sounds, as the other had to find the hidden partner while keeping one's eyes shut. The hidden partner continually roamed around, remaining out of sight, yet confusing the partner with sounds that came seemingly from all directions. L'Asha had suggested it for their activity today, much to Tarsin's chagrin. He had anticipated a light stroll followed by a romp in the grass on today's agenda, only to be overpowered by her strong will and forlorn expression. He hadn't had the heart to tell her no... he never could. So here he was, stumbling through the glade, blindfolded, feeling rather sullen about the overall experience. He only hoped he could catch her soon, so he could kiss her and run his hands over her beautiful form.

Suddenly, the breeze carried a shriek of pure terror, instead of the sweet laughs from only moments ago. Tarsin's eyelids popped open, and he ripped the cloth from his eyes, as he started running toward the source of the noise. All at once, their childish game forgotten, as Tarsin tried to reach L'Asha. Her screams tore at his ears, growing in timbre. A sound so desperate that he knew she was in peril—and in extreme pain. And then there was quiet.

An eerie silence met Tarsin as he crested the hill and came upon a scene so abhorrent, he was momentarily stunned. He skidded to a stop mere inches from the terrifying, hulking beast, which was as black as the obsidian blade at Tarsin's belt. It looked toward him with large red eyes, seemingly irritated by the distraction keeping it from the meal at hand—L'Asha's corpse. It snorted in anger, smoke emitting from its nostrils, before hovering closer toward the corpse possessively.

Tarsin noted that it had taken only a second for his beloved to become scorched by fire by the hideous beast. Her body, what was left of it, lay in blackened earth. Smoke rose from its quick scorch, all hair and clothing burned away, leaving her lifeless form to be torn apart, and consumed. Blood pooled. The creature's huge scaled wings clicked the ground in cadence to its chewing.... Too focused on the meal to recognize the eminent threat.

Tarsin gave no thought to his next action. Instinctively, he reached for the curved blade at his belt and leapt upon the beast, with a savage snarl brimming with molten ire. Blinded by fury, he stabbed the monster deep in its neck. The beast reared on its hindlegs, wings spreading in alarm, desperately trying to claw at the knife in its neck. It spun around, lashing out wildly, and sending Tarsin to the ground. Rising up in a fluid motion, having been trained for combat since his first tottering steps, Tarsin bellowed a war cry and ran at the beast who had taken everything from him. L'Asha had been his life. He had no fear in that moment, only primal fury. The beast, still distracted by the knife in its throat, swung its clawed wing out to block him, but to no avail. Tarsin soared past its wing, fueled by adrenaline, plunging the blade directly into the soft exposed skin on its chest. The creature screamed, then collapsed thrashing. Bloodied flesh clung to the animal's sharp teeth as it let out one last panging cry.

Tarsin tumbled back, avoiding being crushed, as the mysterious creature' s breath gave out, and silence filled the meadow. As if even the birds were paying homage to the brave hero below. On all fours, he crawled toward his love; reaching out as he came upon L'Asha's skull, his tears spilling forth. Sobbing, he carefully lifted her head, cradling it. *You cannot be gone*, he wept, shooting a baleful look at the giant form of the beast still lying where it had fallen amidst death throws. He had never seen a creature such as this, and he was going to make sure he never did again. *That no one did.*

Years of working the earth, left him hardened and resolute in his task. Shame filling him, he wiped his tears with a quick brush of his sleeve. *I failed you.*

He grabbed the pack containing his necessaries. The pick lay wrapped in cloth at the bottom. As he pulled it out from the bag, he bit the inside of his left cheek. Keeping the tears at bay, he welcomed the pain. The iron-filled taste of blood. The work. Idle hands and time would leave him in a puddle of grief. He would see this task carried out. Properly. Then, and only then, would he allow himself to mourn. Turning away from her, he began the chore of digging the grave.

The pick struck the ground and he moved the fertile soil easily to create space for what was left of his beloved. He wrapped her in his spare cloak from the pack, saving her yellow hair ribbon for last. She had given it to him upon their betrothal. She had said he should carry it with him for luck wherever he goes. He remembered her adoring musical voice as she had gifted it, and the kiss and wink she had given him along with the token.

Emotion catching in his throat, he gently tied it around the top of her wrapped skull, creating a loose bow. He could still see how the yellow had tamed her raven tresses. Cradling her small form, he set her in the grave speaking the words over her. His precious L'Asha. Gone.

I will see you soon, L'Asha, he promised softly.

The sequel, *Nav'Aria: The Pyre of Tarsin, is* coming soon! Visit kjbacker.com for details.

Made in the USA
San Bernardino, CA
22 January 2019